THE
DREAM OF
CONFUCIUS

THE
DREAM OF
CONFUCIUS

JEAN LÉVI

TRANSLATED FROM THE FRENCH
BY BARBARA BRAY

A Helen and Kurt Wolff Book
Harcourt Brace Jovanovich, Publishers
New York   San Diego   London

HBJ

22.95 B+T

© Éditions Albin Michel S.A., Paris, 1989
English translation copyright © 1992 by Harcourt Brace Jovanovich, Inc.

Library of Congress Cataloging-in-Publication Data
Lévi, Jean.
    [Rêve de Confucius. English]
    The dream of Confucius / Jean Lévi ;
translated from the French by Barbara Bray.
        p.   cm.
    Translation of: Le rêve de Confucius.
    "A Helen and Kurt Wolff book."
    ISBN 0-15-126570-4
    1. Han Kao-tsu, Emperor of China, 247–195 B.C.—Fiction.
    2. China—History—Han dynasty, 202 B.C.–220 A.D.—Fiction.
    I. Title.
PQ2672.E942R4813   1992
843'.914—dc20   91-40459

Printed in the United States of America
First edition
A B C D E

For Célia and Myrto

The traveler to distant lands beholds
Wondrous things. When he returns and tells
Of them, the people call him liar,
They who in their common ignorance
Accept the evidence only of what
Their own eyes see, their own hands touch.

But I ignore the humdrum disbelief
Of listeners such as these. The clear of head
Will catch the bright truth of my tale.
The clear of head, they are my audience,
They are my reward.

—Ariosto, *Orlando Furioso*, Canto 7, 1–2

THE
DREAM OF
CONFUCIUS

HEAVEN AND EARTH

Heaven created the Ten Thousand Beings
to whom it gives wealth and happiness.
By the course of the sun it establishes the Six Places.
It bestrides Six Dragons, which control the universal norm.
Great and beautiful is the Earth!
Trusty as a mare that never strays from the road.
Find an ally in the South-West, lose one in the North-East.

There were eight guests in the room. Eight enigmatic characters wearing exorcists' masks and the wide-sleeved robes of soothsayers. They were seated on banqueting mats, each in the position indicated by the trigram embroidered on his chest.

They were Heaven, Earth, Wind, Thunder, Pond, Water, Fire, and Mountain. Heaven, who must have been the oldest, judging by the meager wisp of beard emerging from beneath his mask, was seated to the northwest, at the *ying-hai* point of the sexagesimal cycle, the site of all beginnings. Water, to the north, wore a black gown decorated with pigs and ears, and these were balanced by the mouth and sheep on the robe of Pond, who sat to the west of the patriarch. The southwest was reserved for Earth: he displayed the belly of a pregnant woman—is not Earth That-which-bears? Fire, to the south, was distinguished by the flaming red of his silken jacket, patterned with thousands of eyes representing light. To the east, at the *mao* point of the denary cycle, sat Thunder, identifiable by his blue-green coat with dragon-shaped markings. The stillness of his gigantic right-hand neighbor, Mountain, contrasted with the gesticulations of Wind, in the southeast corner.

As soon as they were arranged in the eight corners of the space available, Heaven, exercising the privilege of age, opened the proceedings:

"I am the father, the circle, the sovereign, jade, cold metal, ice, and everything that is hard. My color is royal purple. If I were a horse, I would be a lean horse, a bay. I am fruit or dragon. I am a straight line. . . ."

Earth took up the tale:

"I am the mother, the square, hempen cloth, kitchen utensils, heifer, big square chariot, the mob, black mingled with yellow."

Thunder was next:

"I am the eldest son, the green dragon, flowers, speed, motion, and the foot its agent; I am bamboo, rush, and reed. If I were a horse, I would be a white horse with black fetlocks and a loud whinny, or a chestnut with a white forehead. If I were a plant I'd be one of those that grow upside down—onion, garlic, or turnip—for my diagram is a broad stroke with two soft lines over it."

Then it was Water's turn:

"I am the second son, I am channels and ditches; I am the shapes that bend down and lift up, the harsh law that people must obey—dark jails, handcuffs, and fetters; I am crimson blood, I am gushing red gore. If I were a horse, I would be a horse with a raging heart, lowered head, and slender hooves—the kind that goes around obstacles like a stream. I am that which carries and guides, but also the

2

moon, ambushes, thieves; I am a tree with a dense, tough heart; I am palace, beam, thornbush, fox, and fence. . . ."

And each one of the rest pronounced his own cryptic formula.

The comical getup of those taking part in this performance combined with the seriousness of their attitude to produce a spectacle midway between pantomime and religious ritual. The whole thing might have been ludicrous had these robes and this solemnity not been the distinguishing marks of the eight supreme heads of the terrible and mysterious Hexagram sect.

This secret society, before which all the princes of the Empire now trembled, had been founded by Confucius toward the end of his life, when fate sent him a sign showing it was hopeless to try to restore the glory of the Chous by returning to ancient ritual.

It happened at Lu, in the fourteenth year of Duke Ai. The local potentate's coachman was out in the countryside gathering wood when suddenly he saw a strange beast among the bushes. He rushed after it, caught it, and found it had a single horn on its brow, ending in a fleshy knob. He showed his prize to the inhabitants of a hamlet on the edge of the forest. They had never seen anything like it before, and thought it might bring bad luck, so they stoned it. The animal dragged itself away into the undergrowth to die, and one of Confucius's followers, who had been watching what was happening, hurried off to tell the Master about it.

"There's a strange creature near here with only one horn. It must be an evil omen!"

"Where, exactly, is it?"

"Ten leagues away, in the village of Five Old Men!"

Confucius rose quickly from his mat and told his driver to take him there.

"I'll wager it's a unicorn!" he kept saying as they galloped toward the village.

By the time they got there, the animal was dead. They were soon joined by the pack of seventy disciples who followed the Master everywhere. And when the philosopher, bending over the body, exclaimed, "A unicorn! That's what it is they've killed, the fools!" Yen Yen, standing nearby, seized the opportunity to show off.

"As the phoenix is the most wonderful of birds," he said excitedly, "so the unicorn is the most wonderful of beasts. It is said such creatures are seen only when Virtue reigns. Have you any idea, Master," he asked with a mixture of servility and cunning, "what could have brought a unicorn here?"

Confucius glared at him.

"When the Son of Heaven radiates Virtue and establishes an era of peace," he replied, "dragons, unicorns, phoenixes, and other such creatures all flock to the country and frolic there. So why indeed should we find such a wonder near this village of yokels, at a time when the dynasty is on the point of collapse and there is no wise man capable of taking over?"

He sighed.

"Am I not to men what the unicorn is to beasts? The unicorn appeared, and instead of recognizing it and doing it homage, they attacked it! Is it not a symbol? A sign from Heaven telling me it is my fate, too, to die unrecognized? Perhaps my own end is near."

And, half laughing, half weeping, he began to sing:

> "In the golden past
> The unicorn and the phoenix
> Would visit us arm in arm,
> And dance together.
> But now times are bad.
> So what are you doing,
> Pure and virtuous unicorn,
> In this dungheap?"

Then he went back thoughtfully to his school, followed by his pupils. And that night he dreamed of unicorns.

A reddish mist rose up from a village in the land of Ch'u, and Confucius summoned Yen Hui and Tzu-hsia and hurried thither. As they were approaching a place called Fan they met a young wood-cutter who had wounded a unicorn in the left rear leg and hidden it under a heap of kindling. Confucius leaned down from his chariot and asked the boy his name.

"Red Hymn!" was the reply.

"Have you seen anything unusual?"

"Yes—an animal rather like a kid, with only one horn."

"Where is it?"

"Gone."

Confucius smiled, alighted, patted the boy on the head, and said: "At last the Empire has found a master!"

Then he went over to the heap of wood and found the unicorn. It got up and limped toward him, stretching out its right ear. Confucius pulled the animal's ear, whereupon it spewed forth a book—the *Book of Filial Piety*. Then the unicorn proffered its other ear, and when Confucius pulled that, it spat out another book—the *Esoteric Commentary on the Book of Changes*.

Confucius went back home to Lu, where he summoned his seventy disciples, asked them to face north, and showed them the two volumes. Then he handed them over to Tseng Tzu, who prostrated himself, holding the precious writings high above his head, as one does when presenting a petition to the Emperor or to Heaven. The Master himself, dressed in an unpadded coat of plain red with madder kneepads, bowed to the Supreme God.

The sky seemed to move, and a mist crystallized into a white cloud, which settled on the Earth and turned into a piece of pale jade, onto which a red rainbow descended and formed itself into the following words:

The Sage who came from Water disappears; the trees lose their green foliage; a comet rises through space, heralding the advent of the Black Dragon, who will destroy the Barbarian. When the books have been consumed by Fire, Red inherits power and vernal Green loses it, for the collector of wood has caught the unicorn.

Though unable to rule, one of the Black Dragons who make Red's bed guides mankind through signs and portents, that the will of Heaven may be done; the sixty-four signs attend him, and the Six Dragons are steeds secretly steered by the motions of Heaven and Earth.

As the Master deciphered the letters, they detached themselves from the jade and formed an incandescent sphere, which, when he had finished reading, changed into a red crow. Then the jade sank into the ground, and the bird flew off, croaking "Orient Whet-Iron! Orient Whet-Iron!"

Confucius awoke feeling disturbed. He went out into the cold clear night and looked up. The western part of the sky seemed to shine brightly, but the east was dark. Then it all changed. He stood and thought for a moment, then harnessed his horses to his chariot, and his tall form faded into the night.

For six months he was in retreat. If he had not freed himself of his disciples, whose irksome questions scattered his thoughts as the autumn wind scatters dead leaves, he could only have skimmed the smooth surface of the words, without penetrating the mystery behind the mystery, and would never have reached the image within the image.

He had understood the superficial meaning of his dream as soon as he woke: Seen as an ordinary premonition and warning, it signified that, when he was dead, the Chou dynasty would collapse, and after a merciless king had cowed his subjects by cruelty, a commoner would seize the Empire by violence. The symbols were transparently clear. "The Sage who came from Water" was himself; his given name was Mud, and mud is produced by water. The "green foliage" referred to the Chou, whose coat of arms depicts spring. The fall of the leaves denoted the end of their reign. A "collector of wood" is someone of low degree; the unicorn symbolizes the Empire; a wound suggests violence, which was in the name croaked out by the crow. Black is the color of winter, season of suffering, and the dragon was the emblem of royalty: hence a king would impose a reign of terror. Red is fire and is born of wood: the green of the Chou would be followed by the red of fire, for thus does History follow the pattern set by the begetting of the elements. The fiery nature of the reign in question was also reflected in the name and occupation of the boy Red Hymn: sticks are used to kindle flames.

"Whet-Iron" was a rebus for the name of the Founder, already suggested by the name of the village. Confucius knew well the genealogy of the clans, having studied it since he was four years old. Fan was the appanage of the descendants of Liu Lei. At first, all these parallels annoyed the Master: he liked conciseness, and was vexed that his mind should indulge in prolixity even in the relaxed vigilance of dream. But his dissatisfaction didn't last long: he soon realized that the details concerned the boy's career rather than his identity.

K'ung-chia, a degenerate king of the Hsia dynasty, had lived a life of debauchery and worshiped demons. Heaven sent him a warning in the form of a pair of dragons, male and female. Not knowing how to feed them, the king called in his cousin Liu Lei, who professed to know how to raise dragons; but after only a few months the female dragon was dead. Liu Lei was frightened and fled to Lu. His descendants later found refuge with the Prince of Lin, who bestowed Fan upon them. But the Liu family was in decline. Who would have dreamed they could fall so low?

The title belonging to the ancestor of the Liu could be read as an omen. The words "rises" and "dragon" suggested a breathtaking ascent, such as that of a woodcutter, for example, rising to the dragon throne. They also acted as a genealogical proof, with History at once heralding and authenticating the future: Liu Lei could be seen as a "raiser of dragons" in the sense that his lineage would bring forth a prodigy.

Barbarism begets barbarism, which destroys itself in its own fury. The Master, having studied the theory of discourse, knew that names are never meaningless: reality, moving in its own mysterious ways, influences mankind through names, and is in turn affected by them.

Thus the Black Dragon's descendant would be called "Barbarian," and his murderous folly would bring ruin on his family. The sixty-four signs referred to the divinatory hexagrams: their sequence reflects the course of things as set in motion by the alternation of yin and yang in the three orders of Heaven, Earth, and Man. These three orders are represented by the six lines in the hexagrams, which are like six dragons. The course of things makes and unmakes kings, whose chariots are drawn by six steeds known as dragons.

In addition to the metaphorical interpretation, the Master discovered other implications, as in a nest of boxes. He too was the Black Dragon, linked to it by the water he was made from. And some of his admirers called him King-without-a-Kingdom. Although, unlike his double and opposite, he could not embody a moment in History, he did influence its course, since the Law was but the hidden face of Ritual. So the reference to red took on another dimension. Fire changes the other elements when it combines with them: wood becomes dust; solid metal becomes liquid; water, by nature cold, becomes warm; malleable earth grows hard. Thus he himself might transmute harsh reality, sublimating torment through the soothing vindication of morality and the harmonious form of ritual. But fire, through its brightness, is also ornament, and since all ornament is a veil thrown over reality, it is connected with untruth. And that was why the boy had tried to deceive him.

He was amazed by the subtle construction of his dream, and instead of rejecting its tautologies, as he had done at first, he now accepted and even admired them, as adding to its richness. He realized that repetition, by its very superfluity, was a clue to understanding, giving rise to a network of hidden analogies. Apparently superfluous words, echoing others, were really meeting points of meaning, intersections where various and contradictory senses collided and sparked the ultimate message. Such duplications evoked a myriad of symbols, and smelted them down, as in an alchemist's crucible, into a single substance more precious and rarer than its constituents.

And the simple place-name Fan, a metonymic counterpart of the name Whet-Iron, contained the whole message of the text in concentrated form. But the repetition of the personal name by means of allusion to a family was also tantamount to a recapitulation of the themes of deceit and the flight of dragons. Every founder of a dynasty contains all the vices and virtues of his race, and reenacts in his own life the experiences of generations of forebears. This is because, as is shown by the immemorial ordering of the trigrams, which the Master had made the subject of particular study, the march of time produces a converse movement of contraction, caused by the withdrawal of the ungerminated seeds of destiny. Thus it was always in the past that the future was to be read. Liu Lei was a rogue and a liar. Not content with laying claim to a skill he only half possessed —one of the two animals died—he had also tried to fool his master. To get rid of the evidence of his incompetence he cut up the dragon's dead body, cooked it, and served it to K'ung-chia as snake stew.

The fiery nature of Whet-Iron's reign was confirmed, in its turn, by what happened to the Fans. Before coming into the land from which they got their name, they were invested with the ancient estate of the princes of Shih-wei, descendants of the Invokers of Fire. This place-name carried with it a whiff of usurpation—a lawful usurpation, like all those that History acclaims—for the Liu were in the cuckoo-like habit of taking over other people's properties. So a whole web clearly connected untruth, fire, rising, raising, and dragons. If, as the Master suspected, nothing here was devoid of meaning, he might infer (since past events are repeated in reverse, just as the pattern of growth from seed to plant corresponds in reverse to that of growth from tree to seed) that a snake cut up and presented as a dragon would herald Whet-Iron's ultimate ascent to a throne that rightly belonged to others.

As he delved deeper into the layers of meaning, it struck the Master that the allusion to untruth by means of reference to a family must be intended first and foremost to emphasize the fundamental ambiguity of the name Whet-Iron.

In the place-name, Confucius saw not only one of the flimsy and supererogatory signs that dreams are made of, but also a plan of action—or, rather, the first stage of one. The dream showed him indirectly how to write his books so that their prophecies would be revealed only to the elect. It would be through a tedious and trivial profusion of proper names, a dry listing of unimportant details that he would deliver the key to his writings: their mysterious innermost meaning would be accessible only to those who possessed the secret art of deciphering indirect allusions.

He therefore had to write books. But they would have to be burned if his teaching—aimed at clandestinely promoting the rule of Law, of which he was the practical expression—was to become the basis of a new order—an attractive, because fallacious, version of the old. Confucius was sure the greatness of the coming era would reside in its untruth.

However, just as ornament cannot exist without the thing it covers, morality could not exist independently of the practice it purported to negate. Morality belonged to the realm of words, whereas the laws of History, while acting irrespective of the consciousness of men, express themselves through human will and action. Confucius saw that an efficient and structured organization would be needed if the doctrine shadowed forth by Heaven was to be imposed on Earth.

The outlines of this organization were indicated in his dream: sixty-four plus six makes seventy, the exact number of his disciples. Adding Heaven and Earth gave seventy-two, the number of days in a season, the product of yin and yang, from whence emerges the motion of the universe.

The Master returned home, and that winter, season of withdrawal and death, sensing that his end was near, he called his disciples and dictated his last behests. He bade his followers study divination and inquire into the deeper meaning of the *Book of Changes*, on which he had just completed a brief commentary. He told them that the two books he had compiled during his retirement could be interpreted cryptically as well as literally. The *Book of Filial Piety* used moral exhortation as a pretext for prediction, while *Springs and Autumns*, in the unappealing form of a chronicle history of the principality of Lu, contained a key to knowledge of the future. For to anyone who can make the necessary comparisons to the patterns of the stars, every event foreshadows that which is to come; every moment contains within it the eternity written in the great book that Heaven spreads above our heads and in the no less magic volume that Earth's contours spread before our feet.

As he spoke, the Master crossed two fingers of his left hand and drew in the air, for the benefit of his six aptest pupils, the signs denoting a stag, a horse, a monkey, a pheasant, a dog, and a pig. The next day, between the hour of the stag and the hour of the pig, the six pupils came to see him one by one in secret. At the hour of the rat, when the last of the six had gone away, two shadows emerged from the darkness and moved silently to the dying philosopher's bedside. Not until cockcrow did they slip away like ghosts into the pale mists of dawn.

———

Society was organized into increasing exclusive concentric circles. The sixty-four disciple-hexagrams, effective because of their links with scholars and politicians, formed the main strike force. Their job was to foment conspiracy and faction in the courts of all the princes, to transmit orders issued by the Trigrams, and to supply the leaders of that sect with valuable information about intrigues and changes of alliance.

The second circle, six child-trigrams chosen from among the seventy disciples, were by virtue of their knowledge of the *Book of Changes* in charge of the guild of seers, and could thus bring influence to bear on politics by means of predictions and advice. But they were only a halfway stage between the ordinary members and the "parents." Although they knew the main principles of the organization, were invited to its secret meetings and regularly informed of its passwords, they knew nothing of its practical objectives or even of their colleagues' identities, let alone those of their superiors, Heaven and Earth. The real center of decision resided in this pair: the parent-trigrams, the third circle, which through its undivided authority exercised a formidable occult power over the whole.

For nearly a century the activity of the sect remained so unobtrusive and arcane that its existence might have been doubted had its foundation not coincided with the gradual elimination of Mohism, the doctrines of which were fiercely attacked by every school of thought. Then it was the turn of the rhetors and the sophists to be the target of insidious persecution; the majority of learned men and scholars adopted the teachings of the Master, who was soon venerated like a god, though there was no evidence that their conversions had been brought about by threats or pressure. The name of the sect began to be whispered in well-informed circles. Over the last sixty years or so, its attitudes had undergone radical change. No longer content to operate on the level of ideas, and apparently determined to undo all it had so patiently worked for, it had become a formidable instrument of repression against the learned. Some people had recently suggested that through Chou Ch'u, who succeeded K'an the Huge in the fourth generation of child-trigrams (whose ranks were replenished by transmission from master to disciple), the politicians of Ch'in, who were hostile to the Confucians, had managed to infiltrate and manipulate the group. But this ignored the fact that the second circle played only a secondary role in determining the sect's policy.

Be that as it might, something had certainly happened: not only did Ch'in intrigues seem to enjoy support and collusion throughout the Empire and in every layer of society, but also the evidence pointed to the existence of a powerful association specializing in political assassination and the sale of strategic intelligence. This body was dedicated to destabilizing the Central States, fomenting unrest, and ruining the economy. Only the Trigrams had the infrastructure necessary to operate on such a scale. Naturally, this was only speculation. The sect's activities remained as vague and elusive as ever: some people even maintained that it was no more than a bunch of pompous old fogies whose only concern was celebrating the anniversaries of the Master's birth and death. But the accusations carried enough weight for the Prince of Ch'u to have the society infiltrated by his cleverest sleuths. He hoped not only to free it from Ch'in influence, but also to win it over to work for him.

It would take too long to catalogue all the feats of patience, intelligence, and guile performed by the agents of the northern state's secret diplomacy. Suffice it to say that it took them two generations and thirty years of effort to achieve their goal. But when a certain agent, after making himself expert in all existing methods of predicting the future, and winning a reputation among the learned by writing a commentary on the *Book of Changes*, finally managed to enter the eminent and exclusive circle of the Trigrams, he realized to his chagrin that he had made no inroads whatsoever as far as the sect's real methods were concerned, and that there was no chance of his being able to affect its actions. He had not even been able to find out who his accomplices were, so strict were the precautions taken to conceal the leaders' identity. As for Heaven and Earth, he had never succeeded in meeting them, and received their orders through the oddest and most unexpected channels.

The agent was on the point of giving up in despair, when, in the tenth year of King Kao-lei of Ch'u, a blind seer led by a deaf and dumb child handed him a paper. It was twisted into the shape of a unicorn, and summoned him to a plenary session of the sect to celebrate Heaven's one hundred and twentieth birthday. The gathering was to take place at a particularly propitious conjunction of the stars. The agent's heart missed a beat through joy and apprehension.

———

Now, looking surreptitiously around the room, he wondered for what mysterious ceremony, for what fearful plot, the dread conductor and manipulator had called the whole fraternity together in this seedy tavern in Chung-yang. Neither the unwholesome greasy food, which stuck to the teeth, nor the dark second-floor room, with low rough-hewn beams, nor the view over a narrow alley through which ran an evil-smelling gutter, offered any explanation for the choice of venue. Was it something to do with terrestrial signs? He knew from his studies in geomancy that this was not the answer. Was it because the place was so inconspicuous? But the whole neighborhood could see all that went on there. When the local urchins noticed the way the guests were dressed, they had come running, their faces smeared with gruel, their black eyes glittering with curiosity. They had clambered up to the balcony and were swarming around the door and window frames. Every now and then the innkeeper, a hideous cripple bent double either by his hump or out of respect, tried to drive them away with cuffs and brutish cries. But as soon as his back was turned, they again flocked like flies to a lump of meat.

Heaven, quite untroubled by the publicity the meeting had aroused, signaled for drink to be served. Earth started the guests talking shop. They compared the various types of divination and discussed their respective merits. They listed all the methods of computation from the simplest to the most esoteric, including prognostication by means of intercalary remainders and the mantology of the six letters *chia* and the signs *jen*. They went into ecstasies over the wonders of the extra or "leap" hour, which made it possible to meddle with the interstices of time. Someone mentioned the retrocessive calculus, by which the past melts into the future; another spoke of the technique of vacant signs, and how experts can use it to free themselves from the chain of destiny, escape from temporality for a moment, and modify fate. Of course there was talk of astrology as well: some scholars tried to explain how results depended on whether Jupiter or Venus was taken as the norm. Still more methods were gone into: physiognomy, and divination through wind direction, the song of crickets, ripples on water, tracks left by birds, clouds, mists, and vapors.

All the time the agent himself was speaking, treating of the subject most appropriate to his garb, his mind was alert and his eyes scrutinized and tried to identify the faces behind his companions' masks.

Everyone drank immoderately. The conversation grew warm and less formal. Bodies relaxed, tunics fell open, shoelaces came undone, masks grew sweaty and slipped awry. All these men so accustomed to being aloof and reserved allowed themselves to let go. All except three of them. Mountain towered over the gathering as silent and impassive as his namesake. Earth wagged his head and brooded over everyone with a moist and benevolent eye, like a mother hen; but though he smiled a lot, he spoke little. As for Heaven, whom the agent had at first taken for the dangerous master of all the machinations, he seemed to be lost in some muddled dream. After mumbling a few words about the cycles of hidden hours, he started to burble a series of numbers that had nothing to do with the general conversation.

"Fifty-five is the sum of thirty and twenty-five—but that's really forty-nine, because there are six lines: Heaven and Earth plus one, multiplied by yin and yang, which are two. Nine, six, seven, eight, young and old yang, old and young yin, coming and going from One to Six until nothing, which changes into . . ."

And so he went on, muttering a meaningless string of algorithmic formulas until the whole thing turned into loud snoring.

Earth smiled indulgently.

"He's bound to tire easily," he said. "After all, he is celebrating his hundred and twentieth birthday."

Then all glasses were raised to wish the patriarch long life and good health. Now perhaps the serious business will begin, thought the spy from Ch'u. But he wasn't very hopeful. It was inconceivable that this old dodderer, droning out procedures for manipulating divining sticks as if they were really mysterious and terrifying spells, could be the head of a mighty organization—an organization that had foiled all the princes' attempts to form a league against Ch'in, that controlled the fates of politicians, ordered executions, and fomented unrest in the states. Suddenly the agent caught Earth's eye.

It had a strange effect on him. It struck him as familiar and reassuring—and did he detect a gleam of complicity? Earth was making an almost imperceptible sign, indicating the northwest, where Mountain was sitting, formidable, unwavering, and almost silent. The agent was impressed, and raised an eyebrow. Earth put a finger on his lips, nodded his head slightly, then got up and went out to the latrines. His step was light, almost a caper despite the considerable bulge he carried in front of him. The agent was irresistibly reminded of a filly. . . . Then it came to him in a flash: the Mare! That was what, because of her walk, they called the Princess of P'ing-yang, the great-niece of queen Hsia of Ch'in, a princess of Ch'u married to the King of the West. She had been sent as companion to the queen at the time of the latter's marriage, and since her great-aunt's death she had played a key role in Ch'u's secret diplomacy. The reason for her way of walking was that she was expecting a child. Although she sometimes acted independently, her sympathies were certainly with her native land. The agent felt better. He could count on valuable support in the rough game that was about to begin, for she was one of the cleverest politicians and one of the wiliest negotiators in the Empire, and had managed to surround herself with an extraordinary network of alliances. But why hadn't he been told? If he'd known, he would have been able to operate more efficiently. His ignorance was probably due to the rivalry between the princess and her master, Prime Minister Spring Awakening—unless their canny monarch had thought it best to send two agents unwittingly on the same mission, to keep an eye on one another. . . .

His reflections were interrupted by a whisper in his ear.

"Well, Chou Hui," said a placid voice, "the Earth hexagram fits this little get-together exactly, doesn't it? *'Trusty as a Mare . . . in the southwest one finds an ally. . . .'* It would have been surprising if our dear princess from P'ing-yang hadn't been one of the party!"

The agent's heart nearly stopped. He had been recognized! He turned and looked at Pond; by the languid, reptilian way the man was drooping toward him, he recognized none other than Chang Yeh. Yes, this was his voice, quiet and calm as still waters. How familiar it sounded now that it no longer aped the exorcists' diction. Chang Yeh, his old friend and rival, the gray eminence of Chao foreign policy, clandestine chief of its secret service, the perfect man for difficult missions, a formidable negotiator and subtle strategist. So he too had wormed his way in! How had he been so blind as not to recognize him at first glance in spite of his mask? And to think that he had thousands of eyes in the pattern of his robe, as a sign of vision! He could plead that their last meeting had taken place more than fifteen years ago, and his friend had a stoop now and time had left its cruel mark on his neck and hands. Behind the mask a smile flitted across the old man's face at the memory of their first meeting. It had taken place in the bedroom of the dowager of Yen, a lecherous, decrepit old hag (fifty-five years old at least) whose moist vagina and withered buttocks they'd both worked away at like slaves to get her to put in a good word for their respective princes to her son, whom she ruled with a rod of iron. He shuddered as he looked back at all the ways a diplomat had to use his tongue.

"Have you noticed we're among colleagues here?" Pond went on, interrupting the other's recollections.

And Fire, as if the scales of anxiety had suddenly fallen from his eyes, recognized by the sweeping gesture with which Thunder raised a goblet to his lips that he was really Ch'en Yü, a creature of Ch'i whom he'd often come across in the course of embassies and less official meetings. A sleuth of the first order! It was he who had uncovered the schemes of Su Tai, when he found out that the Ch'i minister was merely pretending to betray Ch'i. So the King of Ch'u wasn't the only ruler who'd had the idea of infiltrating the sect, and other intelligence services had managed to penetrate it too—no doubt with just as much difficulty, thought Fire bitterly.

Meanwhile:

"Don't you remember Tsou Tang of Wei, you old rogue?" Water

was whispering to the noisy character who represented Wind. "We studied diplomacy together under the master of the leagues, Valley of the Demons."

"That dates us a bit! . . . I see our charming Han prince has let Wei get the better of him as usual! But why are you so secretive? Seeing that we're allies—for the moment—we ought to collaborate with one another, or at least exchange information."

This conversation had not escaped their neighbors.

"Do those two whispering together remind you of anybody?"

"Yes! They're old acquaintances. That makes five of us who are agents of the Seven Powers. We could almost hold a peace conference."

"Do you think Mountain is the ringleader, hiding behind Heaven and acting for Ch'in? He has the right figure for a leader. . . ."

Water laughed.

"You're making a mountain out of a molehill!" he punned. "He's only that oaf of a general Fan I. Just because he made his way up by wielding a knife in his butcher's fist, he takes himself for a politician."

He'd spoken a little too loudly. Mountain looked daggers at him.

"If I've gained an ally in the southwest, you've made an enemy in the northeast," said the agent impersonating Fire.

"Which one can be Ch'in's envoy? I can't see anyone it could be except Heaven. But it isn't possible such an old wreck could be the brains of the organization. For that, he'd need to be in his right mind!"

" 'A flock of dragons without a head: extremely auspicious,' " Water murmured pensively. "That's the sixth line of the Heaven hexagram in the Book of Changes. Doesn't it all seem rather sinister? It's as if we were trapped into acting a part."

"That's because we are putting on an act."

"Not in the way you mean. We're doing more than imitate another identity: we are that other identity, as if we were letters forming part of a piece of writing. We didn't choose—we were chosen. We all fit into the trigrams only too well. Even the points of the compass assigned to us correspond to the geographical direction of the countries we serve. The formulas even apply to what we do. The Princess of P'ing-yang's nickname is the Mare, and she plays Earth, the ally of the South-West. Yes, there's mischief in it somewhere!"

"You know as well as I do that the *Book of Changes* is a handbook for sorcerers and charlatans, written so that any maxim will fit any situation. That's all there is to soothsaying. I'm amazed that you're so gullible."

"By all the devils!" exclaimed Wind suddenly, clutching Fire's arm. "We were sent to infiltrate the sect in order to thwart Ch'in, the only country that hasn't thought it worthwhile to send a representative of its own. And the result of all our efforts is that the organization works for Ch'in's benefit!"

"That's precisely because Ch'in *is* absent. The well-known law of the attraction of the void."

"What do you mean?"

"Absence is the reverse side of presence. The presence of others creates absence, through the weight of their being. The force of the negative is greater than that of the positive; so being always works for the benefit of nonbeing."

"Our heads are so full of Ch'in that it doesn't need to be present to exist in each one of us. And we ourselves feel its absence as a kind of void to be filled. So by acting as if it were manipulating the society, we have created its existence in order to justify our own."

Thunder interrupted.

"Doesn't it strike you as incredible?" he said.

Then he broke off, picked up his spoon, and dipped it into a sticky liquid with three maggoty jujubes and two ancient lotus seeds floating in it. While the others hung on his lips as if their slurping might provide the key to the mystery, he suddenly declaimed in a voice that boomed through the silence like a roll of drums:

"Incredible, the rubbish they have the nerve to serve!"

The others chortled, and Thunder, gratified, went on:

"Earth represents Ch'in because of the excess of noblemen; she also stands for the Six States together, which she contains in her huge womb. She belongs to Ch'u by descent, to Wei by marriage, to Han by sympathy, to Ch'i through love, to Yen through interest, and to Chao through politics, while belonging to Ch'in by marriage and residence—hence her being placed in accordance with the direction assigned to Ch'in. But if Earth represents Ch'in positively, Heaven does so negatively. He is the empty space, the void indicated by his nonparticipation in what is going on. That is why the old man is so abstracted."

"Yes, but the negative form of absence is positiveness in Heaven's case, expressed in the direct and immediate form of negation itself, which is vacuity or emptiness. Whereas the positive form of absence is negation, presenting itself indirectly in the shape of the presence of others. That is why the first is Heaven, yang, and the second is Earth, yin."

"You might as well say they are black and white and we are colors. White is colors added together; black is colors canceled out. They are the two extremes that meet, despite the fact that they are opposites, because they underlie the sum of all the others."

"You never spoke a truer word! Ch'in's emblem is *either* black *or* white. White as a symbol of metal and the west; black as a symbol of winter and repressive laws."

Mountain let out a loud belch.

"All that's only after-dinner philosophy," he said. "All I know is that we've fallen into Ch'in's trap. They spread a rumor that they'd infiltrated the sect in order to lure us into it while staying outside themselves. They left us just an empty shell, so we would manipulate merely ourselves, creating our enemy by the mere fact of struggling against him. It's a political application of the well-known strategic principle of setting emptiness against fullness. In the game of *go* it's called the empty-territory technique, and in the game of *liu-pu* it's known as the ploy of the kitten playing with its own tail."

"Yes, of course! Six cats trying to catch their own tails!"

"Unless we're all really double agents in the pay of Ch'in," put in Wind provocatively. "It's happened before. Didn't Su Tai, who passed himself off as a false double agent for Ch'i, work for the power of the West, which had charged him with destroying the two states that thought they employed him?"

"Anyhow," Mountain insisted, "neither sorcery nor mystery has anything to do with it!"

"Tell me, Mountain, since you have your feet on the ground," said the Princess of P'ing-yang, who had just returned to her mat and overheard the last few words, "how many are there of us?"

"Eight, of course," he replied.

"Count again!"

"Eh?"

"Well?"

"Good heavens! I can find only four! But I know there are eight of us."

"Count again then."

"I must have drunk too much. There are only three of us."

Sweat streamed from him.

"Try again!"

"Only two!"

"Again!"

"Only one!"

As one man, they all rose in amazement, upon which Heaven emerged from his torpor and, with an imperious wave of the hand, signed to them to sit down. When they had done so, he heaved a deep sigh, dislodging from his beard a shred of sticky black mushroom and two dried shrimps.

"My poor children, it doesn't take much to surprise you," he said. "But you've sweated over the *Book of Changes* long enough to know that sixty-four, eight, four, and one are all the same—just different modulations of the Tao, which, though it has neither substance nor determination, begets One, which through division produces Two, the emblem of yin and yang. From their union come the four seasons, and their order is reflected in the eight trigrams, symbols of time and space, which are resolved in Unity."

Then, in a voice that rose as he went on:

"No sun, but a dazzling rainbow; no moon, but the tails of comets. What should be hidden is visible; what should be visible is hidden. Corrupt ministers abound; princes wallow in debauchery. The Empire is in the grip of affliction: the mountains collapse, the earth splits open, everything is dark and confused and topsy-turvy. Thunder rumbles, the sky is shaken, stars shine in broad daylight, all walk on thin ice, the people cover themselves with clouds, the prince breathes up the dew. There is no more summer or winter; men no longer recognize father or mother. Everywhere you look there is nothing but darkness. The wise man shuts himself away and sits on his mat, humming softly. Outside, men howl with the wolves, trying to climb onto the jade throne.

"Eight and eight collide to make the sixty-four signs that punctuate the stages. When the Black Emperor dies, two suns shine; when the Black Emperor dies, the eye of the wolf shoots forth its rays, the crossbow looses its arrow, the star of fire turns back its light, and the white snake dies.

"Confucius drew up the rules that will be used during the reign of Red. That is why he wrote *Springs and Autumns*, which sets out the laws of cyclical succession and reveals the future in the traces of the past."

Then he rapped out:

"Orient Whet-Iron! Born of the part of space marked by the star Chen, he will receive the mandate and hand down the teaching. For Fire, through the impenetrable ways of Heaven, will make the dragon spew forth its pearl."

Mountain couldn't restrain himself.

"Gibberish!" he cried.

"Stupid idiot!" howled Wind angrily. " 'Orient Whet-Iron' is a cryptogram for the name of the Liu family, made up of the three roots East, Whet, and Iron. Chen refers to Ch'u, which lies under that constellation. The old man is uttering a prediction: A man of the name Liu will arise in that place and become emperor."

Heaven ignored the interruption, rose from his mat, and walked unsteadily over to the window. The rest of the company got up and joined him, as if drawn by a magnet.

The sinking sun lighted a window in a dilapidated low house opposite, which framed the figure of a woman. The back of her rather plump neck, which stood out against the darker tone of the room, was revealed because of the way her hair was piled on top of her head in two coils, a style favored by the peasant women of Ch'u. She was bending forward, her arms moving languidly back and forth performing some mysterious task. A pale ray of light found its way between the surrounding roofs and lighted up two feet in a bowl of water. There was something intimate and restful about the scene. The masks looked on, touched and amused.

"It's she," Earth whispered to Heaven. "Lady Liu, vessel of the Origin, bearer of the pearl of the Red Dragon."

"Of course! 'Feet in water! Feet in water!' That means gestation: the feet are the organs of movement, indicated by thunder—thunder and water go together—the hexagrammatic emblem of beginnings. In this auspicious conjunction, with the symbol of beginning, the Story may begin."

Then Heaven, eyes half closed, as if inspired:

"In the immutable beginning there was chaos, vast and void— a unique and turbulent mass closed in upon itself, a moist and misty dream giving off no light. The fineness of the spirit filled everything; no lightning flash disturbed the quintessential calm. Before Heaven, before Earth, it was there—the primal Tao, unmoving cause of every transformation. Sometimes yin, sometimes yang, he is the Way, the Great Pinnacle, who by splitting in two expresses himself and acts through the Two Norms, of which Heaven and Earth are the most complete expression. From these two models proceed the four seasons, and they in turn give rise to the good and bad luck that characterize human enterprises. Such is the order of the symbols that

23

govern events: these are the stages by which will arise the Red Dragon, whose reign Confucius predicted! 'Which is why there will be . . .' "

And the old man, listing in order the first thirty divinatory figures in the *Book of Changes*, used his fingers to calculate the vacant spaces, found the chink between the earthly branches and the heavenly boughs, and opened up a breach in time. It was as if six dragons, plain and striped, could be seen writhing themselves into the figure

There was a kind of tremor, and thunder and rain were unleashed. The room disappeared, and in its place was a gray landscape lighted by the pale rays of the setting sun.

BIRTH

Movement is trapped in a pass:
*   whence are born beauty and integrity.*
Hard and soft unite for the first time;
*   it is not easy.*

As she looked at the little dike holding back the water in the dam, she had the absurd thought: *Stone wall symbolizes integrity, good for the founding of a kingdom.* She felt cold. She had fallen asleep near the jetty in the pool that lay to the west of the village. She had taken to resting there of late because whenever she did so she had a dream predicting a miraculous future. Sometimes a red bird dropped a shining pearl into her mouth, and it went down into her belly and came forth in the shape of a flame-colored peacock. Sometimes she would be doing her washing and find a precious stone engraved with the words "Whoever swallows this jewel will bear a king." Sometimes a fabulous animal played with her. She had named the place the Pool of Dragon Dreams. But this time her dream had left her with a weight on her heart.

First there had been a meeting of people wearing masks. As she was washing her feet in warm water and enjoying the relaxation, she had had an uncomfortable feeling on the back of her neck, and when she turned around, there, looking at her from the window opposite, were eight hideous masks. One of the figures pointed an accusing finger at her, and she saw six lines, like six dragons, unfold in the air. Then everything collapsed, there was a peal of thunder, and it started to rain.

Dark masses of cloud coursed over the gray countryside. She went down among the bare fields dotted with pale green shoots of rice and walked along a bank that wound between them, widening as it came to a grove of mulberry trees. There, in the middle of the soaked earth, was a huge footprint. She burst out laughing and started to jump like a little girl inside the strange track. Soon her feet began to act independently of her will, making nimble and complicated movements of their own: first the left foot advanced, then the right; then the left drew level, then the right moved forward again, leaving the left behind. It was a kind of dance, with one foot lagging behind, imitating within the hollow of the footprint the seers' and exorcists' way of representing the Great Bear.

There was a kind of tremor. She was enveloped in a green-and-pink halo, lightning rent the air, and the earth gave way beneath her. Out of its folds emerged a scaly thing the color of flesh but ruddier, a sort of huge serpent that rose slowly, swaying to and fro a long thin muzzle with bulging eyes and a multicolored beardlike fringe. From the monster's body sprang a pair of bright red wings. It knocked her over, gripped her with its four sets of claws, lifted her dress, and entered her. At first she tried to resist, but then she remembered the phrase *"a swirling mass that bestrides and whirls: if not to loot, to wed."* And she ceased to struggle.

Soon she no longer felt how the beast had hurt her while it

moved in her. The clouds coursed across the sky, the thunder rumbled in the distance, and a fine rain sprinkled the black coils of her hair with silvery pearls.

When she opened her eyes, she saw her husband bending over her. Her clothes were dirty, her whole body was covered with shining foam, and all around her the ground was strewn with shimmering pink and red fragments that glowed like carbuncles. She was enfolded as though in a casket of mother-of-pearl set with gems: all made of the dragon's scales and sperm. Her husband looked thoughtful, put down his hoe, and said, smiling: "You will be the mother of an emperor."

She suddenly felt cold again, and woke up. Her feet were still in the basin of water, and her husband's face was leaning over her.

"Do you think the weaving does itself, you lazy creature? Or that the pot can boil without fire?"

She roused herself. She had had a dream of a dream. She'd have to ask a soothsayer if it was auspicious. The dragon was a good sign, anyhow. After she had dried her feet and put on her slippers, she turned toward the northwest, smoothed her hair, and recited mentally: "Go back to the tiger Ch'iung-ch'i, you nightmares, that he may cram himself with your flesh and thank me by sending great happiness. If it's not good money, let it be good cloth; if not wadding of silk, let it be of willow!"

———

The birth of Lady Liu's son wasn't greeted by any particular omens. No new star or phoenix or dragon was seen. But the whole village rejoiced, for on the same day and at almost the same hour a son was also born to the Kuans, the Lius' best friends. The coincidence was thought to be auspicious. It was a good omen that two families so closely linked should each have a son at the same time: Heaven had given their friendship its blessing. Two sheep and some wine were brought in procession, and a feast was held in the Kuans' house, larger than that of the Lius'. The two infants were believed to have excellent futures before them, as civil servants, with plenty of money and long life.

It was *chi-mao* day in the second month of winter, and the local scholar was consulted. The entry he found for that date in the almanac was: *"He will leave his own province"*; so the Liu child was named Pang, which means "country." Another soothsayer was consulted, to read the message contained in the leaves of the yarrow plant. He came upon the mutant line in the Heaven hexagram: *"Dragon couchant is unemployed."* The child's parents were glad about the reference to the dragon, but worried about the word "unemployed."

BLINDNESS

Fine and promising is the blindness of youth!
The Spring under the Mountain:
  the wise man cultivates virtue
  by perfecting his behavior.

Disturbing signs characterized Liu's—Whet-Iron's—childhood. Locusts attacked the Empire, covering it with a gray cloak and laying waste the crops. The sun was hidden by an eclipse. In the twenty-third year of King Kao-lie of Ch'u, a comet blazed through the west and northwest part of the sky, and soon afterward Hsia, the dowager queen and grandmother of King Order of Ch'in, died. The comet reappeared two years later, filled space with a huge yellow vapor, and threw a sulphurous veil over the cold clear night of Ch'in. And this time the false eunuch Lao Ai tried, with the aid of his mistress, the king's mother, to overthrow the king.

The sort of people who believe in immediate cause and effect saw the comet's two appearances as omens presaging the two events.

But more profound thinkers shook their heads and said nothing. They realized that the true interpretation was quite different.

Great shoals of fish swam up the main rivers against the current, the cold-blooded creatures with their protective scales foreshadowing the armed bands in coats of mail that would fall upon the Empire spreading chaos and death. The stars called the Wolf and the Crossbow shone with unusual brightness. Winters were unduly long, and imprisoned the earth in a shroud of ice. Late frosts withered the tender shoots of spring. Men changed into women. There were reports of a girl whose sex organs were on the top of her head, while another's were in the middle of her navel. But all these disturbances of the natural cycle, far from relating to individual circumstances, heralded a whole age of hardship, when the yin principle of winter, cold and dark and secret, would reign unchallenged and plunge the world into darkness.

It was already affecting the way men behaved. The princes lived in a state of blindness. Either—like the Chao, the Han, the Wei, and the Ch'i—they were obsessed by trivial quarrels and rivalries, and plotted against one another, making and unmaking conspiracies, but in the end always coming around to Ch'in, which gradually ate them up like a silkworm consuming a mulberry leaf. Or, like the Prince of Yen, distracted by a humiliation inflicted by a powerful neighbor, they tried to satisfy their hatred by murder, instead of through long-term planning. Perhaps even the King of Ch'in, who prided himself on his clear-sightedness, was really motivated by the pleasure he derived from the immoderate use of force.

The ministers too were blind. The mind of Spring Awakening, prime minister of Ch'u, was so clouded by fear of losing his privileges and by desire for more and more power, combined paradoxically with the illusion of his invulnerability, that he fell into a crude trap set for him by a boor and a coward. And Lü Pu-wei, a bold and perspicacious merchant who traded in princes and had become the most powerful man in the Empire, extracted the post of prime minister from the pale monarch, who owed him his throne. But so in-

30

toxicated was he by his own success that he was incapable of guarding against the perfectly predictable misfortune that lay in wait for him.

The blindness of the great extinguished all light in the world around them. It threw tens of thousands of men into murky jails and dank dungeons where the sun never shone—a darkness as deep, as endless, and as final as the darkness of the blind. Over the eyes of others it threw an impenetrable gray veil of resignation as they groped their way along the desolate road of life, surrounded by the bloody gloom of war and threatened by the indiscriminate executioner's block of the law.

In this somber world Whet-Iron, son of the Red Dragon, lived with the good, healthy, measureless blindness of youth—a temporary state due merely to ignorance, but promising a fine flowering in the gentle rays of the spring sun; a seed in the dusk of its pod, ready to open up to the light.

When he was eight, the age at which the inner breath begins to stir and to make children interested and receptive to instruction, the teachers at the local school set about dispersing the mists of ignorance in young Whet-Iron and in a hundred or so of his fellow urchins. In a big classroom open to the winds they faltered through the *Reading Book of the Great Historiographer of the Chou*, four characters at a time. But in his case the seed must have been surrounded by a particularly tough husk, for when Whet-Iron wasn't having to sit without his shirt to show he was sorry for misbehaving, he was being flogged for idleness or unsatisfactory writing. He was disrespectful, and preferred the company of naughty boys to that of sensible people. Instead of poring over the *Book of Filial Piety*, the *Book of Odes*, or the *Book of Documents*, he roved the woods and marshes in search of birds' nests, crickets, or dragonflies, which he stuck pins through and whirled around on a piece of string. But his family and their neighbors were quite happy, because he and String, the Kuans' son, were friends, and inseparable. Even if so far the only result of this attachment was to lead them into mischief, it was nonetheless a proof of filial piety, a promise of continuity, in that it carried on the friendship between their parents and fulfilled the expectations of Heaven, which had blessed that friendship by causing the two boys to be born on the same day.

And so when the two young rascals left school, after learning very little, neighbors and friends came and made them presents of a sheep and some jars of wine. Feasts were held in both houses, and both families rejoiced that the boys promised to bring their parents great happiness.

———

The ignorance of childhood was followed by its natural prolongation, the heedlessness of youth. At the age of sixteen, when a boy's veins begin to swell with the sap from the north, Whet-Iron started chasing girls, and spent more time entwined with the body of some peasant girl than poring over the eight bodies of scripture. Still, he never went anywhere without his bag of books, and this evidence of his penchant for learning and ambition to become a civil servant enabled him to get out of all domestic chores and decline to share in the work in the fields.

Instead of catching dragonflies, he now went to dog and cock fights. Instead of wandering through the woods, he frequented fairs and markets. Instead of eating birds' eggs, he knocked back glasses of sour wine in Mother Wang's tavern or Mother Wei's shop; they both gave him credit on the strength of his good looks. Besides his friend String, he now had an entourage of happy fellows, drinkers and gamblers always ready to make a bet or fight or have a tumble with a girl. When they ran out of money—which was often, since none of them had a job—they would invite themselves to some random victim's place to eat, and because Whet-Iron had a violent temper they were rarely refused. One day, at the house of his eldest brother's widow, he shoved her face in the cooking pot and smashed all the furniture just because she, having to work hard to support herself, was tired of seeing him and his friends stuffing themselves with her food, and had scraped the bottom of the pot with a spoon to make them think it was empty.

But even if his temper did sometimes get the better of him, and even if it seemed doubtful whether his teachers' efforts would ever succeed in extracting the seed from its husk of ignorance, Whet-Iron was acquiring a great deal of knowledge. In his own way he was "cultivating virtue and perfecting his behavior." His regular attendance at cockfights taught him the fundamental elements of the art of war and initiated him into the rules of strategy, which according to the great master Sun Tzu consists in separating cocks from hens. Since Whet-Iron could distinguish between two cocks, he was certainly able to tell the difference between a cock and a hen. Through his relations with the opposite sex he learned the natural motion of yin and yang, the alternation of which governs the rhythm of the seasons and presides over the upheavals of History. That was his way of learning the laws by which men may rule peoples and nations. His social life brought him into contact with all kinds of people, the dregs of humanity for the most part. He thus followed the rule governing success and failure which holds that you must stoop to conquer, and in so doing he acquired the accessibility and ease of manner that denote a Great Man.

So what looked like folly and incorrigible giddiness helped him, in reality, to grow in experience and wisdom. Yet at the age of nineteen he was far from knowing the nine thousand characters in the *Writers' Manual*. So he couldn't sit for the civil-service recruitment examination, the commoner's gateway to a post as archivist or scribe and thence to a career in provincial government.

WAITING

Fame is at the end of the road
if only one perseveres.
Faced with a ravine, if one stays firm
one need not fall in,
nor meet with any real misfortune.

The sky was still and silent and devoid of any sign, as if waiting. But what can the sky wait for that it doesn't already know in advance?

The Empire that Ch'in had gathered into its power was in suspense too. It was hoping for the end of its sufferings, holding its breath, uncertain what to do, for the slightest wrong move could lead to slavery. People made themselves as small as possible, trying to turn themselves into a cloud or mist or a breeze: to expose themselves as little as possible to denunciation by their neighbors, the vigilance of the authorities, and the harsh force of the law.

In addition to this general, almost cosmic anticipation, there were many individual longings for a breath of change, some alteration that might lift the shroud of repression smothering everyone.

Fathers who had been deported to the borders of the realm prayed to be hit by the arrows of the Huns, so their bones might freeze, ending their suffering. Sons exiled to the sweltering southern marches hoped one last bout of fever would set the final icy seal on their trembling limbs. And those whose families had been doomed to be tradesmen for two generations languished in camps, waiting to be marched to the farthest limits of the Empire, to replace the kinsmen whose corpses bestrewed the wilderness and no longer waited for anything.

Governors of provinces waited for instructions from the central government, which they would pass on to prefects of departments, and they to subprefects. Subprefects would pass them on to districts, where they would be posted to terrify inhabitants, who lived in dread of ever more severe laws.

Brigands who'd taken refuge in the forests and marshes to escape conscription waited along the roads to fall on travelers and rob them.

———

It was a dark night and a lonely place, and a dense fog was drifting up from the river. The man pacing back and forth in this inhospitable spot might have been taken for a lurking robber. He had several things in common with a bandit: he was an outlaw, and he lived in Hsia-p'i under a false identity. Three years earlier he had indeed lain in wait for a traveler, not to rob him, but to beat his head to a pulp with a bronze cudgel.

The moon cast yellow patches on the shroud of fog that lay over the riverbanks. The cold of the night, intensified by the dampness, bit deep into the man's bones. The waiting seemed to have petrified time itself. This gave his pacing a hieratic air, as if it were part of some sacred vigil; so he almost took pleasure in the pain that cramped his limbs.

He had always known that it wasn't just to pay him back in his own coin that the old man made him wait like this: it was a test, intended to put his patience to the proof. But he was beginning to realize that it was meant to be a lesson too, something to make him think. It stretched a short period of his life into an eternity, and made him achingly conscious that this expansion of time-as-experienced—which far from being the fullest form of time is really the most meager—was going to lead to an important turning point. Such suspense was nothing new to him: his whole life so far had been one long waiting.

Chang the Good—for it was he who was kicking his heels here beside the Chih River—was a man of the past who had never resigned himself to the fact that it was over. All he lived for was its return, and he was forever thinking he saw signs of this revival in a present that, on the contrary, only dreaded what he hoped for. He believed in omens and watched everyone else's slightest gestures, not because he was interested in his fellow creatures, but in the hope of deciphering destiny.

He came from a noble family in Han which had supplied that principality with prime ministers for generations. When Ch'in annexed Han, and the August Emperor deposed its princes, Chang saw it as a mortal insult, and after an assassin hired by the Prince of Yen failed in a first attempt to avenge the Empire, he resolved to do the job himself. By chance, he came across Wu Hao, a blacksmith of the Mo-sui clan whose worth was evident from the way he wielded his bellows. Chang made friends with him and got him to forge a cudgel weighing two hundred pounds. The two of them lay in wait for the Emperor as he rode along one day, fell upon his party, and attempted to smash the tyrant's carriage. But they missed their target and had to separate and flee. Chang the Good ended up in Hsia-p'i.

Suddenly he started. His ears had caught a faint sound, like that of oars skimming the water. A shape moved through the mist and then materialized out of it, the play of moonlight soon revealing a human being. The white-haired ancient jumped noiselessly out of the boat and advanced like a drift of denser vapor.

Two weeks earlier, Chang, strolling idly by the river, was crossing a bridge when he met an old man whose sandal had come off and fallen in the water, and who unceremoniously ordered him to rescue it. Chang's first thought was to give the stranger a beating, but out of respect for his age he restrained himself and did as he was asked. When the cantankerous old fellow stuck out a dirty foot, Chang knelt and put the sandal on again. He had already been humiliated; he'd only look more ridiculous, without wiping out the insult, if he beat the old fellow now. And, since he was so interested in omens, perhaps he also had a presentiment. The stranger went on his way, and Chang, intrigued by his haughty manner, followed. As they approached the gates of the town, the old man turned around and said:

"Meet me here in five days' time at sunrise."

Twice since then Chang, arriving late, had been sent away by the old man, who was furious at being kept waiting. So this time Chang had set out before midnight, and by now he'd been hanging around for hours.

When the old man saw Chang standing on the riverbank, by the bridge, his face relaxed.

"We have chosen you to help a king," he said. "A new dynasty will arise thirteen years from now."

"Who do you mean by 'we'?"

"If you don't know, there's no point in my answering; if you do know, there's no point in your asking."

"The Trigrams?"

"You might equally well say fate!"

"So they really do exist! There was a rumor they were just imaginary. But there are so many rumors. Some people say they were working for Ch'in, and disappeared after Ch'in's victory."

"Ch'in is merely the executor of Heaven's will. The ways of fate are inscrutable and may not be revealed."

"How shall I recognize him?"

"It's because you recognize him that he'll be the king."

"And how can I help him?"

"With this!"

The old man drew a book from his sleeve and held it out to Chang. It was *The Art of Strategy of the Eight Trigrams of King Wen*.

"Study, be patient, and your time will come," he said. Then he turned and disappeared, and on that very spot Chang's foot hit a stone shining in the light of the moon. He picked it up and looked at it. It was green, with white veins depicting unicorns, phoenixes, and dragons. And in the middle, quite clearly visible, there was an octagon containing the eight trigrams of King Wen. Chang sighed and slipped the strange object into his sleeve.

Chang waited patiently and took in all kinds of fugitives in the hope of finding the future Son of Heaven—knights-errant, scholars, and others who had abandoned friends, family, the tombs of their ancestors, and even their own identities and fled to this remote region where rough country and a population hostile to Ch'in protected them from pursuit.

———

Whet-Iron too was on the lookout for a sign of his destiny. Some of the men in black coats who traveled the dusty roads in those days of ice and iron, and earned their living by selling that intangible but precious commodity the future, had told him he had a brilliant one. So far, all he'd got was a fine red uniform: he had managed to pass the examination for a post as local police chief in the subprefecture of P'ei. He looked very grand walking around the streets in his uniform, stalking as confidently as a cat on his broad feet in string sandals, throwing out his chest as proudly as a bear, the nose on his big fat face held high.

At meetings of regional worthies and civil servants he was treated with respect despite his lowly rank, though he treated his superiors quite casually. Some people said this was because he was thought to have the makings of a Great Man. Admittedly no one was better than he at arranging a funeral, livening a wedding, or organizing a banquet, private or official. He always shared the bag shrewdly after a hunt, and at local memorial ceremonies and sacrifices to the god of the Earth he divided the offerings so impartially that people exclaimed, "Well, there are never any recriminations when Liu performs the sacrifice!" But others said the consideration people showed him was due to his relationship with the underworld.

And it was true that the room where he put up visiting officials more often offered hospitality to the very outlaws, gallows birds, and brigands he was supposed to track down. He was often seen sitting in low taverns with gang leaders, hired assassins, and heads of private armies. There would have been nothing wrong with this—it was part of his professional duty to mix with criminals—except that some of these hard cases were his best friends. Be that as it might, this way of operating had won him useful protection from certain influential groups, and he preferred to be in their good books than risk being discovered someday with his throat cut or a knife in his back.

Yet another theory was that he was directly linked to the Ministry of the Interior. This wasn't entirely untrue. You still have to live, even while you're waiting for a great destiny to begin: if you don't come to terms with the powers that be, you'll suffer the fate of all who are too virtuous to tolerate compromise. You'll be cut off by a death as obscure as it is sublime before you ever realize your glorious future. Whet-Iron had the courage to be a coward. He wrote reports on all his bosses and the local gentry he rubbed shoulders with. The central authorities had chosen to keep them under close surveillance rather than embark on direct and brutal repression, which in these still unsettled regions could easily lead to trouble. Every so often they did launch a campaign against banditry and crime, and then Whet-Iron would humor his masters and put them off the scent by arresting some of the smaller fry, while letting the larger quarry escape.

Meanwhile, time went by and he had not yet done anything out of the ordinary. He still prowled around like a wild beast seeking its prey, and his tall figure and tigerish countenance were to be seen in markets and taverns, surrounded by young reprobates who half admired and half feared him.

His parents, who had had such high hopes of him after the coincidence of his and String's births, had grown weary and transferred their dreams of advancement to their youngest son, Ramble. He, unlike his brother, had been a brilliant student. Too brilliant, perhaps—he'd spurned a civil-service career in order to follow Wandering Hill, an itinerant teacher from Lu. Wandering Hill was a disciple of Hsun Tzu, a Confucian and an expert in the tradition of the *Book of Odes*. His school had been famous, and his pupils had included such remarkable scholars as Master Millet, Master White, and Master Extension. He had been a friend of Sky Blue, the archivist of the imperial library, and kept in touch with the prime minister, Li Ssu, who had studied with him under the same teacher. This choice might have led the younger Liu to positions of great distinction. Unfortunately, because of the great proscription of the classics, his master's teaching was also banned. Wandering Hill's pupils had abandoned him, his protectors at court were themselves the object of persecution, and it was Li Ssu himself who had organized the hounding of the scholars.

So Wandering Hill and a few faithful pupils, including Ramble, became interpreters of the books of divination, the only books that were still allowed, and earned their living by extracting hexagrams from them. And thus the elderly Lius were disappointed also in their last-born son, whose brilliance at his studies should have led to a distinguished future. They gave up hope of rising in the world through their children, and grew sullen and resigned. Their bitterness and disillusion redounded on Whet-Iron. Whenever he went to see them to fulfill his filial duties, he was followed everywhere by their looks of reproach and disappointment.

Sometimes, in the middle of a merry drinking bout or rowdy party, his brow would cloud. He sensed that his friends' faith in him was starting to fade, and that the civil servants would not put up with his superciliousness much longer: their respect had gradually become tinged with condescension, which was only waiting for an opportunity to turn to outright contempt. And as he squatted in the latrine with his hands on his hips, producing a large turd, he couldn't help thinking, as he felt the rolls of fat beneath his fingers, that he was now over forty and hadn't achieved anything.

There were new candidates, and by no means inconsiderable ones, angling for the admiration of the roisterers and swashbucklers. Yung Ch'ih, known as Barricade of Teeth, was Whet-Iron's most dangerous rival. He was a young man from a family of wealthy potentates in Big Bridge who had fled to Feng, along with many of the noblemen of Wei, when its capital was destroyed by the Great Emperor. Barricade of Teeth had squandered his inheritance maintaining a retinue of toughs; and, in addition to enjoying the support of the Wei émigrés, he had won the respect of the local population for his physical prowess, his good humor, and his liberality toward the knights-errant.

Although Whet-Iron and Yung Ch'ih were secretly hostile to one another, they had tacitly agreed to pretend to be friends. Neither was confident of coming off best in an open struggle, so for the present they preferred to get along with one another.

———

Despite his displays of gaiety and exuberance, Whet-Iron became more and more subject to fits of depression. But his lucky star was watching over him, and to save him from despair it sent him a reassuring token of advancement. As a matter of fact, Heaven often sent the local police chief signs that his present humble position had no bearing on his real destiny, encouraging him and exhorting him to patience through various interpreters of its will—or, to put it more prosaically, through the occult influence of the sect of soothsayers, with whom Whet-Iron was unwittingly connected through his younger brother, Ramble.

Some years earlier, when whispers started to be heard even among his closest associates suggesting that Whet-Iron promised more than he performed, a friend of the prefect of P'ei, who had a reputation as a physiognomist, was so struck by his looks that he offered him his daughter's hand in marriage. Although this seemed to promise much for his career, its chief effect was to tie Whet-Iron down to a nagging wife and the two squalling brats she soon presented him with. Shortly after that, the prefect was deported for embezzlement, and Whet-Iron's father-in-law, who had taken refuge with the prefect after some trouble of his own with the law, was thrown into prison and beaten to death.

This time the prediction was accompanied by a tangible sign. Because his meager salary was not enough to keep a wife and two children, Whet-Iron had started to farm a few acres of land, and often took time off to look after them. One day, on his way to join his wife in the fields, he saw an old man with a white beard coming toward him, his noble bearing emphasized by the poverty of his dress.

"I have just seen a mother and two children destined for great success," said the old man. "You will be the source of their fortune. But if you want to ride in the dragon's chariot, you must win the friendship of the keeper of the Trigrams' charter."

And he went on his way. Whet-Iron, hurrying after him, knocked his foot against a stone on the very spot where he had seen him disappear. It glittered so strangely that he picked it up. It had green-and-white markings in the shape of fabulous animals, and in the middle was an octagon enclosing the eight trigrams. Whet-Iron's heart filled with hope, and he stowed the stone away in his sleeve. Then he grinned cynically and thought: Oh, well, in the meanwhile I can always tie it to my belt to impress my friends.

BRUSHES WITH THE LAW

Even for someone of integrity and circumspection,
processes are not auspicious
if they do not reach their conclusion.
The sight of a Great Man is favorable,
unfavorable the crossing of a great river.

Anticipation turned into impatience, though this scarcely showed itself, because people were too frightened to come out in deliberate opposition. So far there were only tremors.

Then repression struck with redoubled violence, and new fugitives continually swelled the ranks of the outcasts hiding among the hills and marshes. Gradually a network grew, a kind of mutual-aid society for saving victims from the ever hungrier maw of justice, and conveying them to hideouts in the South-East.

So fierce and dense was the jungle of rules and regulations in Ch'in that no one could be sure of escaping all its snares. Men from all ranks of society tried to elude the law by forming bands of looters. Members of such gangs came not only from among minor civil servants and local gentry, aggressive and unruly fellows used to wielding a sword, but also from among artisans, fishermen, and peasants.

The new governor of Low Country rode proudly through the streets of the town under the silver-braided canopy of his carriage, flanked by guards bearing aloft the insignia of his authority. Heads bent like grasses of the steppe beneath the wind as he passed by. Lesser conveyances moved to the side of the road, their occupants spilling out hastily to bow; horsemen made themselves scarce. But one carriage continued on its way, driven by an immensely tall and impressive man with a red face and long mustaches. He not only failed to stop, but also urged his horses forward in such a way that the prefect's were obliged to swerve. The prefect recognized this eight-foot giant as Beam, son of the famous Ch'u general Hsiang the Swallow. He glared at him and hissed:

"How dare you flaunt yourself thus, son of a vanquished general through whom his master lost his altars to the gods of earth and harvest?"

The giant let out a roar and raised his arm as if to strike. The prefect turned around and drove home, where he hastily summoned his officials.

"You know the directives of the central government, don't you?" he stormed. "Ministers, noblemen, and generals of the old kingdoms are not allowed to live in their native provinces. They're supposed to be relegated to the outskirts of the capital and live there under house arrest. And who did I come across no more than an hour ago? Beam, the son of the rebel general Swallow, swaggering through the streets! How is it he wasn't deported with all the rest?"

"We decided not to press the matter for reasons of political expediency. His father is worshiped like a god by the local people, and we thought banishing him would lead to unrest."

"And you don't think his presence here, in defiance of the Law, might do the same? I want him transferred immediately to Yüeh-yang!"

A large troop of policemen was sent at once to the Swallow's palace, where they arrested Beam, Uncle Hsiang, and Plume, a young orphaned nephew whom Beam had taken under his wing. All three were transferred under strong guard to the remotest mountains.

A year later, at the time when accounts had to be presented in the capital, Double Light, the prefect of Low Country went to Ch'in and stopped at the official guest house in the suburbs. On the next day but one, he was found lying in a pool of blood with his throat cut. All his belongings had been stolen. At first the police treated it as an ordinary crime, but an enemy of the Hsiangs sent a letter accusing the Ch'u general's family of having had one of their followers kill the prefect out of revenge. The murderer was found—or, rather, his corpse was. He had cut his own throat so he couldn't be made to betray his masters.

Beam was arrested and questioned, but he managed to get a letter to the head of the crime department in his own province, who had been under obligation to him in the past. Beam asked him to intercede with his friend and colleague in Yüeh-yang. The official back in Ch'u had a high regard for Beam, and also feared that if he were found guilty there would be trouble in his unruly principality. He pointed out to his colleague in Ch'in that there was no proof against Beam, since the only witness had died before confessing anything. So the case was closed.

Beam escaped the vigilance of the authorities and took Uncle Hsiang back to Low Country, where they wiped out the whole family of the man who had denounced them, and then fled. Beam and Plume took refuge in the region of Wu, south of the Blue River, while Swallow's elder brother took a friend's advice and went to Hsia-p'i, where Chang the Good gave him bed and board and treated him with great respect. He could see from his appearance that he was someone out of the ordinary. When Chang heard from some of his

45

own followers that the murdered prefect's relatives were looking for his guest to take revenge on him, he sent some of his mercenaries to kill them, and exterminated all their clan.

———

Ear and Scrap also managed to escape the rigors of the Law. It didn't take them long to find help in doing so. They were scholars brought together by similar tastes and similar destinies. They had both married very beautiful and wealthy wives when they were still quite young, with no advantages but their hopes. Thanks to their wives' fortunes they had each established an entourage and acquired a reputation for being Great Men. Ear had been made a prefect on the strength of it.

After Ch'in annexed Wei, they both went on living there as private individuals, but when the August First Emperor, claiming that they were a danger to society, decided to eliminate all the philosophers, knights-errant, and other distinguished inhabitants of the old principalities, and had his officials draw up a list of everyone who enjoyed any kind of celebrity, Ear and Scrap were on the list. A price was put on their heads. But a civil servant managed to warn them before the "wanted" posters were put up. They changed their names and took refuge in the hills of T'ang, regarded as a haven for all those in trouble with the authorities. An active search was made for them; so they hadn't found the safety they had hoped for. Tracked from village to village, they would have been reduced to the direst straits if Whet-Iron had not intervened.

Ear's and Scrap's reputation for being out of the ordinary had spread far beyond the bounds of their own province, and their wisdom was proverbial in P'ei. Whet-Iron, who prided himself on paying proper respect to philosophers, took advantage of his official visits to the capital of Ch'in to deliver batches of criminals and convicts, to visit Ear and Scrap on his way home, often staying quite a long time with them.

When he learned that they were in difficulties, he used his influence with an assistant secretary of Criminal Affairs in the prefecture of Ch'en and got each of them a job with the city government. Ear and Scrap were thus able both to earn a living and to escape pursuit, for they were put in charge of espionage and denunciation in part of the city.

———

The very officials who were supposed to be carrying out the campaign of repression could also be struck down by it, and their offenses were then treated as all the more heinous because of their position.

Whet-Iron, who had succeeded so well in keeping Ear and Scrap out of the clutches of the Law, came to be harassed by it himself. The first time was for a mere peccadillo. He was in the habit of playing rough games with his friends, and during a bout of singlestick he injured String rather seriously. A witness denounced him, and he was charged with assault. A state official convicted of such a crime was liable to hard labor and branding on the face. But during the interrogation String maintained that Whet-Iron was innocent. Even when a further inquiry was ordered and String was beaten with bamboo rods, he wouldn't change his story. He was charged with perjury, and joined his friend in prison. Whet-Iron's wife, Lü the Pheasant, begged his local police colleagues to do something. Finally they agreed, and Ts'ao the Examiner, secretary to the law courts, had the case closed.

A little while after this misadventure, Whet-Iron was instructed to take a convoy of convicts to the tomb of the August Emperor. Usually he didn't mind going beyond the passes, because it gave him a chance to stroll around the capital looking at the palaces, stopping at shops and market stalls, and drinking in the atmosphere of activity, elegance, and luxury. Not to mention the fact that he could enjoy himself in brothels and dives without having to endure the lamentations and reproaches of the Pheasant. Also, with a little luck, he might see an imperial procession, with the August First Emperor standing in his red-decorated black chariot, being drawn by six black chargers between two lines of Tiger Officer Guards in animal-tail caps and uniforms with striped facings, while standard-bearers carried banners stamped with Black Dragons. It was an imposing and magnificent spectacle, even if it did smell of oppression. But for some time the monarch had given up going out. He wanted to be as inscrutable as the gods; and the ban on private trading had greatly reduced the lively bustle of the marketplace. Moreover, the spirit of rebellion, which had never really deserted the scholars and the swashbucklers, had now spread to the people. Inscriptions predicting the end of the dynasty had started to appear everywhere, echoed in the songs that urchins sang in the streets. All this had nothing to do with the gentry or the nobles, who were only too eager to come to terms with the authorities in order to be left to lord it over the provinces. The local notables were the first to resent the popular unrest: it gave the central government an excuse to intervene in their affairs. Some saw it as the work of the guild of soothsayers, the Hexagrams, but Whet-Iron didn't agree. Their leading lights had posts at court, where honors and gifts were showered upon them, and the only books that remained unbanned were divination manuals.

So he wasn't at all pleased at the prospect of his present mission. The conscripts were difficult to handle, and desertions were increasing. He could understand that: it was better to take off into the blue than let yourself be led like a lamb to the slaughter.

His fears turned out to be justified. Before two stages of his journey were complete, half his men had melted away. At that rate there wouldn't be a single convict left by the time he reached his destination. To take his mind off this, he pitched camp near the marshes to the west of the subprefecture of Feng, and went to see his local opposite number. The two district chiefs of police started to drink while discussing their hopes and fears and how difficult life was. Whet-Iron bemoaned the fate that forced him to take men who were his comrades and fellow countrymen and deliver them to servitude and death under a foreign master. Then they started to play *liu-po*, and quarreled over a move. They'd had a lot to drink, and soon became very heated. The Feng police chief grew abusive, and Whet-Iron replied in kind. The other drew his sword, and Whet-Iron was so angry he wrenched it from him and ran him through. He regretted it at once. Even if he pleaded self-defense, he risked the death penalty!

He went back to his camp and released all the men from their chains.

"Away you go!" he told them. "I'm off myself!"

A dozen or so said they'd go with him.

"Why don't we stay together? We'd make a good team."

They collected some wine and drank until nightfall, praising the exploits of past heroes and saying how much better it was to be robbers living a free and adventurous life than to be respectable citizens, who were much more likely to fall into the clutches of the Law. It was getting late. The moon had risen and was shedding its pale light everywhere. Whet-Iron was afraid someone might give the alarm and catch them.

"Let's go!" he said.

So they set off across the marshes. It was dangerous country, and he sent a man ahead to scout. The man soon returned, pale with terror.

"There's a huge snake barring the way!" he said. "We can't get past."

Whet-Iron waved his hand airily.

"Nothing can bar the way of a brave man," he answered.

Drawing his sword, he set out, staggering unsteadily along until he came to an enormous serpent lying numbed by the cold. He lifted his sword and brought it down on the snake, chopping it into three pieces. Then he stepped over it, advanced a few paces, and fell down by the path dead drunk.

His companions waited for him till dawn, when, out of the gray drifts of mist that hung over the reeds and rushes, there emerged a white-bearded old man with a dignified air despite his homespun tunic. He was carrying the paraphernalia of a soothsayer. Their first thought was to kill him, but they changed their minds: it would bring bad luck, and, anyway, soothsayers didn't give people away to the police. They asked the old man to tell their fortunes.

"Band of runaways," he said, "whose leader is the slayer of the White Serpent."

"Oh!" one cried. "There *was* a huge serpent barring the way, and our leader set out to fight it. Let's go and see!"

They found the reptile in pieces and Liu sleeping it off nearby. They bent over Whet-Iron admiringly, and when he awoke they repeated what the soothsayer, who had disappeared, had told them.

"I had a dream just like that," said Whet-Iron, a sly gleam in his eye. "A woman dressed in white was weeping by the side of the road and saying, 'The Red Dragon has killed my son, the White Dragon!'"

The whole gang, happy now to serve him, hid in the scrubland that lay between T'ang and Mang. But Liu had a hard time of it, with the Ch'in police after him; he suffered from the fear, hunger, and lack of sleep that are the lot of all hunted creatures. He managed to get a message to his friend String, and through him Lü the Pheasant knew where to deliver food and news to her husband. People said she could trace him because of the red vapor he gave off, and the August Emperor, on the advice of his geomancers, set out to find this emanation and slay him. People were starting to talk about wonders and marvels.

More people came to join the band of fugitives. Jen Ao, an assistant secretary at the Ministry of Criminal Affairs and a close friend of the Lius, had been unable to stand by and do nothing when a law officer molested Lü after her husband had fled. He'd fallen on the offender and beaten him so fiercely he broke his spine. So Jen Ao too, in flight from the authorities, joined the outlaws. After a year on the run, Whet-Iron found himself at the head of a couple of hundred brigands.

———

The horse was black with white pasterns, a beautiful creature with a shining coat, a saddle trimmed with gold, and a spray of kingfisher feathers nodding between ears as sharp as bamboo shoots—a mount fit for a prince. Tattooed Face put his bundle of sticks down by the side of the road and caught the magnificent steed by the bridle. It offered no objection, so he stroked its neck; then, unable to resist the temptation, he sprang onto its back. First it reared, then it answered the bit, and Tattooed Face set off at a gallop. The neat hooves seemed to swallow up the miles, and the rider, intoxicated by the thrill of his flight, didn't hear the noise rising behind him. Suddenly he was surrounded by a group of armed men—the escort of the prefect of Six, whose horse had thrown him and bolted. The guards had ridden off in pursuit, and a peasant, hoping to get a reward, had told them he'd seen a man riding off on its back, presumably with the intention of stealing it.

Tattooed Face was hauled off to prison and subjected to harsh interrogation. But no matter how much they beat him, he smiled happily. When asked why, he said a soothsayer had told him he would become king after he had been branded like a convict: he'd been given his nickname because of this prophecy. And he was glad that the first part of the prediction was about to be fulfilled, because now he could no longer doubt that the second part would come true too.

According to the Penal Code his crime was only an "unpremeditated theft," for which the maximum penalty was two years' hard labor without branding or amputation. But the prefect thought the prisoner was laughing at him, so he had him accused of deliberate theft. In such cases the punishment was proportionate to the value of the object stolen, so Tattooed Face was sentenced to have his nose cut off and do three years' hard labor.

He served his sentence packing earth on building sites in the prefecture. Then, because there weren't enough free laborers to carry out all the August Emperor's grandiose projects, he was sent to work on the ruler's tomb, along with two hundred thousand other convicts. But Tattooed Face had presence and authority, which, together with the aura of his distinguished horoscope, greatly impressed the lower ranks of his fellow prisoners. He also made friends with their leaders and with the deported notables among them. These he persuaded to escape with him to the region of the Blue River. They broke their chains, strangled their guards, and, thanks to their contacts among the local potentates, managed to reach the hills of T'ang. Once there they turned themselves into a gang of bandits.

Although by rights he ought to have blessed the prefect of Six for having, by mutilating him, set him on the road to fortune, Tattooed Face was illogical enough to hate him implacably, and he and his comrades mounted a punitive expedition against him. They set fire to his official residence, and in the ensuing confusion cut his throat and seized all his treasures, including his horse, a filly from Ferghana which the Khans had presented to the Great Emperor of Ch'in, who in turn had passed it on to the prefect as a reward for his merits.

THE RISING OF
THE MASSES

The masses are virtuous
and the Great Man enjoys good fortune
without encountering obstacles.
He crosses passes steadfastly.
And thus he rules and is obeyed.
He obtains favorable auguries and meets with no pitfalls.

The death of the First Emperor could not be concealed, and a replacement had to be found. It should have been Fu Su, but in fact it was Barbarian, his younger brother, owing to the intrigues of his tutor, the eunuch Chao the Tall. The succession didn't change anything, and it seemed that everything might—as it should—go on as before. Wasn't the system more important than the individuals who followed one another at the head of it? But the death of the Founder cast doubt on the inevitability of the order he had created, so the continuity, instead of reinforcing its power, undermined it by bringing out the contrast between its precariousness and its violence. Perhaps some radical change, or at least some appearance of change, was needed to wipe out the shame of the August Emperor's defeat by death. Fu Su might have provided this: great hopes had been pinned on him, and on the fact that he'd been critical of his father's severity. Barbarian's accession provided a haughty affirmation of permanence; but the previous order wasn't wanted anymore. The death of its creator had demonstrated in no uncertain manner that he too was subject to the law of change. Li Ssu knew this, and he, the very architect of the terror, found himself starting to think about the possibility of softening the laws and hiding torture under the veil of morality.

However, either because he was the prisoner of his role or because his tongue was stiff from repeating the same slogans over and over again for twenty years, he couldn't change his tune. Every time he was in the presence of that blasé, distant countenance, with its weak and greedy lips twisted in a scowl, he wanted to cry out, "Master, you must restrain your appetites, make the laws less harsh and your exactions less burdensome!" Instead, his lips, as if under a spell, repeated the old refrain: "Make the laws more severe and repression fiercer, deport and kill people, terrorize them so much they dare not even breathe, and thus torture will be abolished by torture, and the Great Peace will reign. Then you will be obeyed without having to act cruelly, and can devote yourself to debauchery, idleness, and vice without bothering to rule."

So the death of the Founder and the accession of Barbarian produced an increase in harsh laws. A number of new building projects were introduced to confuse people's minds and tire their bodies. New victims were needed: more statute labor was exacted. But the fact that the government was persisting so savagely in ways no longer really its own merely served to sharpen popular resentment. And the policy that was supposed to preserve law and order was the very cause of disorder. The raising of the masses to serve the state led to the rising of the masses against it.

———

In the sixth month of the first year of the reign of the Second Emperor, a circular marked "urgent" was sent to the three provinces bordering the territory of Ch'in proper. The governors scowled; they were being asked to raise more statute labor. This meant using the iron fist, but severity now called forth more and more unrest. The governors sighed, but marked the documents "To be dispatched at once to all districts and given top priority."

In the middle of the sixth month, on the *chia-tzu*, or last day, of the period of ten, a notice appeared on the doors of all official buildings in the city of North Bank, in Honan. It read: "Families living to the left of the entrance gates in each locality are required to supply all their able-bodied men for forced labor."

Every civil servant guilty of making a mistake had already been deported, after which it had been the turn of the unemployed— beggars, idlers, and work-shy sons-in-law. Next came the merchants, followed by their sons, and the grandsons of everyone condemned to make a living in trade. Now the whole population was involved —respectable citizens, primary producers, those doing fundamentally necessary jobs. After those who lived to the left of the gates, it would be the turn of those who lived to the right, and all of them would perish in the wilderness of the North-West or the heat of the far South. The disappearance of the merchants had been greeted with applause: they were rich, and other people's troubles can be quite enjoyable. But exultation was short-lived: supplies were difficult to come by, towns became lifeless. The peace that had followed Ch'in's victory had created an illusion of prosperity, but now the people were working like horses, living like slaves, and dying like flies.

The proclamation set North Bank in a turmoil, with denunciations on one side and reprisals on the other. The police searched all the houses, elbowing aside women who tried to stop them and routing out men from their hiding places. Those who'd mutilated themselves to avoid service were executed.

On *chi-chou* day the army was assembled, and Ch'en Take-the-Plunge, a day laborer who had acquired some reputation because he'd learned to read and was ambitious, was put in charge. But it wasn't until the seventh month that the calendar indicated a day propitious for armies to set out on expeditions. The column started on its way, a long line of miserable wretches shuffling along under the eye of guards and warrant officers. They halted near Great Marsh, in the subprefecture of Ch'i, where another column, from the south, was already encamped. Take-the-Plunge struck up a friendship with Vast Wu, its leader.

———

Take-the-Plunge looked anxiously at the lowering clouds. It hadn't stopped raining for six days: rivers had overflowed, roads were impassable, and the troops were bottled up in Great Marsh. They ought to have started out long before, to avoid these autumn rains, but they'd been hampered by resistance on the part of the population and the ten days lost waiting for an auspicious day. It was now impossible for them to arrive at the outpost on time.

Take-the-Plunge went in search of Vast Wu, and they started drinking—drinking to drown their sorrows. But the wine only loosened their tongues and opened their hearts, and so brought them back to their troubles: they'd never get to where they were supposed to be by the date prescribed, and they ran the risk of being executed. Even if they were excused because of the adverse circumstances, their position would be little better. They'd either die of privation or be killed by alien arrows. What if they ran away? But they didn't fancy living like hunted animals, either.

"Let's rebel!" cried Take-the-Plunge, carried away by the wine. "We've got nine hundred men—quite a large army. And they're in such a bad way, they'll turn against Ch'in as soon as they're given a signal."

"They'd need training. And we have no standing or influence to make them do as they're told."

"They're fond of you. You treat them decently."

"Obedience comes from respect, not love."

They hesitated, not knowing what to do, and decided to try divination.

––––––

It was raining, and the marketplace was deserted. The man sat alone on his mat, his soothsayer's equipment beside him. He had a white beard, and the plainness of his dress was in contrast to the dignity of his bearing. He smiled at their embarrassed explanations, then carried out his procedures with long, nimble fingers, turning up a mutant figure, which referred to the sixth line of the Isolation hexagram: *"The Solitary Man meets a pig covered with mud, and a chariot full of demons. At first he draws his bow, but then he changes his mind: They aren't brigands; they're relatives by marriage. When you set out on a journey and meet with a rainstorm, it's a sign of good luck."*

Then the soothsayer added:

"Those who seem doubtful will turn out to be allies, and your undertakings will prosper."

They were so excited that they heard this through a kind of haze, and understood the soothsayer to mean that the fact that it was raining was propitious to great undertakings. But the mention of demons did puzzle them somewhat.

Vast Wu suggested they dress as demons. They would thus be able to recruit more followers, as well as whip up enthusiasm among the existing rank and file, those pigs covered with mud that the rain would transform into loyal comrades.

Take-the-Plunge said it would be a good idea to impress them with signs and wonders. He'd heard that just before the Chou dynasty came to power a white fish had leaped into the Founder's boat as he was crossing a river. He had slit it open, and inside was a red inscription: "The Yin will be destroyed, and the Chou will reign through the will of Heaven."

"And we too," said Take-the-Plunge, "want to raise an army to dispense justice and put down a tyrant!"

So they wrote carefully on a strip of wood: "Ch'u will triumph, Ch'en Take-the-Plunge will be king, and Vast Wu will help him." Since they had no red ink, they used blood. They stuck the strip of wood down the jaws of a large fish swimming around in a tank. But when the cook caught the fish, gutted it, and found a piece of wood inside covered with streaks of blood, he threw the would-be prediction away in disgust.

Vast Wu and Take-the-Plunge didn't lose heart. Take-the-Plunge remembered that when a wise king appears, demons howl in the darkness. Not far from the camp was a deserted temple that was supposed to be haunted. They stole there in the middle of the night, waved some lanterns like will-o'-the-wisps, and barked like foxes.

"Yap! Yap! Ch'in will die, Ch'en will be king, and Wu will be viceroy!"

But this only terrified the troops, who saw it as an evil omen. The next day the two conspirators found their army distinctly unenthusiastic.

The two warrant officers from Ch'in were bored, and drank day and night to forget. One day one of them asked Take-the-Plunge to keep him company. At first they drank together in comradely fashion, as became men who faced fate and the elements together. But as he emptied glass after glass, Take-the-Plunge's cup of bitterness overflowed. They might be brothers in the eyes of destiny, but in the eyes of men they were enemies. He could contain his resentment no longer and flung his plans for rebellion in the face of the Ch'in officer, who promptly lost his temper and grabbed his whip. Take-the-Plunge wrenched the other's sword from its sheath and ran him through.

When the victim's colleague came running, Wu seized him and held him while Take-the-Plunge cut his throat.

The two men, brandishing the two heads, addressed the crowd of prisoners.

"You have all suffered under Ch'in oppression. Now it is time to overthrow the tyrant! Even if they don't kill you, how many of you can hope to return to your own country if you go to the North? Three out of ten? Two? Not even as few as that! If you have to die, it's better to die a hero than a coward! It's better to be a ghost, well fed and honored from generation to generation, a spirit bestowing wealth and happiness on your children and grandchildren, rather than a famished ghost without a grave and without any offerings."

The crowd gave a yell, as if this was the moment they'd been waiting for, and fell on the handful of guards and slaughtered them. Then they marched on and seized the chief town of the region, and, having acquired new supporters there, went on to attack Ch'i, which surrendered to their first assault. Gathering more and more recruits as they went along, they struck at Ch'en, the capital of the province. The governor and the prefect had just been recalled to Double Light and imprisoned there on charges of embezzlement, so the defenses of the city were in disarray. A rumor swept through the population to the effect that the ghosts of Swallow and Fu Su had joined together and were marching on the city to free it from the tyranny of Barbarian's officials: their army, made up of all the warriors who had died in battle, was invincible.

The people rose in revolt. The garrison, bereft of leaders, took flight, leaving the temporary subprefect all alone to defend the gates. He fell, transfixed by dozens of spears, and Take-the-Plunge entered the city in triumph. He called the local elders, the other worthies, and the young resistance fighters together to decide what was to be done next.

When the wise old men, respectable citizens, and heads of families had finished their deliberations, they pronounced as follows:

"Noble General Ch'en, wearing your sturdy armor and wielding your mighty spear you have chastised the cruel rulers who thought they had the right to fleece and oppress us without mercy. Now, having carried out that sacred mission, you are preparing to march against the bloodthirsty monster of the West and to restore the altars of the glorious land of Ch'u. Such virtue calls for proper acknowledgment. The people of this city therefore, in their gratitude, accord you the title king."

Take-the-Plunge lost no time in having himself crowned king of Ch'u and appointing Vast Wu as his viceroy. And his friends set out with suitable bodies of troops to the four corners of the Empire, to liberate provinces and conquer kingdoms.

———

The governor of Wu, after lengthy meditations in the vaulted chamber of his official residence, with its lofty painted rafters, ordered one of his staff to send for Beam, who was said to have considerable influence with the local gentry and among the younger generation. He was also friendly with a certain Huan Ch'u, leader of a band of some eight hundred outlaws.

When Beam presented himself, the governor told him his plans. All the territory east of the river had risen in revolt, and Ch'in had lost control of the area. The governor needed to anticipate events if he wasn't to be their victim. He had thought the matter over at length, and arrived at a firm and irrevocable decision: He meant to raise an army against Ch'in, and he wanted Beam to lead it.

"You should be applying to Huan Ch'u, not me," said Beam.

Huan Ch'u was really only a henchman of the Hsiangs, who through him were able to command the band of cutthroats while themselves retaining the appearance of respectability. The gang killed people, held them for ransom, and looted and pillaged through hundreds of leagues around, all the while proclaiming themselves righters of wrongs, friends of chivalry, and protectors of widows and orphans.

"How can I get in touch with him?" asked the governor.

"He's disappeared into the marshes, and no one knows where he is," said Beam cautiously.

"But he must have spies in town! Let's be frank with one another. I'm not trying to trick you. This alliance is in both of our interests."

"Perhaps my nephew Plume has some idea . . ." said Beam reluctantly.

"Tell him I'd like to see him."

Beam went home and told his nephew what had happened. Then they both went back to the governor's residence: Beam went in; Plume waited outside.

"You want me to introduce you to my nephew so he can lead you to Huan," said Beam to the governor. "But what guarantee can you give him?"

"What are you trying to insinuate?"

"How are we to know this isn't a trap?"

"What can I do to reassure you?"

"Send your guards away."

The governor did so, and Beam stuck his head out the door and called his nephew.

"It's all right—you can come in. Hurry!"

Plume came forward, as lithe as a young panther. He whipped out his sword and cut the governor's throat. Beam bent down over the corpse, took the seals from his belt, and finished severing the head from the body. Some guards came running, and stopped dead at the sight of Beam brandishing the governor's gory head. Plume took advantage of their hesitation to slaughter as many of them as he could. The survivors threw down their arms and begged for mercy. The two men immediately rounded up all the officials, elders, and notables and ordered them to join the rebellion. Because the intruders' hands, faces, and clothes were spattered with blood, and because, glaring horribly, they dangled the seals of office in front of their adversaries, no one dared say no to them. Proclamations were drawn up and posted throughout the province. Seven thousand young men volunteered to fight under the Hsiangs' banner. These, with their former band, gave Plume and Beam an army of some eight thousand men. Ranks were assigned, standards distributed, and military discipline imposed. Beam appointed himself governor, and Plume assumed the title of deputy commander in chief.

———

The prefect of P'ei was sitting on a mat in the main hall of the administrative palace. He sat there like a poisonous lotus with his long white robe, embroidered with flowers and aquatic animals, spread around him. There was a bitter twist to his mouth as he mulled over his plans. Everywhere, colleagues were being murdered, towns were rising in revolt, and hordes of ruffians roamed the country. He could not just sit and wait for them to come and slit his throat.

He beckoned a clerk and sent for Ts'ao the Examiner, head of the Ministry of Criminal Affairs, and Hiao Porter, inspector of the civil service. He knew they had contacts with local swashbucklers and potentates. When they answered his summons, he told them of his decision to turn against Ch'in. He would foment rebellion, take over the province, assume the title of prince, and establish an independent realm.

"But do you think you can win the people over after serving Ch'in so zealously?" the two officials objected.

"That's why I sent for you two."

"What do you want us to do?"

"I need the support of men who are friendly toward the masses and can make the masses accept me. Liu is quite popular with the young reprobates. He has a gang of a hundred armed men that operates between T'ang and Mang. With his help I could do what I want. I know you two were close to him when he was chief of police. I'm sure you could put me in touch with him."

"We severed all connection with him after he ran away."

"Come, come! You're always with String, who acts as his courier and liaison officer. I'm very well informed, you see. So don't try any funny business."

62

"It's only a working relationship; we don't know anything about his private affairs. . . ."

"A working relationship with a junior bookkeeper in the Accounts Department? Anyhow, you're friendly with String, you used to be Whet-Iron's superiors—so just do what's necessary to get in touch with him."

"We'll do our best, but we can't promise anything."

When they got outside, the two officials looked at each other in perplexity.

"What do you think?" asked Ts'ao the Examiner. "It looks to me like a trap. You don't ask a tiger to protect you when you're sitting on a chunk of meat."

"If he calls on Whet-Iron for help, ten to one he'll find his rescuer taking his place instead of pulling his chestnuts out of the fire."

"Our prefect is no fool, and he knows that very well."

"But he *is* a coward, and I don't see him defying the wrath of the mob."

"Be that as it may, if he's setting a trap, it's because he doesn't trust us. And even if we don't take the bait and bring him his man, he'll try to eliminate us. The best thing to do is to act as if he means what he says, but be very careful."

And off they went to String's house.

"Do you know Whet-Iron well?" they asked.

"What a question!"

"So you know where to find him?"

String's eyes narrowed suspiciously.

"Who sent you?"

"The prefect."

He recoiled slightly. The two officials hastened to reassure him.

"He says he wants to join with the brigands and start a rebellion."

"What if it's a trap? What guarantee have we got?"

"None. Except that he's obviously frightened."

"Fear is not a wise counselor."

"Nothing venture, nothing win. You have to enter the tiger's lair to get his cubs."

"Let's hope we're not rushing into the tiger's jaws," said String with a sigh.

Nonetheless he went and fetched his friend, and Whet-Iron, having pitched camp outside the gates of the city of P'ei, accompanied the two officials to the prefect's residence. But the sentries shut the city gates behind them, and as soon as they were inside the palace they were surrounded by guards. Hsiao Porter, however, had taken the precaution of getting the support of the chief clerk and two provost marshals, and these three immediately attacked the guards, who fled in disorder when they saw the officials taking the prisoners' part. The six conspirators, meeting with no further resistance, rushed in to the prefect and cut off his head. Whet-Iron lost no time in waving the head in front of the people and exhorting them to rebellion.

The crowd hesitated. The elders and the notables lowered their eyes and exchanged glances. Even the young rowdies at the back shifted from one foot to the other, looking awkward and undecided. P'ei was a provincial capital with a sizable garrison, and the population was quite small. The outcome of revolt was by no means certain. Then again, Ch'in itself was powerful, Whet-Iron had only a few hundred men, and no one knew much about Take-the-Plunge's uprising.

Whet-Iron had fallen silent, and looked anxiously at that mass of impassive faces swept by varying impulses as they weighed the pros and cons. The attempt was going to fail, he thought; the garrison would intervene at any moment. Suddenly there was a stir at the back of the crowd. Shouts were heard. Newcomers rushed in, out of breath. Soon everything was in an uproar: the rebels were attacking.

"You see!" cried Whet-Iron, seizing the opportunity and going on from where he'd left off. "Everywhere bold and fearless men are on the march against oppression! They'll exterminate you if you don't join their side!"

64

The crowd now made up its mind: they slaughtered all Ch'in's officers and soldiers, then opened the city gates and with great solemnity let in the rebels, who were with Whet-Iron's followers. The newcomers were not a detachment from Take-the-Plunge's own force, but a column from nearby Feng, led by Barricade of Teeth. This young man, at the head of the émigrés from Wei, had had no difficulty in winning control of Feng, which was densely populated and poorly defended, and in raising an army to invest the provincial capital.

———

Once they had gained control of the city of P'ei, the rebels had to choose a leader to replace the prefect.

None of the previous officials wanted to take the responsibility. Some people suggested Whet-Iron; other voices were heard for Barricade of Teeth. There were two parties. Porter and Examiner, fearing it might all end in a bloodbath, suggested solving the problem by divination.

Consultation of the auguries pointed to the fifth line of the Pit hexagram, which merged into Rising of the Masses to give the oracle: *"There is game in the field, and it is well to catch it. Make no mistake. Let the older lead the army and the younger transport a tumbril of corpses. Obstinacy is a source of misfortune."* The verdict was perfectly clear, and Barricade of Teeth had to accept it.

One of the elders recalled that Whet-Iron's birth had been accompanied by signs and wonders. Someone else mentioned the strange story of the White Serpent. A force of three thousand enthusiastic young men was assembled, and under their new leader they embarked on a campaign to establish a territorial base, seizing several small towns. Ts'ao the Examiner, assisted by Hsiao Porter, was made responsible for the defense of P'ei, and Barricade of Teeth, having been appointed assistant to the prefect, returned to Feng.

MUTUAL AID

Excellent and useful
is mutual aid; it produces lasting happiness!

Feng Expulsion, wearing his crimson court dress and bowing his head so as not to cast his eyes on the august countenance, was remonstrating with the ruler—proposing that he should postpone some of his sumptuary expenses and lighten the burdens weighing on his people. It was to be feared that excessive exactions might provoke a population already showing signs of insubordination. Stirrings of discontent were reported from the eastern part of the Empire, and slight though these were, and easily put down, to continue current policy might well cause serious insurrection.

Barbarian scowled.

"My dignity requires ten thousand carriages," he said, his voice shaking with wrath. "And do I have them? By no means! Therefore I will order a column of ten thousand—so that my titles may be matched by the facts. My father rose above the mass of nobles and imposed his will on the Empire. He drove the Huns back from the frontiers and gave the whole world peace. He built walls and cities to show the world his glory. His work will be continued. Not only will I enlarge the A'fang palace and continue embellishing the tombs, but also, to show that the reign of water is ever more splendid and supreme, I shall this very day give orders for the ramparts of the city to be lacquered black."

"Oh," said a squeaky voice nearby, "just what I've been meaning to suggest for a long time, prince! Of course it will impose a terrible burden on the people, but how useful it will be. The walls will be so smooth and slippery, no rebel will ever be able to scale them. It will also show how concerned you are about those of your subjects who wish to approach you. For after all, it's pleasanter to become a painter than to be castrated."

The Emperor turned pale with fury, and signed to one of his officers to take the offender away and execute him. The courtiers tried to intercede for the unfortunate hunchback. The Emperor's august father had regarded the jester as a sage and had always forgiven him his daring sallies. It was not good for a monarch to kill his jesters. But the Second Emperor was deaf to their pleas.

The guard smuggled the offender through a secret door and took him out of the Forbidden City to his own house. There he took some children's clothes out of a chest and said:

"You'll be too conspicuous in your jester's red coat and black trousers. If you put on these things and hide your face, people will take you for a boy. Go and see Chiu, in the western part of the city; tell him I sent you. We learned fencing from the same teacher. He'll either hide you himself or find you a safe place to stay."

"Why do you risk your life for a cripple?"

"Remember that time in the days of the First Emperor when I and three of my friends were on sentry duty at the bottom of the steps? It was pouring, and I was frozen to the bone. And you called out, 'Would you like to have a rest?' When everyone was drinking the Emperor's health, you jumped on the balustrade and shouted out to us: 'What's the good of being fine fellows like you and getting drowned, while I with my hump sit comfortably at the table of the Son of Heaven? It's a perfect illustration of what Master Chuang calls the usefulness of the useless!' And the Emperor ordered the guard to be changed as quickly as possible. You showed then that you were a good man. And this is a way of showing you that usefulness can sometimes be useful too."

———

While at court, people of all ranks were getting together, as they always do when a dreaded despot starts to be despised. As it says in the fifth line of the eighth hexagram, *"The king surrounded the quarry on three sides, but it escaped him because the people of the town did not act as beaters."* The moribund Empire as a whole was also shaken by attempts at mutual aid. It was as if a huge lump of carrion were being infested by worms.

But the gang leaders, soldiers of fortune, and generals did not help each other, as certain birds and animals do when trying to escape a predator: they were more like wolves gathering in packs to hunt in the territory of the tiger.

As a result of the rising of the masses, thousands of men were thrown upon the dank gray roads of Ch'u. They had left hamlets surrounded by pallid marshes to serve under the banners of potentates who, drawn like moths by the fame of the bullies and swashbucklers of Great River, had enrolled in the armies of General Tattooed Face, Major P'eng Yüeh, or the army chief Lo Pu. These worthies, in turn, joined some lord more famous or powerful, among others Beam and Take-the-Plunge. It was a time for alliances, that aristocratic but deviant form of mutual aid, which inevitably leads to betrayal.

Their ingrained habit of bowing to authority and infallible instinct for hierarchy led the rebel generals to pledge allegiance to any leader with enough supporters to make him their immediate superior. Yet, though it was out of their former state that this centrifugal motion had arisen, nostalgia for that state produced a contrary tendency.

This made them detach themselves from their new masters as soon as the latter had rewarded them with territories of their own.

The campaigns carried out by Take-the-Plunge's lieutenants brought about a revival of old particularisms. Sometimes the descendants of former lords took advantage of the rebels' arrival to throw off the yoke of Ch'in officials; then, when the newcomers became irksome, they ousted them and took back their thrones. Sometimes the rebel generals proclaimed themselves kings of the lands they'd liberated, then lost parts of them to one of their own lieutenants, thus receiving the wages of their own treachery.

When the rule of Ch'in ended, the constraint of necessity was lifted, and wide pastures of unpredictability were left exposed to all kinds of predators. The freedom arising from this temporary break in the chain of time opened the way to all kinds of possibility and all kinds of greed. But it also produced spontaneous impulses of solidarity.

The first line of the Mutual Aid hexagram reflects this, and brackets solidarity and trust: *"Wherever there is trust, give help and you will not regret it; wherever there is trust, fill the bowl and you will have pleasant surprises."*

This saying was perfectly illustrated by the mutual aid that benefited a certain worthy from the banks of the Huai, significantly named Trust. The name foretold not only the solidarity based on trust that its possessor inspired, but also the confidence he felt in his own abilities and fate, despite the fact that his chief characteristics were extreme poverty, bone idleness, and a complete lack of business sense.

His belief in his own talent must have been contagious, at least at first, because until he was borne by the wings of the historic moment to the heights of fame, he managed to live entirely off other people.

When revolt broke out in the East, he had been sponging for several months on a local police chief in Low Country—the only person still willing to subsidize him. The police chief's wife had come to loathe the interloper: she resented his continual demands, the casual way he invited himself to lunch and supper every day, and the greed with which he demolished everything set before him. The scrounger's lack of consideration and the domestic scenes his presence gave rise to were wearing even the police chief's patience thin. So the husband made no more than a token protest when one day the policeman's wife declared that she was going to have her breakfast in bed, and requested him to do the same.

Trust arrived at the right moment for sharing some rice porridge with assorted pickled vegetables, perhaps with preserved eggs, dried fish, little mutton patties, and stuffed dumplings. But he found himself all alone with yesterday's leftovers. From the bedroom came the sound of voices raised in a quarrel about him. This was too much for his sensitive feelings, so after eating every bit of his porridge, he left without so much as a good-bye, vowing never again to set foot in the house of such churlish hosts.

He was now in difficult straits. The purses of his friends and acquaintances had been applied to so often to help him provide his mother with a sumptuous funeral and to build her a tomb fit for a queen that any further applications were doomed to failure. He was soon actually hungry, and his only recourse was to fish from the walls overlooking the river.

It was the time of the great autumn housecleaning, and dozens of women were doing their washing on the riverbanks. One of the women working just below where Trust sat was struck by his looks and bearing. When she saw how disappointed he looked at failing to catch anything, she felt so sorry for him that she called to him and gave him some millet bread and salted fish.

The woman had a lot of washing to do, and every day for three weeks she went to the same spot and shared her food with him. Sometimes it was rice balls stuffed with meat, sometimes fried noodles, sometimes rolls stuffed with red bean paste, or millet porridge. Trust was very grateful to the woman, and on the last day, when all the washing was finished, he said warmly:

"You've been extremely kind to me. When I am rich and powerful, I shall pay you back!"

She turned quite pink with annoyance, and cried, with her hands on her hips:

"But now you can't even provide for yourself! If I gave you food, it was because I couldn't bear to see someone who looked as princely as you dying of hunger; it wasn't because I looked for reward. If I gave you such a wrong impression of myself, I must have got a very wrong impression of you!"

Trust apologized profusely. He hadn't meant to offend her, to imply that he doubted her disinterestedness. He just wanted to show her she wasn't talking to someone unworthy of her kindness.

Before they parted, she gave him two jade bracelets and some pieces of silk that she had spun herself, so he would be able to hold out for a little while longer.

———

At the very bottom of the ladder, the confusion brought about by the rising of the masses produced a solidarity untainted by any speculation about the future. This was among men so deprived that no notion of social improvement, ambition, or greatness ever found admittance to their dull brains. These people, devoid of hope, were the only ones who had remained on the east coast and the marshy wastes of the Huai. The more enterprising young men, along with the potentates, gentry, popular leaders, and other people of any character, had left to seek their fortunes at Take-the-Plunge's court or on the western expedition. And since the Ch'in officials and administrators had all been massacred, and all the notables had gone, the people at the bottom, who had always borne the weight of the rest of the hierarchy, were left to their own devices.

At first they sat blissfully watching the sun rise and set. After dark they were ready to contemplate the stars indefinitely, quite happy just to see these festive lanterns lighting the night sky. These people were rooted in the soil, like some meager harvest ripening slowly as the days and seasons passed. Any journey, any change of scene was for them connected with misfortune—with forced labor, deportation, or banishment. Their only thought was to huddle together in their hamlets; to merge with their neighbors in a warm, dense, shapeless mass, all sharing the same punishments and the same toil.

In the autumn the old men would sit in their doorways warming their creaky bones in the rays of the setting sun. But the warmth they felt for one another came from the soul. The younger people worked in the fields, reaping long stalks of millet with sickles of black metal or polished stone. And their hearts too were melted by the warmth of mutual aid into one ball of fire, rivaling that in the western sky.

Sometimes in the quiet of evening they would hear dogs barking or hens clucking in a nearby village, or see the smoke of a more distant hamlet rising from a grove of bamboos. But they had become so close and exclusive a group that they never felt any curiosity about these places, any desire to meet their inhabitants.

But this time of withdrawal was followed by a desire for something different. They grew tired of quiet contemplation, the painful communion of empty minds and empty stomachs. They felt there was something missing; as if they were a severed and dying limb, cut off from the circulation and heat of the whole body. People from the different villages began to visit one another. They exchanged goods and services, showing a humble fraternity. They no longer had to produce things for the gentry or the government. They had time to spare. They began to think and met together to talk. Their thinking was not real thinking. It was more a faint throb or vibration, like the brush of a butterfly's wing against the clumsy fingers of a child.

SMALL
ACCUMULATIONS

How auspicious are small accumulations!
Hurrying clouds that shed no rain,
coming from our western lands.

In rebellions, great victories are made up of accumulations of small gains. Neither the mobility of their armies nor their officers' skill at maneuver was the reason for the rebels' success. It was, rather, the complement, the negative counterpart, of the former government's disintegration. All Take-the-Plunge's victories, which brought in more and more supporters, were reinforced by the repeated errors of Ch'in, paralyzed by Barbarian's stupidity and the despotism of his regime. If the father was able to claim the distinguished title Obscure because no one could make him out, the son could do so as well, not because he was invisible but because he was blind. The eunuch Chao the Tall had so sequestered him from external influence within the double circle of absolutism and the Forbidden City that he could no longer understand anything about the outside world. He saw, heard, and thought nothing except through the eyes and ears and brain of his eunuch.

Chao the Tall had told him: "The greatness of a ruler consists in his inaccessibility—that's why he is called *Chen*, the Obscure. You are still young, and because of your inexperience you may make blunders, may through ignorance be caught out. Then, not only will you expose yourself to mockery, but, by showing that you are not infallible, you will encourage your subjects to neglect their duties. Is that the way for an enlightened ruler to govern? No. Stay in your apartments and let the eunuchs, who know more about it, get on with governing, under my direction. Then people will fear you, and no one will bother you with complaints and petitions and other such foolery. You will be able to devote yourself entirely to your pleasures."

Thus did he keep his master out of public life, manipulate him, and take the reins of power.

———

Sometimes reality would penetrate the walls of the inner palace in the form of a particularly energetic or naive inspector from east of the passes, who forced his way in to the ruler and told him what was going on: the brigands were raising veritable armies; the Ch'in garrisons were helpless; governors and prefects were being murdered everywhere. But the eunuch soon dismissed reality. A commission of inquiry would be appointed and would prove that the facts had been grossly exaggerated: some brigands might have looted a town, but the chief of police and the director of Criminal Affairs had acted vigorously to restore law and order, and the guilty parties had been tried and severely punished. The overzealous official who had misled the Emperor was charged with spreading false reports and executed, and all his relatives, down to the third degree of kinship, were exterminated.

Because no real army was ever sent against it, the expeditionary force led by Chou the Sign, one of Take-the-Plunge's generals, captured city after city and won one victory after another. It kept advancing westward, ever westward, going through the passes from Ch'in into Han-ku, where it thrust aside a weak garrison that had not been reinforced because the court had decided the rebellion did not exist. But with the rebels on Ch'in's territory, and the state itself in danger, increasingly alarming reports began to come in. Finally, persistent rumors of the insurgents' successes pierced the walls of the Forbidden City and the barrier the Emperor had erected against reality. He began to feel uneasy.

Chao the Tall knew he couldn't leave the Emperor in ignorance any longer without imperiling the Empire and putting his own life in danger. He had to find a way of forcing Barbarian to take the measures necessary and at the same time deflect his displeasure onto the prime minister and thus bring about Li Ssu's downfall. He made Li Ssu believe he was anxious about the Emperor's blindness to reality, and arranged for him to be given an audience. Naturally, it took place at a bad moment: the Emperor was delighting in the singing and dancing of some female musicians sent by the southern protectorates. Nevertheless, he agreed to call a council meeting for the following day.

Next morning the scholars of great knowledge, the learned men, ministers, and other dignitaries assembled in the austere council chamber, lit faintly by the first glimmers of dawn. A double row of backs bowed down to the wind of imperial authority blowing from the jade dais under its canopy of thick black silk embroidered with flying dragons. When the Son of Heaven lowered his languid eyes upon his prime minister and was about to grant his request, all the scholars of great knowledge stepped forward and spoke with one voice.

"Your Majesty," they said, "no subject may disobey his prince, but the brigands from east of the passes, not content with rejecting the authority of their master, have raised the standard of revolt; they have organized themselves into armies and are slaughtering their prefects and governors. This calls for exemplary, ruthless punishment! We, your subjects, ask that an army be assembled at once to put down subversion and wipe out the rebels."

The Emperor, very annoyed, flapped his sleeves and remained silent. But as Li Ssu was about to come forward to support what the scholars of great knowledge had said, a learned doctor emerged from the crowd and shouted:

"That's all lies! The Empire is united, like one big family enjoying the Great Peace. Haven't the walls around all the estates and fortresses been leveled? Weren't all the weapons melted down and made into bells by the late August First Emperor to show there was no longer any need for war? When there is an enlightened ruler on the throne, the laws are applied in all their perfection and in all their severity. Everyone is in the place appropriate to his abilities, and receives a salary in proportion to his efforts. Easy, swift, and uninterrupted communications facilitate the circulation of orders, goods, and people. Are we to believe that in such a perfectly regulated world troubles can arise, not to mention a rebellion? No. It's merely a matter of a few wretched thieves, not worth the attention of a prefect's secretary! All that's needed is for all the provinces to send in their police and haul the troublemakers before the courts. What's the point of bothering our Emperor and talking about raising an army? It only causes confusion, and casts doubt upon our ruler's virtue."

The Emperor's frown disappeared.

"That sounds sensible," he said.

And he ordered the council to deliberate on the suggestion that had been put forward. Most of the dignitaries agreed that all they had to deal with was a few ordinary troublemakers. But a few men of integrity persisted in maintaining that it was a genuine revolt.

They were put on trial, accused of spreading false reports and trying to undermine public morale, and executed in the marketplace. Their sumptuous robes were given to the flatterer who had contradicted them—Sun-chu Tung Totality. He was made a scholar of vast knowledge.

Chao the Tall was both angry and worried. Now how was he to persuade the Emperor to take the necessary measures? He had imprisoned his master in a net of lies, but the meshes were closing in on himself as well. He suspected Sun-chu Tung Totality, who had foiled his plan, of being part of a diabolical plot hatched by the prime minister in order to destroy him. Li Ssu also thought he'd been tricked: he believed the eunuch had been behind Totality's intervention. So both Chao and Li Ssu sent henchmen to murder the newly appointed scholar: the two gangs of assassins met outside his door. But he had already fled. Then both Chao and Li Ssu began to think Totality must be a member of the Trigrams, which had been working to destroy the dynasty ever since the First Emperor banished magicians from his court. They even wondered whether the rebellion itself might not be the result of the soothsayers' secret machinations.

———

East of the passes, in the midst of insurgent army chiefs who were accumulating minor successes and adding to their own territories, Beam was preparing to cross the Blue River with his eight thousand men, advance westward to destroy the Ch'in armies, and avenge the death of his father, General Swallow.

The whole of the province he aimed at, however, had already been taken over by other groups of rebels. There, as everywhere else, the young men had murdered the prefect and raised the banner of revolt. Wearing the green turbans that had once been part of the uniform of the peasant militias disbanded by Ch'in, they roamed the country in a leaderless horde, pillaging the houses of the rich and looting public granaries. Then some of them, made uneasy by the beginnings of hostility among the population, decided to provide themselves with a leader. Their choice fell on Ch'en Ying, the local vice-prefect, who had earned great respect for the moderation with which he applied the laws. He agreed to accept the post of leader for fear of being thought to support Ch'in if he refused, though the responsibility daunted him. He consulted his mother, who had always given him sound advice. She was alarmed: for generations none of her kinsmen had done anything outstanding or occupied an important post, and in taking on such a prominent position Ch'en Ying would be going beyond his family's allotted destiny. He must hide himself behind someone else. Moreover, she didn't like the sound of all those young rowdies. He agreed. But how were ten thousand hotheads to be got rid of?

Beam had just crossed the river. His arrival was providential.

"The Hsiang family," Ch'en Ying told his troublesome supporters, "has provided soldiers for generations, and they have a great military reputation in Ch'u. You say you aim at great things—so why don't you choose Beam as your leader rather than me? I'm too timid. With me, all you'll acquire is a prefecture, whereas with him you'll win a kingdom. What's more, the Hsiangs are venerated like gods in Ch'u, and they'll be able to get everyone to help them destroy Ch'in."

So the fiery young men dropped Ch'en Ying to offer their support to the potentate from Ch'u. When he saw this rabble approaching him, Beam frowned: it would be hard work to make them submit to the discipline he imposed on his men.

"Why are you wearing those turbans?" he asked their spokesmen.

This brusqueness didn't go down well. One of the rebels' representatives tossed his head and answered insolently:

"To mark the beginning of spring and the end of the reign of darkness. There won't be any more laws or law courts. And there won't be anyone giving us orders!"

Plume, standing beside his uncle, was not going to put up with this. He stepped forward.

"It's not the reign of green that we'll be imposing," he said menacingly, "but the reign of red. And we'll impose that with our swords!"

The rash youth was determined to have the last word.

"The signs are clear," he said. "The reign of green is about to begin. Water and darkness are finished, and blood, though it may look red, is a kind of water. What we want is wise men, not butchers!"

Plume, beside himself, slit the youth's throat and put his hands in the wound.

"Red!" he roared. "Red as blood! Red as the vengeance that will be our master!"

Some of the rebels counterattacked to avenge their comrade, but Beam and Plume soon slaughtered them. A few of the rest scattered to the north of the Huai River, but most merely yielded in a mixture of terror and admiration, having recognized Beam and Plume as genuine leaders.

———

The Hsiangs' name alone made the whole province tremble, and they won over General Tattooed Face's thousand tall rebels.

Plume was a great connoisseur of horses, and soon noticed and coveted the general's mount. Since Tattooed Face had sworn allegiance to Beam, Plume asked his uncle to get the animal for him.

"You can't be serious!" said Beam. "It's a mare! She'd make the whole of our cavalry ruttish. No. Mares may be all right for tradesmen and robbers, but they're unworthy of a general."

The men laughed, but Tattooed Face looked sour. He didn't like hearing his mare denigrated. It was because of her that he had been punished, but he was more convinced than ever that he owed his rise in the world to her. He resented Beam for his contempt, and Plume for his greed. But he pretended to see the joke, and promised the nephew the colt that the mare would undoubtedly give birth to after she'd been served on the battlefield.

"And I think I know who the father will be," he said, pointing at the white stallion Beam was riding.

Thus, in accordance with the relevant hexagrammatic allusion to gestation (*"Hurrying clouds that shed no rain, coming from our western lands"*), the seed of animosity was sown in Tattooed Face's heart, just as the seed of Plume's future mount was soon to be planted in the mare's womb.

Tattooed Face having just married the prefect of P'an's daughter, the ranks of his supporters were swelled by that official's small army, and with the troops of General P'u, his brother-in-law, who betrayed Ch'in to join the rebels. The Blue River army numbered fifty thousand men by the time it passed through Low Country. Trust, impressed by the organization and the martial bearing and manly vigor of the generals, thought at last his talents would find proper employment. He offered his services to Beam, but was made only a spear-carrier in the Guard. Every time the Hsiangs' army halted, new recruits came to join them, and with all these regiments behind him, Beam marched on Hsia-p'i, where Uncle Hsiang had ousted the prefect and won over the local aristocracy. By now Beam had seventy thousand men, and was able to pick off territories along the Blue River one after the other.

———

Whet-Iron's successes were more modest, but his almost imperceptible beginnings were a promise of greater things to come. At the head of the three thousand rebels who had gathered together in P'ei, he had attacked and captured a couple of strongholds. But when his supply lines were threatened by the superintendent-general of the Ch'in army, he withdrew, like a prudent field mouse scuttling back to its hole, to his base in Feng.

The Ch'in general took this guile for cowardice, and his siege of Feng was halfhearted. Whet-Iron made a bold sortie, broke through the enemy lines, and killed him. Encouraged by this success, Whet-Iron pressed on to Hsieh, not so much for strategic reasons as because he was curious to see the place where his fine bamboo cap had come from. A column led by the governor of Four Rivers was on the move when he got there, and he was able to take it by surprise and put the men to flight. The governor tried to fall back on Parent, but was caught and killed. In this laborious fashion Whet-Iron conquered five or six cities and half a province.

————

While corpses piled up on the battlefields, and the generals won their victories; while the government of Ch'in made mistake after mistake, enabling the brigand leaders to take city after city; at the same time, in the stony soil of humble people's minds, there gradually sprang up tiny shoots of thought. These fragile plants died as soon as they appeared, but by slowly laying down layer after layer of humus they were preparing a rich earth from which one day a great idea would grow.

WALKING

So long as you can walk on a tiger's tail
without getting bitten, everything is all right.

Li Ssu was pacing to and fro in his huge hall decorated with yellow-gold and red lacquer, which was in one wing of a residence filled with the ostentatious luxury that appeals to men who have risen too fast in the world. He stalked like a beast in a cage, shaking his sleeves with the fury of a tiger when someone has stepped on its tail. Once again that vile eunuch Chao the Tall had got the better of him, and he, the prime minister, the most powerful person in the Empire, had to submit to being thwarted by a criminal whose physical uncompleteness symbolized his moral imperfection. Li Ssu had called the Emperor's wrath down upon himself by revealing the gravity of Ch'in's position: it didn't even have a cordon of troops to face the four hundred thousand men who were marching on the capital. Whereas the eunuch had won the Emperor's gratitude by suggesting Chang Han as the man sent by providence to save the situation.

While Li Ssu's embroidered silk slippers trod briskly back and forth over the richly tiled floor, millions of sore bare feet, hampered by clanking chains, were dragging themselves painfully down the slopes of Mount Li, site of the grandiose but sinister funeral mound of the First Emperor. It was because of this slow march that the worried minister was stepping so briskly.

But the thud of hundreds of thousands of feet as they descended into the broad valley of the Wei River brought a smile of triumph to the lips of Chang Han, minister in charge of the Emperor's Exchequer. Here was the army that would halt the rebel forces—the three hundred thousand convicts laboring on the tomb of the Great Emperor and the A'fang palace. The convicts would be reinforced by the criminal population of Ch'in, and all the scum of the earth, all the despair of the Empire would be hurled against the hordes of rogues and brigands and rebels led by nostalgic nobles. It would really be just one army tearing itself to pieces, convicts against gallowsbirds, prisoners against brigands, slaves against paupers; but the cohorts fighting for Ch'in would be spurred on by a greater hope, for Chang Han would promise them freedom in return for victory. There would be a general amnesty: when the hostilities were over, they would be given some money and allowed to go home. They would also be exempt from forced labor for three years.

———

The rebel armies streamed down from the other side of the mountains, but by the time they emerged on the plain of Double Light they had lost their momentum. Chou the Sign had divided them into eight separate corps, officered by former noblemen and their followers. Chou the Sign, who had been a soothsayer to the armies of Ch'u, knew all about this kind of organization: he had studied military strategy in *The Talismanic Mysteries of the Great Yin*, an esoteric treatise given him by a hermit. The eight corps, named clouds, dragon, wind, bird, earth, tiger, sky, and serpent, each following a standard bearing the appropriate emblem, surrounded the commander in chief and his Guard. All the bare feet had been shod in boots, decorated with the regimental symbols. The ragged rush of beggars had slowed down, and began to resemble the elegant and disciplined movement of ballet dancers. The way each corps was deployed varied according to the lay of the land, the time of day, and the positions of the stars. Sometimes it formed a circle, figuring the sky; sometimes a square, symbolizing the Earth; now it would amble like a filly, now go firmly as a stallion; it might spread out wide, twist into a spiral, flow like a torrent, or move in formation like a flock of wild birds.

Chang Han's convicts, on the other hand, were not restrained by anyone except the Guards who followed them, slashing at stragglers with nail-studded chains. They hurled themselves with savage yells upon the enemy lines which were so artistically set out in emblematic formations. Ignorant of all the subtle points of tactics implied in the layout of the rebel battalions—open and closed points, windows of life and gates of death, the path of wounds, the meanders of harassment, the maze of attrition—they broke through the center, knocked down the staff officers, cut Chou the Sign's throat, and massacred lords and churls alike. The gleaming leather boots, the horses' painted hooves, the leggings of the peasants fled to the east, pursued by millions of the sore bare feet that had lately leveled the earthen roads of Ch'in.

———

At the other end of the country, on the borders of fertile, well-watered Ch'u, another pair of feet was on the way, neither bare nor clad in silk, but wearing simple sandals of woven straw. Instead of moving over splendid tiles patterned with birds and flowers, or along a dusty road dotted with sharp stones, these feet were moving over the brick floor of a staging post. They were walking toward what seemed, in the eyes of their owner, the gigantic soles of another pair of feet, the toes emerging silvery and dripping from a bath. As the eyes, approaching, rose and took in the chubby arms of the two pretty maids who were now rubbing the two huge feet dry, the body they belonged to reared itself upright. The feet disappeared from the visitor's view, to be replaced by a penis pointing at him like a great accusing finger. This vanished in its turn, to be succeeded by the broad and angry countenance of Whet-Iron, who shoved away with a crash the bowl in which he had been performing his ablutions. The newcomer's robe was soaked.

"Miserable little Confucius-monger!" roared Whet-Iron. "You know what I do to people like you? I make you take off your hats, all you parasites, cowards, and jabberers, and I pee in them. And think yourself lucky if I don't tear out your heart and eat it raw!"

"Because of your reputation for virtue," replied the other, "I came here from Tan-fu to offer you my services. I'm sorry to find that you do not deserve your reputation. Your ease is just vulgarity, your coolness mere stupidity. You take good care of your feet and like to exhibit them, but you ought to meditate on the third line of the saying concerning walking: '*A blind man may see, a lame man may walk, but both will be bitten if they tread on the tail of a tiger!*' That's what a violent and brutal fellow has coming to him when he tries to rise in the world and rule. What is the meaning of the Ritual in which the feet are planted on the path of virtue? Virtue, of which Humility is the handle, Return the root, and Constancy the rampart. Those are the qualities a leader should display, of which we are reminded in the symbolism of Walking. Do you think you're going to rid the Empire of tyranny and earn yourself a glorious name by lying down and waving your feet in the air? What's more, by being so disrespectful to scholars you are merely aping Ch'in!"

Whet-Iron was about to shut this chatterbox up and boot him out of his tent, thus giving him a lesson in manners, when his eye was caught by something hanging from the rhetor's belt and emitting a curious gleam. After a second look he recognized the same green-and-white markings that were on the stone he once picked up after hearing a prediction from a traveling physiognomist: animal shapes around an octagon enclosing the eight trigrams. He took this as an omen, the more so because, though he hadn't understood what his visitor was talking about, he'd sensed something profound and mysterious in his allusions to divination. Adjusting his clothes, he said:

"You're not being fair to me. How can you think I'd want to be like the tyrant when I've raised an army to help destroy him?"

"If you want to be different from him, start by showing a bit of decorum, and stop having your servants tell people you haven't time to waste on scholars."

Whet-Iron, embarrassed, offered the man a mat. But he refused.

"We'll have an opportunity to meet again, and then perhaps you'll be better able to benefit from my advice."

He turned on his heel and left.

"My dear rhetor," Ramble, who had been present, called after his brother's visitor, "you are a perfect illustration of the next line of the hexagram you quoted just now: *'He treads on the tail of the tiger, but he is so wily he emerges unscathed'*!"

———

Fortunate, the collector of letters on goodness, walked neither with *"the even pace on a smooth road of a freed prisoner,"* as in the second line of the hexagram; nor, as in the third line, with the uncertain step of the blind man or the cripple who treads on the tiger's tail and gets bitten; nor with the stealthy step of the fourth line, which even wild animals cannot hear. No; Fortunate didn't walk—he flew, scarcely touching the road as he swept along, emptying the big boxes of their wonderful suggestions and bringing the flowers of the people's thought back to the new capital. There they would be sorted and set down in a great and sacred book that would ultimately contain the very teaching of the Tao, for Heaven has put a fragment of the goodness of the primal impulse in the mouth of each of the humble and lowly. When all the fragments are put together, they will restate divine morality and its holy precepts.

Fortunate went like the wind. He had to, in order to gather together the brilliant ideas, the sublime and saving ideas that would make possible the compiling of the *Book of Goodness* and the establishment of a government of Wise Men. Before long the hidden saints, the miracle men from foreign lands, the prophets and eccentrics who roamed the markets concealing their wisdom under an appearance of folly would all emerge from obscurity and silence to enlighten mankind. And the king, inspired by these echoes of the cosmic Word, would distribute the book widely and civilize the people. Virtue would prevail. There would be no more thieves or murderers, no more policemen or judges; everything would be sweetness and light. Gone would be the gap between the great and the humble, the prince and his subjects. And since lack of communication is the cause of every kind of disturbance, all natural calamities and disorders would end, harvests would be abundant, famine and disease unknown, and the whole world would be happy. Men, restored to their original simplicity, would live on good terms with animals. They would be able to look in a magpie's nest without frightening it away, hold snakes in their hands without being bitten, and walk on tigers' tails without being eaten.

CONCORD

The small makes way for the big.
Heaven and Earth couple: this is concord.
The prince follows and completes the work
    of Heaven and Earth, helping their alternation
    and supplying the needs of the people.

An idea, a great idea, the same idea that was lending wings to Fortunate's nimble feet, had been born in the dimness of narrow skulls
blackened by sun and wind. Like deep-sea monsters that burst into
a million pieces as soon as fishermen haul them to the surface; like
dawn mists vanishing in the first rays of the sun; like wood mushrooms
that shrivel as soon as they are uncovered; so these efflorescences of
darkness faded when exposed to the harsh light of language. But they
did not disappear. Floating in rainbow-colored drifts in the cold air
of winter and giving out a subtle and elusive fragrance, they condensed, like dew forming on a mirror held out to the moon, into the
utterance of an eccentric character called Li Harmony, basketmaker

by trade and amateur soothsayer. He claimed to be descended from Confucius on his mother's side and from Lao Tzu on his father's.

In the pale light of winter, season of hibernation, but with the promise of awakening, Harmony, like a grub in its chrysalis waiting to spread its wings or a dragon sleeping underground in preparation for flight, had seen a small group of men go by, survivors of Beam's massacre. Misled by accounts of the latter, he also misunderstood the significance of the men's green turbans. He thought they were a protest against violence and an appeal for peace and concord; whereas in fact their meaning was martial, for they were inspired by the uniforms worn formerly by the Wei militia.

Fortunate was transported with happiness when he saw these bellicose and unruly young fellows wearing an emblem of spring. He felt in every fiber of his being that he was witnessing the advent of a new cycle of tenderness and love. So he set out to preach in the countryside, where men left idle by the decay of agriculture gathered in village halls while the women did their household chores to the sound of crickets chirping. And because he held up a mirror to their souls, they listened to what he told them.

"I'm an uneducated fellow," he said, "but there are some things I feel and understand better than any scholar, as if Heaven had caused me to be born on purpose to have these experiences and make them known. I believe it would take very little for the great brotherhood of man to be restored. All that's needed is to give yang back its brightness and to strengthen fire by abolishing everything made of metal. Yes, everything. Metal objects are monstrous symbols of the violence and repression that have the world in their grip every hour of the day and night! Just think! Coins, made of melted bronze, reproduce the shapes of weapons: knives and axes. Can't you feel their cold breath stifling the life-giving breezes of spring, checking the fertilizing flow of the Earth? Look at the suffering and misery of humanity! Poverty, crime, and famine on the one hand; disease, war, and repression on the other. Countless calamities afflict the Empire, frightful omens appear, for Heaven and Earth are repelled by so much bloodshed. My brothers, is it not time for us whose hearts are overflowing with love and tenderness to replace all this cruelty with something else?"

Which was only an introduction to the subject that interested him most: female infanticide. He saw this as terrifying proof of the barbarism arising from the dominating influence of metal.

"The numbers one and two represent Heaven, which is masculine, and Earth, which is feminine: this means that in order to conform to the universal norm there ought to be two women for every man. But in these barbarous times female infants are killed, and as a result there are more boys than girls. This interrupts the breath of yin, which is a terrible offense against the proper course of nature. The shortage of yin causes a drying up, which manifests itself in a lack of rain. The breath of the Earth, itself the mother of all, is contained in women. Killing baby girls is killing mothers—mothers who receive seed into their wombs and make it fruitful. Yes, you are smothering, murdering the good, productive breath of the Earth. Are you surprised, then, that disasters rain down upon you?

"Don't keep putting the blame on government corruption. We alone are responsible; the government merely reflects our own degradation. It is a horrible crime to kill living beings, especially human beings, the most valuable and sacred beings in the universe. I tell all of you that Heaven forbids female infanticide. Do you want your name to be entered in the books of life that the master of fate compiles in its offices in the North? If so, try to save your daughters' lives, and look after their health.

"As soon as this monstrous practice is abolished, the Great Peace will reign anew. The horrible stench of murder will disappear, and everyone will breathe fresh air again—the light and fragrant air of happiness that Heaven in its mercy bestows.

"Instead of killing baby girls, cherish them, that they may multiply. For following the pattern of Heaven One and Earth Two, a man should have two wives."

Occasional murmurs arose from the dark mass of heads. Girls

were a nuisance. Extra mouths to feed, and then when they got married they no longer belonged to their own family or helped to serve its ancestors. And it was even worse if they didn't get married, because then they turned into vindictive demons when they died.

But the preacher had his audience well in hand. As soon as he raised his voice louder and began to denounce the temperance advocated by the authorities, the timid sighs of disagreement gave way to nods of assent. Chastity and virginity, said Li Harmony, interrupted the life-giving connection between yin and yang. They were responsible for the barrenness of nature, the people's loss of property, and the declining population. The harshness of the government was merely the consequence of disturbance in the universe, itself due to lack of contact between the two breaths. Sages and schoolmasters were misleading the people when they advocated chastity and continence. These should be utterly rejected, since they prevented nature from pouring forth its bounty.

The audience was now smiling broadly, thinking of the old-time festivals when girls and boys bathed together naked in the river, and when you could sleep out in the mulberry grove with the partner of your choice. But all these things had been banned, and it was often village leaders or bureaucrats from the local population office who arranged marriages. The prettiest girls were requisitioned for the harems of nobles and princes, when they weren't sold by their parents to some wealthy potentate.

There were titters and knowing winks.

Li Harmony hastened to moderate this reaction.

"We mustn't go to the other extreme! We must harmonize yin and yang and make them merge in the proportions prescribed by Heaven and Earth, so that there are neither any superfluous men nor any superfluous women. Then the creative breaths that fertilize the Earth will flourish, plenty will return, and the Great Peace will reign once more."

Li Harmony's speech had a definite appeal, even a kind of fascination, for his listeners. This was probably because, though he shocked them by arguments that challenged their prejudices, at the same time he revealed to them their own secret thoughts. There was also something spellbinding about his manner. He was, in fact, inspired. It wasn't a case of violent possession or trance—though this wouldn't have surprised anyone. Country people and villagers were always consulting sorcerers and holy men, and sometimes experienced trances themselves on high days and holidays. And the tone of Li Harmony's discourse was comparatively light and ethereal. Instead of talking about ghosts seizing the living with shrieks and threats, he invoked the touch of invisible wings brushing men's souls. It was as if a deity composed of the pure breaths that preceded the creation of Heaven and Earth were whispering its impalpable thoughts into Li Harmony's ear. He always started his speeches hesitantly and laboriously: trying to make contact. At first he'd speak slowly, carefully, delivering the phrases separately, as if they'd been whispered to him from long ago and far away, beyond this world, beyond this age, amid the origins when nothing existed but the purity of the void. Then his voice would grow louder and more assured, and he spoke without hesitation, with conviction and warmth, carrying every listener along with him.

Among his most enthusiastic listeners were Fortunate and Pomp, two young rascals who had given up everything to follow him and serve him as disciples. Pomp claimed to have the power to heal people with magic water, an art inherited from his mother's family, in which the women were shamans. Fortunate had some amulets that enabled him to cover five hundred leagues in a single day. He could outrun a stag or overtake a galloping horse. There was also a disciple called Flash-Pedigree, a distant descendant of the Ch'u royal family. He was a practicing doctor and geomancer, and enjoyed a reputation for wisdom. All three disciples zealously spread their master's teaching, gaining tens of thousands of supporters. These they organized into a kind of commune, dedicated to bringing about the reign of the Great Peace.

Li Harmony's theory on concord had led them to develop a

system to facilitate communication and understanding between superiors and inferiors.

"Heaven issues warnings and advice through the courses of the sun and the moon and the motions of the stars, which inscribe the ideograms of its will across the blue of the sky. Earth expresses itself through the configuration of the land. Man too makes signs and utters sounds to manifest his thoughts. He can convey the motions of things and beings; it is he who gives form to spirit, which is why he is the master of all living creatures. Such is the sanctity of the Word, which reproduces the cycle of the cosmos and communicates it to all.

"A ruler should watch for changes, note them down and convey them to the Empire: he should fix them in writing and broadcast them to the four corners of the world. A word that is not communicated or circulated is a barrier between a prince and his subjects and produces chaos. Nowadays news no longer rises from inferiors to superiors, and this brings down warnings on us from Heaven—meteors, comets, eclipses, and the rest.

"A ruler should never be feared; he should be kind and benign. If his authority or prestige is too great, the people around him are afraid to speak, and terror filters down through the different levels of the administration until it afflicts the common people. They come to fear even such a minor official as a local police chief. No one dares tell anyone else his opinions or give anyone else his advice: they are all too much in fear of their lives. There is no communication; Heaven's intentions are no longer conveyed to the ruler. And the same is true at all levels, including the villages and the family, where virtue is becoming debased.

"When something unusual happens, the villagers are now too frightened to tell the authorities about it. Whenever a decent person tries to break through the wall of silence and report signs sent by Heaven, the whole administration conspires against him, to shut him up and eliminate him.

"The people are born of Heaven and Earth, and Heaven and Earth are their father and mother, keeping them informed of their wishes through signs and wonders written in the great book of nature. The people's vocation is to transmit these messages to their king, isolated and shut away in his palace, so that he may do the divine will.

"Villagers ought to reveal anything that might be considered a symptom: illnesses that strike them down—dysentery, cholera; miraculous signs and wonders that have appeared to them. And they ought to express all the thoughts that occur to them too—divine seeds sown by Earth and Heaven."

It was this that gave rise to the idea of boxes for letters promoting virtue. They were big thirty-foot cubes (thirty being the sum of the three cycles of Heaven, Man, and Earth). In each side there was a padlocked door with a slit in it at eye level, just right for slipping a letter through. Each cube had a notice posted on it, which said in large, readable characters:

"O black-haired people, your prince, moved by the Tao, is looking for good, wise, and pious men to give him the benefit of their counsel. He wants to hear the opinion of everyone, even those in the most remote parts of his Empire, in the humblest classes of his people. Every opinion is welcome, no matter where it comes from; he longs to know what is in every subject's mind. So he is asking each one of you to write down your thoughts, no matter how trivial, and post them in the house of virtuous suggestions, taking care to put your name and address on the back. Government positions will be made available at court and in the provinces for those who make the best suggestions or comments. Even women, children, and the infirm will be eligible for rewards."

The boxes had been set up at crossroads, in village squares and town markets. Fortunate, who could run like the wind, had offered to make the collections.

———

To begin with, Li Harmony's direct influence extended over only one or two prefectures. But then came a sudden expansion. A man called Ch'in the Fruitful recruited among the population in the northern part of Eastern Slope and conquered Burning City, the chief town. The prefect, Congratulation, then joined the revolt and brought all the other towns in the region with him.

Fruitful and Congratulation showed great sympathy for Li Harmony's teaching, out of either sincere conviction or self-interest; or perhaps because they had no choice in the matter, so popular were these doctrines in the province. They even went so far as to offer the visionary the crown of Ch'i, but Li Harmony declined in favor of Flash-Pedigree, who would only accept the lesser title wise prince of the Tao. Li Harmony did not say no to a post as minister, however, or to the title saint. As for Ch'in the Fruitful, he appointed himself general of the One, the Great One.

Fortunate could not collect all the letters of virtuous suggestions by himself, and they piled up in boxes all over. So he recruited help, and soon found himself at the head of a whole postal network, which came to be called the Ministry of Heavenly Communications. Pomp was made head of the Department of Auspicious Signs and Wonders.

———

The brotherhood of Great Peace had thousands of followers. To give new life to the element wood, bearer of the breaths of spring, all weapons made of iron or bronze were abolished, and, instead of metal coinage, the use of barter and cowrie shells was reintroduced. In the hope of creating wealth through a shared enjoyment of poverty, all property was now held in common. Baby girls were no longer killed, and the many concubines left behind by wealthy or eminent men away on the expedition against Ch'in were shared among ordinary citizens. Because there weren't enough women for there to be two females to every male, swapping took place during great local festivities. These were called Banquets to Celebrate the Union of the Breaths. The participants modeled themselves on the great cycle of the universe, and their couplings contributed to the creation of abundance and the harmony of nature. The consumption of alcohol was banned from the markets, because wine was of the same nature as water, and markets attracted crowds just as rivers flow toward low places.

Heaven and Earth were joined together in a gentle embrace, exhaling the damp warm breath of spring. And as the days lengthened, men lifted eyes full of hope to the sun, whose ruddy beams brought peace to their hearts and blessings on their concord.

OBSTRUCTION

Access is denied to him who is undesirable.
Unpropitious for the Great Man.
Obstruction is a symbol of lack of communication
 between Heaven and Earth.
A wise man withdraws his virtue to avoid misfortune;
 he does not allow himself to be tempted
 by remuneration.

"Prince, there are more and more people rising in rebellion despite the repression. The harsher we are, the more the people revolt. They are tired of frontier garrisons, of periods of forced labor that are too frequent and too long, of having their grain and fodder requisitioned for the army, and of all the taxes that rain down on them and reduce them to beggary. We ought to suspend work on the tomb on Mount Li and postpone the extension of your A'fang palace. We ought to reduce the garrisons and cut down on military expeditions on the borders. Then we wouldn't need to levy so many taxes or so much forced labor."

The Emperor shook his sleeves impatiently and cast a melancholy eye around the room. The table was covered with rare dishes and goblets of wine, and around it was every kind of regal distraction—jesters, dancing girls, performing animals. It was just like these tedious old fogies, Li Ssu and Ward-off-Evil, to come and spoil his fun as usual with their stupid complaints. As if they couldn't have chosen one of the all too many occasions when he had nothing better to do. No; out of sheer malice they had to pick the very moment when he was enjoying a new game—a fight between three dwarfs and three hunchbacks. The dwarfs were piled on top of the hunchbacks like three straight lines on three broken ones, echoing, if he had but known it, the symbol of the eighth hexagram, obstruction. Which is what existed between him and his ministers.

He looked at the two old men again, standing stiffly in their court dress of long gowns embroidered with tigers and bears, and tall caps made of stiffened silk. They stood bowed slightly forward so as not to look directly at him, still droning out their sermon and making sinister insinuations about Chao the Tall, his sole protector and support. It was more than he could bear.

"He may be only a eunuch," he said, "but Chao the Tall has always behaved with integrity and followed the path of virtue. That is why he has been able to rise to his present distinguished position. I have the utmost confidence in him. So please stop making these slanderous accusations. Remember, I lost my father when I was very young, and I still have little experience of handling people. You are old, and must soon leave us. Whom shall I be able to turn to then except the faithful Chao the Tall?"

"But he's a villain," croaked the prime minister, "an insatiably ambitious villain! He's on the highest step next to the throne already, and is only waiting for an opportunity to climb to the throne itself!"

"That will do!" cried the Emperor angrily. He clutched his brow.

He had a terrible headache. "I won't hear another word against my counselor!"

With a contemptuous curl of the lip, he went on:

"You're always quoting the great philosopher Han Fei. Well, didn't he write that princes like Yao and Shun, who ate out of earthen bowls and lived like slaves in hovels a swineherd would turn up his nose at, were no good as models, even if they did seek the good of their people?"

Then he hissed straight at them:

"I've been on the throne for two years, there are brigands rising up everywhere, and you haven't done anything to arrest them or nip subversion in the bud. All you do is try to stop the work my father began. You are ungrateful to him and disloyal to me. You should blush to occupy positions you're unworthy of."

And he ordered them to be imprisoned and put on trial.

Opposition, which thus reached a culminating point in the seventh month of autumn, had begun in the first month. Then, as the sap of spring, propelled by the life-giving exhalations of Earth and sky, hung puffs of pale green on the branches and lit great white fires on the magnolias, the black winter forces of Ch'in, having wiped out Chou the Sign's elaborately arranged eight corps, swept down on the eastern provinces.

Ear and Scrap, who were living in Ch'en, had been among the very first scholars to join the rebels, and this gave them considerable ascendancy over the still-inexperienced king. They had at once warmly recommended K'ung Bream to him. K'ung Bream was a direct descendant, in the eighth generation, of Confucius, and had kept up his ancestor's tradition in all its purity. He was said to have connections with the soothsayers' sect, and had sent his disciple Totality to work for Ch'in while he himself became prince of Cultural Diffusion in Lu, under the August Emperor. Through his position he was able to warn his friends Scrap and Ear that they were about to be arrested. When books were banned and he himself was in danger, he had to flee to the Great Cave mountains south of Lo-yang.

For once, paying a debt of gratitude didn't involve injustice. Bream was a remarkable man. Take-the-Plunge, king of Ch'u, asked him to be his guest, and he accepted. And soon the whole group of Confucians in Lu had taken their wide-sleeved gowns and starched silk caps out of storage and showed up with the holy relics: the Master's lute and sandals and ritual equipment. A complicated ritual was introduced, which imprisoned Take-the-Plunge in a straitjacket of etiquette and genuflection. Isolated in regal pomp and circumstance, he drifted away from his former companions in arms and misfortune, and he was equally inaccessible to his learned advisers. Ceremony had stifled the simple enthusiasm and freshness that lay behind his successes, and what now prevailed was his basic stupidity, made worse by his sense of his own importance. He had stopped being a rebel without becoming a king.

Bream, a man of sense and experience, warned Take-the-Plunge about the power of Ch'in.

"Chou the Sign is no match for a general like Chang Han, and you're sending him off so rashly, without even taking the precaution of organizing your defenses, that I'm afraid you may be in for trouble. I know man proposes and God disposes, but if you rely on chance, without doing anything to help it, you'll be inviting disaster. You know the law of strategy: A general counts not on the enemy's weakness but on his own strength."

The king laughed.

"That's too complicated," he said. "Couldn't you descend to my level and illustrate what you mean by a little anecdote or a funny story?"

"Very well. When I lived in Wei, I had a tremendously strong neighbor, all muscles and sinews; he could lift a bronze tripod all by himself. He was very agile and nimble too, and could overcome a wild beast with his bare hands. He was the terror of the whole region. But he couldn't control his wife—a real harpy, always nagging and answering back. One evening some of the neighbors and I heard shrieks coming from their house. We rushed over, thinking the wife needed help. Imagine our surprise when we saw the husband lying on his back and screeching like a pig having its throat cut, with the shrew on top of him, twisting his balls. They'd been having a huge row, and the man had lost his temper and seized his wife by the hair. Clamping her head against the bedpost, he'd picked up a stick and started beating her. But she had twisted free, grabbed him by the testicles, and squeezed with all her might. The husband, taken by surprise, had fallen over backward and was gasping for breath.

"After having a good laugh at the scene, we decided to rescue the poor wretch. But we couldn't make the furious virago let go. Then someone thought of lifting her skirt, and she had to loosen her grip to defend her modesty."

King Take-the-Plunge roared with laughter. The scholar followed up his advantage.

"Do you know why this force of nature was brought down by a weak woman?"

"No. Tell me!"

"Because he thought he had nothing to fear from her, and so he was not on his guard. But Chang Han is no weak woman, and Sign is no athlete. On the contrary! Yet you're so sure of your superiority that you're attacking without protecting your rear. It makes my blood run cold just to think of it."

"Your story's very amusing, but not so strong as its hero. I'd like to see *my* wife try that trick—I'd knock her silly!"

And he took no notice of Bream's pleas for prudence.

———

The obstacle that Viceroy Vast Wu was up against was even more solid than the wall of self-satisfaction that now barricaded the king of Ch'u's heart. For months Vast Wu had had to cope with resistance from Li Yu, son of Prime Minister Li Ssu. Li Yu, in turn, was exposed to obstruction from Chao the Tall's men, who intercepted his pleas for help.

While the insurgents contemplated with growing irritation the lofty ramparts that prevented their advance, another, and invisible, barrier gradually grew up in their midst. A wall of mistrust separated the viceroy ever more widely from his men. Was not Vast Wu the only one of Take-the-Plunge's officers without any notable success to his credit? Had he not loitered in the East while Chou the Sign was advancing into the heart of Ch'in? Now he was stuck in front of the city like a sparrow mesmerized by a snake, while Chang Han's ruffians fell upon the East, destroying everything in their path. If Vast Wu didn't do something, he and his men would be caught between Ch'in's assault troops and the besieged army.

The men started to have doubts about their leader's military skill, and one evening when the viceroy got drunk to forget his frustrations, his lieutenants went into his tent and cut off his head. They sent it to Take-the-Plunge with a letter explaining that they'd taken this drastic action because of the late viceroy's negligence and incompetence, and asking that they be confirmed in their posts.

The king shed a tear over the severed head of his former comrade, sighed at the thought that the past, though still so close, was blotted out by the clouds of glory, and agreed to his generals' demands. They then led the main army against the enemy, but came up against Chang Han's convicts and their iron force, which crushed them like a millstone grinding wheat. Those who tried to put up a fight were slaughtered, and the rest scattered like a flock of sparrows. Ch'in's army fell upon Take-the-Plunge's capital and obliterated their opponents. Soon afterward Take-the-Plunge's coachman, with whom the king of Ch'u had fled, brought his master's head to the Ch'in generals as a token of submission. K'ung Bream was made prisoner, along with many other scholars. He was taken back to Double Light, and there cut to pieces and pickled in brine.

Contradictory rumors circulated about King Take-the-Plunge's fate. Some people said he was dead, others that he had only fled. Ch'in the Fruitful, the rebel from Burning City, thought his opportunity had come. He made Flash-Pedigree temporary king of Ch'u, appointed himself supreme commander, and moved the capital to Remains, not far from Whet-Iron's base.

But instead of contributing to the spread of goodness, the nomination of Flash-Pedigree only severed all communication between the king and the common people, for the generals and other dignitaries in the king's entourage hampered the collection of virtuous suggestions, and the link between the dark heads of the peasants and the silken caps of the officials was weakened. Many of the rebel leaders refused to recognize the new king. Congratulation and Li Harmony were sent as ambassadors to try to win over the ruler of Ch'i, a man infatuated with rank and aristocracy, and who had the most profound contempt for every kind of commoner.

As soon as Flash-Pedigree's envoy had made his bow before the royal dais of purple silk, the king of Ch'i asked cuttingly:

"There are all kinds of rumors going around about King Take-the-Plunge. No one knows whether he's alive or dead. So I find it strange, not to say offensive, that Ch'i hasn't been consulted about the appointing of a new king."

"You didn't find it necessary to ask for Ch'u's approval when you were crowned. So why should Ch'u need your permission? Wasn't Ch'u the first to raise the standard of revolt? All the other rulers ought to follow and obey it!"

"We don't take orders from anyone. Especially not a renegade!"

And he signed to his guards to seize Congratulation and cut off his head.

Li Harmony had preferred to persuade the people. He had rushed through town overturning jars of wine in drinking shops in every narrow alley, making incendiary speeches about the reign of fire, and urging the people to destroy the coinage and put up boxes for virtuous suggestions at every street corner. He expounded his theories about concord between the mighty and the humble via the circulation of the word; he lauded the fertile union of Heaven and Earth, symbolized by the sacred proportion of two women to one man. But the inhabitants of northern Ch'i were tough and often greedy; they liked the cool feel of money in their hands, and haggled more out of cupidity than self-interest. Once they got over their amusement and surprise, they were angry with Li Harmony; the crowd grew restless, shouted, yelled, and threw things at him. Among them were some members of the butchers' guild—rough, violent men who saw this as an opportunity to avenge themselves for the contempt in which they were generally held. Brandishing their knives and cleavers, they rushed upon Li Harmony and dragged him to their stall. There they disemboweled, dismembered, and chopped him into mincemeat, egged on by the enthusiastic cheers of the populace.

———

Whet-Iron too was a victim of the obstruction that prevailed throughout the Empire. The barrier he came up against was not the invisible membrane that may come between a ruler and his subjects because of his position, and not citadels of stone and ramparts of armored bodies, and not a wall of greed and stupidity. No; it was, quite simply, Barricade of Teeth.

The young man who had come out worse in the divination had sought his revenge as soon as Whet-Iron's back was turned; taking advantage of his absence on an expedition, he had seized Whet-Iron's capital. With the support of the émigrés from the court of Wei, he had sworn allegiance to that country, and it had sent him troops. So Whet-Iron turned to Flash-Pedigree. He was quite attracted by Li Harmony's ideas. Admittedly he knew them only by hearsay, but he saw a kind of promise of advancement in the reign of wood, which would usher in the radiance of fire. Flash-Pedigree thought it a good idea to ally himself with someone rumored to be the son of the Red Emperor, and granted him some troops. Then Whet-Iron came up against the walls and barred gates of Feng, behind which Barricade of Teeth had withdrawn. Despite his furious assaults, Whet-Iron could not overcome this double obstacle. He had to fall back south to reassemble his forces and rebuild his reserves. This was made more necessary by the danger of attack from the rear by a Ch'in column moving eastward.

———

Beam, with the seventy thousand troops he had stationed in Hsia-p'i, saw all the territory north of the Huai River within his grasp. But first he must strike down the green turbans Fruitful had quartered in P'eng-ch'eng. Beam tried to negotiate, but without success. He was not disappointed, however: all he wanted was a pretext for eliminating these madmen who were threatening both the hierarchy and the rest of the established order. He issued a proclamation to the Empire:

"The great king Ch'en Take-the-Plunge initiated the rebellion: it was he who raised the standard behind which all men of noble and generous blood have risen. Fortune, alas, did not smile on him, and no one knows what has become of him. Ch'in the Fruitful, a faithless vassal and a traitor, took advantage of his master's misfortune to betray him and place a false king on the throne. He is a disreputable and unscrupulous wretch who must be punished. He is supported by a gang of yokels who preach a perverse and unnatural doctrine. If we do not put all this to rights, the whole social order will be turned upside down. There will be no more princes or vassals, no more distinction between nobles and commoners, no obedience. Your property will be shared, and so will your wives. All will be chaos."

He marched on P'eng-ch'eng in the autumn of the Second Emperor's second year, a time of stagnation and decay, when creative forces were no longer in communion and the fertilizing breath of Heaven no longer filled the Earth. Fruitful was put to ignominious flight, and Beam hunted him down to the Mound of the Barbarians. The vanquished general regrouped his forces, adding to them the supporters of Li Harmony, who, since they would not use any metal, fought with long wooden lances that still had leaves on them. One day there was a terrible battle between the two armies—the upper classes and the masses. Beam won, and his forces inflicted fearful slaughter on the advocates of the Great Peace. The Earth, blackened and bruised by battle, was drenched in rivers of blood. Then Beam and Plume attacked and occupied Remains, the enemy capital, slaying everyone who crossed their path.

———

Flash-Pedigree fled on Fortunate's back. With the aid of his amulets, Fortunate galloped along like a foal of the steppes. He went on and on, along paths lined with somber and excessive lushness that bore witness to the pernicious breath of autumn. He passed valleys and hills, crossed rivers and marshes. He was going through a pass in the tree-clad mountains that overlook the Lin Ch'i plain when the hot breath of a large animal with black and red stripes streamed over his head. But he didn't have time to see anything as he was thrown to the ground. A tiger had Flash-Pedigree by the throat. His lifeblood gushed darkly from a gaping wound. Fortunate got up, shrieked, and fled as fast as his legs would carry him, as the tiger gorged itself on its victim.

Fortunate ran and ran, crossing hills and canyons until he came to Lin Ch'i, where he leaped over the city walls, rushed to the king of Wei's palace, and burst into the royal apartments. King Wei the Unfortunate was alone, weeping. He had just negotiated the surrender of the city to the Ch'in army, in order to save its inhabitants. Fortunate shed copious tears and offered to take the king to Ch'u, carrying him on his back. But Wei the Unfortunate shook his head, conferred the title marquis upon him, and advised him to offer his services to Barricade of Teeth. Then he took off his cap, shook out his hair, and held it over an oil lamp. It lit up like a torch, and a few moments later there was nothing left of the king but a heap of charred and blackened bones.

MEN IN SYMPATHY

Men in sympathy are on the plain:
Excellent! and useful for the crossing of a great river;
integrity is useful to the Great Man.

Barbarian's hand shook with joy. His eyes brimmed. He felt a warm wave of sympathy for the eunuch.

"And to think I almost believed Li Ssu, the traitor!"

Li Ssu had accused Chao the Tall of the very misdeeds he himself was guilty of: as had clearly been shown by a committee of inquiry specially set up in Three Rivers, Li Ssu, using his son Li Yu as an intermediary, had plotted with the rebels. Otherwise how could a group of subversives have reached the outskirts of the capital? A host of memories flooded back, together with a feeling of gratitude toward that smooth fat face with its shaved eyebrows, toward the man who had been a nurse to his infancy, a tutor to his youth, and a minister to his first steps as a monarch. He owed everything to him—his throne, and perhaps even his life. He would certainly have been killed if anyone else had succeeded the First Emperor: he himself had killed his ten brothers. Chao the Tall was the only person he understood, and an attempt had been made to destroy that understanding. . . . He must do his best to make up for his brief moment of doubt. He would make him prime minister that very day.

Thus, in the secluded atmosphere of the inner palace, a bond of deep affection bound the young prince ever closer to the big fat spider who was spinning the web of solitude. It was a morbid affection: instead of being turned outward toward others, it was directed inward, toward Barbarian himself, as in the hexagram *"Sympathy for the tribe: misfortune."*

————

Outside the black-lacquered walls, in the vast spaces swept by the bracing but lethal wind of reality, the obstacles that lay along the paths of ambition created bonds of sympathy between men gathered in bands and armies. Bonds all the stronger because everyone knew they were precarious.

The Great Men just wandered about. Sometimes they met someone like them, their double, and felt a kind of attraction: they were like the big black dogs of the steppes, sniffing at and recognizing one another, then running shoulder to shoulder over the plain, vying with one another in strength, and tearing their prey to pieces with yelps of triumph as if to seal their friendship in blood. At other times in their bold wanderings they came upon individuals so different from themselves it seemed impossible they could co-exist. Then it was the contrast that attracted them.

————

A curtain of rain covered the land with a pearly gray dusk, and through it came a muffled clanking of bits and creaking of damp harness. Chang the Good saw a large troop of soldiers coming toward him, advancing in good order, though with difficulty, along the sodden road. Every so often one of the bronze studs on their armor cast a dull gleam on a streaming sharkskin doublet, bringing out its warmer tones. Fringes and aglets added bright touches of red and gold to the officers' uniforms. In the swirls of mist arising from the warm soaked earth, their tall caps of glossy silk made them look unreal. The forest of spears and halberds made a darker hatching against the bluish curtain of the rain. Although the banners, drenched and dripping on their crimson-tasseled poles, looked as if they were weeping, they had a martial air. And in their folds, quartered with gules and gold, could be divined the double tigers rampant, the flames, the phoenixes *affrontés*, the shadows of suns.

A sudden gust filled the heavy draperies; the commander's flag fluttered in the wind and, scattering silvery drops, stretched out like a long silken snake. Chang the Good saw large white calligraphy on a vermilion ground spelling out "Prefect Liu, Grand General of Fire." It was Whet-Iron, accompanied by one of Fruitful's captains, setting out on an expedition against Chang Han, who had recently encircled T'ang. Chang the Good knew Whet-Iron by reputation, and asked to speak with him. He was led before a strapping fellow wearing a rhinoceros-skin cuirass studded with silver, and sitting proudly on a chestnut horse. His skin was white, and he had a broad nose in a strong square face. Chang introduced himself and offered to join Whet-Iron, along with his own men. The other smiled when he saw how few they were, and how frail their leader was. But Chang had always been one of the heroes of his dreams, so he welcomed him and accepted his offer.

At their next halt, when they had set up their camp, Whet-Iron invited Chang to his tent to share a meal and drink a few cups of wine. As soon as they seated themselves on their mats, a sympathy sprang up between them: this was strange, since they were so different. Chang the Good admired Whet-Iron's tall stature, his strong body, and the rough countenance that was sometimes lighted by a good-natured and charming smile. Whet-Iron was impressed by Chang's exquisite manners and the subtlety and depth of his intelligence.

He was surprised: he'd imagined the hero who had tried to assassinate the First Emperor to be imposing physically; instead, he saw before him a man of moderate height, as delicate and fragile as a girl. He often put his long white hand up to his chest, as if he suffered from some heart complaint. Had it not been for his age— he must be about forty—he would have eclipsed the loveliest damsels in Ch'u and Cheng with his chalk-white complexion, his little red mouth, his bright black eyes and finely arched eyebrows. The years had left their traces at the corners of his eyes, on his forehead, and around his mouth. They had thinned the oval of his face and sharpened his nose. But in so doing they had given him an expression of sensitive melancholy, which, while it made his looks less perfect, brought out their distinction and their owner's spiritual radiance. So the depredations of time only made Whet-Iron admire Chang more. He got the better of his usual boorishness, and behaved with as much consideration and tact as he would have with a woman he was trying to captivate.

He noticed the green-and-white stone Chang wore on his belt, with its octagon enclosing the trigrams. He asked about it. Whet-Iron had found a similar stone after a meeting with a soothsayer, but he had lost it at the gaming table. Could the two stones be, by any strange chance, the same? Chang told Whet-Iron of his tribulations: the unsuccessful attempt on the life of the Emperor, his flight to the South, and his encounter with the mysterious old man. In the eight years he'd spent in Hsia-p'i he'd met many extraordinary men, but none was the Great Man he wanted to serve. When the rebellion broke out, he thought he'd found fit employment at last. He had gathered together a hundred or so young men and set out for Take-the-Plunge's capital. He'd met gangs of looters, and then columns of soldiers who'd been defeated by the legions of Chang Han. When he reached Ch'en, it was only to learn of the disaster in which Take-the-Plunge had probably met his death. A new king—Flash-Pedigree—had been proclaimed and had taken up residence in Remains. What he'd been told about him had given Chang new hope. He had set out once more, and that was how he and Whet-Iron had come to meet.

During the days that followed, Chang expounded the principles of the old man of Hsia-p'i's book on strategy, and Whet-Iron listened reverently although he couldn't understand a word. However, it was with the help of his new friend's advice that he won the city of T'ang back from the Ch'in armies.

The victorious forces returned to P'ei. Chang the Good was struck down by one of his mysterious chest attacks. Whet-Iron had him taken to his own residence, where he charged his family to look after him. He himself had to go retake Feng, the ranks of his army having swelled with new recruits from his recent conquests. Thus Chang the Good got to know Lü the Pheasant. As a physiognomist he noticed that his hostess's every feature bore witness to a remarkable destiny: she had great strength of will and unbounded ambition. To Chang's affection for Whet-Iron was now added admiration for his wife.

As Whet-Iron was deploying his troops around Feng, he intercepted Fortunate, who was hurrying from Wei to offer his services to Barricade of Teeth. Impressed by the strength, physical prowess, and long, regular stride of the collector of virtuous suggestions, Whet-Iron summoned him and felt his calves, going into ecstasies over their size and marveling at the talismans attached to them. He questioned him. The news of the tragic end of Flash-Pedigree and Wei the Unfortunate brought tears to his eyes—the death of crowned heads always made him weep. But he was appalled by the king of Wei's advice to Fortunate, and set about trying to persuade him to join his camp. He succeeded, and had the modest satisfaction of stealing a man of talent from someone to whom he had lost a whole city. Fortunate was made a courier in his army, with the rank of lieutenant.

The former chief of police had been amused by Li Harmony's ideas, but now he began to dream of a perfectly regulated world in which the people governed themselves; a world where, under the influence of a saintly king, everyone kept to the path of virtue and there was no more need for punishment.

The siege was unsuccessful, and Whet-Iron went to Remains, where Beam, the new champion of the rebellion, had set up his headquarters, to ask him for more men to help him drive Barricade of Teeth out of Feng.

Beam, Plume, and Whet-Iron got along with one another from the start. They were alike: tall, imposing, able to wear out other men's bodies and brains to serve their own ambitions. Given this likeness, Beam and Plume might have resented Whet-Iron's preeminence, but he, impressed by their superior lineage and the laurels of their ancestors, bore himself modestly and acknowledged them as his masters. So for the time being they accepted their physical and moral resemblance. Whenever they met, their eyes lighted up and their carnivores' teeth gleamed through their bushy black beards. They let out huge roars of laughter, clapped one another on the back with their enormous hands, and dug their elbows into one another's bearlike ribs. It was as if three huge apes were performing a friendly jig, but at the same time testing each other's strength.

They talked of military campaigns, of rides across the plains, of drinking bouts and friendship. They recalled the prowess of knights and heroes in the past, and revealed the vast ambitions that swelled their own steel-clad breasts. They spoke of food and women, and horses too. They had the same tastes in everything. Whet-Iron was captivated by Plume's exquisite manners toward anyone he wanted to win over. He was attentive without ever being importunate; he refilled empty glasses without forcing people to drink; his horn chopsticks deposited the choicest morsels on the plates of his guests. And this easy, natural considerateness seemed the more delicate and disarming because it came from such a formidable warlord.

The Hsiangs gave Whet-Iron five thousand more men for his campaign.

But the bonds between Beam and his nephew on the one hand

and Whet-Iron on the other were not strong enough to preclude other feelings. Their friendship was the kind that lasts only as long as the circumstances that produced it. So it wasn't surprising that as soon as Whet-Iron had left, Beam and Plume felt their hearts go out to the tall, thin old man advancing toward them with a step still firm despite his age. He was wearing a loose, full-sleeved robe with a turned-down collar, its only ornament a silken border embroidered with occult and animal emblems. Time, which had dulled his eyes with the impenetrable veil that experience lends to guile, had also scattered streaks of rust among the sparse silvery strands of his beard. He had always lived in Nest, never leaving his huge fortified estate overlooking the peaceful waters of a large lake, forever poring over ancient prophetic books given him by a hermit known as the Wise Old Man of the South. A vague but persistent rumor had it that the Wise Old Man was one of the leaders of the Trigrams of the second generation after Confucius. There was no way of testing the rumor, but it probably arose from the fact that the hermit was one of the greatest interpreters of the *Book of Changes*, in the Confucian tradition. There in his solitude among the lakes and hills, the patriarch of Nest had used his knowledge of divination to concoct wonderful plans, which events had hitherto kept from fulfillment. When news reached him of the exploits of Beam and Plume, he thought he had found fit masters to serve, and an opportunity for his plans to take flight like captive eagles freed at last.

Everything about the uncle's and nephew's looks spoke of virility, strength, and ability to sway the mob: their broad red faces symmetrically divided by prominent noses like the muzzles of wild beasts; their big black eyes, narrowed at the corners, flashing out from beneath brows like dark and monstrous silkworms. Fan the Increaser, for such was the old man's name, knew he was in the presence of Great Men as soon as he set eyes on them. And the Great Men knew at once that they were dealing with a sage counselor. They treated him with deference; he told them some of his plans. He said they would be able to master the princes better in the name of some puppet ruler they had removed from contact with reality by means of the very grandiloquence of his name. Beam and Plume, attracted by this idea, asked Increaser to set out in search of a suitable scion of the royal house of Ch'u.

The wise, the all-too-wise old man thought he had found this rare jewel in the person of Intelligence, though only his name possessed that quality. Intelligence was an indirect descendant of King Huai, who had been reduced to the rank of an ordinary commoner when the First Emperor came to power. Having neither culture nor talent of any kind, Intelligence had become a goatherd. Increaser took him back to Remains and had him crowned king by the assembled nobles.

Meanwhile, Whet-Iron had rescued his native city from the greedy maw of Barricade of Teeth, whom he forced to flee ignominiously to Wei. Whet-Iron returned in triumph to Remains, to tell the new king of his exploits. No sooner was this done than he had to embark as Plume's lieutenant on a campaign against Ch'in.

It was then that he discovered what war really was. Hitherto he had experienced it merely as a police operation on a large scale: you drove the enemy into a cul-de-sac as you might a gang of criminals; then you surrounded and closed in on them like a fisherman drawing in his net. But when he encountered a fortified place, he was confused.

Plume never hung back. He always attacked a city at once, encircling it like a hurricane sweeping across the steppes, smashing it and everything in it as if it were in the clutch of a gigantic whirlpool.

His campaigns traced a huge zigzag made up of constant unpredictable movements—lightning advances, withdrawals, and breakthroughs. He was always surprising the enemy in open country, and, instead of taking cities by siege, capturing them suddenly from the rear. Sometimes his army would wind about like a snake and imprison the foe in a loop; sometimes, deployed in a straight line, it would overwhelm its adversaries on their wings; sometimes it would march in columns, piercing its foes like an arrow, then cutting them up like a sword. Plume's army could grind like a millstone, flatten like a flail, penetrate like a wedge.

His opponents either surrendered or were exterminated: Plume gave no quarter. He left a wake of blood and tears behind him, slaughtering whole cities and laying whole countrysides waste. His own blood lust in battle communicated itself to his men, who fell on the enemy like a pack of wolves. When he stood amid the smoke of smoldering ruins, covered with black gore and yellow mud and hacking at heaps of still-gasping, groaning flesh, he might have been Ch'ih-yu, the god of war, himself. This man, so gentle and courteous in private life, so considerate to his friends and his wives, was transformed by battle into a bloodthirsty demon. He must have had the soul of a tiger; his pleasant ways were like those of a wild beast playing with its cubs.

Whet-Iron, proud to be one of the few people for whom Plume sheathed his claws, still reeking from the blood of his victims, let himself join in the intoxication of slaughter. The smell of blood awakened the beast of prey that slept within him, and he took pleasure in carnage, rejoiced in butchery. But in his case they left behind a taste of bitterness. Perhaps it was only because he could see that Beam and Plume would always be infinitely better warriors than he.

They crushed the Ch'in army at the Mound Barrier. Li Yu, the governor in charge of the Three Rivers forces, put up fierce resistance, and when he was captured he was put to death. After cutting his throat, they poured his blood on an improvised altar, and Plume offered it up to the spirit of Swallow. Then he gorged himself on Li Yu's liver and lungs.

———

Beam was sleeping the sleep of the victor in his tent. He had driven Chang Han's forces back to the northwest, and they had withdrawn behind Strength-of-Clay-Pot. His slumber was filled with dreams of battles, triumphs, and glory. Mounted on his huge white stallion, he was cutting heads off as lavishly as a spring breeze scattering camellia blossoms. They fell in graceful curves to the ground, where each one lay like a sumptuous flower with black petals, its stem encircled with crimson, until all were trampled by the massive hooves of the chargers. The headless trunks thudded like enormous stalks. Beam and his men, in complete communion, felled whole ranks of the enemy, rank after rank. What savagery! What joy!

But, they too united in the communion of war, the very men Beam was decapitating in his dream were creeping silently and invisibly forward under the cover of darkness. The horses were muzzled, their hooves muffled with straw. All the bells had been removed from the trappings of chargers and chariots; the metal parts of armor and harness were smeared with soot so that the advance of Chang Han's army would not be betrayed by any telltale gleam. The Ch'in sentries were overpowered as if by the night itself. The horde of dark and silent warriors had already entered the camp, a special detachment had already surrounded the commander's tent, before the signal was given to launch the attack.

Beam was still dreaming. But his dream was now making him vaguely but painfully anxious. The proud general on his white stallion had been unseated; a great blade of steel not wielded by any hand was transfixing his body, striking him down like a sword brandished by heaven. But this poor wretch writhing grotesquely around the shaft that pinned him to the ground could not be he, Beam! It must be the Enemy; the sword was his own, the invisible hand that held it was his own desire to conquer and kill. But why then had the Other taken his features? Why was the identification so complete that he could feel his blood seeping out of his body? Why was he feeling such pity for a vanquished foe? And why, why, this awful, atrocious pain?

Beam opened his eyes and saw the answer in the brutal, merciless face that was bending over to slay him. He took his killer with him into his everlasting sleep.

———

The penultimate line of the hexagram read: "*Men in sympathy who first cry and then laugh: the victory of a great army permits their union.*" The Master expounded it thus: "A wise man must adapt his behavior to circumstance, according to which he is either open or secretive, taciturn or talkative; but when he finds a heart that beats in time with his own, he becomes keener than metal, for the outpouring of a kindred spirit is as fragrant as an orchid."

And indeed, was not the friendship between Ear and Scrap living proof of the power of such close communion? They had had to face many reverses, yet they had always managed to overcome them and change bad luck into good, misfortune into advantage. They had eluded the Ch'in police and risen through Take-the-Plunge's rebellion to become ministers in Chao. They had survived a palace revolution that had cost the life of their king, and succeeded in taking over the reins of power. Yet even the merging of twin souls is not indestructible: it is in the nature of human feelings to be vulnerable to time and circumstance, which sometimes reinforce such bonds and sometimes loosen them. It is against this precariousness that the last line of the incompleteness hexagram warns us, if we can but decipher it: "*Friendship reduced to the outskirts: nothing to complain about.*" Thus, although after the dramatic events that followed the destruction of Beam and his army, Ear and Scrap laughed after having cried, the end of their friendship was nevertheless in sight.

The defeat of Ch'u's main battle force and the inglorious death of General Beam spread terror among the rest of the Eastern army. Its soldiers fled at the mere name Ch'in. Even Plume gave up the idea of leading his troops into battle, and fell back to defend Remains.

Chang Han, sure of having broken the military power of Ch'u, marched against Chao. He advanced with lightning speed, and the capital, Han-tan, was taken in a trice. Ear fled with the king to White

Stag, while Scrap hastened to the north of the country to raise a new army. But when he tried to rejoin his friend, the enemy cut him off. Since the opposing force was too strong for him to attack it, he entrenched himself in a camp north of White Stag, behind the Ch'in lines.

While Scrap was outside the city tearing his hair in despair at the enemy's numerical superiority, Ear, within, could only look on miserably as his reserves ran down. Looking to the north, he saw the earthen walls behind which Scrap was skulking and cursed his cowardice. Looking to the south, he saw dimly through a curtain of rain the black and threatening lines of Ch'in's legions, and he began to tremble.

In his terror and distress he began to feel hatred and scorn for Scrap, who was cravenly failing to honor their oath of mutual aid. He sent message after message through the Ch'in lines, urging his friend to intervene. But Scrap was merely irritated by this lack of composure.

And so, as the weeks went by, the supposedly unbreakable bond between them was worn away by inactivity on one side and fretfulness on the other. Every day of the siege took a fiber away from the cord that had held them together; and the siege went on and on, partly because Ear and the other nobles inside White Stag remained passive, and partly because Scrap too was temporizing. His lethargy angered his deputy, whose wrath in turn vexed his commander, so that through mutual exasperation they came to loathe one another.

It had been decided at the court of King Intelligence of Ch'u that an army should be sent to the relief of the besieged town. A general had yet to be appointed, when the ruler whom Plume and Fan the Increaser thought they could manipulate asserted his independence and named Sung the Just as supreme commander. Plume and Increaser had to serve under him as second in command and master of strategy. Was not Sung the Just better qualified than anyone else to exercise the highest responsibility in a country at war? He had been prime minister when Ch'in annexed Ch'u, and had warned Beam against excessive self-confidence.

Sung the Just set out boldly at the head of his troops, crossed the Yellow River, and penetrated deep into Chao territory. But when he reached the banks of the Chang River, some two hundred leagues from White Stag, he pitched his camp and went no farther.

They had been there in the mud for forty-six days. All that time the rain had poured down in torrents, seeping into the tents, warping armor and harness, and soaking clothes and bedding. It was difficult to start fires, and when they were lighted they gave off clouds of choking smoke. Chariots got stuck in the mud, grain rotted, hay started to ferment. Food was getting scarce; the men were exhausted. Murmurs and complaints were heard in the ranks. Sung the Just merely waited, calm and imperturbable.

Plume urged him to attack, but he merely raised one eyebrow, gave a thin, haughty smile, and uttered one of his characteristic maxims: "You don't bother the fleas on an ox by crushing a tick."

Plume had great consultations with his staff, and Sung began to fear mutiny. He tried to prevent it by intimidation; he issued a proclamation threatening capital punishment for "officers whose tigerish ferocity, mulish obstinacy, and wolfish greed make them reject all discipline."

His fate was sealed. The very same day, Plume burst into his tent, cut off his head, took over the army, and ordered it to march.

Plume won a great victory over the Ch'in army, wiping it out completely. After weeks of cries and tears, there was now laughter, dancing, and singing. But the festivities marked the final break between Ear and Scrap. Ear, who was superior to Scrap in the hierarchy, heaped insult after insult upon him, until Scrap handed back his seals of office and left. The two were now mortal enemies.

GREAT POSSESSION

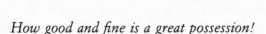

How good and fine is a great possession!

His chariot, drawn by four white horses, sped like the wind. He was driving through parkland well stocked with game and shaded by tall, rare trees. Flowers gave off exquisite scents; the air was made melodious by thousands of birds. He had been hunting since dawn through this reserve stretching to the ends of the earth. He could hear the steppe greyhounds baying; the growling of panthers struck down by his infallible arrows; the cackling of lanky storks, pursued by hawks in a flutter of feathers. Huge birds dripping with blood rained from the sky; the wheels of his chariot rode red to the axles over the remains of deer, leopards, bears, boars, and gazelles. Then suddenly a great pure-white tiger bounded out of the woods, leaped upon his left-hand lead horse, and devoured its hindquarters. The other horses shied, and the chariot overturned.

The Second Emperor gave a loud cry and fell out of bed, clutching a scrap of its heavy silk hangings. The corridor was already full of the sound of muffled footsteps: his eunuch guards running to the rescue. He reassured them—he'd been having a nightmare. But even if it was only a dream, it was a bad omen and left him vaguely uneasy about the stability of his possessions. To exorcise the unpleasant feeling that he was merely the temporary owner of all these riches, and that their profusion was no guarantee that he would enjoy them forever, he began to pass them in review. There was the huge imperial city of Double Light, with its Old Palace, the Six Palaces of the Conquered Princes, the new A'fang palace, and five hundred villas and rest houses scattered throughout the Empire. Inside these residences were millions of curios, vases, and articles of furniture; more than three thousand wives, not to mention dancing girls, singers, and various kinds of maids, companions, and junior concubines; eight thousand thoroughbred horses, kept just for his imperial vehicles and processions; and hundreds of chests full of precious stones, iridescent pearls, carved jade, and golden ornaments set with rubies. And then there were the vast estates at Sang-ling, Yun-meng, and Yung, with their populations of does, bucks, and other animals both wild and tame, birds of every kind, and rare and valuable trees. Beyond the walls of his palaces were lofty mountains and broad rivers, the latter bearing thousands of boats of fretted sandalwood and larger, swifter, vermilion-painted ships. There were the two million soldiers ready to sacrifice their two million lives for him, and the fifty-five million black-haired peasants whose hundred and ten million arms worked endlessly to satisfy his wishes. He owned everything, all the land under heaven. . . . He started to doze off again, smiling peacefully, soothed by the murmured catalogue of his possessions, like an infant counting his toys. Little did he dream that, although he still enjoyed the trappings of the Empire, he had long ago been dispossessed of what alone can lastingly secure them: the affection of his subjects.

While the Emperor fell asleep gloating over his innumerable possessions, the eunuch Chao the Tall, whose sleepless nights were haunted by desires he could never again assuage, consoled himself by listing those same treasures. He planned to acquire them for himself. It was not the things, but their symbolic value, that gave him pleasure, just as he no longer embraced anything but the shadow of desire. Thus, in the vast imperial archives to which as prime minister he now had access, he enjoyed going through the maps: images of the territories he would come into; the registers of births, marriages, and deaths: a dull and motionless reflection of the pulsing lives that would be his; and the account ledgers: records of treasures worthless except as echoes of joys their possession promises but usually fails to give. Constrained, owing to the terrible punishment inflicted on him by his masters, to know only the representation of desire, Chao confused things with the names of things. The symbol of possession is Power, a promise that all desires and appetites will be satisfied—but it is a promise that can remain forever unfulfilled.

Chao thought he could acquire Authority by seizing control of words. He called a horse a stag, and no one, not even the Emperor, dared to contradict him. As the master of language he thought he was the master of the facts it referred to, once more confusing the object and its representation. He was like a hungry man trying to get sustenance from the smell of food.

———

It wasn't only at court that people assessed what they owned in the hope of acquiring more. The whole of the Empire east of the passes was doing its accounts.

The new kings had carved out territories for themselves, conquered cities, and raised armies—fragile enough acquisitions in those troubled times. The generals had troops who seemed to promise territorial gains—though these had to be won through victories, and victory isn't always certain. But Plume, although he had no title of royalty, possessed its reality. He led an enormous army, and enjoyed the trust of his soldiers and the fearful admiration of most of the rebels. He had both the qualities and the means to acquire the greatest possessions and wealth the Earth affords: he had ambition, courage, talent, and people who could give him good advice. There in his tent, sharing the hardships and privations of his men, he counted up his advantages: although he was only a subject, he had an eminent position and was able to win over kings and peoples alike. He thought of the assurance about great possessions in the fourteenth hexagram.

Though it wasn't so evident in his case, Whet-Iron too was endowed with great possessions. He also had wise counselors who *"while following the motion of the Tao, conformed to circumstances."* So was he not also in a position to know the designs of Heaven and to convey its secrets to the people?

There were a multitude of possessions in the Empire, all of them great in their own way but all tinged with unreality: some consisting in the enjoyment of what the possessor no longer had, some in the promise of what he didn't yet enjoy, others in a mere token of future possessions, and others again in what hope alone could afford.

————

Besides these great possessions—really nothing more than the possessions of the great—there were others, more unobtrusive and retiring and promising nothing. These were the possessions of the poor.

The disappearance of the leaders of the green turbans had destroyed the Great Peace movement, but the removal of its most eminent and unusual members had in a way cleansed it of elements that had distorted its real significance. It emerged from the loss of its leaders at once smaller and purer.

The anonymous mass of its adherents, those who leave no name to history, had submitted to events. When the storm had passed over, and government was still not back to normal, they went on living in concord, a down-to-earth village concord, and forgot about spreading it throughout the world.

The marvelous suggestion boxes had been dismantled, and metal coins were used again in the markets, those centers of attraction for wine and theft and murder. There were fewer women again: many had been abducted, raped, and murdered by Beam's and Plume's soldiers. Then, as the still bloodstained leaves trembled in the first cold winds of winter, the humble folk gave themselves over to listing and dreaming of great possessions, huddling their tired bodies together, their brittle bones creaking like crickets or the burning of dry sticks.

First of all, they had—their very own inalienable property, even if they were slaves—their three hundred and sixty bones and joints, corresponding to the three hundred and sixty days of the year; their four limbs, corresponding to the four directions; their five viscera, symbols of the five elements; their six receptacles, their nine orifices, and their three hundred and sixty million hairs. And inside, the eighteen thousand gods inhabiting them; the seven corporeal souls; the three spiritual souls; the gods of sun and moon, which light the eyes; the goddesses of the cycles of the hours, which look down over the ocean of the breath; and so on.

The people knew a fuller and more complete enjoyment of the body all possessed than did the great and the rich. For they were conscious of it all the time, in their aching bones, in their empty, swollen, flatulent bellies, and in their straining muscles and sinews.

In addition to their bodies and each body's divine population (though this was but a potential possession, accessible only through an inner vision not vouchsafed to everyone), they had an immense colony of parasites. This was a secure possession no one would try to take away from them, consisting as it did of fleas, ticks, lice, and innumerable intestinal worms. Besides the attentions of vermin, each man had the affection of his wife and starving brats, dependent on him for their support.

These men too dreamed of possessions, of genuine possession, recalling the theories of Pomp, which matched so well with the vague shadows still floating in their minds. In the beginning, Heaven and Earth had lavished their fullest bounty on mankind without stint, but they had gradually ceased to do so because men began to be greedy, hoarding and monopolizing things for themselves.

The earth had become completely barren, and the unproductiveness of the soil was paralleled by the poverty of the rulers. In earlier times kings bestowed all the goods and wonders of creation upon their subjects, and were able to satisfy all their desires. Then they could provide only two-thirds of their needs, and later only one-third. Things were already tight in those days. But now that the princes could hardly supply their own needs, let alone hand out rich silks and fine pieces of jade to anybody else, it was an age of absolute want, with the ordinary people struggling to keep alive under princes who themselves were bankrupt.

Possession was only genuine possession when it did not exclude wealth in general, when it allowed everyone to satisfy his needs. The phrase "private wealth" was a contradiction in terms, and those who were called rich were really poor. . . . And they sighed for a world in which everything would be given them in abundance, and "thine" and "mine" would have no more meaning; a world where they would all enjoy the plenty which Heaven rained down upon them or Earth caused to spring up at their feet.

HUMILITY

A beautiful thing, the humility by which
a Great Man adds to his fame!

On the yellow immensity of the plain, stretching out under the blue immensity of the winter sky, the white of the procession made a kind of lugubrious stain. Soon the outline of the chariot emerged, with horses and their riders; the rampant dragons, flanked by symbols of royalty, could be seen blazoned on the wan banners of defeat. When he reached a point a hundred paces from his conqueror, whose radiant standards displayed their solar phoenixes on guidons steeped in the gore of glory, King Tzu-ying, dressed in mourning, the silk cord of surrender around his neck, bare-shouldered and carrying the instruments of sacrifice in his arms, alighted from his chariot and dragged himself on his knees to the victor. Raising his hands above his lowered head, he presented Whet-iron with the seals of the Empire.

This was the final and climactic scene in a series of submissions: Two months earlier, another sovereign—that time bearing the proud title emperor—had abased himself before his executioners.

It all began in view of the Barbarians, a country villa surrounded by extensive grounds, to which the Second Emperor, after his dream, had withdrawn to seek purification.

Chao the Tall thought *he* would be able to rule the Empire. He decided to eliminate the person in whose shade he had always stood, not realizing it was this shelter that had allowed him to exist.

One day, on the orders of the prime minister, the prefect of Double Light and the captain of the Imperial Guard took the sentries at the Son of Heaven's house by surprise, burst into the forbidden room, and shot at the eunuchs, who scattered in all directions like a flock of big yellow birds. One of the arrows pierced the canopy above the imperial dais. Barbarian, purple with rage, shouted orders at his entourage, but they were too terrified to do anything but surrender to the intruders. The two officials then broke through the door into the inner apartments, where the Emperor had taken refuge. They seized him by the scruff of the neck and offered him a sword.

"Your love of murder, your pride, and your extravagance are the cause of the rebellion that is laying waste the Empire!" said one of them. "But Chao the Tall, the prime minister, will kindly allow you to settle the matter yourself."

"Let me speak to him!"

"Out of the question!"

"What if I were to abdicate in his favor? All I ask is one province, and the title king."

They shook their heads.

"Just a prefecture, then, and the title marquis?"

"No!"

"A small post as head of a subprefecture? Is that too much to ask?"

"We're under orders from the prime minister to put you to death in the name of the whole Empire."

"Please! All I ask is to be allowed to live the rest of my life with my wife and children. I can keep a little garden to support them. Surely that's a very modest request?"

And he fell down and embraced their knees. But they were inflexible.

"You should have thought about humbling your pride before."

They raised him to his feet, thrust the sword into his hand, and cried:

"Stop moaning! You'd do better to bless the prime minister for letting you kill yourself."

But the elimination of Barbarian didn't produce the desired effect. In the secrecy of a special council chamber in the House of Government, Chao the Tall's two henchmen pointed out to him, not without some satisfaction, that he had miscalculated.

"There are times when one has to stand aside," one of them said. "It would be very rash of you to proclaim yourself emperor in the present circumstances. Didn't you notice the ripple of indignation in the audience chamber when you made as if to go up the steps to the throne? The best thing for you to do is choose some member of the First Emperor's family, and rule through him."

The eunuch glowered at the prefect of the capital and the captain of the Guard, who were letting him know his attempt to usurp the throne was to be thwarted. Then he sighed, but said nothing. They were right. He was doomed to stay in the background.

A few days later, before all the country's dignitaries gathered together in the throne room, Chao the Tall presented his diminished pretensions in the form of a request that Ch'in itself should be more modest.

"We must be realistic," he said. "We are now reduced to our original borders, and the title of emperor strikes me as too grandiose for so small a territory. So let us show due humility and revive the title of king, which was in use before the reign of the First

Emperor and is more appropriate in the present circumstances."

Thus the eunuch, facing north and bowing to the empty throne, presented his request in the attitude of a vassal.

———

Barbarian's cousin Tzu-ying was also bowing his head: but he was gazing pensively into a bowl in which several large gray fish were swimming merrily. Their well-being seemed to derive from their not being aware of existing, and for one fleeting moment he felt his own consciousness, heightened at first by the effort to enter into another mode of being, suddenly vanishing as it merged into a fish's unconsciousness. He was turning into a carp.

He felt a surge of pleasure sublime in its humility. Just as he was blowing out his cheeks as if he too had gills, a servant came in to inform him of the decision the council had taken after Chao bowed toward the empty throne. Tzu-ying was no longer a fish—he was a dragon! He had just been given wings. All his joy ebbed away. He was as terrified as an earthworm suddenly hurled up above the clouds.

Gliding about in a backwater of comfortable mediocrity, he was one of the few members of the royal family to have been spared under Barbarian. Now he was suddenly caught up in glory and honors like a frog in the talons of an eagle. His head swam. His legs gave way. He fainted. He made this an excuse for postponing his investiture, and shut himself up in his apartments, refusing to see anyone— especially Chao the Tall. The eunuch grew impatient. Ch'in couldn't go on much longer without a ruler. Chao was prepared to drag Tzu-ying onto the throne even if he was at his last gasp.

Tzu-ying sought the advice of his sons, and of one of his faithful servants.

"Chao the Tall murdered the Second Emperor in order to take his place," they told him. "He had to postpone this plan because the court was against him. That is why he suggested you, thinking he could get rid of you when he felt like it. People say he and Whet-Iron, one of the rebel leaders, have agreed to divide what remains of Ch'in between them. Your head will be the guarantee of Chao's good faith. If he's in such a hurry for you to complete the rites of purification, it's because he intends to kill you as soon as you enter the temple unarmed and without an escort."

"It's all up with me, then?"

"No. We must turn his impatience to our advantage. If you refuse to leave these rooms, you'll force him to come in, and then we shall be able to kill him!"

Ten days later Chao the Tall managed to force his way into the imperial sickroom. But just as he was reminding Tzu-ying of his royal duties, a servant sprang out from behind a curtain and ran him through with a sword.

At first Tzu-ying refused the throne, though everyone pressed it upon him, saying he was the only one worthy of the honor, and the best fitted, because of his wisdom and moderation, to treat with the rebels. Finally, either through weakness or because he was secretly attracted to power, he gave in to his friends' entreaties and went through the rites of purification and coronation.

———

By some strange repercussion, the word uttered in the dark throne room in Double Light echoed beneath the red-and-gold-painted rafters of the palace in Ch'en.

Humility—again the word was addressed to a council by royal lips—was praised by Intelligence, king of Ch'u, as the virtue from which all other virtues proceeded. Intelligence was a man in whom the vain and glorious dream of a fleeting present had reduced his modest past to nothingness; and the word "humility" billowed forth from the pink cavity of his mouth to fill the enormous void left by that lost reality. Admittedly he wasn't claiming to be modest himself; but even as he lauded humility in another, some of that quality redounded on him like spray scattered by a wave breaking on rocks.

Whet-Iron, he said, would not allow his head to be turned by success: he was a sensible man who knew his own limits and weaknesses. If he sent him across the mountains with an army, he would conquer Ch'in without shedding any blood. It might be objected that Plume seemed better qualified for the job: he was a distinguished soldier and very popular with his men. But he was also extremely violent, and would arouse the people's hatred with his harshness and pride. Moreover, when the present truce expired, Ch'in would fall to whoever invaded it first, and it would be dangerous for the richest province in the Empire to go to a leader whose prestige was already too high: he would be sure to swallow up all the other provinces, and everything would be back to where it was before.

———

Whet-Iron set out for the West, but suffered many defeats and had made no progress at all when he interrupted his oblique approach to the passes to camp outside the walls of Kao-yang. There he was visited by a local official, who turned out to be Li I-ch'i, the scholar he had insulted in P'ei. As he had risen in the world, Whet-Iron had made considerable progress in the art of being a Great Man, and now he was able to flatter his guest by descending to his level. Li I-ch'i chortled happily and whispered something to Whet-Iron that made him smile.

Two days later Li I-ch'i's brother Li Shang, an unemployed rhetor who had become a brigand, led his two thousand outlaws in a bold attack on the warehouses and granaries of Ch'in. This opened the way for Whet-Iron to make a lightning advance, which brought him to the outskirts of Double Light, where Tzu-ying awaited him in the attitude of a suppliant.

Whet-Iron saw this as an opportunity to show his magnanimity. He raised Tzu-ying to his feet, covered him with his cloak, and, like the princes in the chronicles, recited a chant from the *Book of Odes*: "*No, you are not naked and exposed.*" It's not certain whether this was the quotation most appropriate to the situation and to Whet-Iron's secret objects, or whether it was the only one he could remember. In any case, this is what he sang:

"No, you are not naked and exposed.
Do we not wear the same tunic?
If you raise your army,
I ready my swords.
We have the same enemy.
No, you are not naked and exposed.
Haven't we the same shirt?
If you go to war,
I prepare my rapier.
We both do the same thing.
No, you are not naked and exposed.
Don't we wear the same trousers?
If you attack,
I polish my shield.
So we shall set out as friends."

Either out of politeness or because he had understood his victorious adversary's real intentions, Tzu-ying saw fit to answer:

"What is there on the heights of the capital?
Wormwood and sandalwood.
You have come to us
With a red brocade tunic,
A fox-fur cloak, and a rosy face.
Your glory is unique.
What is there on the heights of the capital?
Gorse and foxglove.
You have come here
In shimmering raiment.
May you delight forever
In the tinkle of jade seals!"

A smile spread over Whet-Iron's broad countenance, and he ordered the guards to put the king under house arrest, while at the same time showing him the utmost consideration.

———

The lines rang through the clear winter air and echoed in the hearts of Whet-Iron's lieutenants. The verse *"No, you are not naked and exposed,"* along with Tzu-ying's answer, sounded to Master Li I-ch'i like a secret pact between the two men against the coalition. So he asked Whet-Iron to see that the frontier was well guarded.

Plume, some hundreds of leagues away, was also trapped in the conflict between pride and humility. He would probably have been carried away by the intoxication of victory if he hadn't had before him the melancholy example of his uncle Beam and the admonitions of Sung the Just—he would have done anything to prevent that one from crowing over him in his grave. So he was more cautious than ever and did his best to subdue the ardor of his generals. After winning two victories over Ch'in, he agreed to negotiate with Chang Han, promising him a kingdom in Ch'in in exchange for his surrender. Chang Han's troops were incorporated into the Ch'u army to serve as a vanguard. But before long the Ch'in soldiers and junior officers, harassed by all kinds of vexations on the part of the rebels, grew restive.

Though he was cautious, Plume could also be decisive. He wanted to go through the passes before Whet-Iron became too powerful, and he didn't mean to be delayed by trouble on the part of an army that had surrendered to him. So one night he made a surprise attack on Ch'in's two hundred thousand troops, and slaughtered every one of them. Then he and Chang Han swept down toward the West, only to come up against the cordon Whet-Iron had put in place to keep them out.

Plume's heart swelled with rage when he saw this attempt to stop him from entering Ch'in. He ordered his four thousand men to attack, broke through Whet-Iron's defenses, crossed the defiles, and set up camp at Cranes' Gate, vowing to demand an explanation from Whet-Iron the following day.

———

The verse "*No, you are not naked and exposed*" had echoed also in the mind of Tsao Unwounded, a Left general; to him it spoke of treason. He harbored a mortal hatred of the kings of the West. His whole family, right down to third cousins, had been exterminated by them in the name of collective responsibility. He, still a babe in arms at the time, was the only one who had escaped the fury of the judges, thanks to the devotion of a family retainer, who killed his own infant son and passed Unwounded off as the dead child.

Unwounded joined the revolt at the very beginning, and after the death of Take-the-Plunge fought under the banner of the Hsiangs. During the campaign that Plume and Whet-Iron carried out together, Unwounded served under the latter, and so impressed Whet-Iron with his fighting spirit that he was asked to stay on as his lieutenant. Unwounded's present attitude might have been due to lingering loyalty to his former master.

He sent a reliable aide to tell Plume of Whet-Iron's plans. Plume happened at that moment to be consulting with his adviser Fan the Increaser.

"It wasn't so long ago," said Increaser, "that Whet-Iron was known as a dissolute and venal chief of police. And when he fought with you in the East, all he thought about was burning, raping, and looting. But now, ever since he's been in Ch'in, you'd think butter wouldn't melt in his mouth. Do you know he hasn't abducted one single girl, he's put seals on all the treasures and left them alone, and he hasn't even gone to live in the palace in Double Light—he's camping on the banks of the river? He's abolished the laws of Ch'in and replaced them with three very mild decrees. He's put up soothing proclamations all over Double Light to win the people. That shows he's after something more important than trifles like women and money."

Plume hesitated. The situation was painful to him. His reason told him Increaser was right; his heart shrank from doing anything that might injure a friend. It was almost impossible for him to turn against a man who had been a guest at his table; it was as if liking someone marked him with a protective sign.

But that talisman lost some of its power when he heard from Unwounded's messenger that his friend was preparing to reign over the passes with Tzu-ying as his prime minister. The song he had sung when the king of Ch'in abdicated left no doubt about it.

———

Uncle Hsiang did not forget his friends. Chang the Good had saved his life, had taken him in and supported him when he was in distress. As soon as he heard of the threat to his benefactor, he made his way in secret to the prefect of P'ei's camp, intending to urge Chang to flee and take service with his nephew. But Chang wouldn't hear of it.

"It was loyalty to the house of Han that made me enter the service of the man I thought most capable of conquering Ch'in. And now it's on the pretext of loyalty that you want me, at the first sign of trouble, to abandon the master I chose."

"Do you want to die, then?"

"Let me have a word with Whet-Iron. Perhaps there's some way to mend matters."

Chang hurried to his leader's tent and told him everything.

Whet-Iron turned pale.

"We are lost!" he exclaimed.

"What possessed you to be so foolish?"

"Master Li I-ch'i advised me to keep the passes."

"And you listened to him. I should have guessed as much after that singing from the *Book of Odes!* But tell me, did you stop to ask yourself who is the better general, you or Plume? And who has four times as many troops as the other?"

The answer was obvious.

"Are you prepared to play your only trump card? If so, send for Uncle Hsiang and eat humble pie to him. He's waiting in my tent."

As soon as Uncle Hsiang arrived, Whet-Iron bowed low to him, called him his elder brother, and drank a toast to him. He even suggested they should unite their families by marriage. Then he set out to justify himself. He hadn't touched anything since he'd entered Ch'in. He'd merely put seals on all the government buildings, arsenals, granaries, and stores and waited anxiously for the august general to come. If he'd posted soldiers to guard the passes, that was just a precaution to ward off the gangs of looters who might otherwise have taken advantage of the confusion to make their way into Ch'in. He'd never dreamed of trying to oppose the man he looked upon as his prince—the man whose arrival he was ardently waiting for. He hoped his elder brother would plead his cause with Plume and correct this horrible misunderstanding.

Uncle Hsiang agreed to do so, but told him he would have to apologize to Plume in person.

REJOICINGS

Propitious for the establishing of princes and for war.

There were five of them gathered together for the reconciliation banquet. Plume and Uncle Hsiang sat side by side facing east, leaving the mat of honor, facing south, to Increaser, the oldest person present. Whet-Iron had insisted on facing north, in the vassal's place, while Chang the Good helped and served him, facing west. Some attendants brought lacquered dishes heaped with game, fish, and meat; others poured wine into large chased goblets. The two generals' faces grew lively under the influence of wine and rich food. The joyful fire of alcohol coursed through their veins, and as they each listened to the full, firm voice of the other and looked at his big bluff face, they felt their hearts melt in the warm breath of friendship. Caught up in the pleasure of renewed comradeship, wrapped in a cocoon of shared enthusiasms, hopes, and tastes, Plume ignored Increaser's nods and winks. The longer the feast went on, the longer and paler the old man's face became. He lifted the pieces of jade he wore attached to his belt and rattled them against one another. Plume roared with laughter, his eyes bright as those of a phoenix, his cheeks flaming; he offered his friend more wine. Chang the Good cast puzzled looks at Increaser as he brandished the green-and-white trigrammatic stone warningly in his long, gaunt hand. Surreptitiously he studied Plume's face, bright and crimson as a dragon's, and realized this was the one man who could threaten Whet-Iron's career. And if he, Chang, didn't do something about it, that career might well come to an end in the middle of this banquet.

Increaser left the tent, and Chang the Good took the opportunity to blink his eyes at Uncle Hsiang to show him that he suspected danger.

When Increaser came back, he brought with him Hsiang the Strong, Beam's distant cousin. They offered him a cup of wine. He drank their host's health, and observed that all that was needed to complete their enjoyment was some music and dancing. Unfortunately, there were no dancing girls or female musicians in the army. But he would do his best to take their place.

As Increaser picked up a lute and began to play a martial air, Hsiang the Strong took up his position in the middle of the space enclosed by the tables and became the moving and disturbing center of the scene. Drawing two steel blades from their sheaths, he waved them up and down and in and out around him so that they seemed to create a bluish mist. At first it was a languid, graceful dance; then the pace quickened. As the supple rapiers whirled faster and faster, Hsiang the Strong wove slowly nearer the table set before Whet-Iron, who began showing signs of anxiety. The tension was made almost tangible by the measured twangs of the lute. Then Uncle Hsiang stood up, and two more sinister shafts of steel flashed forth. The cousins pranced around one another like performing bears; or like the wild beasts in the classics who couldn't resist the influence of music.

Hsiang the Strong tried to get past Uncle Hsiang, but between him and his target he always found the older man's broad breast, surrounded by metal vipers giving off showers of silver blossoms. Whet-Iron sat petrified as his host nodded his head in time to the music, spellbound by the warlike mime. The violence simultaneously masked and revealed by the lithe yet lethal motions of the dancers aroused Plume's latent animosity. His eyes went strangely yellow and narrow, as if he were about to bite. He did nothing to stop the deadly ballet.

Suddenly a gust of fresh air swept into the tent; the heavy draperies billowed. A huge figure stood in the doorway, his hair on end, his eyes blazing. The intrusion halted the dance.

"Who is this fellow?" cried Plume.

"It's Fan K'uai, captain of the Guard," said Chang the Good. Fearing his master would come to harm, he had sent for his assistance. "I thought he might join in—there's no one to touch him for swordplay!"

"I can believe it," said Plume. "And I'm sure he's got a champion thirst too. Let's give him a drink."

He held out a heavy wine bowl, which the giant soldier emptied with one swallow. Then he sent to the kitchens for a haunch of wild boar. The newcomer disposed of it in a few mouthfuls.

"I don't suppose you'd shrink from another cup?" said Plume suavely, intrigued by Fan K'uai's capacities.

"I don't shrink from death, so I certainly wouldn't quail at a cup of wine!"

The joke took the tension out of the atmosphere. Plume's momentary animosity faded; his only thought now was to revel in congenial company, the joys of victory, and the pleasures of drinking.

They drank like fish, and the mixture of alcohol and fear produced severe twinges in Whet-Iron's innards. He barely had time to leap up and get to the latrine, where he crouched for some time, panting and voiding his foul-smelling anguish into the tub. Back in the tent, Plume grew impatient with the absence of his friend from the party. He sent Fan K'uai to fetch him.

"Prince," said the captain to Whet-Iron, "don't stay out here, exposed to some dirty trick on the part of Increaser or Hsiang the Strong. Come back to the banquet, where Uncle Hsiang and I can protect you."

"I don't feel well."

"Don't you realize they tried to murder you? And they won't give up just like that! You must get away!"

"I don't want to slink off like a thief."

They were joined by Chi the Sincere, one of Whet-Iron's lieutenants, who combined great physical strength with utter devotion to his leader. He resembled him in looks and stature, and thought he'd found an opportunity to demonstrate his loyalty in a way he'd never been able to do on the battlefield.

"I've received much from you," he said, "without doing anything in return. Change clothes with me, and I'll go and take your place at the banquet while you return to your lines. If General Plume has really decided to kill you, or if he sees through my impersonation, I'll gladly give my life to save yours."

"No. Plume won't be fooled for a moment. And the trick will only make him angrier. I'll have to go and take leave of him in person."

"Take leave! What you should do is flee! Never mind such trifles. Chang the Good will present your excuses," exclaimed a voice behind them.

Liu and Fan K'uai started. It was Ch'en Peacemaker, one of Plume's generals, another messenger sent to bring Whet-Iron back to the banquet. He bore a grudge against his master for not appreciating him properly, and was afraid that in Plume's service he'd never get the chance to demonstrate all his talents. He saw the present occasion as an opportunity to recommend himself to another Great Man, in case his present master went on denying him promotion. So instead of taking Whet-Iron back to the feast, he urged him to leave as soon as possible, adding, to reassure the others about his own intentions, "No point in putting all your eggs in one basket." Then he left.

"I need to change my gown," said Whet-Iron faintly. "It's dirty."

Sincere was already taking off his tunic, but Fan K'uai stopped him and spoke shortly to his superior.

"That's enough fuss! Your horse won't mind. And while you're galloping across country you'll meet only demons."

And taking Whet-Iron by the arm, he led him to his horse and held the stirrup for him to mount. While Whet-Iron rode at top speed to his own camp, Fan K'uai, former butcher, with Dollface, former carter, Hsin the Sturdy, former seller of rice water, and Chi the Sincere, covered his flight from some way behind. They went on foot, swords and bucklers at the ready.

———

Plume made a face.

"I'm disappointed in Whet-Iron," he said. "Three cups of wine and he's ill! I thought he'd hold his drink better than that."

"I think he was afraid you'd be angry with him. He didn't even dare deliver the presents he'd brought for you and Increaser."

And Chang the Good gave Plume a pair of white jade rings and Increaser two agate cups.

Plume shrugged, put the rings in his sleeve, and tottered away to bed to sleep off his excesses. Then Chang the Good turned to Increaser and showed him the green-and-white veined stones he carried on his belt.

"I've taken Whet-Iron's side," he said, "so he's under the protection of the Trigrams, and there's nothing you can do to hurt him."

"Not true! Since the fall of the Ch'in, we can do what we like. The Empire is a wandering stag—it belongs to whoever can catch it. You've backed Whet-Iron and I've backed Plume, so, although we both belong to the society, we're rivals."

"You're wrong! We must obey the decrees of heaven."

"Nonsense! You know as well as I do that omens can be made to mean anything."

"It's precisely because they're ambiguous that we must wait for instructions. Do me a favor, and don't advise Plume to attack my master's camp. It's not much to ask, and it's the best way of leaving things in the hands of fate."

Increaser did not answer. But when Chang the Good left him, he paced the room like a trapped tiger, and dashed the agate cups to the floor.

———

Four weeks later, in the first lunar month, when thunder emerges groaning from the earth, the nobles gathered on the plain east of the Ch'in capital and feasted night and day to celebrate their victory: Plume had sacked the city and razed it. The Empire was for sale. There was something for everybody, whether they were generals, captains, prefects, governors, or gang leaders' friends. There were lands and estates to be acquired; serfs to be given; titles, posts, salaries, and emoluments to be picked up. And the acclamations and shouts of joy that greeted the appointments of new kings and dukes; the shrill music to which the dancing girls seized from Ch'in's palaces performed; the sound of jaws doing justice to the banquet—all these drowned out the resentful murmurs of those who felt they hadn't received their fair share of the spoils.

Intelligence, the king of Ch'u, had been unanimously voted emperor, but it was an empty title, devoid of all power. Chang Han, Tung I, and Hsin were sharing Ch'in—the first for having surrendered, the second for having persuaded him to do so, and the third, former director of Criminal Affairs in Yüeh-yang, for having interceded on behalf of Beam. Tattooed Face and Tsang T'u, the brigands who had rallied to the Hsiangs' banner, had also been given crowns. Ear had a reputation for wisdom; he had followed Plume in his campaigns against the West; so he'd been given part of the kingdom of Chao. Whet-Iron, on the other hand, had got only the remote provinces of Shu and Han—and he could think himself lucky at that. Scrap, who had withdrawn from the battle into the Southern Hide marshes, had been punished for his sulking by the award of a mere marquisate. Descendants of former kings had each been granted a fragment of the land of their ancestors.

For the moment all they thought about was celebrating the fall of the tyrant and the coming of an era of prosperity for those who had purchased it with their blood. A huge tent had been erected in the middle of the camp, and Plume was entertaining his captains under the yellow canopy embroidered with tarnished gold thread. They tossed off fine red-and-black lacquer gobletsful of amber-colored rice wines, pale nectars made from flower petals, millet beer, and heady fruit liqueurs. Like tigers placidly chewing their prey, they gnawed at roast suckling pig, braised wild boar, venison steaks, and sliced reptiles. They noisily lapped up a broth made of beef, mutton, and pork served in enormous bronze bowls. Ivory chopsticks snapped up pieces of lamprey pie, dog stew, fried snake, mutton boiled with jujubes and lotus seeds, oysters baked with dried seaweed, and scallops broiled with winter bamboo shoots. Hands grabbed fried bean cakes, steamed wheat rolls, pastries made with mare's butter, and thin pancakes stuffed with leeks; and they crammed them all into black maws surmounted by feline mustaches. Crouched over tables groaning with regal delicacies, they belched with satisfaction and satiety as they greedily goggled the dancing of concubines from the imperial palace.

Below the dais where the leaders were sitting, lesser generals and their lieutenants and hangers-on leaned over low tables covered with platefuls of beans and millet porridge, fighting over their superiors' scraps just as they had over pieces of land. In the rest of the camp, outside the shelter of the yellow tent, the rest of the soldiers consoled themselves for their wounds and their fears by stuffing themselves with heavy stews washed down with wine from rough wooden pitchers. Every so often a gust of wind would rekindle the embers of the burned-out capital and a fringe of flames, showing above the line of hills between the camp and Double Light, would shed a lurid gleam over the festivities. The sickly stench of burned flesh mingled with the delicious smell of roast meat, the intoxicating scent of wine, and the healthy odor of sweaty armpits upraised in toasts. Amid all the singing and laughter, the guzzling and the clinking of glasses, the toasts recalled the slaughter and destruction that were the pretext for all this spurious mirth, and cast over the rejoicings the sinister shadow of death.

Plume wasn't thinking about death. He let himself be deluded by the constantly renewed spectacle of his power. It was he who possessed the reality of power, and every bit of it that he gave away, far from decreasing his authority, only strengthened it by continual demonstration. His investitures, instead of enriching those who received them, merely showed their dependence and reduced them to the state of vassals and subjects. He gloated over the thought that by giving he was really taking.

———

One evening at a banquet of this kind, the air, heavy with the gruntings of the guests, was pierced by a series of extremely high notes. Plume looked toward the stage. She was slender, but her slimness was accentuated by her luxuriant hair. She wore it in rows of gossamer knots held in place by tortoiseshell combs and pins whose jade heads, shaped like axes, recalled the warlike nature of the age. The massive coiffure lent her an air of gravity that acted as a foil to her extreme youth. A neck white and supple as a swan's supported a long oval face. Her mouth was like a pomegranate, her long black eyes two shining depthless pools that engulfed your soul. Her delicate nostrils quivered like those of a filly.

Plume called her over, and that same night he knew with Joy —for that was her name—all the pleasure of clouds and rain. Her silky black mane, falling free over her snowy back, gave him the same exhilaration he felt on horseback. She even quivered like a mare, and Plume, who loved horses, felt as if he was on Quicksilver, his white charger with a black tail, son of Tattooed Face's spirited filly and his uncle's fine white stallion: thus sensual pleasure merged with martial frenzy. Plume's long days out hunting on Quicksilver were now like a kind of love-making. The horse and the woman, each a reminder of the other, occupied all his thoughts.

Joy was from P'eng-ch'eng. She disliked Ch'in, and longed for the soft misty landscapes of the East. Her homesickness was contagious: Plume too was seized with a desire to see the lakes and rivers of his own country again. Various advisers kept telling him of his mistakes. He ought not to have killed Tzu-ying, king of Ch'in, or massacred the population, or looted the imperial treasure, or set fire to the city. It had been wrong of him to divide Ch'in among the vanquished ex-generals. Ch'in had strong natural barriers, and easily dominated all the other provinces. Its soil was fertile, its people docile and hard-working. Wouldn't it have been better if, instead of destroying Double Light, he had gone to live there? It would have made a good vantage point from which to control the other nobles, and perhaps—who could say?—he might have come to reign over the whole of the Empire. But all wasn't lost yet: they knew how he could oust Chang Han and the rest from their estates, and take them over himself. Of course there was the agreement, on the expiry of which the Empire was supposed to revert to Whet-Iron, but here too they had a plan. "All that was needed was . . ." and so on. These men were the flies that are always buzzing suggestions into the ears of Great Men.

Plume had no time for them now. His head was full of what Joy said, and every day she urged him to go back to Ch'u and rule the land east of the passes. Why did he stay on in this cold, depressing place? What was the point of living where no one had known him when he was only an ordinary person, and an outlaw at that? It was like dressing up in one's best clothes and then staying at home, or driving out in a golden coach when it was dark. What was the point of becoming famous if no one you knew ever heard about it? . . . Whereas he could return to Ch'u in triumph and the whole population would acclaim him. And so on.

One of the master strategists, annoyed by Plume's lack of interest in his subtle ideas, went around criticizing the Empire's new protector.

"These fellows from Ch'u," he said, "they're no better than monkeys in fancy hats!"

When this came to Plume's ears, he had the offender pitched into a boiling cauldron and served up at a banquet by way of example. Then, to avoid any more attempts at persuasion and to please Joy, he dismissed the nobles, disbanded their armies, and went back to the East.

THOSE
WHO FOLLOW

Men follow those whom great and admirable virtue,
  benevolence, and perseverance shield from misfortune.
Thunder in the middle of the pond:
  such are "those who follow."
A wise man goes home to bed when the sun sets.

The men advanced in isolated detachments, in no particular order, straggling out along a sloping road that grew ever steeper as it rose toward the west. The mountains reared higher and higher, their rocky faces interspersed with patches of vegetation in which occasional terraced fields of millet struck a lighter hue. Here and there the cliffs were interrupted, as by some dark eye, by the entrance to a cave dwelling. At the foot of the hills the poverty-stricken villagers sheltered their wretchedness within walls of yellow mud.

About ten thousand of Whet-Iron's ardent followers had volunteered to go with him into what could only be called exile: it was customary in Ch'in to send influential families to Chou when their influence had grown too strong. The army included some of Whet-Iron's oldest comrades—those who had known him when he was a local police chief and then a criminal, and whose trust in his gifts was all the stronger now for having wavered during his reverses.

Whet-Iron's chief minister, Hsiao Porter, former inspector of the civil service, belonged to this group, as did his steward, Ts'ao the Examiner, once the director of Criminal Affairs in the prefecture of P'ei. Their present enthusiasm for Whet-Iron's cause was a kind of expiation for their patronizing ways in the past. But he saw these specialists in the penal code and administration as valuable colleagues. The proper organization of Ch'in was an absolute obsession with them, and having learned their trade in the hard school of the law, they were unrivaled experts in solving problems of supply and managing all those minor details that if neglected can bring the delicate machinery of a whole army to a halt. They kept the accounts of military equipment, cereals, and fodder, recorded all payments in money and kind, supervised supplies and communications, and decided on the location of granaries, storehouses, arsenals, and even latrines.

When the rebel army took Double Light, and the generals—Whet-Iron first and foremost—thought only of flinging themselves on the treasures in the palaces, the sole concern of Hsiao Porter and Ts'ao the Examiner was to get hold of the accounts and statistics kept in the imperial library and archives: they believed numbers were the key to domination.

There was also Chou Pao, a basketmaker from P'ei who played the flute at funerals to make ends meet. It was at a funeral that he had first met Whet-Iron, whose duties had often included organizing such ceremonies. Chou Pao had been very impressed, and became one of Whet-Iron's most ardent supporters. He joined his rebellion and fought in his campaigns, showing such ability that he was made general of the Tiger Officers Guard. He'd followed his master on the road to Han-tchung without a moment's hesitation. Dollface, once a carter in the same subprefecture Whet-Iron worked in, had been promoted to be his assistant secretary. He came very opportunely to his master's rescue when he fell into the trap set by the prefect of P'ei, and then took part in all his campaigns, exhibiting particular skill in the use of chariots. On the strength of this he'd been made general in charge of cavalry. Whet-Iron had shown him great generosity, and Dollface thought him one of the favorites of destiny and would have followed him to the ends of the earth. Other old comrades included Kuan Ying, who had been a peaceful silk merchant in a nearby village until he saw Whet-Iron's army go by, when he promptly joined it; String, a lifelong friend; Fan K'uai, huge and faithful, who would have burned himself alive for his leader; Li I-ch'i the rhetor, and his brigand brother; Jen Ao; and many other brave and devoted men, including Fu the Broad, Hsin the Sturdy, T'ung the Ribbon, and Chi the Sincere.

Chang the Good was with Whet-Iron too, but for the last time. He came from a family that had served the kings of Han for generations, and believed it to be his duty to help their descendant when he asked for help. Everything he ever did in his life had been dictated by this loyalty, which also coincided with his filial duties. It was for the Han that he had tried to kill the August First Emperor; for them, that for years he had led the life of a wandering exile, breathing and eating only in the hope of revenge; and it was for the same reason that he had been a disciple of the old man of Hsia-p'i before offering his services to Whet-Iron as the man most likely to bring down the despots. Not to be at the disposal of the Han would be to betray the allegiance of a lifetime. But, though he still obeyed this basic impulse, it was now only out of habit: he no longer believed that the former state of things would ever be restored.

This slow transformation, of which he himself was not yet fully aware, was the result of his study of the trigrams. At first he had seen them as an instrument of his revenge, but gradually, through those abstract formulas, he became disillusioned, and acutely conscious of the vanity of earthly desires. Because of the otherworldliness this produced in him, he became, by a curious paradox, capable of the very deeds he had come to see as futile. He would have liked to flee the world and live as a hermit, devoting himself to the absolute, which the trigrams had revealed to him. But such a disavowal would have been a denial of all he ever stood for. The only solution was to go on as before, pursuing his quest whenever he had time to himself.

———

They came to the Li passes, where bamboo bridges suspended over deep gorges led to the capital, Han-chung. At the entrance to the defile, there were five enormous rocks of green schist that looked like crouching buffaloes.

"What are they?" asked Whet-Iron in astonishment. "Are they man-made?"

"The story goes," said Chang the Good, "that the August First Emperor planned to annex Shu, but there wasn't a road wide enough for his chariots. So he had these rocks carved to bring out their resemblance to buffaloes, had gold ingots placed underneath their posteriors, and ordered his propaganda services to spread the rumor that there had been a miracle: the stone had been changed into magic buffaloes that shit gold. The people of Shu built a secret road along which to take the buffaloes back home, but the Emperor had massed Ch'in troops behind the rocks, and as soon as the road was finished, his men swept down it and invaded Shu. The road you are about to embark on is called the Road of the Stone Buffaloes."

Whet-Iron gave a short laugh.

"The story of Chih-p'o and the king of the Chiu-yu all over again!" he said. "Chih-p'o coveted the area around the passes, and gave the king a huge bronze bell to build a road through them. But the king of the Chiu-yu had an adviser who would have helped him discover the trap if he had only listened to him."

Then, suddenly serious:

"If it weren't for your help, wouldn't I fall into traps just like the master of Shu and the king of the Chih-yu, and let myself be blinded by pearls and jewels or a woman's smile?"

"Such desires lie in wait for masters of men," replied Chang the Good, "to make them forget their real possessions and seek illusory treasures. Han Fei was right: Princes should have no passions or emotions; they should close themselves against feelings that come from the external world, and identify themselves only with the void."

Whet-Iron pressed his hand. Chang the Good went on:

"You are pleasure-loving, sensual, and dissolute, but you never let your passions get the upper hand. Fortunately you have enough strength of character to forgo short-term advantages, and would be able to spurn victories that only conceal defeat."

Whet-Iron's tears fell like silver pearls to his slashed vermilion doublet. He clasped his counselor to him warmly. Chang blinked, and before long his tears were mingling with those of his master. He assured him of his unfailing loyalty, and to show his complete obedience offered to go with him. But as he did so, he remembered his original devotion. The agreement with Increaser stipulated that he should leave Whet-Iron's service as soon as he had acquired a kingdom west of the passes. He had agreed, on condition that the Han kings were restored. But he had been tricked. Although the outlying kingdoms of Shu and Pa were indeed west of the passes, no one could genuinely maintain that the agreement had been carried out. Nonetheless he had to give in: the other had might, though he didn't have right, on his side. As he had climbed the mountainside and looked down on the surrounding hills, Chang the Good had caught a glimpse of pikes glinting as they caught the light. They belonged to Plume's sixty thousand men, deployed behind Whet-Iron's twenty thousand, and ready to annihilate them if they showed any signs of turning back.

"Prince, we are being followed by the men from Ch'u. Let us not give Plume an excuse for destroying us. He would be only too glad of the opportunity. You and I must part. Don't forget to cut down the bamboo bridges after you've crossed them: that will hinder your pursuers, and also show that you mean never to return to the East. Yes, there is a kind of moral in all this: You escape by destroying the road that owes its existence to the greed of the invader. And if homesickness ever gets too much for you, remember there is another route, via Ku-tao."

Whet-Iron held Chang to him for some time; then, with heart-rending sighs, let him go. He watched until his counselor's chariot disappeared around a bend in the road; he dried his tears and continued on his way.

It was with a heavy heart that he entered the narrow gorge shaped like the jaws of a wolf. Soon he and his men were enclosed by sheer cliffs smooth as metal: their path lay along the side of the mountain, with dizzying precipices above and below. Every so often a river glinted faintly in the distant depths. A few stunted pines clung to the rock with their gnarled roots, throwing their branches up toward heaven like victims of torture. It was as if, fallen from the sky, they had been trying through all eternity to save themselves by clutching at some invisible crevice. The soldiers were seized with dizziness when, as they edged across a chasm on a bridge made of bamboo planks held together with vines, the fragile structure swayed and reared and writhed like a restless dragon. Some of the men fell into the void. Others sat down, hung on to the rope that served as a handrail and refused to budge. With the sappers hacking up and setting fire to the roads behind the army as it went along, they were left hanging helpless over the abyss.

Coming from the East, the men were overwhelmed and depressed by the wildness of the mountains and the difficulties of crossing them. It seemed like a journey from which there could be no return. They thought of the wives and children and friends they'd left behind, and of the tombs of their ancestors they'd abandoned. They were homesick for their own pleasant landscapes: for lakes; lazy rivers; checkerboard rice fields glittering in the sun between black earth embankments; little villages, with pools of sleepy carp, drowsing behind their bamboo fences. And the farther they advanced into this hostile territory, the more they believed their leader to be doomed to failure.

The ranks of this leader had been swelled by newcomers recruited as the result of battles, binges, and chance encounters. Some had been dazzled by Whet-Iron's meteoric rise to fame, but most had rallied to his side in the hope of getting something out of it. Now they had lost faith in him, and their one thought was to desert a man whose kingship was that of an exile; to get away from a country whose rocky walls enclosed them like a prison. At every halt some of the army melted away. Every day there were defections. Whet-Iron was afraid he would be completely alone by the time he reached the capital, Han-chung. He ordered the execution of any officer or soldier who tried to desert. The day after this proclamation, twenty men were caught escaping, and Dollface was put in charge of their execution. Nineteen had been decapitated; one remained. It was Trust. He looked the general straight in the eye.

"Doesn't the fourth line of the 'Those who follow' hexagram say *'To capture those who follow is an evil omen; but what misfortune can ensue when one makes a vow with a prisoner'*?"

"What do you mean?"

"Your master wants to dominate the Empire, so why does he deprive himself of the help of a brave man?"

Dollface liked this answer, and was impressed by the soldier who made it. He freed him from his bonds, talked with him, and found what he said so remarkable that he introduced him to Hsiao Porter. The minister learned that Trust had followed Plume at first, but left him because he didn't make proper use of his, Trust's, talents. He had then taken service with Whet-Iron, hoping to be appreciated; but he had only been given a brigade to lead. Whet-Iron was not a Great Man, and didn't deserve support.

Porter, dazzled by Trust's profundity, interceded for him with the king, who said he'd make him a captain of supplies. But the minister said that wasn't enough: Trust wouldn't stay unless he was made a general. Whet-Iron's face turned red.

"What!" he cried. "Even captain of supplies is too good for him! Don't you know he's a good-for-nothing, a scrounger, and a coward? He once begged for mercy from a Huai-ying butcher who'd set upon him. Plume told me about it. He deserted because all the other soldiers looked down on him."

"That's another proof that he's exceptional."

Whet-Iron thought his minister was making fun of him. Furious at being both abandoned and thwarted, he flung out of the inn where he had set up his headquarters, had his horse saddled, and galloped off across country to calm himself down.

———

He was riding by the Han River, which flowed between rugged hills dotted with precipices and cliffs, when, at its confluence with the Vast River, which meandered through a broad valley covered with rice fields, a sudden turn in the road brought him to the water's edge. A girl was making her way along in a little boat. Whet-Iron couldn't see her face because she was looking toward the other bank, but her handling of the boat pole showed off the slenderness of her waist and the curve of her hip. She must be beautiful. Wanting to know what her little face was like, he urged his horse on, to overtake her.

Just upstream from the Vast, the Han went through a belt of steeper hills; the road made a detour away from the river, and the girl was hidden by a rocky promontory. The king of Han-chung cursed. He *must* see whether the face kept the promise of the body! He thought he'd noticed that the valley widened a bit farther up; he'd be beside the river again then. He spurred his horse on. But the road was difficult and wound in and out among the heights: he'd never see the river again! He was about to abandon his vain pursuit when another turning brought him out on the bank just as the boat passed by. He caught the profile of a nose and a glimpse of a rounded cheek, which only whet his curiosity. He urged his horse forward in an attempt to see her better, but again the path turned away from the river and headed for the slopes. Uttering horrible oaths, Whet-

Iron continued the chase. He glimpsed the girl two or three times more, now between two rocks, now between bamboos as slim as she was. At last, near the town of Stable, a curve in the river brought them face to face.

She had the most delicious little countenance he'd ever had the good fortune to contemplate: it was round and white as a full moon, with bright eyes, brows slender as a butterfly's feelers, and a tiny mouth with cherry lips. She was like a plum blossom under snow.

The girl, who had seen all along what the horseman was up to, burst out laughing when she saw him wide-eyed and gaping with surprise.

"Perhaps you have dishonorable intentions," she said, half in anger, half in jest, "following me like this! It's a good thing I'm on the river—you'd have to get wet to reach me."

"And perhaps *you* are a fox, going around by yourself and bewitching poor travelers."

"Pooh! Foxes don't go in boats."

"Otters do, though! They use a water-lily leaf, with a willow branch for a parasol, and they sail around on rivers and lakes making boatmen fall madly in love with them."

"My cargo of vegetables would soon sink a water-lily leaf. And it's not very polite of you to compare me to an otter. They have short little legs and smell of fish. If you keep comparing me to animals, it must mean you just want to make fun of me."

"Quite true. It doesn't do you justice. But you're too beautiful to be a human being. You must be a fairy. Perhaps the queen of the river Han, or a nymph of the Vast?"

"If I'm the queen of the river, you, with your height and your embroidered tunic and your tiger's mustache, must be the king of the brigands!"

Whet-Iron laughed.

"Right about the king. Not entirely wrong about the brigands."

"He confesses! I believe you about the brigands. If it's true about the king, I'll give you my hand."

"A promise is a promise! I'll hold you to that!"

"You're not taking much of a risk!"

And so they moved along the river, chatting, he on his horse and she in her boat. He learned that her name was Ch'i. She was seventeen, lived in the small town of Yang-ch'uan, and was on the way to sell produce from her garden and some of her handiwork in the market at Stable. Her family had once been well-to-do but had suffered reverses and was now ruined. Her father had fallen ill and died; her brothers were all away doing forced labor. There'd been no news of them for years.

Suddenly, as they came in view of the walls of Stable, they heard the sound of cavalry and were overtaken by a small band of guards carrying royal banners. When they recognized their lord, they sprang from their saddles and prostrated themselves before him. String, their leader, stepped forward and exclaimed:

"A nice scare you gave us! Your whole staff has been scouring the country for hours looking for you. What are you doing here? It's not very sensible for a king to abandon his ministers and his army without a word and go riding alone!"

These words were accompanied by a loud plop. Ch'i, hearing the true identity of the stranger to whom she'd been prattling so familiarly, had fallen into the water with surprise.

Without a moment's hesitation, Whet-Iron, still on his horse, jumped into the river and brought her to the bank safe and sound.

"A promise is a promise!" he cried. "You're mine!"

"Without even asking my mother's permission?"

"I'll send a go-between to see her, but I don't suppose she'll object. . . . You're soaking wet! Let's go to the inn in Stable—it's only a few leagues. You can get dry there, change your clothes, and rest until the yellow coach comes to take us to my palace in Nan-cheng."

He was so absorbed by his new conquest that when he sat down to a meal and was told that Porter, his prime minister, had left, he didn't pay much attention.

———

The annals tell how King Wen, founder of the Chou dynasty, came back from a country excursion with a wise man he'd met fishing from the riverbank. Whet-Iron came back with a concubine: he had ministers to deal with wise men.

Porter hadn't gone off because of a pretty woman; he was in quest of a man of valor. He and a small detachment of followers galloped toward Stone Fountain: a group of runaway officers had been seen riding in that direction. They'd had almost a night's start, but, because of his official position, he hoped he'd be allowed to use government post horses and so overtake the deserters.

It wasn't until sunset—just when, hundreds of leagues upriver, Whet-Iron was enjoying the reward of his long pursuit—that Porter saw a cloud of dust, sure sign of a group of horsemen. With a mixture of hope and fear, he urged his horse on and caught up with the fugitives. Trust was one of them. The minister and his men captured Trust and let his companions escape.

"This is like the second line of the seventeenth hexagram," said Trust with a shrewd smile. " *'They seize the grown man and leave the children!'* "

Porter continued the quotation.

" *'They are easy to catch if you take the trouble to run after them.'* But don't worry—we're not going to treat you like the prisoner in the last line: *'They take him and tie him up, and make him follow them in fetters for the king to use in sacrifice on the Western mountain.'* "

"You'd be wrong if you did. The allusion is to a consecration, not an execution. When a ruler wants to honor a minister or make his army accept a new general, he presents him to the gods in the sight of his people."

"What nerve! Do you think I'll get Whet-Iron to swallow that?"

"You'd better, if you want me to fight for him. It's the only way he can show he appreciates me properly at last. That's the condition I attach to my services from now on. Things are valued only by the price put on them."

GREAT DESIGNS

Big and fine are great designs,
   auspicious for the crossing of wide rivers,
   three days before
   and three days after the beginning of the cycle.

Whet-Iron's worried look disappeared when, in the audience chamber of what had once been the prefect of Nan-cheng's residence and was now the royal palace, a herald announced that Porter was about to enter. And when his minister came into the room, he scolded him in tones in which annoyance was mingled with relief.

"Vanishing like that without saying anything! Everyone said you'd deserted! I felt as if I'd lost my arms and legs. If it's not too much to ask, would you mind explaining what came over you?"

"You don't think I'd abandon my post, I hope. No. I was trying to catch a defector we couldn't afford to lose."

"Fortunate? I haven't noticed him among the other officers

lately. But he was invaluable during what can only be called our retreat to Han-chung. If it hadn't been for him, we'd have lost a lot more men than we did, negotiating those cursed bridges across the ravines."

"I'm not talking about that useless incompetent. It's Trust I've brought back to you!"

"What! Thirty or more good generals have deserted, and you make me go through agonies just to catch the most undistinguished of the lot. You can't be serious!"

"Trust is the only one who's irreplaceable. As for Fortunate, in my opinion he does more harm than good. He'll never produce anything but trouble and anarchy. Remember the suggestion boxes and those wretched green turbans! If you have cranks like that for courtiers, you could easily lose your crown. Even if he was any good, how can you expect loyalty from a crackpot who cares more about other people than himself? No post or title or possession will ever make him forget his barefoot friends in the East. But before I go on, allow me to ask you a question: Are you going to be satisfied with ruling Han-chung, or do you have more ambitious plans?"

"You know very well I want to rule over the entire central plain!"

"In that case you need Trust to be in Han-chung, and Fortunate to be with Plume."

"What do you mean?"

"Lu and Ti made Earl Wen of Wei lose the west bank of the river. Nao Ch'ih was responsible for the death of King Min. But the founder of the Chou was able to rule the Empire because he took on Lü Wang, and King Chuang of Ch'u reigned over the lords because of Sun-shu Ao."

"Speak plainly! You know classical quotations give me a headache."

"Fortunate is a troublemaker, and he's hated Plume ever since the massacres of the green turbans. As soon as he gets back, he'll stir up revolt, rouse the partisans, try to restore the age of the Great

Peace and other such nonsense. I don't think he's up to doing Plume any serious harm, but he could be a nuisance, a thorn in the tiger's foot. As for Trust, if you really mean to conquer the Empire, you must make absolutely sure of his services. Otherwise, resign yourself to ruling over your own little plot until Plume comes to relieve you of it—and of your life in the bargain!"

"You can't make me believe that a man who humiliated himself like that could ever amount to anything."

"To tell the truth, I thought the same until recently, but then Chang the Good made me see that what he did was really noble. Chang says a man capable of abasing himself in that way probably does so for some lofty purpose that prevents him from risking petty quarrels. His prudence is like that of a queen who's carrying an heir to the throne in her womb, and takes care that he is born safely. Remember Ch'ing Ko, who endured insults from Ko Nieh in Yü-tse and from Lu Kou-chien in Han-tan, and then went on to win universal admiration by trying to assassinate the tyrant of Ch'in. And think of yourself! When you were still unknown, in P'ei, you sometimes put up with affronts without doing anything about them."

Whet-Iron lowered his eyes and thought for a moment.

"You may be right," he said. "Will a generalship do?"

"*That* won't be enough to keep him!"

"All right, I'll make him commander in chief!"

"Good!"

"Call him in and let's put an end to this."

"No. You aren't finished yet. Trust is very touchy, and you'll only offend him if you act in your usual way. You don't whistle for someone as if he's a little boy when you're going to make him your commander in chief."

"Well, what else do you want me to do?"

"If you really mean to appoint him, have the soothsayers choose an auspicious day and put up an altar. Then offer a great sacrifice and name him commander in chief with great pomp and ceremony in front of all your troops. The appointment will mean something only if all the proper rituals are observed."

———

At the banquet that followed the ceremony Porter had insisted on, the king invited Trust to occupy the place of honor and sat beside him and showed him every kind of attention. When many cups of wine had been emptied, Whet-Iron leaned toward the new general and spoke.

"Chang the Good and Porter never stop singing your praises," he said. "So I'm eager to hear what you have to suggest to me."

"Who else besides Plume, to the east of the passes, is capable of seizing the Empire?"

"No one," Whet-Iron admitted.

"And which of you two is the braver, the more magnanimous, the stronger?"

Whet-Iron was silent for a moment. Then:

"I'm not his equal in any of those things," he whispered.

Trust smiled and nodded.

"Good," he said. "I see you judge yourself severely. I agree with you that you're inferior to him in all those things. But I've served under him and I think I know him. I'll tell you the sort of person he really is. He's a man who yells and threatens so loudly, he can rout an army—but he can't appoint a competent general. He's brave, but with a bumpkin's bravery. He treats guests with courtesy and is full of tact and consideration. He can turn a compliment, is never lost for a pleasant word, cries his eyes out over you if you're ill, and is always ready to give food and wine. He'd give his own cloak to a friend who was cold. But as soon as it comes to rewarding his generals with titles and lands, he closes like a miser's purse. He is generous, but with a womanish kind of generosity. He dominates the Empire, but he's made the mistake of setting up his capital in P'eng-ch'eng instead of staying within the passes—and this just to please a concubine who can make him yield to all her whims and fancies. Kings and princes obey him, but he hasn't any real legitimacy. He has disregarded the agreement about the nobility and handed out kingdoms to his entourage and his relations and friends, thus causing unrest among the feudal princes. Everywhere he goes he leaves death and desolation behind him and arouses hatred among the people. Yes, he may seem to have won power over the Empire, but he has already lost the people's hearts. And that's why I say his strength is really weakness.

"You ought to do exactly the opposite. Give jobs to officers who have shown their valor. Give cities and lands to generals who have covered themselves with glory. On the pretext of restoring the rule of law, spread your homesick henchmen around, and by so doing you'll quell your rivals and control the Empire. But remember that before you can conquer the East you must conquer the West. Ch'in is Ch'u's weak point. The three princes it has been divided among were officials under the Second Emperor. Not content with having gone over to their country's enemy, they stood by while Plume murdered their two hundred and fifty thousand men. So, believe me, they're not very popular with the people of Ch'in, who would have overthrown them if they hadn't been afraid of reprisals.

"But you, owing to your levelheadedness, are quite popular. And according to the terms of the peace treaty they might have expected to have you as their leader. Unfortunately, that didn't work out, and they are very disappointed. You ought to exploit the situation, and go back to Ch'in at the head of an army. It would be a pushover; you wouldn't even have to fight."

"Marvelous! You make me sorry we didn't meet earlier. We could have done great things together."

But Trust tried to moderate his enthusiasm.

"That's all very well, but we'll have to guard against Plume's reaction. If he intervenes in the West before we have it completely under control, he could be a serious threat."

"So what are we to do?" said Whet-Iron, suddenly cast down.

"Pin him down in the East. And to do that we need the help of Chang the Good."

———

Whet-Iron was lying with his head in Ch'i's lap, humming a lament from the East, when a page came in to announce the return of the secret emissary he had sent to see Chang the Good. The concubine was annoyed and threw her arms around Whet-Iron's neck, whispering, "Can't it wait?" But he put his hand over her mouth and answered in an undertone:

"Don't you want me to work for our son and heir?"

At that she dimpled and let him go. He got up, straightened his robe, and showed String into a small study.

He could tell from the look on his face that things hadn't gone according to plan. His friend didn't beat about the bush.

"The king of Han's position is precarious," said String. "Plume has kept him in the capital and prevented him from going home, and he's just reduced him to the rank of marquis. Chang the Good is afraid he may meet with the same fate as Intelligence and be murdered by Tattooed Face on instructions from Plume. He has his work cut out pleading his master's cause with Plume, and can't devote himself entirely to ours. If he tried to stand up for us *and* for the king of Han, he might harm both parties. For the same reason, he can't leave P'eng-ch'eng and go to Ch'i and Chao, where he might have been able to talk Scrap and T'ien Yung into revolt. But to show his goodwill he's going to try to stir them up by letter."

"That's not the same thing! A plague on Chang and his loyalty to a lost cause! What on earth can be done to make him abandon the Han's sinking ship? Doesn't he realize he'd serve them better by serving me?"

"Is your wife, Lü the Pheasant, still in P'ei?

"Why do you ask? You know very well she stayed there to look after my old parents."

"She has great powers of persuasion. Perhaps she could succeed where your humble servant failed—especially since Chang the Good has the greatest respect for her. P'ei isn't far from P'eng-ch'eng, and if you sent an emissary to see her, it wouldn't arouse suspicion."

"It would look fishy if she went to see him."

"Who said anything about that? He'll go to see her as soon as she says the word."

———

As usual, Chang the Good felt his willpower weaken under the influence of this woman, whose square face and large features lent her a kind of massive beauty. You could tell from looking at her that she had a lust for power that the whole universe couldn't satisfy, and was capable of both the greatest self-sacrifice and the blackest infamy.

"Don't desert us," she implored, kneeling before him. "Even if you don't take pity on us, who are helpless orphans without your support, think of the Empire, which you'll be handing over to blood-thirsty hyenas. Surely you won't be so cruel?"

Chang summoned up his loyalty to the Han to help him resist the Pheasant's pleas. She gave a bitter laugh.

"Well," she said, "since you can't do anything for us, I only hope you succeed in your efforts to save your master."

Alone again, she remained deep in thought, her white brow clouded by vast and murderous designs. Great undertakings often involve the use of poison—as is suggested by the hexagram known by the name *ku*, which can mean both enterprise and bane. As it implies in its every line, poison is what lies behind most of the machinations that put Great Men on their thrones.

———

In the middle of the summer, when both animal and vegetable matter rots in the heat and produces fevers, noxious fumes, and poisonous insects, the women of the southern provinces collect scorpions, snakes, and lizards and concoct deadly potions from them. It was now the fifth month, when pestilence and its noisome exhalations were at their height, exacerbated by the heat and humidity. And so it was that an idea germinated in the mind of the Pheasant, who, like all the women of Ch'u, was partly a witch: the idea of using the black magic of *ku* to ensure the success of her plans.

After consulting the calendar to find an auspicious day, she crept out of her house one sweltering afternoon, carrying a clothes basket and a big flat bowl. She went up a hill and, selecting a lonely place near a spring, took from the basket a silk robe freshly washed and scented with wormwood and spread it carefully on the grass. She filled the bowl with water from the spring and put it in the middle of the expanse of silk. After this she removed the pins, one by one, from her hair, letting it fall in a mass over her shoulders; she took off her clothes, and, when she was quite naked, began to dance and sing:

"Psst, psst! Come, all you toads and scorpions, all you snakes and centipedes and other foul creatures! Come and infect this basin with your poisons! May everything be steeped in the foul miasmas of summer and help secrete my *ku!*"

Soon a big spider let itself down from the branches into the basin, and it was followed by vipers, centipedes, and scorpions. When the water was covered with them, the Pheasant overturned the basin in a damp, shady corner, reciting a spell as she did so.

Two days later she went up the hill again and picked the mushrooms that had sprung up on the spot where she had emptied the poisoned water. She ground them up and put the resulting paste into the hollows of some goose feathers, which she stuck in her hair. There the heat of her body produced maggots that were like silkworms, and these she put into an earthenware pot, which she kept in a warm dark place in the house until they became poisonous. For *ku* isn't deadly to begin with; on the contrary, women in the South use it for making love potions. It takes at least ten days for the worms to secrete their poison.

As soon as she was sure the powder she'd made from them

would really work, the Pheasant went to P'eng-ch'eng in disguise and managed to get into the kitchens of the marquis of Han. Telling one of the maids she was acting for King Plume, she managed to sprinkle the master's food with some of the powder she'd concealed in a box in her chignon.

————

In the little room set aside for secret deliberations, Increaser looked worried.

"I agree we had to get rid of the Just Emperor," he whispered to Plume, unable to conceal his irritation. "Sooner or later he would have made trouble for us. But by poisoning Marquis Ch'eng of Han you've made a monumental error. Don't you realize you've provided Whet-Iron with the services of a remarkable man he'd have had to do without so long as there was a survivor of the Han dynasty? The death of Ch'eng not only frees Chang the Good, but also turns him into your mortal enemy. If you hated the marquis so much you couldn't bear him to go on living, you should have killed Chang, his faithful counselor, at the same time. I've tried to find him to make good your mistake, but it's too late—he's disappeared. He must be in Han-chung now, and out of our reach."

"What are you talking about?" cried Plume angrily. "I had nothing to do with the murder of Marquis Ch'eng! I was as surprised as you to hear he'd been poisoned. Poison is the weapon of cowards, and I'm not in the habit of using it. Anyhow, he may have died of some mysterious illness, or of food poisoning or something."

"No. The doctors are sure. You need only have seen him, as I did, with his tongue all blue and his stomach swollen."

"That'll do. I won't tolerate these suspicions! Anyway, he was such a nonentity I don't care to waste time discussing what happened to him. We've got other things to think about. Whet-Iron has seized Ch'in. Ch'i and Chao are seething with unrest. Tsang T'u and Luan Pu, his right-hand man, have taken all of Yen. T'ien Yung has killed two of the rulers of Ch'i, driven out the third, taken over the whole kingdom, and started challenging my authority. He's made P'eng Yüeh a general and sent him to stir up Wei. Scrap, with the help of the Ch'i army, has overthrown Ear, who's taken refuge with Whet-Iron. And to crown everything, the prefectures in the coastal provinces are being looted and destroyed by gangs of yokels led by a crank called Fortunate, who claims to be establishing the reign of the Great Peace! What should I do first? Deal with the rebels in the East or attack Whet-Iron?"

"What do you really want? Will you be satisfied with ruling Ch'u? That means leaving the Empire without a master and provoking the envy of all the ambitious lordlings who are only waiting for an opportunity to scramble for the spoils. No, you must conquer the Empire, and once you've set your seal on it, the pretenders will have to swallow their greed. And who is there to rival you for the Empire? Just one man. The one you've already let escape you: Whet-Iron. Don't miss the target twice. Heaven never forgives those who don't seize the chance it offers them. He's the one you must turn your weapons on, and at once, and not bother about the others. They're merely jackals."

At any other time Plume would have listened to what Increaser said. But he was so incensed by his counselor's suspicions concerning the marquis of Han that he needed to contradict him.

"And leave my own land to those vultures? That's just what they'd like! No. I have a plan. It won't take me more than a week to get the better of that handful of rebels. And then I'll lead my victorious army against Whet-Iron and make him bitterly regret his treachery!"

DOMINATION

Domination calls for great qualities
of endurance and generosity.
But the eighth month is unpropitious to it.
The earth above the pool:
A wise man teaches and educates all the time,
tirelessly supporting and protecting the people.

"Brothers," said Fortunate to the tattered crowd, "in the government of Heaven a prince treats the elderly as his masters and teachers, even if they're of humble origin. For he knows that the most brilliant virtues may be met with among those of low degree. He doesn't think he is abasing himself if he asks them for their advice. That is how he establishes his domination over the Empire, without slaughter or punishment, so that the Great Peace may reign. There is, also, a less perfect but still very good form of government, the government of the Earth: subjects have the same wishes and feelings as their ruler

—they might be comrades—and he is a mother to them all, loving, protecting, and sometimes even consulting them. One degree below comes the government of Man, which, as you brothers and sisters of the Tao know, is the third part of the triad. In the government of Man the ruler treats his subjects as though they were children. He looks after them, he doesn't molest them, but he doesn't tell them his plans. Those are the three kinds of government, the three forms which correspond to the three states of the universe, and it is this cycle that ought to have been perpetuated. Unfortunately, because of men's greed, virtue decayed, and a fourth kind of government appeared in history and has lasted for centuries. This is the government of contempt. Subjects are regarded as things and treated worse than dogs, inanimate objects, or plants; they are subjected to all sorts of cruelty and humiliation. It is the reign of metal, which causes war and pitiless punishment. Ch'in has collapsed, and pretenders have arisen wanting to rule the land-beneath-the-sky. Who are these pretenders? I'll tell you—and don't think they're your kings, for *they* are a thing of the past. No, there are only two men who can lay claim to the Empire: Plume and Whet-Iron. You know Plume already—you've seen him at work, leaving ruin and desolation behind him, slaying women and children. What sort of order will he impose? The order of contempt, of course. Plume is a butcher; he spreads terror and rules through metal. He will merely continue the oppression of Ch'in!

"Fortunately there is another pretender. He was once lieutenant to our wise prince Flash-Pedigree. I met him during the campaigns against Ch'in, and would be with him now if I hadn't thought it my most sacred duty to let you know his worth. I'm talking about Liu. He was the first to go west of the passes. So, according to the agreement, he had the right to the Empire. I've seen old weeping men in Ch'in, who for long suffered the oppression of the tyrants, throw themselves at his feet as he went by. He wept too when he heard what they had endured. He abolished the unjust laws, and instead of mistreating the old men and chaining them, he consoled them, listened to their advice in the schools, and gave them a glass of wine and two helpings of meat at local banquets. 'Old men,' he used to say, 'what suggestions have you, what advice would you give me? I'm listening.' So is Liu a typical prince of the government of Man? He is better than that: he doesn't treat people like children. Is he a typical prince of the government of the Earth? He is better than that: he regards his people as more than companions and friends. He is a prince of the government of Heaven: he treats the village elders as his masters. What's more, he is predestined: he killed the White Snake, and his name indicates that he will usher in the reign of the virtue of spring. Liu is Mao-tao-chin, Orient Whet-Iron!"

The sea of grubby turbans, with its lurking undertow of indignation or despair, began to stir. So far they had been lethargic, each concentrating on the slow and difficult process of digesting a mass of grain and wild herbs. Because of this fare, their only reaction to speeches was usually a series of brief farts and plaintive belches, like the bleating of goats, which might express either dumb protest or deep inward approbation. Now, they suddenly uttered a long articulate cry: "Long live Whet-Iron! Down with Plume! Kill Plume the butcher and give his head to Whet-Iron!"

The boldest among them wanted to revive the militia and set out to make war without more ado. Others, for whom the world ended at their own borders, talked of enrolling in Whet-Iron's army as if they were only a bowshot away. Soon they were arming themselves with sticks, great stone sickles, sharp iron spades, and long hoes edged with shells.

Fortunate, who still recalled with horror the great massacres perpetrated by the green turbans, tried to calm the crowd. His own idyllic visions had been modified by the former police chief's dreams of order; he had acquired a taste for discipline.

This may have owed less to the influence of Whet-Iron than to a change in the general atmosphere. The longing for liberty that had arisen in reaction to the Ch'in's attempt to imprison the future within the tyranny of the predictable, and the monstrous killing to which it had led, had gradually been replaced by an intense desire for standards and constraints, even if that meant giving up the unexpected —which, anyway, brought them nothing but unpleasant surprises. And what could be better for getting things back into shape than the methodical approach of a policeman? In a nutshell, the spirit of the age chimed with Whet-Iron's ideas and ensured their success.

But Fortunate warned the green turbans. They mustn't make the same mistake as before and rush into violence. They must organize themselves properly this time. This meant setting up a local police force to stop wrongdoing. For it is men's crimes that bring down Heaven's wrath and the natural calamities that cause poverty. And poverty, as he had explained in his sermons, was itself the cause of the struggle for rare commodities. Because Whet-Iron was too far away for them to join him, it was a tactical necessity for them to swear allegiance to the new king of Ch'i, even if he was the son of T'ien Yung, who'd been no friend to them. But he had raised the banner of revolt against Plume, and this was the best way of ensuring the victory of King Liu, their liberator.

Meetings were organized to promote virtue and punish vice. The whole population, from provincial civil servants to simple peasants, joined together to prevent infractions of both the laws of the land and the laws of morality.

On a prearranged date, a magistrate would go to any village where a crime had been reported and summon all the inhabitants to the Chamber for the Promotion of Virtue. Retired civil servants and other former administrators sat facing east in the western part of the room, the cardinal point of justice: thus, even though they were no longer in office, their position indicated where right was to be found. The scholars, those who had studied the classics or had a reputation for virtue, sat facing north along the south wall of the room, at the cardinal point of penetration: for their intelligence could help find evildoers. In the eastern part of the room, facing west, were dutiful sons and obedient brothers at the cardinal point of roots and origins, since goodness consists in soul-searching. Hardworking plowmen sat against the wall in the northeast corner, the direction of growth and germination: this position indicated approval of their conscientious carrying out of fundamental tasks. Good-for-nothings were relegated to the northwest corner, the point where evil desires and punishments begin, since that is where yang and yin are reversed: thieves and profiteers went and sat there instinctively.

When everyone was suitably seated, with virtuous men to the fore and rowdies at the back, wine was passed around. When there wasn't enough, they warmed one another's hearts with good words. Then came an address to the assembly, asking everyone to back the law to the best of his ability. After that the visiting magistrate went into a kind of wooden cabin in the northern part of the room and turned his face to the south, in the position of the king he represented, and asked everyone concerned in the case to come into the confessional and give his information in private: honest citizens must not be exposed to the malice of villains. The various statements were compared. Witnesses whose evidence did not agree were cross-examined, to find out who had been lying or playing tricks. When the investigation was finished, the meeting was closed. Youngsters enrolled for the purpose set out to track down miscreants who hadn't yet been apprehended. For Fortunate, the main attraction of this whole business was its educational aspect, the way it brought out parallels between morals and the cycle of nature. The local worthies and magistrates approved of the arrangement because it was a marvelous way of keeping the villagers under control. As for the villagers themselves, they put up with it out of fear and hatred of Plume, who dragged old men, women, and children off into slavery, burned cities, razed villages, and killed soldiers after they had surrendered. All the people who lived in the provinces of the East and the North were joined in opposition to such bloody tyranny.

———

Despite Increaser's admonitions, Plume, the warlord used to ruling through military violence, could not understand that police surveillance was a better way of managing the population during a period of political restoration.

And, indeed, King Whet-Iron, the former local police chief, seemed to be on the point of wresting supremacy over the Empire from him. He'd conquered the three kings of Ch'in and installed on the throne of Han a vassal of his own who was vaguely connected with the former royal family. Wei the Panther, Wei the Unfortunate's younger brother, who had hoped to inherit his kingdom, was furious when, because of Plume's greed, he was exiled to P'ing-yang after the victory over Ch'in. He had therefore ranged himself on the side of the king of the West. The kingdom of Yen, separated from Wei and awarded to a Chao general, soon shook off the ruler under Ch'u's control. Ch'i, Chao, and Yen in turn went over to the other side. And Whet-Iron was marching on the capital of his former friend, now his rival, at the head of an army of five hundred and sixty thousand men.

A sign of the times was that even Plume's former comrades and favorites were turning toward Whet-Iron. Tattooed Face, worried by the march of events, had provided Plume with a few back-up troops and then pretended to be ill and went to ground in his kingdom of Nine Rivers. Ch'en Peacemaker had given up his post as commandant and joined Whet-Iron's army under an assumed name.

They had all dug up ancient grudges to justify their defection in their own eyes. Tattooed Face ground his teeth as he recalled how Plume had tried to get hold of his mare, and later, despite his pleas, had grabbed Quicksilver, whose birth had cost his mother her life. Because of the prophecy, the horse and the throne Tattooed Face had won were so closely connected in his mind that it seemed to him Plume had been trying to steal his kingdom when he annexed the mare's offspring. Ch'en Peacemaker was frustrated by his master's military skills: every honor lavished upon him lessened his own standing: although Plume multiplied his titles, he made sure Ch'en had no opportunity to display his talents.

There were other, equally unmistakable, signs. Wang Ling, a rich potentate in P'ei who had always refused to submit to the authority of a parvenu, had offered Whet-Iron his support, along with that of his Nan-yang prefecture. Scrap, deceived by a severed head, apparently Ear's, that Whet-Iron sent to him, had now also swelled the ranks of the conspiracy. Even Barricade of Teeth, who occupied an important post under Wei the Panther, was making overtures to Whet-Iron.

———

Whet-Iron ordered mourning to be observed for the Just Emperor. All his soldiers had to wear white armor, and those responsible for the abominable murder of a prince chosen unanimously by the lords were to be punished. He wooed the old people, widows, and orphans in the villages his army passed through. His proclamations were full of virtuous resolutions and references to aid, amnesty, and bounty. The allied troops reached the walls of P'eng-ch'eng almost without opposition, found that the city's defenders had gone off to quell the rebels in the East, and captured the place in no time at all.

Whet-Iron decided to live in Plume's palace in P'eng-ch'eng, and annexed all the women, horses, and treasures Plume had looted. But he was unable to find either Joy, Plume's concubine, or Quicksilver, the horse he had ridden in all his campaigns.

He threw himself hungrily on the ladies in the palace—Plume's splendid girls, selected wives, and first-class concubines—not so much because they appealed to him, as to leave behind the evidence of his victory. But each infidelity only brought him back, more in love than ever, to Ch'i. The favorite's curves grew fuller, making him hope for an heir. To assure that the child would be a boy, the heads of tigers and bears were hung over the doors of the private apartments. Lady Ch'i set up a chapel dedicated to Ku-chih, a woman who died in childbirth and had become the patron saint of pregnant women in Stable. Whet-Iron, enjoying all the delights of court life, seemed to have forgotten that Plume was still alive and in possession of an army, even if his troops were pinned down in the East by the Ch'i rebellion.

———

Plume was angry. He could not put down the rebels, and this was the kind of war he hated, full of skirmishes and interminable sieges. When he thought of Whet-Iron lolling about in *his* palace with *his* wives, riding *his* horses, and drinking from *his* goblets, he was seized by a longing for murder and carnage. But he knew he must wait until his enemy grew soft through pleasure, relaxed vigilance, and came to believe that victory would be easy. In order to seem weak, Plume deliberately accepted some reverses. Exaggerated reports of Ch'i successes added to Whet-Iron's confidence, and he remained in P'eng-ch'eng, waiting for Plume to be worn down so that he could deliver the final blow. He offered strategic explanations for his failure to act, but in fact it was partly due to a secret fear that his presence on the battlefield might reveal Plume's superiority. He kept putting off the moment of confrontation.

———

Plume's offensive took Whet-Iron by surprise. After rounding the Ch'i peninsula from the southeast and skirting P'eng-ch'eng on the west, he and his thirty thousand men routed the troops defending Whet-Iron's supply lines. The very same day, he crushed the main army, driving it back into the rivers Ssu and Ku, where a hundred thousand soldiers died. He chased the survivors to the banks of the Sui and forced them into the river, again causing more than a hundred thousand deaths.

Nothing was left of Whet-Iron's former power. He fell back on Yung-yang and fortified his positions. It looked as if Plume would dominate the Empire again, since this depended to a considerable extent on military success, and although Whet-Iron was better at organization, he was definitely inferior when it came to strategy. After his defeat, the princes who had enrolled under his banner deserted him and crawled back to the victor to beg forgiveness.

Scrap suddenly discovered that he'd been fooled, and that the head that had been presented to him as that of Ear had really belonged to someone resembling him. Ear's own head was still safely on his shoulders, and he enjoyed the esteem of the king. Claiming to be outraged by the deceit about the head, Scrap broke with Whet-Iron and offered the services of Chao to Ch'u. Wei the Panther found that he was urgently required in P'ing-yang, where his old parents were ill and in need of their son's help. As soon as he got back to his own territory, he demolished the fords across the Yellow River and entered into negotiations with Plume for a new alliance. The proposals Whet-Iron sent him through Master Li I-ch'i he firmly rejected.

"Master Li! Master Li! The life of a man passes by as swiftly as the shadow of a galloping horse glimpsed through a doorway. It's too short for me to waste it putting up with the shouting and bawling of a vulgar boor who never stops nagging and treats me like a slave. Whet-Iron doesn't know the first thing about good manners. It's impossible to work for him."

Even Whet-Iron's rear base in Ch'in was weakened. Ssu-ma Hsin, whom he'd left to guard Yüeh-yang, fled from the passes and joined Plume. Chang Han raised the flag of revolt in Yung, and Whet-Iron had to divert the course of a river and flood the town in order to put down the rebellion.

To cap all this, some of his own family had fallen into the hands of the enemy.

Plume was a smart enough general to restrain himself and wait for the right moment, but he was too vindictive not to seek an immediate outlet for his anger. Because Whet-Iron had occupied his capital, he naturally thought of taking revenge on his enemy's family, who were all in P'ei and exposed to his fury.

But the detachment he sent there arrived too late: Chang the Good, anxious about the Pheasant and her children, had got there first. Since the roads to P'eng-ch'eng were constantly patrolled, the fugitives, afraid of being recognized and arrested, headed for a village farther south. During the debacle, Whet-Iron met his two children, running away in charge of a faithful servant, but his wife and her parents had taken another road, and were caught by one of Plume's patrols. Soon Plume taunted him, threatening to force him to drink a broth made from the dead bodies of the three captives.

VISIONS
FROM ON HIGH

A libation may be made without an offering,
so long as there is sincerity and respect.

The terrace of the pavilion overlooked a vast prospect of steep ridges dominated by the western and southern peaks of Mount Fleuri. Swirls of cloud, flushed with crimson in the last rays of the sun, thinned out to drape the cliffs with long strands of silver, or condensed in puffs of white around the summits. Six old men leaned on the marble balustrade and gazed thoughtfully at the scene. With their bulging brows wreathed in wisps of gray, they were like six miniature summits glowing in the waning light of existence.

They wore the long wide-sleeved robes of soothsayers, decorated with black-and-white stripes arranged in trigrams, and the gold braid on their collars depicted the heraldic symbols of direction. They were all very old. After a long silence, the most ancient of them spoke in a deep voice.

"Does not this spectacle, seen from a terrace built between

Heaven and Earth, remind you of the twentieth hexagram: '*Modest and adaptable, but always righteous, he contemplates the Empire from the heights of his observatory*'?"

"But it would also have to correspond to the second interpretation of the hexagram, as given in the commentary, '*Lesser people gaze at it and are transformed,*'" quibbled another old man.

"The second meaning is contained in the first," said a third, "because the master adds: '*He contemplates the divine way which governs the changeless course of the seasons; the holy man takes that way as the model of his teaching, and subjugates the whole Empire.*'"

"We mustn't argue over something we all agree about!" a fourth said, laughing. "Let's get down to serious matters. The walk has given me an appetite, it's getting late, so why don't we warm ourselves with a few glasses of wine and watch the sun go down behind the mountains?"

They gathered around the low table where their young slaves had already set out goblets of warmed wine. As they drank and nibbled wild berries, pine kernels, and dried mushrooms, the fine layer of mist was tinged by the last fires of the setting sun.

The servants brought in torches and lit the strangely contorted bronze incense burners. And the grave countenances of the six men, thrown into weird relief by the flickering lamps, emerged from the many-colored clouds of incense like effigies of wise men in a temple.

Four of them—Master of the Eastern Orchard, Master of the Village of Chiao, Venerable Doctor of the Village of Ch'i, and Master Yellow Stone—were hoary-headed scholars. The other two were the patriarchs Flower of Reality and Save-Your-Life.

They talked of various matters, including the different ways of preparing *Polygonatum giganteum* and *Pachimas cocos*, the relative merits of mineral and vegetable drugs, and divination. Also of dietetics, and of physical exercises for getting rid of intestinal worms. They discussed ritual and music, expressing surprise that these should have been different under the three holy dynasties, and lamenting their decline since the Chou. This brought them to the main business of the evening.

Master of the Eastern Orchard, known by his hexagrammatic name, Top Line, recalled how the sect had taken a new direction since the meeting in the Kao-lie period, when the six agents impersonating six trigrams were discovered. Since then, Earth and Heaven had abandoned their masked meetings with the members of the second circle and made their directives known by means of messengers. The new council was reduced to six venerable scholars known to one another and recruited from various places in the Empire; they now represented the directions instead of the trigrams. Their main function was to choose remarkable men and to serve as guides to the Great Men who were expected to appear after the fall of the dynasty of the First Emperor, whose accession they had favored in the hope of silencing the rival schools that threatened the teachings of the Master.

Although the first part of their program had been crowned with success, the same could not be said of its second stage. Interminable rivalries and wars had so impeded life that, instead of being strengthened, the Master's doctrines were in danger of being forgotten. Worse still, neither of the two most serious pretenders could properly be described as a sage.

Master Yellow Stone felt that this criticism was aimed at him: his perspicacity was in question because his protégé, Chang the Good, to whom he had once given the book of the eight trigrams, was now in the service of Whet-Iron. He objected strenuously, pointing to Whet-Iron's exemplary behavior during the invasion of the passes, and his longing to be surrounded by wise men. To emphasize Whet-Iron's virtues even further, Master Yellow Stone contrasted him with Plume, who slew women and children, who threw Whet-Iron's faithful followers into boiling cauldrons, then devoured their flesh and sent what was left to their master!

Now it was Flower of Reality's turn to be offended, for he had been Increaser's teacher under the name Old Sage of the South, and

Increaser was now in the service of Plume. He called attention to Plume's urbanity, his generosity to his friends, his great courage, and his respect for the hierarchy. He listed his enemy's many defects: debauchery, coarseness, boastfulness, lack of any real talent.

Speaking of cruelty, was Master Yellow Stone aware of his protégé's latest exploit? With gusts of laughter that made him spit bits of pine kernel all over his goatee, he told how, during the rout at P'eng-ch'eng, Whet-Iron, that impassive hero, had come upon his two children running away. His driver gave them a place in his chariot despite the protests of the king, who didn't want to encumber himself with extra weight. And a few leagues farther on, when the clouds of dust sent up by their pursuers seemed to be getting closer, Whet-Iron threw the children out! Dollface stopped the chariot and gathered them in his arms, disregarding the yells of his master, who threatened to lop his head off. The same thing happened three or four times, until the enemy seemed to have been shaken off, and the king calmed down.

The best of it was that the danger was quite illusory: what they thought were enemy soldiers was really a herd of buffalo, frightened by the noise of battle.

Flower of Reality warmed to his theme. How could a man who in a moment of panic was ready to sacrifice his own children act as a model for the people of the Empire? How dare anyone put him forward as a paragon of all the virtues? Was it not impertinent to regard him as the Great Man capable of spreading the teaching of the sacred kings as transmitted by the Master? A man who, whenever he saw a scholar, relieved himself in his hat, and received the sages with his feet in a bowl of water! How could you take such a person seriously?

Master Yellow Stone turned pale at this insult. Words were exchanged. The other ancients, heated by their numerous libations, soon joined in. One thin arm reached out and threw a punch; he got a slipper back. The six old men rolled on the floor among overturned platters and pitchers. They pulled one another's beards, tweaked one another's cheeks, tore out tufts of hair. Save-Your-Life was the first to calm down, and this shamed the rest into straightening their disheveled clothes and sitting down again on their mats.

Master of the Village of Chiao—Third Line was his name in the sect—had till then been silent. He now recalled the dictum of the leaders: "The stag of the Empire has escaped from the hands of Ch'in; it belongs to the first person who catches it." Neither Earth nor Heaven had ever mentioned the pretenders' virtues. Possession of the Empire was proof of virtue in itself. So it wasn't that "the Empire should go to the most virtuous," but, rather, that "whoever gets possession of the Empire will have been by that very fact the most virtuous." Moral qualities could be measured only by results. The deeds of both Plume and Whet-Iron were worthy of blame only inasmuch as they weren't yet complete; nor did the mere possession of a disputed part of the land beneath the sky justify deeds as yet unjustified by their final effects. But as soon as one of the two men mounted the dragon throne and spread his phoenix wings, every previous action of his, good or bad, would be cleansed, sanctified, sublimated; his least gesture would take on a secret meaning authorized by his apotheosis. The predestination that seems to characterize a great career is due merely to a retrospective view in which a man's behavior is bathed in the light of his later glory.

Fourth Line—the Venerable Doctor of the Village of Ch'i—objected to this pragmatic approach, which according to him was nothing but sophistry, even tautology. Very helpful, to say that the person best qualified to possess the Empire was the person who would possess it! A strange profession of faith for a soothsayer, who was supposed to know the future, to admit that not only could he not foretell the future but that even the present could not be properly understood until it had become the past! He, Fourth Line, believed in omens: there were such things as signs foretelling fate for those who knew how to interpret them. And everything to do with Whet-

Iron portended a remarkable destiny. Admittedly Plume too gave off unusual vibrations, but that was only to be expected in someone capable of challenging Whet-Iron for supremacy.

Then Line of the Beginning entered the fray. Everyone was talking as if the Empire must be one and undivided—but why shouldn't it be broken into parts? Didn't Confucius's appendix to the *Book of Changes* begin: "A time of yin, a time of yang, that is the Tao," thus expressing the necessary alternation between light and shade, hot and cold, unity and division? And the *Book of the Way and of Virtue* said: "The One gives birth to the Two, the Two produces the Three, from which proceed the ten thousand beings." This shows that one of the manifestations of unity is division, the second being latent in the first.

The reason the Empire was undergoing such convulsions was the attempt to impose a structure on it that didn't match the natural course of things. In the natural way, since duality was the mode of instability, the Empire would necessarily revert to unity so long as there were two pretenders to the possession of the land beneath the sky. But if a third claimant were to be put forward, the Empire would be more stable under partition. Line of the Beginning would maintain, no matter what anyone else might say, and contrary to common opinion, that the most perfect form of the Tao was not unity but trinity, because it included both the other two (unity and duality, the One and the Two). Trinity was not one broken down into three, but One and Two co-existing and mating to make Three.

"That's all very well and good," said Top Line, smiling shrewdly, "but I don't see who could rival Plume and Whet-Iron. So all those arguments are academic."

Now it was the turn of Save-Your-Life to wear a mocking smile. They were, he said, all so intent on Whet-Iron or Plume that they failed to see there were others besides those two—people tall as towers, solid as oak, straight as marble columns, who could do great things, could even found dynasties. There was Lü the Pheasant, for a start! At the name of Whet-Iron's wife, the five lines all cried out in horror. But Save-Your-Life went on deliberately:

"Yes, yes—the Pheasant's horoscope is just as brilliant as her husband's! She might well steal the Empire from the Liu and give it back to the Lü! Besides, as you know, my dear Master Yellow Stone, your disciple has the greatest respect for her, and serves her just as much as he serves Whet-Iron."

"But her future seems terribly uncertain," said Second Line. "Plume threatens to throw her into a cauldron and send her flesh to her husband for him to eat!"

"That's mere swagger! Plume knows Whet-Iron would be ready to devour his father and mother and both his children in order to get the Empire. And now that Lady Ch'i, by whom he is bewitched, has just given him an heir, he'd be delighted to make a meal out of his elderly wife."

"I wasn't thinking so much of the Pheasant—that would be keeping it in the family—as of other worthies: Fortunate, for example . . ."

"That troublemaker! All he cares about is spreading chaos and overthrowing the hierarchy. If he were to win, it would be the end of the Master's teaching."

Line of the Beginning smiled. He had mentioned Fortunate only to annoy them. The one he really had in mind was Trust. He had to admit he had once believed in Plume and even suggested certain plans to him; unfortunately, the general hadn't been able to understand them. He had then turned to Whet-Iron, but he hadn't proved any more worthy. Finally he had found in Trust a really remarkable man, someone who had to be taken into account. He thought him capable of leading men, of civilizing them and changing them by his own example, like the Great Man depicted in the twentieth hexagram: *"The sage contemplates the divine law, and all submit to his teaching. . . . Wind over earth: as in this symbol, the former kings inspected the lands, examined the people, and transmitted their teaching."*

"But at present he is under Whet-Iron's orders."

"Every founder of a dynasty is a vassal before he is a king."

"He lacks humility!" said Flower of Reality.

"He hasn't enough ambition!" exclaimed the Venerable Doctor of the Village of Ch'i at the same time.

"And he hasn't been able to attract any support," said the Master of the Village of Chiao.

"I beg your pardon—he attracted the washerwoman from Nan-yang."

"Pooh, a woman! And from the common people too!"

"That shows he could attract the trust and hopes of a whole nation."

"Quote the name of one remarkable man who respects him."

"K'uai Understanding!"

"Who's he?"

"He's my disciple. A rhetor from Fan-yang. It was he who got Chao to surrender by his words alone, while Ear and Scrap were cooling their heels outside all the fortresses. He went to Chao with Ear, as his adviser, and when Ear was defeated by Scrap, K'uai persuaded him to enter Whet-Iron's service. He did so on the strength of all the stars of the first magnitude in the constellation of the Well, which presides over the territories of Ch'in and Shu. It was at Whet-Iron's court that K'uai met Trust and recognized him as a superior man. He's waiting for an opportunity to speak to him and tell him of the great things he has in mind for him. And then we'll see Trust take flight like a crane and equal the two phoenixes!"

"Barricade of Teeth!" whinnied the Master of the Village of Chiao, opening toothless jaws so wide he almost revealed his innards. The other five followed the last line of the relevant hexagram—"*The sage does not think it wrong to enjoy the spectacle of the living*"— and, far from averting their eyes, feasted upon the gruesome sight.

"Yes," went on the Master of the Village of Chiao, "you were forgetting Barricade of Teeth. He has already proved himself by opposing Whet-Iron and wresting the town of Feng from him. And he was more popular there than Whet-Iron! Now he crouches, calm and silent as a lurking tiger, on the frontier between Wei and Chao, waiting for the right moment to leap on his prey."

"He has not one decent adviser!"

"It's better to have no one than someone like Li I-ch'i!"

"It isn't the adviser that matters, it's what you do with the advice! Need I remind this learned gathering of what it says in the *Book of Documents*? *'The wise man can apply low suggestions to lofty designs.'*"

"A worthless saying!"

Flower of Reality flew to the defense of Li I-ch'i, who'd been one of his favorite disciples.

"If Master Li's advice isn't good, it's because he wants to harm Whet-Iron. He's never forgiven him for the rudeness with which he received him the first time, and he's really working for Plume."

This brought forth vehement protests from the Master of the Village of Chiao, who had also taught the rhetor at one time. He knew Li I-ch'i well enough to be aware of his connections; if there was any question of treachery, it could be in favor only of Barricade of Teeth, with whose father he had been very friendly.

"That's enough about Barricade of Teeth!" yapped Master Yellow Stone. Fury made his skin turn the color of a white-hot rock. "Let's be serious! You're talking nonsense and behaving like a lot of urchins. You claim to be experts in the secrets of divination, so reflect on the saying *'The sight of children is harmless for a nonentity but dangerous for a wise man.'* At this rate, why not suggest P'eng Yüeh, Tattooed Face, Tsang T'u, or Wu Juei, king of the savages? All are waiting like jackals to prey on the remains of tigers fighting among themselves. That's not the sort of person we ought to wish on the Empire! It needs a guide who can gather capable men around him, who can draw on the efforts of all to help civilize the people and improve their manners. Let us agree upon a name and come to a decision. Haven't you had enough of endless discussion?"

"I don't see why! Everyone's free to support whomever he likes!

Our instructions are clear: We are not supposed to interfere, we are supposed to leave it to history."

"You might as well say our role is perfectly useless! In which case, what's the point of these meetings?" cried Third Line angrily.

"Haven't you realized yet that our role is essential not because we act, but because everybody thinks we do?"

"Anyway," said Line of the Beginning, "who knows whether destiny may not make its way better through our disagreements than through our concerted action?"

The lamps were almost burned out, and now mingled only the odd sooty gleam with the growing pallor of dawn. The mountains began to be outlined in a glow of red. A peal of thunder was heard, and a ray of light flashed down from the peaks on the six soothsayers. At first they flinched. Then they relaxed and formed themselves into six lines, some broken, some unbroken, then took off like six dragons and vanished into the clouds.

———

The new day streaked the tents of the army with red. Plume had reinforced the siege of Yung-yang. His men had just finished their morning meal of rice; drums and bugles were sounding the charge. A very old woman woke with a start and tried to lift her head. Her weary eyes, which age had veiled with gray, sought the distant battlements of Yung-yang, where Whet-Iron was besieged. She was near death; might she allow herself to be reassured by what she had dreamed about her son's destiny? It was absurd—but then, so were all her dreams. Oh, was the dragon going to crash almost as soon as it had taken flight? She would never find out. Anyway, what did it matter? He'd kept her waiting too long, and even if he did succeed and ascend the jade throne, that wouldn't alter his real nature: he always had been and always would be a bad son. Her head fell back on her breast, her body slumped, and she lost consciousness with her feet still in the bowl of water with which she had been performing her morning ablutions.

Chang the Good went into the oratory and looked around. The walls were freshly whitewashed, the well-rammed earthen floor was clean, a thick soft blanket lay on the bed of meditation. Apart from the bed, the only furniture was a bookcase, a low table, a small alchemist's kiln, and an incense burner of gilded bronze in the shape of a mountain. It was giving off clouds of scent.

He sat down on the bed, loosened his tunic, did a few breathing and other exercises, and began to meditate. The yellow arsenic began to do its work. He felt an intense heat in his chest, he could see his own entrails, and, when he was surrounded by the heraldic spirits of the directions, he breathed forth the red and yellow vapors of the sun and moon and let himself be swept up by them. Rising within himself he encountered his three ethereal souls, dressed in red, with red caps, and holding red seals in their hands. He led them into the palace of a superior one, where they met the hundred gods of the mind. Then all of them left his body.

The meditation chamber was filled with a blinding light given off by the primal breath from three fields of cinnabar. Chang rose up through the ether, through the different stories of the sky, passing thousands of divinities of all kinds, some grimacing and grotesque, some without heads and with eyes in their breasts. Some were tiny, some huge; some were terrifying, others wonderfully beautiful. Many had only wisps of hair like tangled hemp, and their eyes were only gaping holes in hollow sockets. But he wasn't afraid.

Up he went, higher and higher, and soon found himself on a mountain looking down on the world, full of the spirits of the lower spheres. Looking up he could see two shapes, one green, one white, facing one another and towering above him. One stood on the left wing and the other on the right wing of an enormous magpie with a bald head. Chang recognized Duke of the East and Queen Mother of the West, who are sun and moon, yin and yang, father and mother. Duke of the East wore a robe made of beads of five different colors, and a hat with three iridescent crests. In his hand he held a green standard bearing the arms of spring, with blazing suns. Queen Mother of the West, also called Empress of the Great Yin, was dressed in an incandescent gown of sulphur yellow, with a diadem of black beads in the shape of a weaver's bobbin. In her hand was a white feather fan with a long ivory handle, which she waved languidly to and fro.

Between these two appeared Child of Immortality, who was none other than Chang's own self. He concentrated his thoughts on this image and made it suck the primal milk, a distillation of the mystic essences of the jade fountain. But as he put his lips to Queen of the West's nipple he thought he recognized her as Lü the Pheasant. He drew his head back in terror, and his eye lighted on Duke of the East, who had begun to look strangely like Whet-Iron. The pallid faces of both figures twisted in a ghastly grin. Their eye sockets grew hollow, their flesh withered and fell away. They were soon only a couple of skeletons rattling their bones with a sound like the rustle of dry leaves. Letting out a horrible laugh, they croaked: "Images are created by those who look at them. Yours will always be of putrefaction." And loathsome worms, nameless insects, slimy reptiles, and monstrous parasites started to creep out of their every orifice and to swarm.

Chang the Good's ethereal souls, overcome by the awful stench emanating from this vision, took fright and dispersed. The breath he had been imprisoning in his belly escaped with a sinister hiss from his nose and mouth, and he felt himself falling as if into a bottomless pit.

As he hurtled down, he saw the divinities of the parts of the body he was falling through whirling madly around him: the gods of the hair winked like malevolent stars; the sun and moon shed a grim light on the eye sockets; he dropped like lightning through the labyrinths of the brain, full of lurking reddish gods. He fell through the nape of the neck and then the chest, passing the spongy lobes of the lungs, where two white dogs were barking. The heart flashed past in a gleam of crimson. The spleen was a gleam of green. Then he plunged into the foaming sea of the spirit between the two black rocks of the kidneys, where the six divinities of the hours greeted him with a sinister laugh. They all looked like the Pheasant, and as he went by they lifted their ledgers of death and marked down years of life for him.

Suddenly there was a great thump. He felt himself being lifted up, on the back of an enormous tortoise. Its shell was decorated with the seven stars of the Great Bear. He rose up from the navel into the stomach. A sun was blazing there. Then he plunged down again into the vermilion below, where in a fold of the kidneys he found Confucius spilling his seed into a dark woman with shining curls. And her womb opened and gave him birth. . . .

He emerged from his own body, panting for breath and covered with sweat. The hills were already growing pale in the dawn, and the incense burner gave forth only occasional puffs. He felt a kind of lump in his innards, and he only just had time to lift his gown and sit on the pot before the lump fell out with a dull thud. He went over to the window and examined it. It was like a hen's dropping, bloody, with yellowish streaks in it, and had a strong smell of fermented grain. There was no doubt about it: it was the husk of the lower corpse, the demon produced by the spirit of cereal food. It was this that had been disturbing his meditations. The drug had weakened it, but hadn't been able to get rid of it completely. Chang sighed and wrapped it carefully in a cotton bag, slipped furtively out of the palace, and threw it into a tributary of the Ssu.

"Bloody corpses," he muttered, "go back to the earth to which you belong. I shall leap up to the sky. *That* is my home." And he returned to the palace by another path, taking care not to look behind him.

Back in his oratory he felt at peace, as if he had been cleansed of his earthly desires, his murky and evil passions. Then the disillusion that was becoming more and more of a habit with him reasserted itself, and he began to reflect that the famous people who ruled over and were admired by the Empire might, like his own visions, be nothing but worm-eaten carrion beneath their gorgeous robes. As he saw the east light up with the first of the sun's rays, he could not help looking at them and thinking of Whet-Iron shut up in Yung-yang, and of Whet-Iron's wife imprisoned scores of leagues away, beyond his help. Had his dream been a warning?

RUMINATIONS

It is good to ruminate.
It helps to resolve conflicts.

The war dragged on, and no one could tell which of the two lights that illuminated the Empire with their glory was going to win. Whet-Iron was on the defensive in Yung-yang; Tattooed Face, his ally, had had to withdraw beyond the passes after a bloody defeat on the Huai River. Plume's flanks were being continually harassed by P'eng Yüeh and Fortunate. Both leaders looked down on the war-ravaged Empire and reflected on the inconstancy of victory. From the ruminations of the Great Men at bay there arose the sound of jaws working. It soared over the emblem of the moment and even muffled the clash of arms.

———

Whet-Iron was gnawing gingerly at a piece of tough and stinking chicken, trying to avoid the rotten flesh next to the bone. Every mouthful brought home to him his present distress. While his teeth grappled with the tangible evidence of his lamentable situation, his mind dwelled on it and found no solution. As he pondered, he inadvertently bit off a large piece of meat that tasted definitely bad. He spat it out, wryly recalling the third line of the Rumination hexagram: *"As he ate some dried meat, he came upon a bit that was rotten."* In it a female stroke was in a male position, like someone invested with a responsibility that was beyond his abilities. In a sudden fit of humility, Whet-Iron thought this applied to him. He had tried to rise too high and overestimated his powers. He ought to have been satisfied with being Plume's vassal. After all, the title king wasn't bad for an outlawed district police chief.

But no. He would have been at the mercy of his master, who'd soon have got rid of him: he'd have come to a bad end, to the great amusement of the other higher-ups. No one could say he hadn't done his best to win honor for his family. But Heaven had decreed otherwise, and although you were supposed to act as if you were master of your own fate, you couldn't fight destiny. Cudgel his brains as he might, he hadn't been able to find any way of loosening his enemy's grip. To ease his helpless frustration he began to turn over in his mind the answer he would send Plume. Plume had taunted him, saying that to save him from hunger he'd send him his relatives served up in a stew. He would reply: Were they not sworn brothers, according to their agreement? Well, since his dear brother obviously longed to boil his aged parents in a cauldron, he himself would gladly drink a bowl of the soup—not to assuage his hunger, for Yung-yang was brimming with food, but out of curiosity, to find out what human flesh tasted like.

As he tried to banish a vision of his father's and mother's skulls, their boiled eyes looking up at him from a pot of turnips, he sniffed another piece of meat and bit at it warily. Then Li I-ch'i came in and interrupted his train of thought. When Whet-Iron told the rhetor what had happened, Li I-ch'i's shrewd eyes narrowed enigmatically.

"You ought to be pleased. The omen isn't unfavorable; it heralds no more than a temporary difficulty, and I am here to get you out of that."

And he explained that the thing to do was to have seals of investiture made, hand them out to all the princes who'd been despoiled by the First Emperor and disappointed by Plume, and promise them that he, Whet-Iron, would give them back their kingdoms. The lords would then raise an army and attack the besieging army from the rear. Plume would be caught between two fires and heavily defeated. Whet-Iron was so delighted, he nearly choked on a drumstick.

———

Li I-ch'i tripped off to order the seals, leaving Whet-Iron to tackle the rest of his meal with more zest than before. When Ch'en Peacemaker dropped in unexpectedly to see him, he gaily told him of the plan. Peacemaker was furious.

"How ridiculous! Do you want to hasten your own downfall?"

"What do you mean?"

"You can't promise land until you're sure of victory. No one who's ever founded a dynasty has given away territory until after he conquered the Empire. Who's going to take any notice of an investiture coming from someone in your position? Even if people did take you seriously, don't you see that your plan would only disperse your supporters? Many of them, including Chang the Good, are former servants of the Six Kingdoms, and the first thing they'd do is rush back to their old masters!"

The king was so cross, he spat out what he was eating.

"The idiot—giving me false hopes! But how *am* I to get out of this trap?"

"It was Increaser who advised Plume to reject your offer of peace, and it's he who's urging him to finish you off. Make Plume suspicious of him. Plume's one of those rulers who like to do everything themselves, and feel it casts aspersions on them if any of their subordinates is too efficient. So although he seems to trust Increaser completely, he'll be only too glad of an excuse to dismiss or humiliate him. Anyhow, so many of his supporters have betrayed him already that he can't have any illusions left about their loyalty. Give me thirty thousand or so gold pieces and I'll see he has plenty of rumors to get his teeth into."

———

Whet-Iron frowned as he listened to Kuan Ying, the silk merchant, and Chou Pao, the basketmaker. He was still trying to do justice to the peach with which his cheeks were bulging: as he crunched its downy skin, his mouth was filled with the delicious juice. But the complaints of his two generals were turning the fruit to dust and ashes. Stiff and red-faced in their court dress, they were indignant at his having trusted someone like Ch'en Peacemaker. Imagine giving forty thousand pieces of gold to such a crook! And all because he was handsome, white-skinned, and fat. By all the devils, do you expect to find jewels inside a cap just because it's got a jade brooch on the outside? Peacemaker had lived off his sister-in-law and been driven out of the house when his brother found out he was being robbed. After knocking around for some time doing nothing in particular, he'd offered his services to Wei and been turned down. The same thing with Ch'u. He had taken refuge in Shu as a last resort. Did Whet-Iron know the rascal was taking advantage of his position in the army to extort bribes, assigning the worst chores to those who failed to pay? He must have amassed a nice little fortune.

"Don't forget he saved my life at Cranes' Gate!"

"Yes—and he betrayed his master at the same time!"

Whet-Iron reflected that he might indeed, as in the case of Plume, have put some of his eggs in other baskets, and resumed his ruminations, mulling over his setbacks and disillusions. Peacemaker had food for thought too: he was vexed at his master's change of mind. And the king's men pondered the trouble they'd taken and the dangers they'd faced. All of them were plunged in thought because hunger, herald of defeat, was on the prowl. When they ground their teeth, they could feel that their gums were swollen, and the only seasoning they could add to their meager broth was bitterness.

In the midst of all these musings a heavy train of supplies managed to get through Plume's blockade, its escort an army led by Chang the Good and Tattooed Face.

Rumination gave way to cheerful chomping as they all devoured meat, cracked bones, and much kale and cabbage. Wine and millet beer, and the singing and laughter they produced, made the soldiers forget their troubles for a while.

———

But this didn't banish Whet-Iron's anxieties. Unlike his men, he couldn't take refuge in the present and forget the future. And the outlook was still grim. When Tattooed Face went to see him, he was having his feet washed. Whet-Iron was rude, distant, haughty. Tattooed Face had done him a service by creating a diversion when Ch'in was being annexed, and the grain he had just brought was a great help in time of need—but Whet-Iron knew he wasn't a man of ideas. And the king was too worried about the future to be grateful for services rendered in the past. Tattooed Face, who hadn't seen Whet-Iron since the distribution of land, expected to be welcomed with open arms, and was chilled and disappointed by this unenthusiastic reception. He felt he'd been used. He'd lost everything: his kingdom had been invaded by Ch'u and his army defeated; Uncle Hsiang had wiped out his whole family—parents, wives, and children. And all for an ungrateful boor! And a fool into the bargain, who was in danger of losing the war!

———

In the staging post where he had set up his headquarters, Tattooed Face unburdened himself to Peacemaker, who had arrived just in time to stop the King of Nine Rivers from doing away with himself.

Peacemaker was astonished, and Tattooed Face told him what had caused his despair. Peacemaker added his own recriminations, and they joined together to work out plans for revenge. Why not take advantage of an audience to approach the king and cut off his head? They could then brandish it at Whet-Iron's terrified generals and urge them to go over to Plume. He would be grateful, give them appointments, restore their estates. Their plan, for all its boldness, was not unrealistic: many of Whet-Iron's officers were disaffected, and some doubted he could win. The army itself was in disarray and wouldn't oppose a coup.

———

The subject of the two plotters' discussion was closeted with Chang the Good, talking about *them*. Although he wasn't exactly ruminating in the intellectual sense, he was illustrating the second line of the relevant hexagram: *"His nose disappears as he bites the meat, but he escapes misfortune."* Whet-Iron's nose was buried in a large meat pie as round and smooth as a baby's bottom. Of course, some people might quote the commentators and say the image refers to the fate of a subordinate who usurps the privileges of his betters and gets let off lightly by merely having his nose cut off. This argument is backed by the fact that in the hexagram a feminine line overlaps a male line, like an inferior trying to climb above his superiors. But couldn't the image apply equally to a strong nose diving into soft pastry so that the teeth can get at the stuffing and the jaws chew it? Especially when the nose belonged to Whet-Iron, all of whose efforts were directed toward wresting power from the monarch currently ruling the Empire. As a matter of fact, Whet-Iron's action marked a change in the situation, as foretold in the hexagram. When his face emerged from the pie, he was smiling with satisfaction at something Chang the Good had just said.

———

"But, my dear Tattooed Face, what are you doing here in a staging post?" said Chang the Good. "We've been looking for you everywhere to show you to your apartments! Do you imagine the king is so ungrateful as not to provide you with more luxurious lodgings? Your coach awaits you below. Rest awhile to shake off the dust of your journey, and get your strength back for the banquet Whet-Iron has arranged in your honor."

Then, turning to Peacemaker:

"I'm delighted to find you here. The king is eager to make final arrangements for the business you discussed with him. The amount you mentioned is at your disposal. Of course you are cordially invited to the banquet: Whet-Iron means to distinguish you before all the court, so as to put a stop to any scandalmongering. After all," he said with a wink, "as the proverb says: *Who cares what color the cat is so long as he catches the rats!*'"

———

Chi Pu, the ambassador sent by Plume to tell Whet-Iron his mother had died in his camp, was ruminating on the implications of the tough, stringy pieces of meat that had been served him. He had noticed the servants' panic when they realized he was Plume's special envoy. They had hastily removed the ceremonial plate, rolled up the best mats, and taken away the cauldrons in which broth made from the three sacrificial meats was usually served. It was as if there'd been some mistake. Yet how was that possible? He had introduced himself as an emissary from Ch'u, and there was only one kingdom of Ch'u. But perhaps there were two ambassadors. . . . If so, who could have sent the other one? There were rumors circulating about Increaser. . . . Unless it was a maneuver on the part of the enemy, to create division among them: a ruse to imply that they had contacts with someone close to the king of Ch'u, whom they chose to honor in preference to him, Chi Pu. But Whet-Iron was so uncouth—would he have the presence of mind for such playacting when he'd just been stunned by the news of his mother's death? His sorrow seemed sincere. He'd presented a striking picture of filial grief, with a band of hemp around his head, his hair disheveled, and his left arm bare. He'd stopped hopping and beating his breast only in order to prostrate himself before visitors come to offer their condolences. His voice was one long wail; his eyes were gruesomely red from crying; he refused all food, even thin gruel. If he was showing more pain than he really felt, the effort involved in putting on such an exhibition would have left him little energy for concocting so wily a stratagem. Anyhow, Chi Pu's job was simply to report to his master. It was up to Plume to decide what to do.

———

Increaser had only a few stumps of teeth left. All he could eat was rice, exceptionally tender meat, very light white fish, and, in particular, fried stag. When this was ground up, flavored with honey, and dried, it formed a highly nourishing paste, rather like oakum, and melted in the mouth without having to be chewed. But now Plume could hear his adviser's six teeth being ground with rage. Increaser sensed that his master mistrusted him: on the pretext that he ought to be taking things easier, because of his age, he was being given fewer and fewer important responsibilities. And then there were all those rumors he could feel being whispered behind his back, those silences and meaning looks when he passed by.

"The Empire is quite peaceful," said Increaser bitterly. "You can take care of the business of governing it all by yourself. As you say, I am old and need rest. I'd be obliged if you would release me from my duties and allow me to end my days quietly at home, looking after my few acres of land."

Plume went on crunching the soft bones of a chick still in its shell. He was thinking of Joy, back in P'eng-ch'eng, kept away from him by this stupid siege. He made no objection to what Increaser said, and as the old man left, he almost envied him for being able to return to the capital, where his own beloved lived, while he himself was stuck here thousands of leagues away. He decided he'd join her if he didn't capture Yung-yang in the next four days.

————

The patriarch of Nest loved Plume like a son, and was appalled by his ingratitude. Throughout his journey he dwelt on his humiliation and resentment. They formed a sort of lump of pus in his mouth, which, when he swallowed, went down his gullet into his stomach, where it mingled with air and was expelled as explosive farts. But the mixture was so dense that some of it remained, and found its way through the intestines and up the spine, where it accumulated between the shoulder blades. And as he kept mulling over his wrongs, chewing them over night and day between his toothless jaws, the corrosive humors of indignation and rage grew into a mass, which erupted as an enormous tumor on his back. It was horribly painful, and the pain increased his resentment. When he drew near the hills that rose south of Nest and saw the cool terrace and dainty pavilions that Plume had built for Joy and Quicksilver, he remembered the princes of olden times who would sacrifice their favorites in order to regain the respect of the least of their vassals. But Plume would have no hesitation in killing the wisest of his counselors just to please his horse. What wouldn't he do for his concubine?

Brandishing his stick at Joy's summer residence, Increaser cried: "Plume will be conquered, not by Whet-Iron, but by you, Joy! By you!"

He was overcome by a fit of fury, and under the pressure the abscess burst. Black pus ran over his back and clothes; even his cap was splashed with it. And a gaping hole was left in his spine. He lost consciousness, and gave up the ghost before his retinue reached P'eng-ch'eng.

ORNAMENT

Fire at the foot of the mountain.

It is said that wise men are the ornament of Great Men. With the death of Increaser, Plume lost one of his finest jewels: a gem that had been worked on and improved with the years. Increaser's mind had been sharpened by long contact with men and events; time had strewn his beard with spangles of silver, and deposited the gold dust of experience in the depths of his heart. He could have brought his master a halo of glory. As it says in the second line of the hexagram: *"Flowered beard helps his prince to rise."*

But Plume had scorned him, either because he thought his own splendor might be outshone by so rich a setting, or because he was concerned exclusively with the other jewel in his crown.

For he possessed another treasure, whose chief value was its youth. Joy had the kind of beauty that needs no artifice, like a fine pearl or piece of jade that a wise jeweler refrains from setting or carving. Joy required no ceruse to whiten her skin, no ink to correct the curve of her eyebrows. Her lips were scarlet, her cheeks pink without the help of cosmetics. Yet, as a precious stone has to be extracted from the ore and polished, and as its splendor may be brought out by a beautiful setting, so Joy's loveliness was enhanced by fine ornaments. Thin rings of chased gold showed off the slenderness of her fingers; the tinkling of bracelets and earrings accentuated each graceful movement; tortoiseshell combs studded with pearls gleamed in her artfully disarranged hair; plumes made of kingfisher feathers swayed as she walked. She had silken shawls of many colors caressing her white neck; gowns of crepe or gauze; wide-sleeved jackets embroidered with water lilies and pheasants; long brocade belts with jade clasps; high-heeled slippers with turned-up toes; sachets of compressed perfume at her waist so that she floated about in invisible drifts of sweet nard and strong musk.

Less than two days after Increaser's death, Plume, tortured by the thought of his concubine, was back in the capital. He wanted to surprise her, so instead of going to the palace he went straight to the pavilion at Nest. Dismissing his escort as soon as he reached the hills, he galloped alone through the gardens to Joy's apartments. She was sitting with her back to the window, combing her hair, which fell down to the floor in a thick, shining mass. She saw Plume in the mirror, and turned and smiled at him. Neither hair nor teeth create beauty in themselves, but they do increase it. With that double row of pearls on a bed of coral, framed by the raven black of her hair, Joy was a living illustration of the words of the hexagram: *"Without any artifice her beauty is irreproachable. . . ."*

The hangings were like a cocoon of foaming silk. The counterpane surrounded her body with a thousand flowers and birds. Stretched languorously on curved pillows of whispering silk, she was clad in a beauty enhanced by passion alone. But passion alone was enough to anoint her with something richer than any cream, to flush her cheeks more sweetly than any powder, and to fill her eyes with an elixir, "gracious and moist," that nothing but love can distill. She was the only treasure worth the sacrifice of Plume's own life. She was more precious than the Empire, for she herself embodied all its wonders.

———

A woman is man's ornament when she is as light as the fire that burns off the scrub on the hill, making way for trees to green the steep black slopes. But an ornament that is too heavy can destroy what it is supposed to deck. From being his companion in pleasure and the delight of his nights, Joy became the very center of Plume's life. He had meant to pay her a brief visit, but he stayed with her for days that stretched into weeks.

———

The captains surrounding Yung-yang, deprived of their leader, lightened the siege, and Whet-Iron seized the opportunity to slink quietly out of the city one starless night, leaving behind his regal trappings, the gold-hung chariot, the Tiger Officers Guard, and the axes with crimson fringes.

It might have been thought that this pitiful escape, with Whet-Iron bereft of the splendid signs and ornaments of power, contradicted the current hexagrammatic trend. But in reality it had hidden and secret parallels with the six lines, as became clear a few months later in a nearby town and identical circumstances. Before they could become manifest, however, another latent modulation had to develop out of them with which the more obvious themes might braid the rope of destiny.

———

As soon as he was back within the passes, Whet-Iron organized new levies of troops, and he was gradually joined by the generals he had left behind in Yung-yang. Because he had always come off worst in direct confrontations with Plume, he decided to wear him out by operating on several fronts at once. If he was inferior to him as a general, he was infinitely better equipped in terms of supporters. A truly great sovereign's worth is brought out by the worth of his subordinates, and the brilliant and varied talents of Whet-Iron's followers added luster to his throne just as the jewels, rather than their setting, make up the value of a crown.

While he himself immobilized most of Ch'u's troops in a war of position, his lieutenants harassed the enemy on the borders. P'eng Yüeh was charged with ravaging the Sui valley. Trust and Ear joined to conquer Chao, then make contact with Yen and Ch'i and support subversion there.

———

Scrap stared haughtily at his aide, Count Military Greatness, and curled his lip disdainfully.

"I shall do nothing of the sort," he snapped.

"But don't you see," replied the other impatiently, "it's the only solution! How can you resist the onslaught of a victorious army? It has the great disadvantage of operating on uneven terrain thousands of leagues from its base. Let me attack its wagons and cut its supply lines, and I guarantee to defeat it in less than ten days. All you'll have to do is remain in your position."

"We've got two hundred thousand men, whereas the enemy claims to be putting fifty thousand in the field, which means not more than ten thousand. And yet you ask me to shy away from them! Do you want me to look ridiculous in front of the whole Empire? Anyway, a decent man fights openly; he doesn't resort to tricks and traps, even if they're to his advantage. When Confucius came across the hexagram Ornament, he frowned and said, 'Bad.' Tzu-kung, his disciple, was surprised. 'But it's supposed to be all right,' he said. 'White should be white and black black,' the Master replied. He meant it is always wrong to misrepresent the nature of something."

The authority of Confucius silenced Military Greatness.

As soon as he heard from a spy that that the count's suggestions had been rejected, Trust marched on the city, ambushed two detachments of household cavalry on its outskirts, and deployed a regiment before the citadel, with its back to the river. The next day he emerged through Rift-in-the-Wall valley with banners flying. It wasn't until then that the Chao army, hoping to capture the enemy generalissimo, burst out of the fortifications, leaving the city unprotected. Trust's troops recoiled and fell back behind the regiment by the river, which fought on with the energy of desperation. Meanwhile, the household cavalry managed to force its way through the Rift-in-the-Wall fortifications, tore down the Chao flags, and covered the city walls with two thousand banners of their own.

Scrap, unable to find the Han officers and seeing no hope of overcoming Trust's army, sounded the retreat. As his men withdrew, they saw that the whole city was draped with the red dragons of Han, which were like a sheet of flame devouring the ramparts. Thinking this meant that the city had fallen, Scrap's soldiers dispersed; their officers were powerless to stop them. Trust then counterattacked and cut off Scrap's head, and the entire Chao army laid down its arms.

When he saw the head of his former friend stuck on a pike, Ear couldn't help shedding tears, though he was grimacing with satisfaction at the same time. When asked about this, the graybeard explained:

"I rejoice in the death of an enemy and weep for the death of a sage. A man who scorned artifice is worthy of praise!"

"Rubbish!" cried Trust angrily. "Anyone who can't take advice from an intelligent subordinate is a fool! A man who rejects guile isn't fit to be a general. The whole art of war is based on deception. If his lordship wanted to remain pure, why didn't he become a hermit? You can't be a leader of men without soiling your hands. All this reminds me of Prince Sung, who brought his country to ruin because he wouldn't attack an enemy until he was lined up for battle. No, I have neither respect nor pity for men who deck themselves in the banners of virtue to hide their basic incompetence; all I feel for them is scorn and disgust. They're a disaster for their people if they're princes, and a bane to their masters if they're ministers. They're the pack asses got up in grand principles referred to in the first line of the hexagram: *'They abandon their coach in order to show off their fine shoes!'* But Count Military Greatness deserves to be spared. He isn't responsible for his master's foolishness, and though his services were worse than useless to an incompetent, they could add luster to an intelligent ruler."

———

Whet-Iron, encouraged by P'eng Yüeh's and Trust's successes, ventured too soon into a war of movement. He wanted to mass troops in Ch'eng-kao and take Plume from the rear, but his rival anticipated his maneuver, overcame P'eng Yüeh, captured Yung-yang, and laid siege to Ch'eng-kao. At this point Whet-Iron was short of men. Trust and Ear should have joined him before the troops stationed in the South did so, but they had lingered in Chao to pacify all the provinces, hoping to be able to use it as their own base.

So the King of the West was trapped again by the wretched Plume. And this time he had no army, apart from his bodyguard and the local garrison. As in Yung-yang, Whet-Iron gave way to despair. This greatly afflicted Chi the Sincere, the only high-ranking officer still with him. Chi loved Whet-Iron with a doglike devotion: before every battle he wept and wrung his hands and begged him not to run unnecessary risks. It was this devotion that had won him promotion, for his prowess as a warrior and his talent as a strategist were by no means distinguished. Whet-Iron's present anguish brought home to Chi his own uselessness and incompetence. He tried to cheer his master by pointing out that the situation wasn't hopeless: he could still count on the help of clever strategists like Chang the Good, Peacemaker, and Trust, who would find a way of extricating him. But Chi couldn't help remembering that he himself hadn't had a single real success in three years of campaigning, and that his rank and emoluments were far beyond his deserts.

The situation was urgent. Chi must find some subterfuge to get them out of the trap they had fallen into. His master's mind was a blank, and his own blanker still. But he did know a little about divination, and he decided to resort to that. When he came upon the Ornament hexagram, it seemed like a gift from heaven: here was a way of showing his fidelity to his lord by means of a great sacrifice, making up for the missed opportunity at Cranes' Gate. What he couldn't be in life he could become through his death: a jewel in the crown of the Great Man, even if he gleamed only for a moment before being swallowed in everlasting darkness. He hastened to show Whet-Iron the hexagram and explain his own interpretation of it.

" '*Fire at the foot of the mountain . . .*' A forest fire attacks everything indiscriminately. So we ought to spread confusion. The image can be broken down as follows: the lower part consists of a yin stroke between two yang strokes, making fire, which is brightness, shimmering, and beauty; the upper part consists of two yin strokes with a yang stroke, making mountain, the ornament of the Earth. Thus, '*the soft comes to the aid of the hard, and the hard alights on and adorns the soft.*' The present situation is approaching a crisis; the paroxysmic form of ornament is disguise. We are at war; armor is to a warrior what ornament is to a woman; thus women in armor and a subject disguised as his prince will bring about a satisfactory conclusion."

Whet-Iron believed in omens. He had no other suggestion to offer. He agreed to Chi's plan.

———

Sincere was haranguing two thousand girls on the parade ground. They'd been issued short trousers, leggings, and narrow-sleeved jackets. They also wore sharkskin breastplates and carried short spears and light shields of woven bamboo.

He began by threatening them, telling them how Master Sun had punished the king of Wu's concubines for laughing at such things by decapitating the two favorites, who'd been put in charge. Then he made them carry out maneuvers at the command of standards and drums, and taught them the rudiments of fighting with spears.

After three days' training, when they'd learned how to march in time, they were let out through the city gate at night, and the royal chariot followed them into the surrounding countryside.

Their ardor inflamed by their armor and their weapons, they fell on the enemy like she-wolves. It was as if the deceptive element in the hexagram were taking heart from its military disguise to fight against its own falsity. The women charged so fiercely, they recalled the elite Tiger Officers Guard.

Taking the enemy by surprise, they drove deep into his lines. Just as success was within their grasp—and revelation of their stratagem almost inevitable—the royal chariot gave the signal to withdraw. They faltered, and the Ch'u army gathered itself and counterattacked. Reinforcements came to their aid, and the female warriors, assailed on all sides, put up a fierce resistance. There was terrible hand-to-hand fighting. Helmets fell to the ground, armor was wrenched off. Then, about to run their adversaries through, the Ch'u soldiers saw. Cries went up everywhere: "They're women!"

At this, the women's military ardor vanished as if by magic: it was their military disguise that had transformed them into lionesses. The men laughed with relief. No longer afraid, they seized their enemies' weapons; some tried to take off their clothes. It ended as in the fourth line of the hexagram: *"All white and adorned, the horse gallops up. Is this war? No, a revel."*

By the flickering light of torches Plume's officers saw the royal chariot of Han, hung with yellow silk and with the great standard flapping: blazing suns on a ground of gules, quartered with phoenixes and dragons. A figure wearing a tall cap with twelve lappets leaned out of the chariot and cried:

"The city has no food left! There are no soldiers left! We tried a desperate sortie with the women, but it has failed. The king of Han surrenders to the king of Ch'u!"

The troops exploded with joy. Shouts echoed through the camp of the besieging army: "The king has surrendered! The king has surrendered! He hasn't any soldiers left but women!" And they left their posts and ran to a part of the wall from which they could enjoy the spectacle.

When the Ch'u army was concentrated around the eastern towers, a score of horsemen slipped out of Ch'eng-kao by the opposite gate and vanished into the night.

The yellow chariot was escorted to Plume's tent. The vanquished enemy alighted and crawled to the dais where the king of Ch'u sat. Plume signed to him to stand. Then he saw that, instead of Whet-Iron, it was Sincere.

"Where is your master?" he thundered.

"By now he'll have left the city!"

"War may depend on deception, but this is cheating and lying!"

And he ordered his guards to prepare the stake, and had Sincere burned alive. The flames adorned the neighboring hills with a bright and tragic beauty.

DIVESTITURE

Mountain resting on the earth: even if there is erosion,
the upper part lies on a stable base.

The rider stopping at the staging post of Military Preparation in Chao must have come a long way that day; his horse was exhausted, his clothes were covered with yellow dust. But he must be someone important, for his bearing and manners were those of a man accustomed to be obeyed.

He went up to his room without waiting for it to be ready, and ordered a meal, a bath, and maids to help him with his toilet. Everything about him suggested he was a royal messenger, so the landlord made no objection and did as he was told. When, a little while later, a servant took up the food, he was greeted by a pair of feet emerging from a bowl of water and being energetically dried by a couple of maids.

The courier rose before dawn, woke up the ostler to saddle his horse, and rode off like a fury toward the camp of King Ear and

General Trust. Presenting himself as a messenger from Whet-Iron, he was admitted into the camp—the entrance was made of two chariot shafts propped against one another—and went straight to the generals' tent. He crept into the room where the two leaders were sleeping, stole their seals of office, seized the supreme standard from where it stood in the middle of the camp, and waved it back and forth to summon the officers. When they were all gathered, he gave them their new orders.

Meanwhile, Ear and Trust had awakened. Finding their seals gone, they rushed out of the tent. They saw an imposing figure dressed in the madder gown of a high-ranking officer addressing the troops. The seals hung at his belt.

The two exchanged uneasy glances. At first Whet-Iron looked at them severely; then he smiled.

"So that's how you stand up your master, is it? I bet you were getting ready to celebrate my death!"

Their faces were covered with sweat as they prostrated themselves before their king and tried to excuse themselves. He cut them short.

"I was only joking," he said. "In war nothing happens as expected, and if I had to punish every mistake, I wouldn't have any officers left. Be that as it may, I'm taking over your army. I'm going to the defense of Three Rivers, which commands the entry to Ch'in. Ear, you're to watch over Chao, and Trust, you're to enroll all the eligible men not already in the army and march against Ch'i."

———

Master Li I-chi thought this would be a good opportunity to regain some of the esteem he'd lost in Whet-Iron's eyes because of his failures at Double Light and Yung-yang. Chang the Good was confined to his room with one of his terrible and mysterious attacks. Most of the king's other captains and advisers were away, either campaigning in the East or attending to supplies in the rear. Whet-

Iron himself was distraught after his latest setback. So the rhetor burst into his tent and addressed him boldly:

"Wei, Chao, and Yen are yours. Only King Kuang of Ch'i is still hostile. You have sent Trust to overcome him. But that was a great mistake! Ch'i is a strong country, and the T'ien family have been established there for centuries. King Kuang has two hundred thousand men massed at Passage, ready to face your army. He has a common frontier with Ch'u, which will certainly come to his aid. Even if Trust were victorious, the people of the peninsula are restless and fickle, and it will take years to pacify them."

Then, leaning toward Whet-Iron, he added:

"Besides, would it be a good idea to let yourself be eclipsed by the exploits of one of your own generals? It would be much better to send an ambassador to negotiate with Ch'i."

"But who could take on such a mission?"

"I'd take it as a favor if I might go."

———

It was the ninth month. The murky waters of the Yellow River reflected a leaden sky and flowed between poplars and willows stripped of leaves by the winter blasts. Floating bridges bobbed up and down on the waves as if in mute appeal for soldiers to cross them. But none did. Whet-Iron's secret envoy had been successful in his bargaining with Ch'i.

Trust stood on the bank and looked longingly toward the east, where the plain stretched away to the horizon. Turning back to his camp, he cursed the rhetor for cheating him of another success.

———

"I'm told you're abandoning your campaign—is that possible?"

Comprehension gazed with disappointment at the leader of the expedition to the East.

"Li I-ch'i and his sharp little tongue have been too quick for us," said Trust. "He's managed to extract the promise of an alliance from the king of Ch'i."

The scholar gestured toward the general's entourage. There might be spies among them—henchmen of the Minister of the Left, Ts'ao the Examiner, sent by Whet-Iron to keep an eye on him.

Trust asked everyone else to withdraw.

When he and Comprehension were alone, he gave free rein to his resentment. His own successes reflected on the king, and Li I-ch'i, the slimy rat, had taken advantage of the situation to deprive him of his rightful laurels. But he hadn't spent all his energy and faced all those dangers to let a suspicious monarch slink into his room while he slept and steal his seals of office.

Comprehension interrupted him.

"But why should you put a stop to the expedition?"

Trust was taken aback.

"Whet-Iron treats with King Kuang," the other went on. "All right—that's his business. But why should it affect you? You have a mission to carry out, and nothing should stop you except an order from your king himself."

Trust burst out laughing,

"And we'll make sure that no such message reaches us!"

Then he added: "Never let it be said that a scholar with no weapon but his tongue, and no protection but his wide sleeves, could conquer more cities in one day than I could in two years with an army of a hundred thousand men."

Trust's army had set up camp two days' march to the west of the Ch'i capital. Scented Grass and Offering of the Dragon, whom Plume had sent to Ch'i's aid after Trust captured Lin-tse, had established *their* camp to the south of Top Secret, where they were to effect a junction with King Kuang's two hundred thousand men.

They met to discuss their plan of campaign in a large tent decorated with the bright barbaric emblems of the Ch'u armies. In the dim and flickering light of lanterns, distorted by the night fog, these trappings looked even more strange and fantastic.

"We won't be able to stop Trust's army," said Scented Grass. "His soldiers are two thousand leagues from their base, and victory represents their best chance of ever going home. Our men, on the other hand, are fighting on their own ground, and as soon as they meet with a reverse they'll disperse and go back to their villages. So let us strengthen our positions. Meanwhile, the king of Ch'i will let the vanquished cities know he's still alive and fighting. If the people of Ch'i rebel, the enemy army's supplies will be cut off, and it will break up."

Offering of the Dragon frowned scornfully.

"I know Trust," he said. "He's weak. A man who's been kept by a washerwoman and groveled to a butcher is a fool and a coward. And if Whet-Iron's army surrenders without a fight, what credit will I get?"

Then he added:

"But if we fight, I'll grab half the kingdom of Ch'i."

Scented Grass had to give in.

Offering of the Dragon, having got his way on strategy, dismissed his lieutenant and went to bed. He was a stout man, and the bed was eaten up with rot: one of the struts broke as he lay down.

When Scented Grass heard of this incident from the general's orderly next morning, he made a face and quoted the second line of the Divestiture hexagram: *"The bed lacks its struts: destruction of perseverance: extremely inauspicious."*

———

From the top of the hill overlooking the river, the head of Trust's regiment of sappers looked down on the two armies: in the distance the soldiers looked like ants. After a heavy hail of arrows from the crossbowmen, he saw a mass of bright spots ford the river, gain the opposite bank, and fall to the ground, disappearing like snuffed-out torches. Then the colored dots returned like flying foam, pursued by other, darker, dots: the Ch'u army was making a counterattack. A third of them had already crossed the river when the leader of the sappers signaled with his flag to the men stationed on the sandbags damming the current. They *"raised the heavy strut that lay across the bed"* of the river, and the water rushed through the breach.

All the Ch'u soldiers crossing the ford were drowned, the regiments led by General Scented grass went over to the enemy, and the Ch'i troops still on the eastern bank surrendered without a fight or ran away.

———

"You know how fickle the people of Ch'i are," said the messenger. "They're always ready to cheat and intrigue and go over to whoever is stronger. Trust will never be able to keep them in order while he's only a minister. He needs more authority. That's why he's sent me to ask you to give him the temporary title of king."

King Whet-Iron was dumbstruck at first. His face turned red, and he began yelling: "To think that just as I'm up to the neck in muck, that fool of a Trust . . ." but he felt someone tread on his right foot and someone else nudge his left thigh. He looked in surprise at his two counselors, Peacemaker and Chang the Good, who stood on either side of him a little behind. He realized he'd been about to make a mistake, and changed tack: "That fool of a Trust asks only for a temporary title, after he's pacified three kingdoms and got me out of a hole. He ought to be given the full title once and for all!"

When Trust's messenger had withdrawn, Whet-Iron had a heated argument with his two advisers.

"I listened to you, but I don't know why I don't make mincemeat of that ass of an envoy while I'm waiting to get my hands on Trust himself and devour his liver. Not content with getting Li I-ch'i thrown into a cauldron of boiling oil, he now has to claim a kingdom, no less. If every general behaved like that, I wouldn't have a shirt to my back!"

"You're well rid of Li I-ch'i. He was only a schemer and a fool. Imagine him wanting to steal Trust's glory and get land from the king of Ch'i! He thought himself good enough to be a prince, when all he deserved was to end up in a stew."

Thus did Chang the Good settle his accounts with Li I-ch'i; he'd never liked having to share with him the reputation of being a shrewd politician.

"Why do you think people serve you?" he asked. "Out of the nobility of their hearts, or because they hope to get something out of it?"

Peacemaker backed him up.

"You complain about your subordinates' greed, but would they serve you at all if they were perfect saints? What dutiful son would trail around the Empire after you instead of looking after his aging parents? What man of integrity would agree to lie and intrigue as we do? What loyal subject would help you to seize what doesn't belong to you? Don't you see it's *because* they're mercenary that your followers serve you so well?

"Would you take into your army a paragon of loyalty and filial piety who had no military talent? You're not in so brilliant a situation that you can afford to do without the help of your best general. Anyhow, what could you do against him? The best thing is to agree to his request with a good grace. If he's king of Ch'i, he'll do all he can to hang on to it; otherwise he might turn against you. Remember the third line of the hexagram: *'He avoids misfortune by divesting.'* That's how one gains the support of one's subjects."

———

When he learned that Chang the Good had gone to Ch'i to give Trust his seals of office and Whet-Iron's congratulations, Comprehension's face lighted up. His smile grew broader when the arrival of an ambassador from Ch'u was announced. Trust now held the fate of the Empire in his hands.

As soon as Plume's envoy had gone, Comprehension asked for an audience at the palace. It was granted at once.

"Did Plume make overtures to you?"

"How did you guess?"

"What did he say?"

"He said the king of Han was insatiable, and his only thought was to strip all the princes of their kingdoms and and swallow up the whole Empire. He said I survived only because he was so afraid of Plume, and that as soon as *he* was eliminated, Han would get rid of me and take over Ch'i. Plume suggested that he and I should make an alliance and share the Empire between us."

"What did you say?"

"I refused."

The sage nodded toward the king of Ch'i's entourage.

"Couldn't we have a little more privacy?"

Trust dismissed his suite.

"Why didn't you agree?"

"I didn't really refuse. I asked for time to think it over."

"I was once taught the art of physiognomy. I can read people's fates in their appearance—their bones, their complexion, their figure."

"And what does my appearance tell you?"

"Face to face I see merely a marquisate that will bring you only misery, but when you turn your back I divine unimaginable glory and distinction!"

"Explain!"

"When the rebellion began, thousands of remarkable men rose up with the sole idea of throwing off their yoke. People got on with one another, they clung together like clouds, they were as close as scales on a fish. Bands of brave men swept back and forth across the Empire like gusts of wind. Then Ch'in disintegrated; there was land to be had; the leaders competed with one another for the remains of the Empire. Plume and Whet-Iron emerged from among the rest, and now the struggle between them soaks the country in blood without ever settling the issue. Whet-Iron has lost all his battles; he was miserably defeated at Yung-yang and Ch'eng-kao. Now he's lurking beyond the river with neither courage nor strength. As for Plume, for all his power and prestige, he's no good at choosing generals, so he too has suffered bloody reverses and was unable to press home his advantage and get through the passes. After three years of continual fighting he's at the end of his tether. His people are exhausted and his granaries empty.

"Neither of these two has the makings of a real king. Neither is strong enough to put an end to the war. And now their fate is in your hands and yours alone. If you favor Whet-Iron, the Empire is his. If you take Plume's side, he can strip Whet-Iron of all he owns. But if you remain neutral, they'll have to give you part of the spoils. The Empire will be as firm as a cauldron on its three legs. Neither of them will dare attack you, for fear of your making an alliance with the other. You'll have a strong territorial base and a large army, and if you rule wisely, you'll control both Chao and Yen, and the whole Empire will look to you."

"It would be a dangerous decision to make, though, and might anger Whet-Iron without surely pleasing Ch'u. I'd rather temporize. Let's wait and see what happens."

"Be careful, though. Heaven punishes those who don't take what it offers, and woe to the fool who doesn't seize his opportunity! Don't put off your decision too long!"

The rhetor took his leave and strode out of the palace. He was extremely disappointed and annoyed. At the door, a woman in the holiday dress and apron of a peasant from Huai was arguing with the guards, who wouldn't let her in. Comprehension noticed her hands, red and swollen from housework, but, although he was usually very observant, he went on his way without seeing the shiny green-and-white octagonal brooch on her jacket.

Trust had meanwhile changed his mind, and he started to go after his counselor, but his attention was caught by the sound of the quarrel. He was about to shout to the guard to chase the intruder off with their pikes when he recognized her as the washerwoman from Huai-yin. He signed to the guards to let her pass, and led her to the audience chamber. There she took a purse full of gold from her sleeve and threw it at the king's feet.

"Did you think you were repaying your debt by sending me this?" she cried angrily. "Didn't I tell you I didn't want any reward for what I did for you? If you really wish to show your gratitude, do me a favor. See that you don't disappoint my trust by acting contrary to virtue or morality. Be a faithful servant to our prince, Whet-Iron, the hope of the people of the Empire."

And, having given back the purse and had her say, she turned on her heel and left.

The next day Comprehension returned to the charge.

"What's the use of having a brilliant mind if you don't have the willpower to do what it tells you? A tiger which hesitates is weaker than a wasp which stings; a frisky thoroughbred is less reliable than a nag that scents its stable. Action is everything. And knowing how to pounce on one's prey. Strip the others before they strip you!"

But this time he met with a flat refusal.

"I served under Plume, and the best he could do in return was make me a captain of the king's Guard. I was just a spear-carrier! He would never listen to my advice, still less adopt my plans. That's why I abandoned Ch'u for Whet-Iron. Without even putting me to the test, *he* made me general over all his armies. I've worn his clothes and eaten his food; it's thanks to him I am where I am now. If I betray someone who's shown me such kindness and friendship, I'll call down the punishment of Heaven. No, I couldn't go back on my allegiance, even if it meant being stripped of my land and my life!"

"Nonsense!" said the counselor severely.

"I owe too much to the king of Han," said the king of Ch'i with some embarrassment, as if he were ashamed of his own rectitude. "There's a proverb that says, *'If you've shared someone's chariot and food, you should share his trouble and toil.'* I can't turn my back on principle just for the sake of profit."

"I suppose you think that by being loyal to your master you'll win his sympathy and ensure the safety of your descendants. How wrong you are! Were there ever greater friends than Scrap and Ear, before they became important? The bonds that united them were supposed to be stronger than life or death. But as soon as they were bitten by the desire for glory, a mere peccadillo was enough to set one against the other, and they fought mercilessly until one of them had his head cut off. Isn't it comical? And what's it all for? It's because men are consumed by ambition, and because there are few dispositions that can resist the temptation of a throne. Remember the tragic example of Chung, a senior officer murdered by his master as soon as he'd got what he wanted. *'When there's no more game they cook the dogs,'* as the saying has it. A subject who makes his ruler fear him puts his life in danger. If you turn toward Ch'u, he will mistrust you; if you remain loyal to Han, he will be afraid. And you have too much power and glory to stay as you are. The last line of the Divestiture hexagram says: *'He doesn't bite the fine fruit: if he's a prince he will live in style; if he's a yokel he'll lose the roof from over his head.'* When you give, you get something back only if you've got something already."

"I have qualms of conscience about betraying a benefactor. I can't make up my mind to it just like that!"

"How wrong I've been about you! Your behavior toward the butcher from Huai-yin was just what it seemed—the instinct of a coward! Your present dignity can't make up for it. On the contrary! If you'd refused all honors and publicity and advancement, it might have been seen as one of the highest forms of self-respect, of lofty and firm belief in one's worth, unmoved by setbacks, by other people's contempt, or even by one's misdeeds. If you'd done that, you'd have been one of those proud beings who rightly consider themselves better than everyone else. If the whole Empire had been too small to contain your ambition; if, not content with being great, you had wanted to be equal to Heaven, vast as the firmament, bright and solitary as the sun, then what you did would have had another meaning. For un-bounded ambition, like excessive pride, exempts a man's deeds from the judgment of his fellows. But you . . . by remaining satisfied with a meager kingdom, you show that you seek honors merely to impress washerwomen and dog-killers! How feeble! How low! You demean yourself by needing other people's esteem."

"I'd demean myself much more by stealing from someone who has given to me!"

"What craven talk is that? If you let Whet-Iron strip you of your wretched kingdom, you'll lose all the dignity you've acquired so painfully, and die amid the scornful laughter of the whole Empire."

Whereupon Comprehension bowed curtly and left. Trust was too taken aback to tell his henchmen to seize the impertinent wretch at once and put him to death. As soon as he was outside the palace, the rhetor dived into an alley, took off his robe, his cap, and his sandals, loosened his hair, and covered his body and face with mud. Then he started wandering around the market, half-naked and gibbering.

By the time the king of Ch'i's guards started to look for him, Comprehension had vanished.

RETURNING

Success. One can safely entertain people;
    the visits of friends will have
    no undesirable consequences.
He retraces his steps,
    for seven days is always the time for returning.
It is a good thing to have a goal.
Thunder in the bosom of the Earth:
The ancient kings used to close the passes at the winter solstice;
    no one went on journeys
    and the ruler did not inspect the provinces.

There had been a change in the balance of power, though it could not be explained in terms either of one particular event or of a combination of factors. It was simply that the new configuration lent everything that happened a meaning that was slightly threatening for Plume. As always, facts were signs rather than causes.

P'eng Yüeh had started raiding again in Wei, and was wrecking the lines of communication. Fortunate, at the instigation of Trust and with the aid of the regional worthies, was trying to found a new independent kingdom in the south of Ch'i, on the Huai. His former supporters, regarding this alliance as a betrayal, were restless. And these local disturbances made it difficult to collect the goods and taxes necessary for the war effort.

Eventually Plume, facing Whet-Iron outside Ch'eng-kao, became uneasy. Handing the defense of the citadel over to his two generals—the former directors of Criminal Affairs in Yüeh-yang and Ti, who had aided him in the past—he ordered them to refuse battle and merely hold their positions until he had worsted P'eng Yüeh and pacified all Liang. He would be back inside a week.

While Plume was turning in the direction of Ch'en-liu, Wai-huang, and Sui-yang, Whet-Iron was provoking the Ch'u army. Plume's two officers bore the taunts of their enemies unflinchingly for a few days, until they could stand them no longer and sallied forth to do battle. But they were so cruelly defeated and humiliated that they cut their own throats. Whet-Iron entered the city, seized all the wealth the king of Ch'u had stowed there, and encircled General Chung-li Mo on the outskirts of Yung-yang.

This was a serious reverse for Plume, but he had experienced setbacks before: hadn't his capital been sacked, the East laid waste several times, and Wei conquered? At the worst, this mishap merely forced him to return to the West before he had settled P'eng Yüeh's hash. As suggested in the third line, *"He frowns and turns back: danger but not disaster."* As soon as news of his approach became known, Whet-Iron fled to the hills and stayed there. They were back where they were before.

If all these contretemps reflected a great lack of talent among Plume's supporters, they also resulted from his own excess of it. All too self-sufficient, he exemplified the line *"Though he marches forth among others, he returns alone."*

———

The essential change in the situation consisted in the inability of either protagonist to break out of his current position. They could only mark time. All their maneuvers swiftly took them back to where they started. It was as if everything were trapped in the icy grip of the eleventh month, which *"imprisons the thunder in the bosom of the Earth."* But this immobility, far from being a temporary suspension of movement, was really the most concentrated phase of action itself. Great changes were evolving in the cold dark underground cave where dragons coil among the secret springs, just as the advent of spring is prepared in the heart of winter and the darkness of the solstice. A multitude of comings and goings heralded a swing of history's pendulum.

Meanwhile, the fighting went on, with its train of massacre and death. Bodies returned to the earth and changed back to dust. Flesh decomposed and blood soaked into the soil, descending through layers yellow and black, fine and coarse, to dissolve deep down in the hidden green, brown, and red springs that color all vegetation.

The shamans summoned by the families of the dead went to the rooftops and cried, "Soul, return! Soul, return!" Their cries echoed through the pure, barren winter air, the icy air no longer warmed and vivified by lightning. But the souls had departed on a journey from which there was no return. They were vanishing into the cruel gaping maws of the monsters that live on the borders of existence, or sinking into the sands of eternal night. And however much sorcerers and priests and their own relations shouted themselves hoarse in the cold air, the souls did not come back: they were *"lost on the way back"* in conformity with the last line of the hexagram and the *"disastrous omens of final military defeat and of great misfortune for the ruler."* There were a multitude of disturbing signs: giant rainbows with crimson or purple halos; monstrous stars winking over the West; celestial bodies falling over Ch'u; unicorns fleeing to the West. The prediction might apply to all the war chiefs, but it seemed aimed especially at Plume, who had authority over the Empire and was regarded as the one mainly responsible for all the slaughter. So it was his destiny, rather than anyone else's, that had undergone an imperceptible but decisive change. This showed itself in the form of a vague uneasiness, a disinclination to fulfill his raison d'être—which was to kill.

He was irked by the way he and his enemy kept being forced back to their original positions. He liked war to produce the unexpected. That gave him the feeling that he could snatch a measure of virgin time from fate and mark it with his own signature.

Plume's lack of interest in the matter at hand was also evident in his obsessive fear that something might happen to Joy if he wasn't there. Because he felt she was safe only with him, his concubine accompanied him on all his campaigns; she filled the void left by his distaste for military operations.

And there was an even more obvious sign of the change that had taken place in him—a revolution all the more momentous because it masqueraded as political expediency.

The city of Wai-huang held out for several days before it surrendered, and this unusual resistance made Plume furious: when it did capitulate, he resolved to put every inhabitant over the age of fifteen to death. But as the prefect's adolescent son was being taken from his father and put among those to be spared, the boy managed to attract Plume's attention and spoke to him. He pointed out that Wai-huang had yielded to P'eng Yüeh only because it had been forced to. If the king of Ch'u, whom it had looked to as a liberator, now acted as its executioner, none of the fortresses that had gone over to Whet-Iron's general would want to return to the fold. It was the old argument of the rhetors, but coming from one so young it made an impression on Plume. He objected for form's sake:

"Everyone would think I was weak if I went back on my decision."

The boy smiled, bowed, and responded thus:

"Confucius said of his favorite disciple: 'He is all but perfect. He always knows when he has made a mistake and hastens to repair

226

it. As it says in the *Book of Changes,* *"He turns back in time; no regrets; highly favorable."* ' "

The quotation overcame Plume's last reservations, and for the first time in his career he did not massacre the population of a place he had had to fight against. Other towns vied with each other now to surrender, and Plume's entourage rejoiced and thought he had acted wisely. But they were wrong. His magnanimity was unsound. A man who owes his triumphs to violence cannot convert to kindness with impunity. His gesture was seen as an admission of weakness. By putting himself on the same footing as his rival, he appeared his inferior. Worse still, his clemency showed to what extent his determination was undermined by a desire for peace. People could say with reason that Whet-Iron had won, by taking possession of Plume's soul if not of his kingdom.

——

There were other, intangible and evanescent, symptoms of this imperceptible but decisive turn of fortune. They belonged more to the order of rumor than of fact, but for that very reason they were more convincing. As all things turn toward the yang at the winter solstice, though no pressure is put upon them, such is the power of the current configuration that it *"summons without calling and dismisses without sending away. It is dark and muddled; no one knows where it comes from; yet through it everything happens."* And the Return of the Strong, expressed misleadingly on the human plane by kindness, was inevitable, because it obeyed the laws of the cosmos. *"Returning follows the cycle of heaven,"* as it says in the *Book of Changes.*

Various insidious events helped to bring this about, as shadowed forth in the hexagram: *thunder,* which is movement, *beneath the earth,* which is restraint. Shadows were at work underground. The sect of the soothsayers was said to be active again. There was a smell of secret confabulations in the air, a permanent whispering coming from dark corners. Yet as soon as anyone tried to listen, all was silence. As soon as anyone tried to distinguish those vague shapes, they vanished into the gray of winter.

All this might have been put down to imagination, to illusion conjured up by the strain of apparent immobility, if one of the squalid mud huts that clung like a disease to the walls of the capital of Ch'i hadn't been the scene of a certain strange meeting, which brought together the most venerable soothsayers, physiognomists, geomancers, and astrologers in the Empire. Anyone familiar with the secret motions that prepare the future would have recognized the figures in this learned assembly, sitting among the cabbage leaves and fish bones and bits of broken pottery. One was Wandering Hill, a former fellow student of Sky Blue, whom Whet-Iron had made prime minister of Chao (he was expert in the arts of divination, and observed the cyclical alternations of the elements). There too were Masters Extension, Millet, and Light, all members of the Great Ridgepole sect, as were Liu Ramble, Whet-Iron's younger brother, and Why, passionate consulter of yarrow and annotator of the *Book of Changes*. Also to be seen there were Culmination, who had done the state of Ch'in some service; his assistant was a hunchback, Barbarian's former jester, recommended to Culmination by fencing master Chiu. Just visible in the gloomy northwest corner of the room was an extraordinary long, thin countenance with a high, bulging, wizened forehead reminiscent of some pallid mountain peak: this was Master Yellow Stone. He merged so completely with the roughcast wall that he might have been dismissed as an optical illusion were it not for some slight tremors—but might not even they have been due to the flickering of the light? The real or imaginary face was gazing mockingly at another person, whose words were making him shake his head doubtfully. This person was a poor fortune-teller in a patched and dirty sorcerer's robe. He had so grimy a face that his features could not be descried. Anyone who took the trouble to examine him carefully, however, would recognize Understanding, returned to his original profession.

He had seen that Trust would never have the nerve to turn against Whet-Iron, and that the alternative of the Three and the One would never be anything but one of History's unrealized potentialities. He had been obliged to admit that fates were already fixed, and so had left the Ch'i court to pronounce oracles in the marketplace. Some people said he was crazy, others said he was a saint. Because it was a good time for contacts—witness the third line in the relevant hexagram: *"One can safely entertain people; the visits of friends will have no undesirable consequences"*—he took up with the soothsayers again and organized a grand reunion in his own den.

It was impossible to make out what was being said there: everybody was talking at once, regardless of whether anyone was listening. The clucking of the hens running about the room, the howls of hungry babes, and the sound of raised voices coming from neighboring shacks drowned all the monologues in the familiar, soothing racket of poverty. Yet every so often a phrase tinged with both mystery and menace could be heard.

"The cauldron has lost one of its legs. . . ."

"As the movement ends with six, seven is the first again. . . ."

"The seventh from the longest is still the shortest containing the longest. . . ."

But these absurd-sounding phrases had a practical application. An exceptionally sharp ear might have discerned, enveloped in hexagrammatic formulas and almost swamped by the racket from the street outside, some forthright judgments on the protagonists of history.

"The deadlock is Plume's fault, not Whet-Iron's. . . ."

"He's trying to draw it out because victory would be as fatal for him as defeat. It would mean the end of war, and that is what he dreads; war is life itself to him. . . ."

"Yes, he's in a very awkward position. He needs successes, but not anything decisive. . . ."

"Which is why he's always let Whet-Iron escape!"

"So the stag of the Empire must be his, not despite but because of his failures. . . ."

"The world needs a man of peace. The six dragons have made up their minds at last. . . ."

"Good omens are beginning to appear. . . ."

"The monster won't confound divination forever!"

"Let's undermine his morale by spreading predictions of woe!"

OPENNESS

*Openness is a noble, great, and profitable characteristic,
but used wrongly it can produce unfavorable signs;
and then nothing good can be attempted.*

Vast War Pass was walled in on each side by steep hills and open above only to a narrow chink of pale sky. The ravine was edged with black both east and west by Plume's and Whet-Iron's fortifications —crenellated walls bristling with pikes and banners. Protruding rocks intercepted the sunlight, causing the pass to be always in semidarkness even at noon. The sides of this gash in the earth's flesh were as steep and naked as a hyena's vulva, and sometimes from its depths the stars of the Wolf and the Crossbow could be seen twinkling like a pair of malevolent eyes.

Today, however, the murky gorge was brightened by two red trails, one crimson as blood, the other orange as flame, descending slowly, the first from the east and the second from the west, in a splash of colors and a rustling of fabrics. The two processions and their motley trains came to a halt on opposite sides of the stream that ran through the bottom of the ravine. Whet-Iron leaped from his curly chestnut on the right bank while Plume, on the left, dismounted from Quicksilver, his proud white, black-maned charger. At a sign from their leaders, the standard-bearers and Tiger Officers retired and arranged themselves in an arc on their respective slopes. The enemies advanced and bowed to one another across the stream. They eyed one another thoughtfully for a moment, perhaps remembering their first meeting, in days when they were only minor leaders who had taken to one another and fought shoulder to shoulder. But six years had passed since then, six years that had been enough to clothe both of them in the red tunic of kings, and to dig an abyss between them even deeper than the one that now separated their two camps. Time had left its mark on their flesh as well as on their positions and their relationship: Whet-Iron's hips and waist were thicker, and it was a portly, almost potbellied figure, weighed down with years and importance, who faced his adversary. Plume's once rosy cheeks were now quite crimson, as if flecked by the blood he'd spilled. The physical changes each saw in the other gave them an acute sense of fleeting time, just as the wake left by junks on the Great River bears witness to their swift motion.

Plume was the first to break the silence. He spoke with feeling. Perhaps the narrow, tomblike valley filled him with secret dread; perhaps the babble of the rushing brook reminded him of time's flight; perhaps, deep down, he had a vein of sentiment in his character. Whatever the explanation, he opened his heart warmly and sincerely to Whet-Iron. He recalled their former friendship, when, under his leadership, they'd put the East of the Empire to fire and slaughter. Why, when they had once shared the same griefs and the same joys, should they now oppose one another? Didn't this reduce them to the same level as people like Ear and Scrap? By squabbling like jackals over wretched bits of land, they were in danger of becoming the laughingstock of the Empire, though once they had been its terror. It was time to end this stupid conflict: after all, the world was big enough to hold them both. He was ready to forgive Whet-Iron, and even to hand over all the provinces west of Vast War Pass if he would accept his supremacy. If not, let them settle the matter in single combat, so that their rivalry might trouble the people no longer.

Coming from the fiery Plume, the suggestion of a duel was not so much a show of hostility as an offer of reconciliation and a token of esteem: for him, peace and jousting were one and the same. But his rival—was it from fear or did he misunderstand deliberately?—took his proposal amiss. Whet-Iron, with a stern expression, delivered a rebuff: a genuine Great Man relied on intelligence rather than force, and a king worthy of the name fought not with his own hands but with those of his subjects. Plume had been talking like a roughneck or a braggart.

The blood rushed to Plume's face. It was Whet-Iron who had asked for this interview, in order to negotiate a compromise, and he, Plume, who had been kind enough to agree. True, the main reason had been his own situation: his troops were exhausted by an unending series of campaigns, and his supplies were threatened by raids by enemy generals right in the middle of his own territory. But that did not mean he was prepared to swallow snubs from someone who was really a petitioner! The resentment that had accumulated within him as a result of their quarrel overwhelmed his earlier impulse toward sympathy for a former comrade. The veins in his neck swelled with rage, and he told Whet-Iron just what he thought of him:

Not content with enjoying the title king without having done anything to deserve it, Whet-Iron had laid claim to Ch'in on the grounds that he had been the first to cross the passes. But would he have been able to advance an inch if he, Plume, hadn't conquered the hordes of Chang Han? Plume had had Whet-Iron's life in his hands several times, but each time he had allowed him to live. Remember the banquet at Cranes' Gate, and the siege of Yung-yang!

"You are base and ambitious, and for you there's no such thing as either good faith or gratitude. Far from feeling any obligation because of my kindness, you've always betrayed your duties as a friend and a subject and tried to aggrandize yourself at my expense. You're also an unnatural father and a bad son. In a moment of panic you were prepared to sacrifice your own children, and you wouldn't have hesitated to eat your father's flesh if it could have won you the Empire. You act the man of integrity only as a matter of expediency: not long ago you were murdering the inhabitants of any city you conquered, raping the women, burning the crops, looting and kidnapping like the brigand you really are. Today you have a weakness for scholars; only yesterday you couldn't stand the sight of them. Mere playacting, on the part of an old scarecrow who wants to get hold of chestnuts that other people have pulled out of the fire! You're a nasty, greedy old thief and a fifth-rate general! Why should I listen to a word you say?"

Whet-Iron straightened his tunic, put on a solemn, dignified expression, pointed an accusing finger, and launched into a diatribe of his own:

"Miserable ruffian, you always reduce everything to sordid personalities! Heaven gave you authority, and you didn't know how to use it. Haven't you heard that *'Heaven withdraws its support from a man without integrity, and sends him disastrous omens'*? And the list of your crimes and infamies is so long that if I had to name them all, the stream at your feet would have frozen three times before I reached the end.

"In order to take over Sung the Just's post as head of the Ch'u army, you accused him of being a traitor and had him put to an ignominious death. You rushed across the passes to take my possessions away from me. You want to get hold of the whole Empire for yourself, and yet if anyone tries to defend his own, you accuse him of greed! You're worse than a wolf!

"Everywhere you go you leave death and desolation behind you. You can do nothing but pillage and kidnap, burn and massacre. You have the soul of a brigand, and almost make people wish they could have the Great Emperor and Barbarian back again!

"You're a butcher dripping with gore from head to foot! After murdering Sung the Just, you kept up the good work by slaying Ch'in's two hundred thousand soldiers after they'd surrendered, outdoing in ferocity even General Peace of Arms, of sinister memory! You treacherously poisoned the king of Han, drove the Emperor Spirit from his kingdom, and had him executed by your henchmen. You're a traitor and a regicide!

"Greedy dog! After dispossessing your sovereign, you couldn't wait to seize the former kingdoms, keeping everything for yourself and giving nothing to anyone else. You're a stupid and avaricious brute, and your monstrous misdeeds alienated the Empire and made it choose me to defend it against your rapacity. So it was in answer to the call of both gods and men that I raised an army and look forward to punishing you as you deserve. But how can such a ruffian as you understand that anyone can be motivated by concern for the common good and not by personal ambition?"

Whet-Iron was one of those people who have the wonderful gift of always believing in what they say and do. So what was intended as no more than a rhetorical introduction became in the process of being spoken the speaker's real meaning. It was as if the longer he went on, the more he convinced himself of his rival's villainy. He ended by making a real indictment, and got so carried away that he was actually insulting the person he'd meant to come to terms with.

Plume gave as good as he got.

"Crow in phoenix feathers!"

"Tortoise in dragon's scales!"

"Rope-maker's fart!"

"Loser's turd!"

And so the two negotiators railed at one another across the stream, faces red, necks outstretched, flapping their stiff silk sleeves at one another like a couple of fighting cocks, until Plume, exasperated to the point of madness, lost patience, picked up a large rock, and flung it wildly at Whet-Iron. It hit him right in the chest and knocked him to the ground, and while Whet-Iron's guard gathered around the motionless form, Plume got on his horse, rejoined his escort, and rode back to his camp.

Whet-Iron, lying supine, should have found himself gazing at a narrow strip of pale blue, but, instead, what met his eyes was an expanse of blackness dotted with specks of light. Gradually the darkness changed into a wan half-light in which throbbed two large stars. His chest was pierced by a sharp pain, like that of an arrow: an arrow shot from the Crossbow, he thought, the unlucky star that hung, with the Wolf, over the ravine. Then he noticed a severe white face bending over him. He heard it murmur the last line of the Openness hexagram: "*Too much sincerity is harmful.*" Chang the Good, looking down with a puzzled and disapproving expression, put a hand over his king's mouth to stifle his cry of pain.

"Don't let anyone guess how seriously you're hurt," he whispered in Whet-Iron's ear. "It would have a terrible effect on the army's morale!"

The king, responding almost instinctively, called out, "Ow! My ankle—I think it's broken!"

"Fortunately, the king isn't really hurt," said Chang jubilantly, for the benefit of the escort. "It was the surprise that made him lose his balance, that's all. He twisted his foot as he tried to right himself, and he's only stunned by his fall."

Reassuring the bystanders with more soothing phrases, Chang helped the king to his feet and hoisted him into his saddle.

The ride back was torture for Whet-Iron. Clinging to his horse's mane as it jolted painfully up the steep rocky path, he could feel his face twisting and sweat pouring down his forehead as he bit back howls.

As soon as he reached camp, he made for his tent, to lie down, but Chang the Good trailed after him, scolding:

"Come, a little more courage and dignity! You must stay on your feet and review the troops if you want them to be properly reassured."

236

"Do you want to kill me?"

"I thought *you* wanted the Empire!"

"Have you no mercy? I'm dying! I'm spitting blood!" wailed the king.

"The army will be in disarray if they find out. Do you want the enemy to take advantage of their confusion?"

"Leave me alone! I need rest. You're not the one who's suffering, and you're heartless, pitiless! You don't even know what it means to live. You've never loved anybody except your precious Master Yellow Stone. . . . No wonder you're hard!"

The minister's mouth twisted in a curious smile. His lips first opened and then closed, as if to retain some momentous secret of which they were the guardians. All they allowed to escape was a sigh—a fleeting breath of a wordless mystery that lingered for a moment like the scent of absence, and then was caught up in caustic utterance.

"Allow me to be frank. Why do you think I serve you? Because of your worth? Why, you're a coarse, stupid brute—eaten with ambition but without the talent or stature that should go with it! Are you conceited enough to think it's your virtue that has won you the support of your betters? No! It was despite or perhaps even because of your mediocrity that I took you for the chosen instrument of fate. What I admired in you was not yourself, but the mission you were entrusted with, which, while it annihilated you as a person, sublimated you as a Great Man. But the fulfillment of Heaven's purposes must not be prevented by the unworthiness of Heaven's instrument."

He brought his face close to that of the king.

"Wet hen trying to act like fighting cock! Do you think an Empire can be won without some tears and sweat? Get up, you fat lump! Or do I have to *kick* your royal backside into the saddle?"

By dint of pushing and pulling, he got Whet-Iron, stupefied with pain and mortification, back on his horse. Then he gave the animal a thump, and it set off at a gallop through the camp. As he was swept back and forth, pale, in front of his troops, Whet-Iron's groans were greeted with enthusiastic cheers.

———

While Whet-Iron was galvanizing his men with sounds worthy of a castrated boar, Plume, when he got back from the interview, worried his generals by going to bed. His face was drawn, his expression melancholy, and he refused to eat. Even Joy's singing and playing failed to cheer him up. He was suffering from a malady—referred to in the fifth line of the Openness hexagram—that only time can cure: hurt pride. Whet-Iron's words had wounded Plume's spirit much worse than Plume's stone had injured Whet-Iron's flesh.

And while the sensitive warrior refused to leave his room, strange rumors began to spread throughout the Empire. They soon reached the army, where both officers and men believed them, for their general's odd behavior seemed to corroborate them. So although it was Whet-Iron's supporters, with their leader really hurt and writhing on his couch with an injured chest, who should have been dreading disaster, it was Plume's camp that was haunted by presentiments of defeat, as if *"his frankness had brought him bad luck,"* as it said in the last line of the hexagram.

A story ran through all the provinces that said Plume had tried to murder King Whet-Iron during a peaceful meeting in the Vast War Pass valley, shooting an arrow at him from a bow hidden under his armor; but a ray of light from the star of the Wolf had diverted it, and a mystic dart from the star of the Crossbow had transfixed the traitor. The astrologers had observed a halo around the two stars the previous night. Scholars and soothsayers recalled ancient predictions said to emanate from the Trigrams, or even from Confucius himself: "The sky is below, the earth is above; stars appear in broad daylight: the winding Arrow glides to the west; the eye of the Wolf begins to shine, the Crossbow begins to plot." The prediction had already been applied to the fall of the Ch'in, but it was just as valid for the struggle between the two pretenders to the land beneath the

238

sky. When Plume, hastening from the east to the aid of the Great Stag, had defeated Chang Han's armies, a falling star with a pointed top and a plumed tail like an arrow had looped across the sky toward the west. It was one of the comets known as "winding arrows" that heralded ruin for the country toward which it headed, while its meandering trajectory reflected a lack of straightness on the part of the person who was to inflict the disaster. When Plume destroyed the Ch'in army and entered Double Light, he had left ruin and desolation in his wake; and the devious trick he had played on his enemy resembled the comet's twisted flight. Although Whet-Iron was the embodiment of fire, as ruler of the western lands of the Empire he was symbolized astrologically by the constellations in the western quarter of the sky. So he enjoyed the help of the Crossbow and the Wolf in the matter of the kingdom of Ch'in: their unwonted appearance in the sky foretold the protection they would afford him. Other signs acted as confirmation: when he entered Ch'in, the Five Planets were arranged in the constellation of the Well, one of the astronomical reference points of the country. Calculation had demonstrated that the planets had arrived in this mansion after having followed the motions of Jupiter. The ruler of the country above which the Five Planets grouped themselves after Jupiter attracted all the lords of the Empire to him by his rectitude . . . And who was the lawful king of Ch'in but Whet-Iron, according to the agreement signed by all the princes. The stars did not lie. The signs were crystal clear. Everything heralded the advent of Whet-Iron.

But if the stars in their courses infallibly portray the future of nations, that which is to come is also heard from the mouths of babes and sucklings, whose innocence and frankness make them the special spokesmen of fate. And now, as the little boys with shaven heads and the little girls with braids hopped and skipped in the marketplaces, their piping voices shrilled out rhymes that rejoiced in the coming downfall of the wicked Ch'u.

GREAT ACCUMULATIONS

It is good to abstain from family meals.
Crossing a great river brings advantages.

The Great Accumulations hexagram is simply the Openness hexagram the other way up. Although the two figures generate one another by inversion, the situations they refer to, while they may be subject to the same process, seem to evolve incoherently, because of the complex nature of both causes and life itself. Yet behind the veil of arbitrariness and chaos with which fact disguises reality, the same inexorable principles are at work.

The porcine screeches Whet-Iron uttered by way of war cries while his enemy took to his bed, victim of *"one of the maladies medicine cannot cure,"* acted as a kind of prelude to the next configuration, of which the fifth line may be interpreted, *"The castrated boar is in the sty,"* and the fourth, *"The horns of the young bull are blunted."* As a matter of fact, Whet-Iron was no longer in his first youth; he was more of an old dog. But the quotation refers not so much to the animal's youth as to its temporary immobilization, which is of benefit to all concerned. The pig imprisoned in its pen will recover from the wound that drove it crazy, and if well fed will become a fat porker whose throat will be cut for the New Year celebrations or some seasonal sacrifice. Similarly, the leather tips on the young bull's horns will protect both it and its keepers from the effects of its wildness until it has grown into a placid and profitable ox, drawing a plow.

Whet-Iron's wound was a blessing in disguise: it forced him to abandon the struggle for a while and find a refuge west of the passes where he could get well again without fear of enemy offensive or attack. But, since all divinatory sayings are ambiguous, the boar and the bull might also refer to the unfortunate Plume, cooped up by melancholy in his room and behind his fortifications, and thus unable to charge his enemy.

But the exchange of home truths in the Vast War Pass, after the abortive attempt at peacemaking, was not the only cause of the great advantage Whet-Iron was to secure. It was also the result of a huge accumulation.

In the Great Commentary, compiled from the lessons of the Master on the *Book of Changes*, we read: *"The great virtue of Heaven and Earth is called Life, and the great jewel of the saint is called Position; men are what allows the saint to preserve it, and wealth is what attracts men."* Indeed, it is by amassing property that kings have managed to gather enough supporters to enable them to rise in the world. And by ensuring in this way the subsistence and survival of their subjects, they model themselves on the action of the universe, the object of which is to maintain life.

———

Hsiao Porter, having been a model civil servant in the model state of Ch'in, was convinced that the fate of monarchs depended on their building ample stocks of grain. When Whet-Iron consulted his generals and strategists in the course of his campaigns, Hsiao was in the habit of exclaiming: "So long as you have grain you can do anything! You can capture any fortress, defend any citadel, defeat any army. You can win over enemy troops and attract the support of foreigners."

So when Li I-ch'i advised Whet-Iron to attack the granaries of Ao, rather than fall back on the Ch'in defile, Hsiao, though he didn't like Li, agreed.

"Your fate is in the hands of the people," he said. "And all they think about is scoffing. Make yourself master of their bellies and you will control the Empire. All the stocks of grain are in the Ao granaries. Seize them, and dig in behind the Yellow River, and the whole Empire will come and eat out of your hand."

Peacemaker and Chang the Good nodded their approval: victory was won by reaping ears in sun-gilded rice fields rather than heads on blood-flecked battlefields. And Hsiao Porter did his best to encourage the necessary activity. The uncouth, mulish men of Ch'in, crouching over their plows behind their massive oxen, wrested Earth's plenty from the soil. The grain, carried in boats and carts or on the backs of human porters, accumulated in the public silos, forming first a heap, then a pile. Ten "piles" made a "load," and was kept under padlock; ten loads filled a silo. The silos were kept in enclosures near the homes of local officials and were protected by armed guards. Each silo contained just one kind of cereal, the name of which was clearly written over the doors. This made it easier to check how much went into the stores and how much went out.

Although taxes had been reduced by a tenth of what the Ch'in had exacted, the surpluses flowed in. Ch'in law had made agricultural labor second nature among that frugal and narrow-minded population: they sowed, hoed, weeded, harvested, and garnered as naturally as they breathed, ate, and slept. Stultified by field labor, the men let themselves be recruited into the army as tamely as cows. And the mountains of grain, overflowing through the doors of the silos, spreading across and even climbing up the walls of the courtyards, served to maintain the human horde which, after harvesting and storing the cereals, flooded to the east to be cut down themselves in battle. There were three agricultural campaigns and three conscriptions. Although not one soldier survived out of the three armies, the granaries were full to bursting, and fresh troops continued to arrive. It was as if supplies of grain and of men accumulated and disappeared according to the same pattern; as if the first were produced only to vanish into the bellies of the second, who were doomed to rapid death; as if the provisions necessary to support life were transported on tumbrils full of corpses.

The sight of these huge quantities of cereals might have caused someone like Han Fei or Li Ssu to meditate on the cruelty of an age in which happiness and peace were replaced by a tedious alternation of agricultural and military campaigns, an age in which production was directed only toward destruction. More probably, after sighing over the sad fate of the poor, doomed to live in a world made by but not for them, they would have shrugged cynically and thought that Order is its own justification, and a system that ensures Order possesses the same sublime and inhuman beauty as does nature. Anyway, what did it matter? If they themselves rejoiced in this world, it was not because they owned riches or other goods wrested from its reluctant soil, but because of their mastery over the material universe.

Hsiao Porter had no such thoughts as he inspected the doors of woven bamboo, bulging from the pressure of the stores they contained: millet, rice both long and round, glutinous rice from the Szuch'uan basin, green rice for making different kinds of beer, wheat of every sort, and an infinite variety of beans. There were also haylofts for storing forage. He always marveled at these vast and tangible signs of the government's efficiency, reflected in carefully filed invoices, conscription ledgers, police records, civil servants' meticulously up-to-date logbooks, not to mention the material on the shelves in the imperial library in Double Light and in the provincial archives. All these gave him the kind of delight a craftsman gets from contemplating work well done.

He organized a visit to the granaries in Ao, the largest warehouses in all the Empire, in the hope of raising his master's spirits: Whet-Iron was depressed as a result of his many defeats and of the wound he had suffered at the hands of Plume. As they inspected the various silos and stores, Porter tried to communicate his own enthusiasm to Whet-Iron and Chang the Good. For him, war was merely a series of problems concerning supplies and lines of communication—challenges to his own department that he found exciting as well as terrifying. These enormous thatched storehouses made him think of the distribution of levies and the exchange of circulars between headquarters and the prefectures; he could almost hear the creaking of wagon wheels as they brought longed-for sustenance to tired and hungry soldiers.

"Look at all that grain!" he exulted. "With those stocks you couldn't possibly lose the war!"

But the king couldn't bring himself to share his minister's enthusiasm. He thought of the entire armies he had led to destruction. Of course, he'd always been able to raise fresh troops and amass fresh supplies. Almost as soon as they were wiped out, his forces reformed. And so, although he'd lost almost all his battles, his potential remained intact. However, there was little comfort in a success that merely emphasized his failures. He felt he was nothing but a foil, there to let his subordinates show off their skill at repairing the damage. He must put them in their place.

"Yes, they're excellent stocks," he said to Porter, "but they'll soon be shrinking. I intend to launch a campaign right away. You amass stores and I use them up—that's why I'm a king and you're a minister."

Porter nearly choked on his surprise.

"Do you really mean to lead an army? You haven't recovered your health properly yet. Besides, it would be better if we temporized. The longer we wait, the more wealth we accumulate and the more Plume expends. Our rear is protected by strong natural barriers, and P'eng Yüeh and Tattooed Face are devastating the enemy provinces all the time. When our economy is at its highest and the enemy's is at its lowest, all you'll need to do to conquer the East is stroll through the passes. The Empire will fall into your hands like a ripe fruit."

"And then? Anyone will be able to challenge me for it, because I won't have done anything to deserve it."

Whet-Iron tossed and turned on his litter. His doctors' prescriptions had still not cured the inflammation of the pleura caused by his wound. A movement of the arm was enough to make him grimace with pain.

"You see," cried Porter with a triumphant smile, "the slightest gesture hurts you! You could never endure the strain of a campaign. And it's bad for an army's morale to know that its leader is ill."

He turned to Chang the Good for support, though he knew his own arguments had already impressed Whet-Iron. Chang was as pale as death. He wasn't upset by the theory that war was dependent on agriculture and that sweat was followed by blood, but the sickly smell of grain is nauseating for someone no longer used to it: he felt as if he were in the middle of a huge charnel house. The insidious odor spread through his nasal membranes to infect the whole of his body, from the brain to the five entrails, with a putrid exhalation. His vital spirits were in disarray. He could hear the Three Corpses, loathsome parasites from the Fields of Vermilion, grating and sneering. His whole organism writhed; the Three Burners were racked with spasms; the medullary vein had contracted and wouldn't let the Primal Breath through; and from the earthly and perishable part he hadn't yet been able to eliminate from his self there arose fearful visions casting morbid and monstrous shadows like jets of dirty water. He had a kind of waking dream: he was climbing up the stony sides of a high mountain, and just as he thought he had reached the top and attained immortality he saw that the summit was shaped like a woman's head—and Lü the Pheasant, the image that always troubled his meditations, gave a disagreeable laugh. Her face started to decompose, and she was soon no more than a skull half eaten by worms. Meanwhile, he could feel the slopes on which he stood collapsing or, rather,

slithering away beneath him like sand. Or like grain. It *was* grain—
a mountain of wheat and rice pouring over and stifling him. And as
the brown grains buried him, they too turned into skulls.

His repugnance was so great, it covered everything to do with
grain. He had a sudden horror of war: for once, he saw in it the
hideous face of death. Distraught, almost swooning, he panted out:

"Peace! We must make peace! There've been enough deaths,
enough blood!"

Whet-Iron was amazed at his vehemence. With a grim look at
his adviser, he curled up on his seat and said nothing. His chest was
hurting, and he was no longer so sure he wanted to fight.

———

In the Ch'u camp all the Hsiang clan had come together for a
family meal. The atmosphere was tense. Plume was in an extremely
bad temper: the East had been reduced to a heap of smoking ruins;
P'eng Yüeh, Tattooed Face, and their ruffians were laying waste the
most prosperous provinces, burning the crops, terrorizing the people,
cutting communications, and seizing all provisions. And none of the
cousins, brothers, nephews, and uncles on whom he had showered
estates, emoluments, and promotions had been able to stop them.

While his eyes roved over their rough-hewn features with a
mixture of affection (they were, after all, his kinsmen) and exasperation (but what a bunch of incompetents!), he diverted the scorn he
could not allow himself to feel openly about his family into threats
against that of his rival. Once again he talked about having them
boiled and served up for his dinner. And men like Fearless, Fame,
Cap, and Strong belched with glee at the thought of the sufferings
they were going to inflict on their enemies. They urged their kinsman
to be firm and not to be held back by scruples. He must slay the
whole enemy crew! He must raise an army and engage all his troops
in a decisive struggle against his one real adversary; the others were
only gadflies. Once Whet-Iron was destroyed, everything would return to normal.

Maybe they and their brutal, oversimplified ideas were right. War is a brutal and simple business. And if Plume had attacked then, confronting Whet-Iron's private army before it had time to call on all its reserves, he would have had every chance of winning.

One of those wily gleams you see in the eye of a fool when he's about to say something really outrageous lighted up the face of Hsiang Proud, Plume's prime minister. He wanted to reinforce his relatives' ranting with a logical argument.

"Do you remember Whet-Iron's answer the last time you threatened to boil his father? He bragged that he'd be glad to drink a cup of the broth. Take him at his word. If he keeps it, he'll alienate all the scholars and the aristocracy, and that will make it easier for you to destroy him. Doesn't it say in the *Book of Changes* 'It is good to abstain from family meals'?"

Uncle Hsiang, the only one in the family besides Plume who had any head for politics, had up till now said nothing. But this absurdity forced him to break his silence.

" 'Family meal' means eating *with* one's family, you dolt, not consuming the family itself! And even if the quotation meant what you say, it would be contradicted by most of the historical examples. Moreover, you pack-ass, eating with one's family doesn't refer to sitting at the same table; it signifies sharing land and revenues among one's relatives. A wise monarch rewards virtue and merit first; he provides for the maintenance of wise men before he supports his own kin. By attracting men of talent to his court with the promise of rewards and distinctions, he increases his power and wealth. But all of you, guzzling away at our prince's table, enjoying his gifts and emoluments, what have you done to deserve it? What prowess have you shown? None whatsoever! As for you, Hsiang Proud, you come from a family who've been generals for six generations, but you've been defeated three times by a draper!"

He looked around at the rest of the guests.

"No need for you to snigger, Cap! You were trounced by Fu the Broad at the granaries in Ao, and by Kuan Ying at Strength-of-

Clay-Pot. And you haven't anything to boast about either, Fame and Fearless!"

He turned to Plume, anticipating his objections.

"Yes, I know—all those things were the hazards of war, and a general shouldn't be reproached for his defeats. But still! The result of it all is that our granaries are empty and our soldiers exhausted. We need a truce to get our strength back. We can make use of the respite to attract some able officers, and I'll wager the Empire will be ours in less than a year."

Perhaps Plume's bluster had been meant to conceal a secret remorse for the hasty action that had put him in the wrong; perhaps he didn't want to be distracted even for a moment from his passion for Joy; or perhaps he was afraid that if he disagreed with Uncle Hsiang, he would expose him to the resentment of all the nephews and cousins he'd just insulted. Whatever the reason, Plume was ready to agree to his suggestion.

"But will Whet-Iron agree to negotiate?" He sighed. "He must be furious at my having thrown a rock at him."

"They say he was only wounded in the foot. Nothing serious. And he's too good a politician to reject an attractive offer of peace."

"A little wound in the foot! I thought I'd broken three of his ribs at least! I must be losing my touch. . . . Well, if that's how it is, we'll negotiate."

―――

Uncle Hsiang was appointed to start the peace talks. On the other side, Chang the Good persuaded Whet-Iron to let a scholar conduct the negotiations, to avoid any risk of repeating the Vast War Pass incident. And the rhetor managed to extract from Plume's representative a treaty handing over all the provinces west of Big Bridge. All the members of Whet-Iron's family being held as hostages were also to be returned.

When he read the terms of the treaty, Whet-Iron felt his eyes fill with tears. Half of the Empire was his. He thought of his modest beginnings and of all the way he had come. He thought how a Great Man, as he rises in the world, passes from little gains to great accumulations. But when it came to the reunion supper with his wife and his father, and he had to listen to the moans and groans of the latter about how badly things had gone in his absence, and to the recriminations of Pheasant, full of jealousy and apprehension of the influence Lady Ch'i might have acquired over the king during her captivity, he was in a good position to appreciate the truth of a maxim in the *Book of Changes: "It is good to abstain from family meals."*

FULL BELLIES

Integrity always rewarded.
Instead of looking in someone else's belly
    think about filling your own.
Heaven and Earth fill the bellies of all creatures.
The saint feeds the sages and thus reaches all the people.
At the foot of the mountain, the thunder.
Thus the sage watches over words and hands out food.

Banners bearing symbols of the directions picked out in heraldic golds, ermines, greens, and reds advanced in perfect formation across the landscape. In the midst of them, beneath the yellow canopy of his chariot, the supreme commander in chief stood on tiptoe in boots hung about with charm. With one hand resting on the crossbar and the other arched against his royal headdress with its dozen lappets, he gazed into the distance at the disappointingly empty horizon. From time to time, when he descried a cloud of dust far away on the plain, his shoulders stirred with hope; but it was only the northwest wind disturbing the parched earth.

"What are those swine up to? Just wait—I'll give them what's what when they do show their stupid snouts! I'll skin them alive! Hang them by their balls! Make them eat their own stomachs! . . . They fall all over themselves when it's a matter of receiving land, but when you need them, they're nowhere to be seen. They vie with each other to feed their faces, but ask them to show a little gratitude and risk their skins, and you can whistle."

Disappointment, fear, and rage cracked the veneer of pomp with which Whet-Iron had embellished his speech since he'd come to the throne, trying to speak as a divinely appointed king ought to speak. Now it was with the obscenities and in the accents of a drunkard and frequenter of low dives that he abused his allies—Trust, Tattooed Face, and P'eng Yüeh—who hadn't turned up to meet with him. His army had followed Plume at a distance as Plume, having signed the peace, withdrew toward the Blue River. The idea was to attack Plume from the rear at a given point with the aid of the other three. Their late arrival put Whet-Iron in a difficult position.

As the king gave vent to his wrath, three columns of dust arose in the distance, tinged with gold by the rays of the setting sun.

"About time!" exclaimed Whet-Iron when he caught sight of them. Then he added in ringing tones: "But woe betide the last to get here!"

Far away, a body of scouts galloped into view, tiny gray dots that grew clearer as they approached, standards flapping in the wind. Behind them the three clouds of dust grew darker as they swept closer to Whet-Iron's army. Soon, through the dust, the watchers could make out a great black mass, shining and compact, like dragon boats in the fifth month, when their white-hot prows turn the waters of the Blue River to steam.

The three divisions, now giving off the scent of death, swirled around into battle formation. A hail of arrows was unleashed from their midst like a tornado. Plume and his generals, Chi Pu and Lord

Ting, had taken advantage of the fact that Whet-Iron's men were exposed and numerically inferior; they had turned back to attack them.

The elegant formation of the eight army corps wavered. The squares disintegrated, leaving the center open. Ting was the first to ride in. His column surrounded Whet-Iron's Royal Guard. There was fierce hand-to-hand fighting, in the course of which Whet-Iron and Lord Ting came face to face. Whet-Iron looked his adversary straight in the eye.

"Is it possible two good men can conspire to harm one another?" he asked, and sighed.

Ting lowered his sword.

"Yes, it would be better if they helped one another," he said. "But as it says in the *Book of Changes*, '*The tiger glares fiercely; he gets ready to pounce on his prey; it is best to make sure that his belly is full.*' "

"I answer with the second line of the quotation: '*He fills his belly at the expense of his subjects.*' Doesn't that remind you of someone? Someone who keeps everything for himself and never gives anything away?"

Then Whet-Iron added in a whisper:

"But *I 'know how to fill the bellies of those who have helped me in adversity'*! I'll give you a kingdom if you let me go."

Ting ordered his troops to withdraw, and Whet-Iron was able to escape.

———

"If you were conspiring to bring about my destruction, you wouldn't act any differently! First you advise me to negotiate, then when peace is concluded, you urge me to break it and attack Plume. And it all ends in a fine muddle: my allies didn't show up, I only just managed to save my own skin, and my reputation is finished!"

King Whet-Iron, gray with dust and green with rage, looked daggers at Chang the Good and Peacemaker, his two strategists, as he showered them with reproaches. He would really have let himself go, and perhaps even have gone too far, had he not been restrained by Chang's air of detachment tinged with suffering. He also needed his subordinates' advice in getting out of the quandary their calculations had got him into. So he remained within the bounds permissible to any master who has to put up with the results of his servants' negligence.

In a faint and uncertain voice, for he had only recently recovered from a particularly severe attack, Chang tried to excuse himself. He had advised Whet-Iron to negotiate because at that moment peace was more attractive than war, and Plume was very likely to have agreed to it. But now the signing of the treaty had completely changed the situation and made recourse to arms desirable. By agreeing to negotiate, Plume had made a dual admission, which should be taken advantage of as soon as possible: first, he needed to restore his forces, and, second, he accepted as a *fait accompli* his rival's claim to a right to intervene in the affairs of the Empire. Thus, though he hadn't lost any military campaigns, Plume emerged from the peace negotiations as the loser. But to win the peace it was necessary to make war, and that was why Chang had pressed Whet-Iron to launch a campaign and ask for help from the other generals, who would certainly support him now that he appeared in the role of victor. But he must act swiftly and not miss the opportunity Heaven had offered him. That would be storing up trouble by cherishing a tiger. . . .

Whet-Iron interrupted.

"Talking of tigers, because of your clever machinations I've had to promise one of them a kingdom to stop him from devouring me."

"Who was that?"

"Chi Pu's maternal uncle—Lord Ting."

"He's not a tiger, he's a hyena, and a toothless one at that! A tiger would never have let you escape. Give thanks to Heaven for sending you the uncle rather than the nephew. *He's* a real fighter!"

"By all the devils, I know about him—he hounded me during the retreat from P'eng-ch'eng."

"You wouldn't have had to throw a kingdom to a hyena if you'd made it your business to satisfy the real beasts of prey! They ask nothing better than to help you, so long as you let them fill their maws."

"What do you mean?"

"Allow me to ask you a question: What message did you send to P'eng Yüeh, Trust, and Tattooed Face?"

"I told them to be at Mount Strong on a certain date so that we could launch a coordinated attack on Plume, after I'd joined them from Yang-hsia and we'd established our main camp. But why go back over all that? You know as much about it as I do—we planned the operation together."

"Unfortunately," put in Peacemaker, "we didn't actually say you should throw in the promise of a province if you really wanted them to keep the appointment. We thought it could be taken for granted. Didn't we go into the question at length when we discussed what Trust was angling for?"

Whet-Iron groaned.

"Haven't they all got a kingdom apiece already? What more do they want?"

"It's precisely because they've got a kingdom already that they *do* want more."

"But what have I got to give them?"

"The spoils from Ch'u. Let Trust have the strip between Ch'en and the sea, and give P'eng Yüeh the provinces from north of Sui-yang to Grain City. Tattooed Face can be king of Huai-nan and have all the territory south of the Huai River. And you can suborn Plume's officials, who are dissatisfied with their present possessions, with the promise of new estates. If you do as I say, I wager you'll have laid your enemy low once and for all in less than a month! It's a very sound principle—using people in such a way that they think they're putting their own interests first. And let me remind you of the true meaning of the last line of the Full Bellies hexagram: '*He takes the*

food out of his own mouth in such a way that his difficulties meet with
a satisfactory resolution.' "

"Very well," sighed the king. "You're right, as usual."

Envoys were sent to Tattooed Face, P'eng Yüeh, and Trust, and to Chou Ying, Plume's minister of war, who was stationed with part of the army near Nine Rivers. The ambassadors were given a sumptuous welcome everywhere, and the promises of lands and estates that they brought with them were celebrated with much gorging and guzzling.

The night the envoys left, Whet-Iron, who ate prodigiously and hardly ever dreamed, dreamed that his innards had disappeared and that all the food he'd swallowed emerged through a hole, to be consumed by a horde of starving, squealing monsters. Chang the Good, who ate nothing and was always dreaming, dreamed that he was being stuffed with cereals through a funnel by two gods whom he recognized beyond any doubt as King Whet-Iron and his wife, Lü the Pheasant.

GRIEVOUS ERROR

The roof beam sags: better move away,
and then things may turn out all right.

The flames of the camp fires rose up straight and high in the darkness. Weary men crouched around them, eating their millet gruel in silence and trying to keep warm. No matter how energetically their leader went from one group to another, sharing their meal, joking, referring to everyone's past exploits and slapping them on the back, the soldiers seldom laughed, and when they did, it sounded forced. Plume was more worried about his army's dejection than about his actual defeat. The reverse he'd just undergone at Kai-hsia was not irreparable; he even regarded it as a partial success. His enemies, though they enjoyed fourfold numerical superiority, hadn't been able to break through his lines. Admittedly Chou had had to give ground, but he had fallen back in good order to prepared positions. While he warmed himself and tried to warm the hearts of his men, he went over in his mind the various phases of that morning's battle, and reflected on the operations that would take place in the next few days. Trust might excel in indirect maneuvers, but Plume was better at direct confrontation: he must lure him into fighting on his, Plume's, own ground. But to do that he needed his men to be keen. And he thought again of those haggard faces.

All around him thousands of lights pierced the darkness like watching eyes: the camp fires of the enemy hemmed him in on three sides, three cordons of troops on each. Every so often the sound of singing and laughter and drunken shouting drifted across. Whet-Iron's men were celebrating their victory. *They* didn't seem short of meat or rice. Plume gave a shrug. Full bellies don't make good soldiers! He went toward his tent.

Just as he was raising the canvas flap, he heard familiar accents. They were coming from the enemy camp. The voices were faint, confused, and mixed with other sounds and other singing. Perhaps his imagination was playing tricks on him. Then the chorus grew louder, swelled by more throats joining in, and the song rose loud and triumphant through the night.

Plume summoned his staff together and told them to listen. His lieutenants agreed: it was a song on the lines of "Cock Crow," typical of the provinces of the South. The king turned pale, and his face streamed with sweat despite the winter cold.

"So many people are singing it!" he exclaimed. "Whet-Iron must have won over all my southern provinces!"

In fact, the only Ch'u soldiers in the ranks of his rivals were the regiments from Nine Rivers, which had been raised by Chou Ying, the minister of war. But when they sang songs from their own country, the other men, most of whom came from within the passes, joined in the chorus just for fun and out of camaraderie, strange though the words and tunes were to them.

If he'd been in full possession of his faculties, Plume would have sent a spy or a scout to find out the truth of the matter: adversity would have galvanized his energies. But, as a roof beam finally sags in the middle after it has been weakened at both ends, so Plume's courage faltered when he'd been softened by passion and undermined by the insidious rumors, circulated by the Trigrams, of his inevitable defeat. The king of Ch'u was afraid. He thought all was lost.

If he'd had a man of good sense at his side, a wise counselor like Increaser in whom he might have trusted, he probably would not have made the mistake he did. But now his entourage consisted almost entirely of mediocrities—kinsmen or old friends who had curried favor by flattering his whims—and the few honest and upright supporters he had lacked the character and authority to impose any point of view that contradicted his own.

He had bent them to his will by his courage, and none of them now had the spirit to cast doubt on his fears. Seeing someone who was always so calm on the battlefield so troubled by a mere soldiers' song, his lieutenants accepted his mistaken conjecture as the truth. It never occurred to any of them to check whether Ch'u really had been lost, though the only evidence lay in the accents of the singing in the opposite camp. They merely discussed how to react to the uncertain situation fostered by the soothsayers' propaganda.

Even so, all would not have been lost if Plume had adopted the plan suggested by his loyal generals. Instead, he followed the advice of a traitor, and committed his sole, but fatal, act of cowardice. For that is what it must be called, whatever arguments were adduced to excuse it.

———

Lord Ting hadn't forgotten the promise he'd wrung from the hard-pressed Whet-Iron, and now, anxious for the success of the contender who would bring him the greatest advantage, he suggested that Plume take the worst possible course: flight.

Plume's men had come to the end of their strength and their supplies, he argued; they were listless and dispirited. A battle on open terrain would inevitably end in defeat; moreover, since his rear base had fallen completely under enemy control, Plume's lines of defense were at risk of attack from behind. The only sound solution was to leave his army behind and attempt a breakthrough with a corps of crack cavalry. Then he could raise fresh troops on the Blue River and drive enemy elements out of the province. Having regained his own territory and with new forces behind him, he could embark on a triumphant reconquest to the north. Lord Ting, as a token of his loyalty and gratitude, was prepared to defend Plume's camp, with its hundred thousand men, to his last gasp; his sacrifice would give his master time to gather fresh troops.

This suggestion called forth angry protests from the bold Chi Pu, Ting's nephew. If Plume abandoned his army, the troops, far from fighting to the death, would scatter like a flock of sparrows at the first enemy charge; he would be dooming to destruction a hundred thousand of his brave and loyal soldiers, veterans who had followed him through all his campaigns. And if the southern provinces had already been conquered, how could he raise new troops there? No, he would find himself a fugitive without an army, hunted throughout the Empire, and would meet an ignominious death.

Plume still had a large army at his disposal, and shouldn't be daunted by the enemy's numerical superiority. Hadn't he defeated the coalition's five hundred thousand men at P'eng-ch'eng with only forty thousand of his own? And if he wasn't victorious, what better death was there for a soldier than to perish in battle leading his army?

Lord Ting pointed out that all this was mere bravado: a real Great Man could subdue his pride and act even in a cowardly fashion in order to achieve his purposes. The end justified the means.

Plume's friends, with the exception of Chi Pu and his younger brother Chi Hsin, agreed with Ting, whose age, rank, and military experience gave him the advantage over his nephews. Yet Chi Pu and Chi Hsin weren't just anybody: Chi Pu had won the support of all the knights of the province by his rectitude and authority. As for Chi Hsin, he had killed a man with his fist at the age of ten, and since then had acquired a reputation for courtesy, benevolence, and courage. He had been lieutenant to the famous bandit leader Yuan Silk. The king of Ch'u held both Chi Pu and Chi Hsin in great esteem, and their fierce opposition to their uncle's proposition left Plume in a quandary. He decided to resort to divination, and found himself confronted with the Grievous Error hexagram, which suggested: "*The roof beam sags: better move away, and then things may turn out all right.*" Everyone saw this as a clear direction to Plume to abandon his camp, where the defenses threatened to prove inadequate. Unfortunately, no one bothered about the symbolism of "*Wood under the Pool.*"

Plume still hesitated. Joy was with him, and he hated the thought of leaving her. If Whet-Iron captured his headquarters, wouldn't she become the property of the victor? The mere thought of such a thing was unbearable. But how on earth could he take her with him? There could be no question of encumbering his sortie with a palanquin or special coach. And could a frail and sensitive young woman gallop across difficult country on horseback, followed by merciless pursuers? Wouldn't it be criminal to let her take such risks? She might be wounded or killed in the kind of skirmish that was all too likely to arise, or break some bones in falling from her mount.

The king of Ch'u gave orders for his flight to be prepared for darkest night, and went back to his tent. He told his concubine what he had decided, and reveled one more time in her face and voice and movements.

He wept, and Joy wept too. They shared the same goblet of sweet wine as a token of undying fidelity, and tried to dull their sorrow in drunkenness and song. Plume composed a poem and accompanied it on the lute: he praised the days of his success, when he was full of ardor and energy and bent the Empire to his will. He lamented the cruel fate that was about to part them.

Joy took up the refrain, and their voices mingled, each making up words as their tears ran together into the earth.

Joy sang:

> "*King Whet-Iron has conquered Ch'u,*
> *and the songs of Ch'u are heard everywhere.*

If the king has lost heart
where will his servant-maid find refuge?"

Plume improvised in reply:

"The lovely maid need have no fear.
She will find refuge
in Whet-Iron's heart.
Lady Ch'i is really to be pitied."

His voice changed into sobs. And Joy said, in a voice choking with emotion:

"A loyal subject does not serve two masters; a faithful wife does not have two husbands. Having once belonged to you, I shall never belong to another!"

"I know, Joy, I know. Do you think I could bear the thought of your being in Whet-Iron's power?"

And he sang:

"A dire moment!
My horse has the bit between its teeth.
If Quicksilver will not speed,
what, Joy, will become of us?"

Joy guessed the hidden meaning of his words, and was overcome with shame and remorse. Instead of helping and supporting her prince, her love had brought him misfortune. For was it not this exclusive passion that had reduced a proud and mighty king to the condition of a fugitive? And now, instead of thinking of saving himself and his kingdom, this once formidable warrior was proposing to endanger all by saddling himself with a woman. Joy wasn't overburdened with intellect, but she didn't lack heart. She wanted to show her devotion by freeing Plume of the burden of her presence.

Thus, that dreadful night, full of misunderstandings and errors of judgment, Plume's fate finally came to depend on a magnanimous decision. But nothing is more fatal to a Great Man than magnanimity. If Joy had been fiercely ambitious like the Pheasant, or frivolous like Lady Ch'i, Plume might perhaps have been saved. Either from expediency or from selfishness, either of the other two women would have made him stay with her in the camp. But Joy was neither the Pheasant nor Lady Ch'i, and Plume's already storm-tossed barque was engulfed in the swamps of good intentions, as shadowed forth in *"Wood under the Pool."* But should poor Joy be blamed for her self-sacrifice? The last line of the Grievous Error hexagram is quite plain: *"Submerged while crossing the ford: bad luck, but no one's fault."* Fate alone was responsible.

Plume went out to issue fresh orders, his mind full of dreams of sublime devotion. . . . As he rode away on Quicksilver with Joy clinging behind him, her hair fell loose and mingled its dark strands with the horse's coal-black mane. Plume, half-rising in the stirrups, brandished a large sword that glinted whenever the moon emerged from the clouds. Sometimes enemy soldiers tried to stop them: Plume felled them in swathes, like an elephant charging through reeds. At other times, fleeing before his pursuers, his mount fallen under him, he strode through woods and fields with Joy clasped in his strong arms and fainting with weariness, fear, and love. With her held to his heart he crossed rivers and lakes, climbed through passes and up mountainsides. He defended her against tigers and other wild beasts; he frightened off gaping crocodiles, lowering buffaloes, and sharp-horned rhinoceroses by shouting war cries at them. Ever southward he pressed, far from the sound of armies, the fatigues of war, and the intrigues of politics, toward some magical land where the flower-scented air was stirred by the wings of countless birds of every color. Cool streams flowed through groves of orange, peach, and more exotic trees. The people welcomed him and made him their king. He raised an army and reconquered the Empire. . . .

As he walked he muttered to himself and waved his arms: "I won't leave you, Joy. I'll take you with me even if I have to carry

262

you in my arms night and day for thousands of leagues. You are my Joy, my life, my crown. . . ." And so on.

When he had made his arrangements, he returned, in a calmer frame of mind. But Joy was hanging from a long silk belt attached to the frame of the tent. The body swung there: her face was white, her eyes rolled upward, her tongue hanging out. Her hair, unfastened in her dying struggle, reached to the ground. A faint rattle still issued from her blue lips. Plume pressed his mouth to hers as if to receive her soul. But it was his own soul he felt escaping from his body, dragged away by the corpse. There was nothing left for him to do but leap into the saddle and ride off into the night at the head of his eight hundred troopers.

THE PIT

They bind the prisoner and slay him:
an expedition will bring a reward.

In the morning an emissary from Lord Ting informed King Whet-Iron that Plume had abandoned his camp and fled in the direction of the Huai River. Whet-Iron sent Kuan Ying, the cavalry commander and former silk merchant, after him with a force of five thousand men, while he himself attacked the Ch'u positions. Lord Ting and the regiments directly under him laid down their arms, and the rest of Plume's army, uneasy at their leader's absence and demoralized by Ting's treachery, put up a strong but brief resistance and fled in all directions. The troops of Trust, P'eng Yüeh, and Tattooed Face pursued and slaughtered them. There were eighty thousand dead. But most of Plume's generals and a handful of partisans managed to escape. A price was put on their heads, and a detachment of fast cavalry was sent after them.

After the victory, Lord Ting presented himself before the king, expecting to be rewarded for his crime. But Whet-Iron signaled to his guards to seize him and put him to death. This, he explained, was so that treachery wouldn't be rewarded and to show everyone in the Empire how he meant to deal with traitors.

Turning to the victim, he flung at him:

"I promised you a kingdom. Well, I am keeping my word. I appoint you king of Liao-tung and governor of Lang-ya. You have only to present your seals of office to the governor of Hell, with my compliments! Meanwhile, know that your blood will serve to appease the angry shades of the thousands of noble soldiers who died because of you."

They slit Ting's throat, and as the blood spread over the ground a priest prayed for the repose of the souls of the warriors dead in battle. The body was minced and made into croquettes, which were placed on the altars among the other offerings. Thus the offended spirits could avenge themselves by consuming his flesh.

———

Meanwhile, Plume was riding at the head of his eight hundred mounted guards. As they galloped silently—the horses were muzzled and their hooves encased in straw—they looked like a horde of ghosts, casting upon the darkness the colder, blacker shadows of another world.

Plume dashed along heedless of everyone and everything. He fled toward the southeast like an animal rushing to die in its lair. Quicksilver took all obstacles in his stride, crossing hills and valleys, leaping over canals and dikes, a white ethereal shape flying over the earth like a specter. Those behind had difficulty keeping up with him: some horses dropped exhausted; some riders fell, or lost their way among the woods and thickets. Only six hundred men got as far as the Huai River, and of them a mere two hundred managed to cross. Plume took no notice. He rode ahead like a madman, never looking back. By morning they'd reached Dark Mountain. It was foggy, and they couldn't find their way. After wandering for some time, they met a peasant, an old man with a white beard whose noble mien shone through his poor appearance. A keen observer would have noticed the strange green-and white-streaked stone that hung at his belt, but Plume wasn't in the mood to see anything. He asked the old man the way.

"To the left," he said.

They obeyed, and found themselves in a hollow full of reeds, rushes, and dense vapors broken here and there by the black shapes of trees, their spindly branches reaching out like phantoms. The fugitives wandered around the marshes; every so often a horse and its rider would vanish down a hole. Soon they were surrounded by marsh and quicksand, and couldn't move in any direction without falling into a swamp. Plume ordered his men, now even fewer in number, to dismount and wait for the fog to lift. They would then send out scouts to find a way through.

The penultimate stage in the process that leads from Heaven to Fire is inevitably the Pit: *"Water before and Water behind."* If destiny is to be fulfilled, there has to be a passage through a hole—that is, the marshes where Plume now found himself trapped, as in the fourth line in the last but one figure in the cycle of the world: *"He has gone where there is nothing but many deep holes; if he enters the pit, he will be hurled to the bottom of the abyss. He must not move."*

By the time the fog had lifted and Plume's party had found a way out, they had lost most of their lead and King Whet-Iron's five hundred troopers were hot on their heels to the south. When they changed course and made for the coast, they were driven back against a hill in East Town. Kuan Ying began to gloat, already imagining himself made a king as a reward for his prowess; his lieutenants were whetting their long swords ready to take Plume's head back to their master, who'd set a price upon it. Little did they know Plume still had enough obstinacy and fervor left to plow a deep and deadly furrow through their ranks, like a torrent that rushes through narrow passes and defiles regardless of any obstacle. Beset by thousands upon thousands of soldiers advancing on him obliquely like a pack of threatening but nervous hounds, he shouted to the twenty-eight faithful comrades pressing around him:

"In eight years of war I've never lost a single battle. I've exterminated every army that's been sent against me. If I've been reduced to this extremity it's because it's Heaven's will, and not through any strategic error on my part. And I'll prove as much by inflicting a bitter defeat on these vermin!"

The troopers hurtled down the hill in four groups, now joining together, now separating again, swerving to and fro like a swarm of wasps. The enemy was taken by surprise, and scattered. Plume laid about him lethally: arms and legs, ears and heads flew like dead leaves in winter; he left torrents of blood in his wake. Three times he charged the fine flower of Whet-Iron's cavalry, sowing terror and destruction in its ranks. When his men regrouped around him, more than three thousand of the enemy lay in the dust, and Plume himself was brandishing the heads of two generals and the standard of the cavalry commander, whose horse had tumbled down with terror at his terrible war cry, leaving his rider to flee on foot, abandoning all his badges of office. Plume's companions fell at his feet, crying enthusiastically:

"You were right! You were right! We'll follow you anywhere!"

Plume resumed his journey eastward to the Wu River, a wide deep tributary of the Huai. A man was waiting for him on the bank with a barge and some armed guards.

"Get aboard quickly!" he said. "I'm the district chief and I'm here to help you. This is the only boat available for miles around. Your pursuers won't be able to cross and follow you. The land of the Blue River is big enough for you to found a kingdom there and raise an army of several hundred thousand men."

So once again the current configuration was offering Whet-Iron's rival a means of escape, in accordance with the dual symbolism: "*Every passage that is narrow and difficult is at once a threat and a protection.*" At this moment, thanks to this providential aid, the king of Ch'u might change danger into defense, as the old man explained in terms recalling—was it merely a coincidence?—the commentary of Kan Pi, Master of the Bow and second-generation disciple in the tradition of the Confucius of the *Book of Changes*. The ancient said, glossing the Pit hexagram: "*Mountains, rivers, and other physical features are the Earth's difficult passages, on which the early kings based the protection of their lands.*"

But was the old man really here to help him? Perhaps he'd been put here by wily fate to open up in his soul the pit he was about to fall into: "*Trap within trap, at the bottom of which whoever enters there is crushed,*" to quote the first line of the current sign.

Plume looked at the man for a while, frowned, then exclaimed:

"Weren't you once a district police chief in Low Country? Yes, I recognize you. I met you at my uncle's house—you were always there. You helped a good man, but you didn't manage to carry it through. How do I know you won't do to me what you did to Trust—change your mind, cut my throat in midstream, and give Whet-Iron my head?"

"I was wrong about Trust, I admit. But I wasn't the only one, was I?"

"I don't blame you for being wrong—I didn't recognize his gifts, either. But I do blame you for lack of perseverance."

"Is my name to be accursed just for a moment's impatience? I came here to redeem myself. Perhaps *this* will serve as a token of my resolution."

And taking a bloodstained cloth from his sleeve, he undid it and produced a woman's head. The district police chief seized it by its heavy chignon and threw it at Plume's feet.

"It was because of her I neglected a good man. So I killed her. Is that proof enough?"

Plume lowered his eyes. He thought of Joy, and quailed: he could never have brought himself to kill her, even to win the friendship of a knight. He shook his head.

"What would be the use of going home? Every day of my life I'd be full of shame and remorse for having set out with eight thousand young men full of hope and enthusiasm, and brought none of them back. Heaven has vowed my destruction, and I will not go against its will. But don't think I'm rejecting your help because I don't trust you. To show my admiration for what you've done, here's my horse. I've ridden him for five years, and there's none to equal him. He can cover a thousand leagues in a day; his hooves scarcely touch the ground. I don't want him to go to my conqueror, but I haven't the heart to kill him. I make you a present of him."

The district chief of police bowed, took the horse by the bridle, led it onto the barge, and set off across the river. When he reached the middle, he took his knife, cut Quicksilver's throat, then jumped into the water and drowned.

Plume, watching from the bank, wiped away the tears that were dropping onto his armor.

"Oh, Quicksilver," he said, and sighed, "I was right—he was a noble fellow after all!"

He ordered his remaining handful of loyal comrades to dismount and fight Kuan Ying's column—now returning to the charge—hand to hand. There was a terrible melee. Plume slew a hundred or so of his assailants and received dozens of wounds. Among those still pressing him on all sides he noticed the familiar faces of some former comrades who'd forsaken him for his rival.

"Well, you old swine, in memory of your good and faithful services I mean to give you a present. Here's my head—you can collect the price that's on it without having to work for it. Whoever catches it can have it!"

And, lifting his heavy sword, he drove it through his throat. But his great body did not fall. It remained propped against a tree, and a stream of crimson blood flowed from the gaping wound. The staring eyes looked furious and astonished; the teeth were bared. The enemy soldiers fell back in a circle and didn't dare approach, until Wang Ti broke through the ranks and with his own curved blade completed the work Plume had so well begun.

The head rolled along the ground. Everyone sprang aside as if it could still bite. But the lips were now closed, and the eyes had rolled upward so that only the whites gazed at them. There was a wild rush: hundreds of men trampled one another to grab the poor dead thing.

A young lieutenant managed to get hold of it; but not for long. As he clutched it to his chest and dodged hither and thither, trying to elude his companions, he was felled to the dust by a treacherous sword thrust from behind. The head fell out of his arms and bounced on the ground. Dozens of hands stretched out, and some actually touched it, but a skillful kick liberated it and sent it flying into the air. The author of the kick, the Marquis of High Pebble, deputy general of light cavalry, ran to catch it as it fell, but while he kept his eye on it he failed to see that his friend Breath, commander of a platoon of household cavalry, had stuck out his leg to trip him. Breath, losing his balance, fumbled the catch, and the head fell among a group of ordinary soldiers. They just kicked it at random to make sure none of them could get it for himself.

The royal head, thrown in the air, carried in men's arms, rolled in the mud, thrust along by hands and feet, finally bowled down the slope to the river, pursued by a crowd of soldiers clutching, clawing, and collapsing on top of one another. The ball of flesh and bone rolled faster and faster, bouncing now and then as if of its own volition. With one last bound it rose into the air, arched over the trees, and fell straight into the water. The soldiers shut their eyes and held their breath. There went the prize money! . . . But there was no splash. Only silence. The head was swinging back and forth over the river, caught on a willow branch by the hair that had escaped from its cap. The tree was soon almost invisible as men swarmed up it and tried to impale the head on their pikes or swords. It was as if a crowd of monkeys was trying to get at fruit that was out of reach. But the men had neither monkeys' tails nor monkeys' agility, and when the branches gave under their weight, they fell into the river and drowned. At last an officer who was small and light managed to creep out far enough on the branch to twist the hair around his lance, pull the head toward him, and get hold of it. But someone else reaped the benefit of his efforts. As he was descending the tree in triumph, the head opened its chops, and its eyes rolled around in their sockets. The man dropped his booty in terror, and it fell into the hands of General Wang Yi. No one dared to challenge *him* for it.

Meanwhile, the body was being fought over just as hotly. As men seized it by the limbs, it was torn in four pieces. Each of the pieces gave rise to mortal struggles, from which cavalry General Lü Palfrey, imperial cavalry officer Yang Satisfied, and palace guards Lü Victorious and Yang Warrior emerged successful.

———

Whet-Iron was much amused when he heard of the fierce battles that had taken place for possession of Plume's remains.

"An excellent form of exercise for the army!" He laughed. "Don't they say the Yellow Emperor celebrated his victory over the monster Ch'ih-yu, who had challenged him for the Empire, by letting his men play football with his head?"

Chang the Good sighed.

"Isn't it a fine end for a warrior to have his corpse help in training the troops? Ch'ih-yu was god of war, and Plume rivaled him in military valor!"

"Use his remains to terrify the Empire," suggested Peacemaker, "and build him a monument that will remind everyone that you were able to vanquish the greatest general of all time."

"Very well," said the king.

The dismembered corpse was fitted together and buried in Plume's country, Lu; a burial mound was raised over the grave. The land that had been promised as a reward was divided among the five men who'd fought and won a piece of Plume's body. And Whet-Iron toured the rebel provinces carrying Plume's head impaled on a pike, to serve as an example.

FIRE

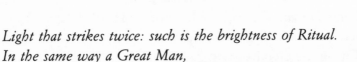

Light that strikes twice: such is the brightness of Ritual.
In the same way a Great Man,
   by his constant radiance, illuminates the four quarters.

The victorious king had to make an incursion into Lu, the native
country of Confucius, which curiously enough Plume had chosen as
his stronghold. Whet-Iron needed to pacify the local population,
which had remained loyal, and to reassure the scholars. He ranged
the countryside exhibiting Plume's head to every set of village worthies, regaling them with a banquet in the local school hall, and
lecturing them on mercy, justice, and forgiveness, and on the close
link between rulers and subjects, superiors and inferiors.

   Then he went on to Strength-of-Clay-Pot, where his supporters,
with all the village elders and other worthies, unanimously begged
him to proclaim himself emperor. He finally yielded to their pleas,
and had himself crowned. But because this little town was too small
to contain his new dignity, he took up residence within the extensive

ramparts of Lo-yang, with its many palaces and towers dating from early dynasties.

The onerous and irksome ritual that used to prevail in Ch'in had been abolished, and life in the Forbidden City was no longer restricted by any rules of precedence, courtesy, or etiquette. More often than not, meetings and banquets ended in fistfights. If the manners of the Emperor himself were less than exquisite, most of his generals and ministers behaved like brute beasts. They were always squabbling about the privileges due them for their various merits, and as soon as they started drinking they tended to leap at one another's throats. The silver goblets in the great banqueting hall were hurled across the room so often they became full of dents, and the pillars that supported the lofty carved ceilings had gashes in them from the frequent occasions when court dignitaries swiped at each other with their swords and missed.

The continual brawling worried Whet-Iron: he wondered how he was going to rule the Empire and make law and order prevail if he couldn't control his own entourage.

Totality realized that his time had come. He had fled Barbarian's court—even though he'd won favor there by his sycophancy—when Take-the-Plunge's rebels were marching on Double Light. He'd taken refuge in Hsieh, his native city, and when it fell into the hands of Beam, he'd entered his service. After the disaster inflicted on his new protector by the Ch'in army, he'd followed the Just Emperor, but abandoned him in turn when he went into exile, and then went over to Plume. After the sack of P'eng-ch'eng he surrendered to Whet-Iron, and went with him when he retreated west of the passes. There he exchanged the scholar's long robe for the short narrow-sleeved tunic of a Ch'u swashbuckler. Instead of speaking of ritual and morality and his own disciples, he urged Whet-Iron to employ brigands, mercenaries, warlords, and other gallows birds.

But when peace was restored, he realized that the Confucians would again have a role to play. So he got his old scholar's robes out of their chest, put on a tall clerical cap, and went to see the Emperor.

"A throne is conquered by the sword," he said, "but kept by ritual. Any ruler who wants to last must swathe his authority in ritual, for that alone lends power beauty and therefore legitimacy: '*Dual splendor of light, adorning integrity, perfecting and civilizing the Empire,*' as the *Book of Changes* so admirably puts it."

Whet-Iron was quite ready to listen to him. Although he'd once despised the Confucians so much that he belched at the sight of a shiny silk cap, now that peace had come he found that he was interested in matters of ritual and felt quite tolerant toward the scholars. So he instructed Totality to draw up, with the aid of his disciples and the other learned men of Lu, a new ceremonial. Totality and a hundred and twenty experts on ritual addressed themselves to the subject of court genuflection in an area close to the palace specially set aside for the purpose.

Sky Blue, who'd been imperial historiographer and astrologer under the Ch'in, was made responsible for the calendar. He decided not to change the existing rules: he had blown down tubes and observed the winds and the course of the sun, and found that sounds, emanations, and the motions of the planets still corresponded to the element of water, as under the Ch'in, even though Whet-Iron was the crystallization of fire. The year would still begin in the tenth month, and prison sentences begin from then. Six was to remain the standard number, and metal the favored element. But, as most honored color, red was to supplant black, which was relegated to linings.

After a month, when everything seemed ready, the Emperor and his suite rehearsed the new ceremonial.

Whet-Iron's ministers had taken their places in the great throne room. They were slightly apprehensive: this was their first solemn audience under the new protocol. Outstanding generals, feudal princes, and other army officers were ranged, in accordance with their military function, to the west of the throne. Ministers, senior officials, tutors, and the most important members of the civil administration were placed to the east, the direction ruling the things of peace. The Guard regiments were drawn up outside in the courtyard, chariots to the right and cavalry to the left. In the middle stood the infantry, composed of giants eight feet tall carrying banners and long gold-tasseled halberds. Suddenly a shout went up: "Make way! The dragon's chariot!" As the yellow palanquin went by, all heads were bowed, bent by the great wind of Authority. Whet-Iron's chair was borne up the aisle reserved for the Emperor alone, depositing him on the dais, where his special mat was spread. He looked down with satisfaction on the perfectly ordered pattern of his ministers and nobles. Their ceremonial robes formed a pattern of bright colors, undulating as the wearers bowed or genuflected and straightened up again.

Whet-Iron took his place upon the throne, his vestments shining like the sun. When he sat, the audience could see his feet, now no longer bare and soaking in a bowl of water, but encased in elaborate shoes adorned with pearls and precious metals glittering like stars.

Either those proudly displayed feet inspired the respect and dread due to any divine attribute, or the onlookers were obeying the first line of the Fire hexagram (Fire being also the Brightness of Ritual): *"By revering the man with golden shoes, you save yourself from misfortune."* Whatever the reason, the knees and teeth of the lesser persons present could be heard knocking together with terror.

Just as Whet-Iron was yielding to the intoxication naturally induced by the spectacle of one's own power, a noise arose outside in the courtyard, and guards surged into the audience chamber, jostling aside the courtiers. The elegant pattern was disrupted; confusion reigned. People shouted and waved their arms; there was even a hint of panic. . . .

Gangs of ruffians, led by Fortunate, had irrupted into the city and invaded the palace, felling the sentries who tried to stop them and swarming in through doors and over walls.

———

The tidings of Whet-Iron's final triumph had been greeted with great enthusiasm. The coast was swept by religious fervor, stimulated by Fortunate's preaching as he took the news from village to village, telling everyone that an age of gold had just begun: Whet-Iron had won and his goodness was already spreading through the world, fertilizing plants and herbs, animals and men like sweet dew. The age of the Great Peace was beginning at last: there would be no more mine and thine; the world was one big family again; no more quarreling or fighting; everyone sharing equally in the fruits of the Earth and the gifts of Heaven. And so on.

Other beliefs, spread by Li Harmony to lend transcendental authority to his theories about the Great Peace, had taken root in ordinary people's minds and had intermingled with hope of the Great Peace and become indistinguishable from it.

Li Harmony maintained that he was inhabited by a god—not a mere demon, but a transcendent entity, Red Fir, an igneous embodiment of Lao Tzu. Red Fir, in accordance with the fire cycle, had crystallized his incandescent spirits in human form so that he might be tutor to the Red Emperor. Then, when his work was done, he had swallowed the drug of immortality, been consumed by fire, and entered the paradise of the Queen Mother of the West. He had fused with her into a single being, for she was none other than the female form of Lao Tzu, and it was through her he had given himself birth.

Li Harmony's sermons often dwelt at length on the life of delight and happiness that prevailed in the land of the Queen Mother of the West, and mention of the golden age came to be linked to the idea of the goddess and her mountain of endless felicity. So when, later on, Fortunate announced the imminent advent of the color red and the rule of Heaven, thanks to Whet-Iron's victory, the king came to be associated with the goddess.

The Queen Mother of the West would soon come down from her enchanted country, bringing immortality to her followers and misfortune and death to the rest of sinful humanity. To become one of the elect you had to wear amulets depicting her around your neck, make sacrifices to her, and sing hymns in her honor. Whet-Iron was just one of the manifestations of the Duke of the East, husband and counterpart of the goddess. An age of happiness would begin when, on the seventh day of the seventh month of the first year of his reign, he and the queen were mystically united.

Some people even whispered that the Pheasant was her incarnation.

Fortunate's speeches had done their work. The East was ready to see Whet-Iron as the good king who would usher in the reign of Heaven on Earth. The poor and underprivileged had been patient in the expectation that they would soon be happy. They had collaborated with the local potentates, their oppressors, submitting yet again to taxes and other exactions in order to support their blessed monarch's war effort. Must not everything possible be done to hasten victory for the man who was to bring the age of gold?

When that victory was actually announced, they had formed into groups and marched forth. Most went on foot, but some of the better-off traveled by cart or on horseback. They wore their hair loose to symbolize a return to simplicity, carried sheaves of rice or wheat as a sign of prosperity, and wore amulets made of peachwood. They climbed fences, emblems of usurpation of the land; smashed tollgates, barriers to the free flow of goods and other desirable things; and hanged countless dogs, those overzealous guardians of private property. They poured away all the wares in the wineshops; confiscated the hated metal coinage. They handed out talismans against every kind of malady and recited spells over water to cure fever; heard confessions from invalids, thieves, and rich men; sang hymns to the glory of the king; displayed the holy book containing the sublime thoughts of the poor; and brandished pictures of the Queen Mother of the West come down from her paradise to spread universal happiness.

By the time this procession, with Fortunate at its head, arrived in Lu, its beloved sovereign had already left the province. He'd gone to Strength-of-Clay-Pot and proclaimed himself emperor.

The crowd, its numbers swollen by new recruits who had been handed sheaves of cereals, likenesses of the goddesses, and all kind of good-luck charms, resumed its march westward to meet its savior. But once again it arrived too late. Emperor Liu had left Strength-of-Clay-Pot to set up his temporary capital in Lo-yang.

But the worshipers of the Queen Mother of the West were undaunted. On they marched, sleeping in the open, drinking from streams, inhaling the dew, and living off loot or alms. They arrived in the capital just as the solemn audience was being held in the palace.

Everyone thought it was a riot. Reinforcements were sent in to help the Guards. There would have been bloodshed if Fortunate hadn't managed to restrain the crowd's ardor. He persuaded most of his supporters to withdraw from the Forbidden City while he and a delegation of elders handed over the book of marvelous suggestions to Whet-Iron.

The Emperor signed to his suite, who had resumed their former positions, to admit the newcomers to his presence.

Chang the Good nearly swooned when he saw the likenesses of the Queen Mother of the West and the Duke of the East being borne along by this ragtag mob waving sheaves of grain. Although the pictures were painted in a naive and sketchy style, he recognized Pheasant and Whet-Iron as they had appeared to him in his dreams. And for the first time the true meaning of these dreams was clearly revealed to him—a meaning he had hitherto refused to understand or admit, though he had always known it.

It wasn't by his fondness for the Pheasant that his vital spirits had been troubled; if that had been the case, he would have been worried now only by the pictures of the queen. No, it was by a realization of his own baseness. He had entered Whet-Iron's service, not because he thought him virtuous or chosen by Heaven but because he himself was secretly attracted by oppression. His action against the First Emperor, far from being dictated by hatred of tyranny, had been no more than a gesture of revolt against his own predilections. Just as one might break a mirror that gives back too true an image, he had been trying, in the person of a despot embodying power in its crudest form, to destroy himself—or if not

278

himself, at least that part of himself that was attracted by cruelty. His aspiration to austerity was doomed forever; he would never be able to rid himself of the real foundation of his being. His devotion to Whet-Iron, like his relationship with the Pheasant, was a kind of slavery. But he enjoyed being a slave, just like the mob of yokels now groveling before a man who would keep them in chains for centuries. They had chosen to worship him not because he was their liberator, but because he would bend them under the harsh yoke of Authority. That, in their heart of hearts, was what they really desired.

The Trigrams had shrewdly chosen him, Chang, as the one most likely to choose someone able to restore order; the one most likely to deck that terrible order in pleasing appearances—for he loved power too much to let it be seen naked. At last he understood the meaning of Master Yellow Stone's phrase "It's because you recognize him that he'll be the king." He now realized that the Trigrams' mumbo jumbo did not contain a recipe for strategy or a principle of government—they had nothing to do with Whet-Iron's victory. Now he could admit it: the Trigrams' stock-in-trade was just a jumble of vague sayings and general maxims that might have provided him with mental gymnastics but had nothing to do with long-term strategy, which had, in any case, resulted only in resounding failures. None of that was of any importance. The mere fact that he, Chang, had chosen Whet-Iron had, in itself, designated him the victor, *in advance*. In short, he had been no more than the dog who had flushed out history's prey.

And just as he had loathed the First Emperor, so he now loathed the crowd which sent him back his grotesque but true reflection, a deformed and horrible image, as if he were looking at himself in the side of a bronze cauldron. His face was pale, haggard.

"It's unbearable!" he croaked. "They should all be slaughtered. . . ."

Whet-Iron needed no persuasion. He was outraged by the intrusion that had disturbed the pomp and circumstance of the audience. He called out to Fortunate, who crouched at the bottom of the steps to the imperial dais, overwhelmed by the display of so much power and luxury, and trembling from head to foot.

"You wanted to undermine the Emperor's prestige, did you?" yelled Whet-Iron. "Well, you'll soon find out who you're up against! The crime of lèse-majesté is punishable by instant death, without appeal or reprieve. Your corpse will be burned, and the ashes scattered by the wind."

As the guards were dragging him away, the condemned man caught snatches of the Emperor's speech to the elders, and of the praise his ministers lavished on him for his firmness and moderation.

"I hope my clemency . . . Out of consideration for your great age . . . On condition that you dismiss this mob and give the authorities the names of the ringleaders . . ."

"A wise sovereign punishes only one offender. . . ."

"And all of them are paralyzed with fear. . . ."

"Confucius had only to quarter Judge Mao Miao to restore order in Lu. . . ."

"Great Emperor, you are like Yü, who when he came to the throne put down the lewd princes of Miao and achieved a Great Peace that lasted for centuries."

"They bless the hand that punishes them, for they know they deserve chastisement. . . ."

Fortunate saw in a flash that he had misunderstood events completely. This was not the kind, compassionate ruler who would bring about the reign of Heaven on Earth, but a tyrant who would impose a government based on contempt but disguised in fine words and pious speeches. A hypocrite—that's what Whet-Iron was—a double-faced villain! Wasn't there a lie in his very name? Liu could be interpreted in two ways: Orient Whet-Iron or Whet-Iron Orient. And he, Fortunate, fool that he was, had chosen the wrong one! Liu couldn't be the gentleness of spring that ends the harsh reign of metal; how could that be broken except by force of arms? He was the steel that slashes and cuts to strengthen the trunk of Authority. As it must be, as it always has been, and as it always will be . . .

Instead of causing resignation in Fortunate, this bitter recognition of the world's invulnerability filled him with a profound impulse to revolt. If nothing in the existing order could be changed, at least one could exploit the weaknesses that offered liberty its chance. But one must choose the right side. As the heavy blade came down upon the back of his neck he cried:

"Down with Liu! Down with Whet-Iron! Long live Plume, the king of fire and blood!"

THE TAO

All that was left was a red glow, and on that bloody background some straight and some broken lines. Then the shapes grew clearer, and six hoary, thoughtful heads stood out within a window frame, bathed in the fires of the setting sun. Behind them the voice of Heaven could be heard mockingly quavering out the third line of Fire:

" *'In the brightness of dusk, bang on a clay pot and sing rather than complain about old age.'* Yes, gentlemen, let us follow that wise maxim and drink and sing, for this meeting will soon be at an end, and so, for all we know, may our own lives."

"Not so fast!" cried Earth. "They haven't finished yet! You've only dealt with the first half of the cycle. There are still thirty-four figures left."

"Not nearly so many, my friend! You know as well as I do that signs can be interpreted in two ways: from top to bottom, or from bottom to top."

"Yes, but in that case there should be thirty-six in all."

"Sharp, aren't you! Well, my answer is that we're concerned only with the figures in the first *Book of Changes*—those that deal with the Empire. The others relate to family affairs; we don't have to bother with them."

"I beg your pardon—they *do* matter, because relations between men and women determine the fate of the Empire."

And before Heaven had time to reply, Earth called out to the other six:

"False soothsayers! True masks playing at being men, signs hastily sketched in blood and flesh on the pale silk of existence, you who will sing your parts in it without even realizing it and without anyone knowing about it, look and take heed, for what you learn may one day be of use to you!"

She lifted her robe. The six agents of the powers turned and looked. The Mare's belly was like a huge convex bronze mirror; or like one of those deep, dark wells down which people shout to recall lost souls. The images it gave back seemed to be below the surface, as if inside the material it was made of; they were at once very distinct and very distant, like pebbles or fish at the bottom of a deep, clear pool. They showed a swift succession of scenes, a long series of murders and other misdeeds perpetrated by Whet-Iron and the Pheasant, together and separately.

Heaven shook his head in annoyance.

"Didn't you know, stupid," he cried, "that the second cycle of changes is merely the lived aspect of the first. That is why the appendix to the *Book of Changes*, on the order of the figures, says that one deals with Heaven and Earth and the other with the relations between men and women. Which simply means that the first thirty outline things as they are in the realm of potentiality, and as they may be revealed in dreams or predictions, whereas the last thirty-four are their realization on the plane of fact. If these gentlemen want to know what all this really means, they'll have to live it themselves! But that's another story."

His voice took on a menacing tone as he addressed them all:

"The game is nearly over. You can't get away with trying to deceive destiny by passing yourselves off as what you're not. Henceforth you will be exactly what you wanted to appear, though you didn't know it."

He snapped his fingers, and the mirror became an expanse of stretched white skin again. The robe fell down and covered it once more. Then Heaven uttered a strange whistling sound, made curious gestures in the air, and shrank into a shapeless round mass. And one by one Pond, Thunder, Wind, Mountain, Fire, and Water flew to join that lump to form a single gigantic hand, which started to flutter clumsily around the room like a moth, banging against the walls and the crockery, then flapping awkwardly out the window. Up it flew into the dusk, getting bigger and bigger, until it covered the whole sky. Then it disappeared into space.

————

Just as the woman with the plump neck who lived opposite the tavern in Chung-yang was emerging from the drowsiness induced by her foot bath, the window was blotted out by a bright, velvety, transparent film, covered with the kind of dust that colors butterflies' wings and human dreams. The red, black, and gold marks on it formed a sort of octagon enclosing eight groups of straight and broken lines. But at the same time the woman, still only half-awake, thought she saw the window space fill with the word DREAM.

Later on, some old men, who'd been warming their creaking bones in the wan sun of twilight, said they'd seen an enormous shape with a word inscribed on it in vermilion letters: DECEPTION.

MAIN CHARACTERS

BARBARIAN (HU-HAI): Second Emperor, son of the founder of Ch'in
CHAO THE TALL (CHAO KAO): eunuch, Barbarian's tutor
TZU-YING: Barbarian's successor
CHANG HAN: Ch'in general

WHET-IRON (LIU PANG): founder of the Han
LÜ the Pheasant (LÜ Chih): Whet-Iron's wife
CH'I: Whet-Iron's concubine

STRING (KUAN YUNG)
EXAMINER (TS'AO TS'AN)
PORTER (HSIAO HO)   Whet-Iron's
CHANG THE GOOD (CHANG LIANG)   supporters
PEACEMAKER (CH'EN P'ING)   and friends

BARRICADE OF TEETH (YUNG CH'IH): Whet-Iron's enemy

PLUME (HSIANG YÜ): Whet-Iron's rival
BEAM (HSIANG LIANG): Plume's uncle

Joy (Yü): Plume's concubine
Increaser (Fan Ts'ang): Plume's adviser

Take-the-Plunge (Ch'en Ch'ih)
Trust (Han Hsin)
Tattooed Face (Ching Pu)   rebel chiefs, later
P'eng Yüeh   kings
Ear (Chang Eah)
Scrap (Ch'en Yü)

Li Harmony
Fortunate   green turban
Flash-Pedigree (Ching Chiu)   leaders
Ch'in the Fruitful (Ch'in Chia)

Li I-ch'i
K'ung Bream (K'ung Fu)   scholars and rhetors
Comprehension (K'uai T'ung)

AFTERWORD

The society established in China in the third century B.C. by Emperor Ch'in Shih Huang Ti is as clear and spare as an architect's drawing. It is illuminated by the cold light of a reason quite conscious of the inhumanity of its actions. This gives it the firmness and aridity seen in winter landscapes, where no softness, vagueness, or superfluity comes between the eye and the object, and the crystal transparency of the air produces a sense of almost aggressive precision. Order and clarity—these were what the despot and his philosopher-advisers tried to impose on the land beneath the sky, and it was this process of purification, of rarefaction of the atmosphere, that I tried to depict in my previous book, *The Chinese Emperor*.

Seen from above, this order and organization looked so perfect that they seemed unalterable. But that was only an illusion. Society as seen through the eyes of the authorities and decision makers might convey the impression of some *1984* universe, but in reality, or at least as I see it, it was more like the world of Zamiatin's *We*. The changes and chances of this fleeting world had not been overcome;

nor had death. If proof were needed that history still went on, the Ch'in dynasty fell as a result of an uprising in all the eastern provinces of the Empire. I was tempted to elaborate this summary account in a second volume, relating the collapse of the Ch'in order. *The Dream of Confucius* is the result of this desire to strike a balance. Its main theme is the rebellion that shook the Empire in the year 209 B.C., and the struggle for power between the two chief rebel leaders, Whet-Iron (Liu Pang) and Plume (Hsiang Yü), after the fall of the Ch'in. Whet-Iron finally prevailed after six years of war, and in 202 B.C. he founded the Han dynasty. It lasted four centuries.

As well as providing a sequel, the present volume involves a change of perspective. *The Chinese Emperor* described order and power; *The Dream of Confucius* depicts disorder and popular uprising. In tracing Whet-Iron's career from his birth, well before the revolt and the fall of the Ch'in, this volume reveals the cracks in the monolithic and seemingly invulnerable order that dynasty had imposed. Chaos is the ultimate outcome of the profound and ancient process involved in totalitarianism; the seeds of chaos are there from the beginning. The cracks in the foundations that ultimately undermine the state are not mere defects in construction; they are an integral part, at once inevitable and lethal, of the order itself.

Bureaucracy is a self-sufficient entity, turned inward, living and reproducing itself independently. It would be completely cut off from society if it didn't have extremities that adapt to it like synapses: these are the minor civil servants whose job it is to watch over and maintain law and order. These officials occupy a sort of watershed between the two worlds; they are attached to both, but don't quite belong to either. In ancient, classical China, outlaws came chiefly from among those who were responsible for applying the laws—junior judges, prison governors, local police chiefs. They weren't full members of the bureaucracy, for the energy of that bureaucracy was much enfeebled by the time it had filtered down to them through all the innumerable layers of the hierarchy; nor did they really belong to the people. They were there to supervise and control, though they had to operate carefully with the local powers and small landowners, to whom they were linked by common interests and complicities. And so, in this no-man's-land there were little areas where liberty could live, beyond the reach of the usual surveillance. These spaces acted as a safety valve for the most turbulent elements in such a highly policed system. They were as necessary, even indispensable, to that system as corruption, moonlighting, and terrorism may be to modern societies; but they are also a threat, a source of subversion that can explode at the slightest sign of weakness in the central authority. The career of Whet-Iron, who was first an ordinary local police chief and became emperor after a long period as a rebel leader, shows the way such forces of destruction sap the basic principle of a totalitarian society, setting the seal of its end on its very beginning.

These minor officials, responsible for the collapse of the order they are supposed to preserve, are also the most active factors in its restoration, even though they are unconscious of the fact. Knowing nothing of this type of organization, they reproduce it as they try to change it. The fact that they participate simultaneously in society and in the machinery of the state means that they have neither the disillusioned and cynical attitude of senior officials nor the critical if passive vision of the lower classes totally excluded from the exercise of authority. The confusion inherent in the collapse of order is reinforced by the confusion due to the difference between what is said and what is done. The officials lie because they deceive themselves. Their already chaotic actions are blurred further by the mists of spuriousness.

Instead of producing real individuals, the disintegration of order produces only shadows, vague outlines. The leading actors, masked by the cloud of ideological justifications concealing them both from others and from themselves, lose all distinctive features and are as difficult to tell apart as figures glimpsed through a fog.

The chronicle of this period, as supplied by the historian Ssu-ma Ch'ien, is a confused series of battles, alliances, and quarrels, a list of nameless faces impossible to organize coherently. Questions hang over this confusion. Why did Whet-Iron win? his advisers keep asking. Why did he win? rage his rivals. Why did I win? he never stops wondering. Well, why *did* he come out on top, rather than one of his rivals? echoes the historian. He lost all his battles; he was neither good nor generous, nor even a real cynic. He was without any special talent or distinction, except for his exceptional coarseness. And yet it was he, always vanquished in war, who triumphed; he, the worst of boors, who established Confucian ritual. What can you do with a muddled story ending in a dénouement so fortuitous and undeserved as to seem quite arbitrary?

It is precisely the inexplicable nature of this victory that constitutes what Henry James called a seed or germ, one of the subtle particles or catalysts that turn a story into a fable, making it possible to give it a form that will not falsify its content.

With no objective factor to explain the success of one contender, I had to fall back on some occult power, some will that intervened in events unknown to the people concerned, something like a secret society, an anthropomorphic manifestation of fate.

Fate, in China, is synonymous with the *Book of Changes*. So I could replace historical chronology with the hexagrams, a series of divinatory figures; could, instead of attempting a linear plot, use links subtler and more secret than those of chronology or cause and effect. These figures punctuate my story, dividing it into emblematic moments. While the hexagrams are dynamic images, representations of the trends governing the phases of time, the trigrams they derive from are simple elements, independent entities; the trigrams are to the hexagrams as the characters are to the episodes. They provided an ideal instrument for converting a cosmic and celestial destiny into human incident. Whether presented as leaders of a powerful secret organization dressed up as divinatory emblems, or as the transcendent executors of fate embodied in individuals, they undermine the notion of character, of people acting as autonomous agents in a historical drama. With the discursive method abandoned, the question "why" gives way to the tautology by which all historical explanations may, basically, be resolved: "Whet-Iron was the right man to win the Empire because he won it"—a materialistic and empirical reversal of ontological proof, made possible by an approach abolishing the distinction between fact and reality. Events, instead of being organized in accordance with a historical sequence, which made them seem confused and absurd, are arranged in a pattern that has validity both as a political fable and as a meditation on History.

But, it may be objected, isn't it just an artificial exercise to take a divination manual and juxtapose it with certain historical events? It isn't so artificial as it seems: the ideology of the *Book of Changes* is exactly the one the Han used to establish their legitimacy. It was under that dynasty that a massive upsurge of esoteric and prophetic literature was used to explain things as they were—the rise of a mere district police chief to the supreme position of Son of Heaven—in terms of a Divine Will deciphered through the signs and symbols of divination. Admittedly, it was the only way you *could* explain Liu Pang's success. And it gave me a mischievous pleasure to serve up this character, whom I did not like, in his own ideological sauce, referring to the great mechanism of destiny hiding, under the lofty patronage of Confucius, behind the grimacing masks of the Trigrams.

The chronicles of the period contain little of substance. They consist largely of an anarchic and repetitive mass of meteoric figures, murky battles, and sordid rivalries, often lapsing into mere catalogues of names of people and places. They are also contradictory whenever there are two versions of the same event. Ssu-ma Ch'ien's *Historical Memoirs* are the only documentary source for what happened between the fall of the Ch'in and the accession of the Han. The main facts are set down in chronological order, year by year, in the "Annals" recording the reigns of the Second Emperor, Hsiang Yü, and Han Kao-ch'u (Whet-Iron); these facts are arranged in diagrammatic form in the "Tables." Supplementary details are in the "Biographies." But the Annals and the Biographies often give differing or even completely contradictory versions of the same event. Frequently the facts seem quite incredible, or are presented so elliptically that it is impossible to tell what actually happened. Take the account of how Whet-Iron captured the prefecture of P'ei. Sounded out by the prefect, who finally retracts, about persuading the people to rise in revolt, Whet-Iron gives the signal by shooting a proclamation over the city walls attached to an arrow. Then he conquers several fortified positions and "goes back to Feng," where he entrenches himself. It is surprising that his arrow wasn't intercepted, unless he bombarded the population with tracts. But then the prefect would have been alerted. Unless the arrow was supposed to fall into the hands of an accomplice. We are reduced to conjecture. Ssu-ma Ch'ien never mentions the taking of Feng, which plays an important part in the story, though it must have been taken for Whet-Iron to be able to withdraw to it and defend it. But when and how? Why not invent another and more satisfactory version, based not on probability—fact, as well as fiction, is made up of strange and incredible events—but on the allegorical message? After all, the only testimony, in the *Historical Memoirs*, written a hundred and twenty years after the events, is not fact, but a representation of fact.

So what part does history play in this novel? How much is "fact" and how much imagination? To satisfy readers who like to know if they're standing on the quicksand of invention or the terra firma of reality, let me say that most of the characters are historical, in that they are vouched for by the chronicle, but that what happens to them is invention, inasmuch as mere names are given personalities and lives. Sometimes it is a detail, mentioned in passing, that gives rise to a character: I constructed Chang the Good (Chang Liang) on the basis of the observation with which the historian concludes his biography: "I always regarded him as a man remarkable for his stratagems, so what was my surprise when I saw his portrait: he looked like a woman, a beautiful young girl." This exclamation, juxtaposed with his bizarre illnesses, his diet, his gymnastics (also mentioned in *Historical Memoirs*) and his ambiguous relationship with Liu Pang's wife, Lü the Pheasant, made it possible for me to create a less conventional human type than the unemotional superman so often met with in traditional Chinese literature.

Although the main course of events is followed (an act of rebellion by one peasant really did set off a general revolt against the Ch'in, which was taken over by small landowners, feudal chiefs, and brigands), the rising of the poor and the theories of Fortunate, along with the character himself and his followers, are invented. But the popular rising does have a point of departure in history: Ssu-ma Ch'ien, in the Annals concerning the reign of Plume, mentions "a gang of young men who wore green turbans and fomented an insurrection of their own." The commentators, unsure what this refers to, cite the green turbans worn by the Wei paramilitary militias, and various millenarianist rebellions, such as those of the Red Eyebrows in the first century and the Yellow Turbans in the second. Green is the color of spring, gentleness, and great riches.

There is a huge literature of apocrypha and prophetic and utopian books giving elaborate descriptions of the idyllic visions suggested by the color green. Although this material was written some time after the advent of the Han, it is representative of Han society's deepest concerns. Therefore Ssu-ma Ch'ien's reference was a boon. I needed, from a purely formal point of view, something gentle, peaceful, disinterested, and at the same time rather passive, to contrast with the warlords' warlike frenzy, sordid intriguing, and ambition. For the ringleaders, the rebellion was a chance to rise in the social scale; for the people, an opportunity to affirm its hopes, its faith in a world of harmony, equality, and peace.

The unleashing of all possibilities sharpened every kind of greed and envy. Chaos turned out to be as terrifying and deadly as order. But it had the great advantage of letting everyone dream—the leaders, of advancement and greatness; the ordinary people, of the Great Peace. These dreams were to wither at the harsh touch of reality. Except those of Whet-Iron: his would come true in the deviant but persistent form of deception. That's one of the explanations of the first noun in the title of this book. As for the second, following the sage advice of Umberto Eco, who says a title should mislead rather than reveal, I leave the reader to find the explanation for himself. Just to point him in the right direction—unless it is to plant a red herring—I'll add that in the course of the book Confucius has a dream.